Emmeline K

"Revenge and murder are served up at a cracking pace as Emmeline unites with Gregory in...Daniella Bernett's [intriguing] mystery series."
Tessa Arlen, author of the Woman of World War II series

"Scintillating...theft, murder and general mayhem.... styled to mirror the writing of classic Golden Age authors. With strong characterization...Daniella Bernett has enhanced a series which...has the potential to gain a strong following." -*The Dorset Book Detective*

Other Books

in the Emmeline Kirby/Gregory Longdon Series

Lead Me Into Danger

Deadly Legacy

From Beyond The Grave

A Checkered Past

When Blood Runs Cold

Old Sins Never Die

Viper's Nest of Lies

A Mind To Murder

An Emmeline Kirby/Gregory Longdon Mystery

By: Daniella Bernett

A Black Opal Books Publication

GENRE: ROMANCE/MURDER MYSTERY, INTERNATIONAL
THRILLER, AMATEUR DETECTIVES

A MIND TO MURDER
Copyright © 2022 by DANIELLA BERNETT
Cover Design by Transformational Concepts
All cover art copyright © 2022
All Rights Reserved
Print ISBN: 978-1-953434-87-6

First Publication: SEPTEMBER 2022

Published by Black Opal Books **http://www.blackopalbooks.com**

To my mother and my sister Vivian, with love.
I would be lost without you.

Acknowledgments

I would like to thank Editor Susan Humphreys, who gave my book the extra polish it needed and created the beautiful cover.

My continued gratitude to the International Thriller Writers and Mystery Writers of America New York Chapter for their support.

I would like to thank bestselling author Tracy Grant, who has been on this journey with me from the beginning. My deepest thanks also go to former BBC Asia and World correspondent Humphrey Hawksley, and authors Alyssa Maxwell, Emma Jameson, Tessa Arlen and Kate Quinn, with whom I became friends via Facebook and exchange lively ideas about writing and life.

Prologue

Torremolinos, Costa del Sol, Spain June 2002

Another angry breaker lifted her up and then dropped her with a vicious crash. Tendrils of panic and icy dread clutched at the woman. She struggled to draw in a ragged breath. However, her lungs nearly exploded with the effort, as sharp needles of pain radiated down her left side. She gratefully sank into oblivion's comforting embrace where there was nothing. No love. No lies. Only numbing blackness.

She was dragged unwillingly into consciousness again by a shuddering cough that rumbled and rattled her already battered body. Saltwater erupted from her nostrils. Its briny stickiness mingled with the coppery, metallic tang of blood on her tongue. Tears seeped from the corners of her eyes. She had always loved the sea, but the high tide was cruel. It hissed and mocked her as if it knew what an utter fool she had been.

The next wave flipped her onto her back. She blinked. Salt and grit from the ocean floor made them sting, but she managed to open her eyes a crack. She gasped. The creamy orange moon loomed above her, a celestial pearl reclining on an inky pallet of wispy cloud.

One provocative strand of light tumbled from the sky and sliced a path through the waves. "Come to me," the moon beckoned. "I will help you forget."

The woman laughed and instantly regretted it. Every part of her body throbbed. Not only was she broken physically and emotionally, now she was losing her sanity.

Come to me.

The woman squeezed her eyes shut again and tried to block out the seductive voice.

Leave me alone, she cried silently.

But she didn't want to be alone. In the terrifying chambers of her childhood dreams that had been her greatest fear. Being left alone.

He had already left her alone. He...She choked on an excruciating sob. It had been their honeymoon.

And he had tried to kill her.

She felt his hands grab her in a vice-like grip and shove her overboard as if she had been a rag doll. Her eyes burned with tears. Tears of shame. Of stupidity. The worst thing was she had believed all his loving words. But it had all been a *lie*. In this cold, watery hell in which she now was trapped, she saw it all with crystalline clarity.

So, with her last ounce of strength, she called out to the moon, "Wait. Don't leave me."

She didn't know whether she had uttered the words aloud or only in her mind, but she felt her lips curve into a smile.

At least she wouldn't die alone.

Chapter 1

London, December 2010

W hat a filthy night," Emmeline said, as she stepped into the welcoming—and warm—embrace of the St. Martin's Theatre's brightly lit lobby in the West End. She gave her umbrella a brisk shake, before furling it up tightly.

It had only been a five-minute walk from the restaurant, where she and Gregory had dinner with Maggie and Philip. But the dampness had seeped into her bones. She rubbed her fingers vigorously. They were chilled from gripping the umbrella in a fierce tug-of-war against the snarling gusts of wind. Mother Nature was in a particularly foul mood this December evening, lashing buildings, cars, and the hapless citizens of London with icy sheets of rain. No, rain was not the right word, Emmeline thought. *Winter monsoon.* She tossed a glance over her shoulder and peered at the murky deluge. She nodded. Yes, definitely monsoon.

"Forget the weather," Maggie ordered, her green eyes alight with excitement. "We've stepped into the magical world of the theatre." Her arm swept in an arc that encompassed the entire lobby.

"Absolutely right, Maggie. For the next two hours or so,

we have no cares," Gregory concurred, a smile curling around his lips. "Come along, ladies." He inclined his head toward Philip. "And gentleman. Let's get to our seats. Agatha Christie's *The Mousetrap* awaits."

Emmeline looped her arm through the crook of his elbow. "I've been counting the minutes all week. You know how much I've always adored Agatha Christie's work. This was a lovely surprise. I still can't believe that you were able to get tickets to this gala performance. I know the proceeds are going to the Mousetrap Theatre Projects, which seek to expose disadvantaged young people and those with special needs to the theatre, but I thought it was sold out."

He waved a hand dismissively in the air. "I can't take the credit, darling. We are here tonight because of the largesse of one of Symington's clients. He wanted to show his gratitude because I was able to recover his stolen property."

Emmeline tilted her head back, her mouth wreathed in a broad grin. "Indeed. Symington's should be in your debt. In the five months since you joined the firm, you've been instrumental in solving a series of major cases and in the process saved them from making hefty payouts."

"Here, here," Maggie echoed. "Superintendent Burnell and the rest of the Scotland Yard must be singing your praises too."

Gregory bit back a smile, as he caught Philip rolling his eyes toward the ceiling.

"As you ladies know, old Oliver is not the most effusive of fellows."

"Yes, well," Emmeline murmured. "Perhaps, you shouldn't needle him so much." She gave him a pointed look. "His job is hard enough already with Assistant Commissioner Cruickshank breathing down his neck, just waiting for a chance to pounce."

"Emmeline, you must admit," Philip interjected. "Prat, though Cruickshank is, he behaved rather decently when it came to the Jardine murder."

She stiffened. She didn't want any reminders of the recent tangled case that had ensnared them all with its ugly claws. She and Burnell had been accused of murder; Special Branch had come with a warrant to arrest Philip for some unspecified crime; and Laurence Villiers, the deputy director of MI5, had been threatened with blackmail. And a fifteen-carat, fancy pink diamond with the provocative name of the Pink Courtesan had men salivating and willing to do anything to get their hands on it. She and Gregory were forced to sift through layer upon layer of lies, family resentment, and rivalries. After a harrowing couple of days in Malta, where they nearly lost their lives, they discovered the truth. At the heart of it was a carefully orchestrated scheme by Alastair Swanbeck to exact revenge.

Swanbeck.

She shivered involuntarily. Was he really dead? *He has to be*, a voice inside her head scolded. *He couldn't have survived the explosion on the boat.* But his body still hasn't been found, she argued with herself. *There was nothing to find*, the voice snapped.

But everyone thought Swanbeck was dead once before. And that's what worried her.

Gregory bent down and brushed a kiss against her cheek. She felt his warm breath as his mustache tickled her ear. "He can't hurt us anymore," he whispered.

She drew back and met her husband's steady cinnamon gaze. It was as if he had read her mind. She touched his arm lightly. The arm where he had been shot when they were in Malta. But it was healing. *They* were healing. He gave a faint nod. They would be fine.

She lifted her hand and pressed it against his cheek. "Yes, of course you're right. I'm just jumping at imaginary shadows. We're here to forget." Philip caught her eye and winked. "For one night at least, all the nastiness in the world is on the other side of that door." She jerked her thumb over her shoulder. "Sloshing around in the rain at its own peril."

Gregory slipped his arm around her shoulders. "That's the spirit."

He drew the tickets out of the inside breast pocket of his suit jacket and handed Philip and Maggie theirs. They chatted idly as they shuffled along with their fellow theatergoers, who were streaming toward the door to the left that led to the seats in the Stalls.

Out of the corner of his mouth, Gregory said in a soft undertone, "As I'm a neophyte and you're the expert when it comes to mysteries, Emmy, you must promise to go over the finer points of the story in detail. I wouldn't want to miss an important clue." He paused a beat, his lips convulsing mischievously. "In exchange, I'd be delighted to tutor you in the finer arts of a different kind."

He pressed a quick kiss on the sensitive spot just behind her earlobe. She felt her cheeks flame as her gaze shot to his face. One of his eyebrows arched up suggestively.

"Ahem." Maggie cleared her throat loudly. "That's quite enough of that you two. I know technically you are still newlyweds, but I suggest you continue the rest of your conversation later. At home. In the privacy of your bedroom. Mind you, if you had taken a *proper* honeymoon. Ahem." She cleared her throat again, her gaze flickering between them. "You would have gotten some of this out of your system."

Here we go, Emmeline thought.

"But no," Maggie harped on this old theme. "Instead of enjoying the Lake District, the two of you decided to chase after an international assassin. I've made my feelings quite plain on this sad subject."

"Yes, you have," Philip interjected hurriedly. "Many, *many* times in the month and a half since Emmeline and Gregory's wedding. Their married life is their own to make."

Maggie would not be fobbed off again. "Hmph. And if that wasn't bad enough. Then you immediately became embroiled in that sordid Jardine murder my darling husband alluded to a few moments ago. *All* of you ran off to Malta, while I and the boys were shunted off to Helen in Swaley." She halted, her probing stare locking on Emmeline's face. "Now, you know I adore your grandmother, but I was going out of my mind with worry. I'm still waiting for an explanation. The three of you have been *particularly* vague, when I've tackled you on the subject."

Emmeline opened her mouth, but Maggie put up a hand to forestall her. "Don't tell me that everything was in your article. Because I don't believe it. I *know* there was more to it."

Maggie was right. There was more to the story, but they couldn't tell her. Emmeline sighed inwardly. *Secrets.* How she despised them.

"I'm beating a dead horse since your lips are not only sealed, but wired shut, on the subject. I will content myself with reminding you and your"—she shot a sideways glance at Gregory—"I will content myself with taking every opportunity of reminding you that it is time to devote all your energies to a baby."

Gregory chuckled, as Emmeline's gaze darted to her right and left to make sure no one else had heard.

"Really, Maggie," she chided. "You're as bad as Gran."

"Can you blame her? The poor woman has been waiting ages and ages for the two of you to produce her great-grandchild. It's extremely unfair. You're married now. It's time to get cracking."

Philip gave a disapproving shake of his head. "You will forgive my wife. Her tongue often intrudes, where it's not wanted."

Maggie's eyes narrowed and she gave him a withering look, but he ignored it.

Gregory leaned across and gave Maggie a peck on the cheek. "Thank you for putting us in our place. We will take your um…*advice* to heart. We know it was said out of love."

Maggie sniffed. She was slightly mollified. "Good." Her gaze landed on Emmeline again. "Helen and I will be deeply disappointed, if you don't demonstrate the same enthusiasm as your dashing husband."

Emmeline groaned inwardly. She had learned that it was the better part of valor not to argue with Gran and Maggie on this subject.

Over Maggie's head, Philip mouthed "Sorry."

They fell silent as they approached the shallow steps where an usher was standing and checking tickets.

From somewhere behind them, a woman's silvery laughter mingled with the low murmur of desultory chatter. Emmeline knew that laugh. She craned her neck around to chance a peek.

"Oh, no," she mumbled.

Gregory grasped her by the elbow and asked, "What's the matter, Emmy?"

She turned her head back and stared straight ahead. "Do you see that slim woman with the dark hair cut in a sleek bob standing in the middle of the lobby?"

Gregory, Maggie, and Philip all glanced around.

"Yes," Maggie said leaning her head close to Emmeline's. "Who is she?"

"One person I wish wasn't here this evening. That's Verena Penrose. Gossip extraordinaire, who has dedicated her adult life to skewering people with a few strokes of her keyboard. Oh, why did she have to be here? It had been such a lovely evening until this point."

"Do you know her?" Maggie asked.

"Our paths have crossed. I try to give her a wide berth. I always feel so dirty, after I've been in her presence. Beneath that elegant and cultured exterior lurks a vicious and vindictive woman. Salacious exposés are her forte. She sullies the name of honest, hard-working journalists." Emmeline tucked her chin into her chest. "I hope she hasn't seen me. I'm not in the mood to do verbal battle with her tonight."

Gregory squeezed her arm. "You won't have to, darling. She just disappeared through the door to the Dress Circle."

A smile spread across Emmeline's face. Her good humor was restored once more. "Right." She plucked her ticket from his fingers and tugged at his sleeve. "It would be a crime to keep Dame Agatha waiting."

An usher checked their tickets and directed them to take the door on their left to reach their seats in Row J. Snippets of conversation drifted to their ears as they wended their way down to their seats, with Emmeline leading the way. Row J was just below the overhang of the Dress Circle, but it didn't obstruct their view at all. They quickly shrugged out of their coats and settled into the worn crimson velvet seats. Emmeline and Maggie sat next to one another in the middle, while their husbands flanked them, with Gregory on the aisle and Philip on his wife's right.

Maggie flipped through the program making comments about the actors, Agatha Christie, and mysteries in general. Emmeline was only half-listening, as her eyes roamed around the theatre, drinking in the highly polished wood paneling and crimson silk wallpaper scattered with golden flower medallions that matched the carpet. A faint smile touched her lips as her gaze traveled on, following the graceful curve of the wood railing as it swept from an invisible point above their heads in the Dress Circle until it reached the boxes overlooking the stage.

Her gaze narrowed into a frown, when she saw the notorious Verena Penrose leaning perilously far over the railing to Box B in a bid to be the center of attention, as usual. There was a man with her, but from her vantage point all Emmeline could see was his arm because he was sitting back in the shadow of the wooden column.

She nudged Maggie with her elbow and gestured with her chin. "There she is again making a spectacle of herself."

Maggie glanced up. "Verena Penrose?"

"Hmm," Emmeline murmured, as they watched the woman wave to someone across the theatre.

Maggie bent her head closer and whispered, "If she's as awful as you say—and I have absolutely no doubt about your judgment—I wonder if that chap with her knows what he's let himself in for tonight."

"I don't fancy his chances," Emmeline remarked, "Verena devours men and spits them out when she's finished with them. She's had a string of husbands, each one richer than the last. And in between, to keep herself from getting bored, she's thrown herself into several affairs that had nothing to do with love and everything to do with lust, power and shock value."

"In other words, a barracuda," Maggie ventured.

"Precisely. If that weren't bad enough, she's anti-Semitic."

Maggie's jaw tightened, as she cast a glance up at Verena Penrose's box. "Is she? Well, that's not surprising."

"That's another reason I can't stand the bloody woman. I've been on the receiving end of some of her venomous barbs on more than one occasion."

"Hmph. That woman likes living dangerously.

Obviously, she's not acquainted with your temper. Personally, I would have throttled her."

They both giggled.

"You don't know how much the idea of doing her bodily harm captivated my imagination. I was very creative."

Maggie smirked. "I'll bet you were."

Emmeline exhaled a long sigh. "However, in the end, it wouldn't have solved anything except making me feel better for the moment. We both know from experience that you can't change people like that."

Maggie slipped her arm around Emmeline's shoulders. "Unfortunately, no." She paused. "But we can still dream about her painful demise. After all, what goes around comes around."

Emmeline smiled and touched her head to Maggie's. "I knew we were friends for a reason."

The lights dimmed. A hush descended upon the audience. Time for the play to cast its spell.

Chapter 2

The red velvet curtains came down, signaling an end to Act 1. The audience began to stir. A few stood and stretched but remained at their seats while many spilled into the aisle. Some hurried to the toilets before the queue got too long and others ambled leisurely toward the door to the Stalls Bar.

"Emmy, are you enjoying the play?" Gregory asked as they rose to their feet.

His wife gave an enthusiastic nod. "Oh, yes. It's wonderful. I hope the rest of you are too."

"How could we not?" Maggie countered. "Miss Investigative Journalist, I bet you've already figured out who the murderer is."

A sly smile curled around Emmeline's lips and her shoulders twitched up in a sheepish shrug. "I have a fairly good idea. Shall I tell you who I think it is?"

Maggie flapped a hand in the air. "Certainly not. You, like Helen, are always right. I don't know how, but you are. I don't want the play to be spoiled. Therefore, you will keep your lips sealed."

Emmeline sketched a little salute, mimed locking her mouth and tossing the key over her shoulder.

Philip shot his cuff and checked his watch. "Well, now that we've settled that question. The interval's supposed to be twenty minutes long. How about a drink."

This suggestion was met with hearty approval.

The crush in the bar wasn't too bad. Emmeline and Maggie spied a quiet corner, while Gregory and Philip waded across the room to the bar.

Maggie had been regaling Emmeline with the twins' latest naughty adventures when a husky female voice intruded upon their conversation. "Emmeline Kirby, I'd know those dark curls anywhere. I see you still haven't managed to tame them. Pity." This statement was punctuated with a laugh.

Emmeline's spine stiffened. *Bloody hell*, she swore silently. Her gaze locked on Maggie's for an instant, before she slowly pivoted on her heel.

She gritted her teeth, steeling herself for the inevitable confrontation with Verena Penrose. The tall, impossibly slim woman with hardly any curves, was swathed in a mauve dress that accentuated the blue-violet hue of her eyes. Her trademark sneer was firmly in place upon her lips, while her eyes held a mocking glint.

Emmeline cleared her throat. "Verena, what an unexpected…surprise."

Verena tossed her head back and laughed. "For a Jew, you're a very poor liar. I thought you people were supposed to be experts when it came to lying and cheating." Behind her, Emmeline heard Maggie draw in a sharp breath at this offensive remark. Verena, however, was oblivious and went on, "You knew I was here. You saw me in the lobby earlier, although you pretended not to. I hope you weren't trying to hide from me." She batted her eyelashes coquettishly over the rim of her glass as she took a sip of her martini. The gesture only served to send Emmeline's pulse racing.

She drew back her shoulders and sliced the odious woman to pieces with her gaze. "I don't need to hide from anyone," she retorted in clipped tones. "But we have nothing to say to one another, so if you'll excuse us. My friend and I will be going. Come along, Maggie."

She attempted to sweep past, but Verena blocked her path. "Coward," she hissed.

"What do you want, Verena?" Emmeline snapped, her efforts to tamp down her temper abandoned. "If you're bored, why don't you leave the theatre right now and allow the rest of us to enjoy the play in peace? I assure you no one would miss you. I wouldn't have thought Agatha Christie was your cup of tea to begin with."

Verena peered down her nose at her with disdain. "You'd like that, wouldn't you, Miss Prim and Proper? I'm afraid I must disappoint you. I have no intention of leaving. Tonight is a work outing." She sighed melodramatically. "A journalist is a slave to the job."

Emmeline laughed, but rage bubbled in her throat at the woman's audacity. "Journalist? Ha. You call what you do work? You're nothing more than a spiteful gossip, who derives pleasure from ruining people's lives."

"Aren't you being a teeny-weeny bit hypocritical?" Verena asked. "You write reams of column inches about corrupt politicians, unscrupulous businessmen, and murderers. How is that different from what I do?"

"Not that I need to justify myself—"

Verena interrupted her, "But I've struck a nerve and you have to save face."

"How dare you?" Maggie exploded, outraged on Emmeline's behalf.

Emmeline patted her friend's arm lightly. "It's all right, Maggie." Then she rounded on Verena again. "As I was saying, my job is to see that the truth is told, to hold those in power to account for the public's sake, and to ensure that justice is served."

Verena clapped her hands. "*Bravissima*. You said that

with such conviction. Did you practice that speech in front of the mirror until you actually believed the drivel you're spouting? Perhaps if you ask nicely, they'll find a part for you in this dreadful play."

She barreled on, without giving Emmeline a chance to respond. "Let me tell you something. Your precious public doesn't care a damn about the truth. All they want to read about is someone else's problems so that they can feel better about their empty, dreary lives." She took a breath and scoffed, "I despise people like you, who think that they're superior to everyone else. The only difference between us is that you're a scheming little Jew." Her voice rose an octave and her nostrils flared. "You'd steal my scoop in a heartbeat. Don't try to deny it. We're both willing to step on whoever stands in our way to get ahead in this man's world. It's nothing to be ashamed of. Gossip and scandal are my bread and butter. As it is yours if you're honest. You can't trust anyone in this world."

Her blue-violet gaze surveyed the bar. "Look at all those smug faces." She gave a disapproving shake of her head. "They think they can get away with anything because they have in the past. Infidelities, gold-digging, and even murder. Each person is harboring a dirty secret. When you trade in scandal, all sorts of evil truths come to light. Think of it like the old superstition about the ravens in the Tower of London flying away, and the Crown and Britain falling as a consequence." She pressed a hand to her chest. "I'm the one who can set the ravens free. All I have to do is twist the key and the box is unlocked. Everyone must pay in this life. Some sooner rather than later."

"You've made a lucrative career—if you can call it that—out of innuendo and rumors without bothering to check pesky things like the facts. I always corroborate every story with multiple sources, as a good journalist should. Not a word goes to print otherwise."

Verena rolled her eyes. "Spare me your holier-than-thou sanctimony. There's nothing wrong with making money. It's awfully amusing to have people groveling on my doorstep, begging for a dispensation to allow them to go on pretending that their reputations are unsullied. Why should I?" She gave a nonchalant shrug of her shoulders. "So, I've made a few enemies. It makes life more interesting."

"You prey on people's misfortunes."

Emmeline was blinded by the whiteness of Verena's reptilian grin. "It's called power. It's the only thing worth having. Power is deliciously thrilling. And I intend to have as much as possible."

"You're willing to write anything if it will set tongues wagging. Most of it is titillating lies, but it doesn't matter as long as your name gets out there."

Verena tossed her chin in the air. "You're one to talk," she mocked. "I wonder how much that story of yours over the summer about Victor Royce and his family was true. Don't misunderstand me. I found it fascinating. It had shades of a James Bond thriller. Russian spies, poisonings, family disputes, and a trail of bodies. Deliciously wicked. And at the end of it all, you, dear Emmeline, ended up as the prime beneficiary of Royce's will." Her voice dipped to a sinister hiss. "As an outside observer, something smells a bit fishy. Or is that a whiff of blackmail? We all know how greedy Jews are. Always playing the victim and claiming other people's property is theirs."

Emmeline felt the sting of these words as surely as if Verena had slapped her face. She knew the vile woman was alluding to the story she had written back in the spring about Maggie's quest to recover her Great-Aunt Sarah Levy's Constable painting, which had been looted by the Nazis.

A caustic rejoinder danced on tip of Emmeline's tongue, but Maggie was quicker to lash out. "Why don't you crawl back under the rock from where you came, you bitch?" Every word dripped with icy malice.

Verena had the temerity to laugh. "Oh, wait, I remember." She made a show of squinting at her. "Yes. You're poor Maggie Roth. The one who caused all that fuss over the Constable painting. You were a darling of the papers for a few weeks. Do you miss all the media attention? Or now that you have your grubby hands on the painting, that's all that counts? As I said before, it always comes down to money for you people."

Emmeline's fingers flexed open and closed. A primitive voice inside her head urged, *Go on. Punch her dead center in the mouth. You'll barely notice the blood for that heavy coating of red lipstick.*

"Ah, Emmy, there you are." Gregory's voice drifted to her ears.

The tension from her muscles uncoiled. She glanced around and he was suddenly by her side.

"Sorry, it took so long. The barman got in a bit of a muddle. Here you go." He handed her a glass of golden Sauvignon Blanc and flashed her a smile that sent that familiar warm glow spreading through her body.

"Thank you," she murmured as she accepted the glass and leaned into him slightly.

Philip was right on his heels and handed a glass to Maggie. He raised an eyebrow in askance, but Maggie was still fuming. She flicked a glance at Verena and then took a long, fortifying swallow of her Bordeaux.

"Where are your manners, Emmeline?" Verena prodded. "Who are these delightful creatures?"

Gregory extended a hand. "Forgive me," he replied. "I'm Gregory Longdon."

Verena clasped his hand and held onto it longer than was strictly necessary. "Verena Penrose," she murmured. "Longdon." Feigning concentration, two vertical lines appeared between her perfectly plucked brows. "I've heard that name somewhere before."

"He's Emmeline's husband," Maggie blurted out.

Verena's blue-violet eyes widened and her mouth curved into a smile. "Oh, yes, of course. My, my, Emmeline, still waters run deep. How *did* you manage to catch such a criminally attractive man?"

Emmeline felt the bile rise in her throat. Although Verena's comments were directed at her, the woman's gaze never left Gregory's face. Her tongue even flicked out for an instant, like a rattlesnake, to moisten her lips.

Gregory, always an astute judge of character, sensed something was not quite right despite the playful tone. He slipped his arm around Emmeline's waist and drew her close to his side.

"Ah, Ms. Penrose, fortune smiled upon me the day Emmy dropped into my life. In fact, I still can't believe she agreed to be my wife. Every day is still like our honeymoon."

Emmeline tipped her head to one side and beamed up at him. She couldn't love him more than at that moment. His words were a reminder that now they faced everything together. Good and bad.

Verena chortled. "Please call me Verena. Everyone does." She paused for a beat and then continued, "One of the world's most handsome men and a charmer. I take my hat off to you, Emmeline." She stared at her intently. "I suppose there must be something behind your insipid façade and that superior manner. But for the life of me, I simply can't see it."

Gregory gave his wife's waist a squeeze, a gentle warning. She glanced at his profile. Although his smile was still firmly in place, the planes and angles of his face had hardened.

Verena abruptly tore her gaze from him and settled on

Philip. "This is my lucky night for meeting dishy men. I know exactly who you are. Philip Acheson."

She proffered a hand. He hesitated for a fraction of a second, before reluctantly shaking it. Emmeline bit back a smile at the revulsion etched on Philip's features. He looked as if he wanted to wipe his hand on his trousers, but deemed it impolite to do so.

Verena's eyes drifted back to Maggie. "I remember seeing pictures of the two of you in the papers at that time your wife caused that big scandal about the Constable."

This was too much for Maggie. "The painting belonged to my family. It was stolen from my great aunt."

Verena gave an exaggerated yawn. "Yes, yes, dear. I've heard that old, tired story before. It's wearing rather thin."

"No one is interested in your bigoted opinions," Philip shot back.

She shook her head. "It's a tragic shame to see two otherwise intelligent men taken in by these scheming Jews. You'll regret your foolishness one of these days."

Gregory took Emmeline by the elbow. To Verena, he said in crisp tones, "You've insulted my wife and Ms. Roth out of sheer bloody-mindedness. A gentleman never strikes a woman, but I fear if I linger here a minute longer you will leave me with no choice. I have no doubt Mr. Acheson agrees with me completely on that point."

Although she was more than capable of fighting her own battles, Emmeline found it extremely nice to have a champion.

Verena's eyes narrowed, but she kept her counsel.

They had only taken a few steps when she hurled at their retreating backs, "Mr. Longdon, I'll find out your secrets. I'm *very* good at ferreting out dirty laundry. And I'll take great pleasure in reminding you of this night when I reject your pleas not to publish them."

Gregory gracefully spun around on his heel. Emmeline

put a restraining hand on his sleeve. "Don't," she implored. "She loves baiting people."

He patted her hand, a faint smile touching his lips. "My life is an open book, Ms. Penrose. You'll only end up with egg on your face, if you take it into your head to smear me or my wife." He flicked a sideways glance at Maggie and Philip. "Or our dear friends."

"Hmph," Verena snorted. "If that was a threat, it failed miserably. I expected better of you." Her gaze roved over the entire bar, before once again latching onto Gregory's face. Her voice rose an octave, drawing a few curious stares. "Secrets and lies have a funny way of rising to the surface. Always. People are deluding themselves if they think that they can get away with murder. In the end, everyone has to pay the price for their crimes."

Gregory gave a curt nod. "Thank you for that bit of wisdom. I'll tuck it away and ponder it at my leisure when I find I have nothing better to do. Good evening."

Without another word, he turned his back on her and guided Emmeline to an empty corner at the opposite end of the barroom. Philip and Maggie were close on their heels.

"Ooh," Maggie fumed when it was just the four of them. She rounded on Gregory. "Why did you wish her a good evening? I would have wished her straight to the hottest corner of hell."

Gregory chuckled, as he took a sip of his Scotch. "It wouldn't have made a difference." However, his eyes were full of concern for Emmeline. "Darling, are you all right? Don't let that odious woman upset you."

"I'm fine. I should be used to Verena by now." The hand that wasn't holding her glass curled into a fist at her side. "But she always knows which screws to turn. I try to let it wash over me—"

Maggie took a deep swig of her wine and cut across her. "Huh. The woman deserved to be sliced to pieces. I'm surprised she wasn't a pool of blood at our feet. I would have gladly been your accomplice."

"You don't know how close I came," Emmeline admitted sheepishly.

"Then it's a good thing Longdon and I arrived when we did. Neither of us would have fancied visiting our wives in jail. I'm certain Superintendent Burnell wouldn't have been too pleased to have the two of you as guests of Scotland Yard."

This remark had the effect of lightening the mood. Their conversation turned to the upcoming holidays and plans for the new year. Emmeline injected a comment at the appropriate juncture, but she was only half-listening. Instead, she watched over the rim of her glass as a distinguished man dressed in a navy suit strode forward and clasped Verena by the elbow, an expectant gleam in his intelligent brown eyes. He had closely cropped sandy brown hair and a neatly trimmed beard, both of which were threaded with strands of gray. He bent his head close and whispered something in her ear. Verena looked annoyed by his appearance. She shook her head, hissed something out of the corner of her mouth, and extricated her arm from his grasp.

Verena's voice floated to Emmeline's ear above the low buzz of conversation swirling around them. "No, I am staying for the rest of the performance."

"But Verena," he pleaded, twisting his signet ring around his pinky and inadvertently bumping her arm in the process.

"Now, look what you've done," she scolded. "You've made me spill my martini." She tamped at the droplets on the back of her hand with a napkin. "Just leave. I'll be home late. You needn't wait up for me."

Ah, that must be the husband. The poor chap, Emmeline mused. As if somehow sensing her sympathy, his eyes found hers. Before she averted her gaze, she caught a glimpse of sadness mingled with regret in their depths.

She was glad when the bell rang signaling that the play was about to resume.

They dutifully trudged back to their seats. Emmeline was determined that the ugly confrontation with Verena would not spoil the play for her. As if drawn by a magnet, her gaze snaked toward Verena's box in the Dress Circle. The woman was already installed in her seat, one hand resting casually on the railing. She suddenly swiveled her head around, as someone entered the box. Emmeline couldn't see who the new arrival was. But she caught a quick flash of a man's arm, as he caressed Verena's face.

Dear, oh dear, Emmeline clucked her tongue silently. A rendezvous with a lover in plain sight. No wonder Verena didn't want her husband lingering about. It would have been more than a tad awkward.

Maggie's voice broke into Emmeline's thoughts. "Why does she have it in for you?"

"Hmm," Emmeline murmured, tearing her gaze away from the box to look at her friend. She exhaled a weary sigh. "It's sheer pettiness. Verena was at *The Times* for about a year, when I was still there. She was always trying to inveigle herself wherever she could. I'm certain she had her eye on becoming the editor-in-chief. Well, one day, James Sloane, my former editor, assigned a hot story to me that Verena was foaming at the mouth to cover. She became my enemy from that moment on. I did my best to steer clear of her, but it was inevitable that we would see one another in the newsroom. You won't be surprised to learn that Verena and Ian Newland, my other nemesis"— she rolled her eyes in disgust—"were thick as thieves. They always had their heads bent together plotting my downfall no doubt. I was relieved when she left the paper a few months later."

Philip leaned across Maggie. "Never mind. The cream inevitably rises to the top, as it was bound to do in your case, Emmeline. You had a distinguished career at *The Times* and now you've cemented your credentials as the editorial director of investigative features at *The Clarion*. Don't allow anyone to belittle you, especially someone like that." He jerked his thumb over his shoulder in the direction of Verena's box.

Emmeline smiled and reached across to squeeze Philip's hand. "Thank you. What a lovely thing to say."

Maggie pressed a hand to his cheek. "My husband has his moments."

"That's quite enough flirting with my wife, Acheson," Gregory said playfully. "Now hush all of you, the play's starting."

Right, Emmeline thought as the actors gathered on stage once again. *It's time to focus on murder.*

Chapter 3

It was barely ten minutes into the second act when Emmeline became aware of a low ripple of voices coming from the level above. She tilted her head back and silently cursed the rude people in the Dress Circle. Their conversation could wait until after the play. And if it was so urgent, they could have the common courtesy to step outside and allow the rest of the audience to enjoy the play.

She settled back in her chair and directed her attention at the stage, hoping the chatter would cease. Major Metcalf had just entered the scene, when there was an ominous *whoosh* from the Dress Circle, followed almost instantly by startled gasps and screams.

The performance halted, as the bewildered actors stared out into the theatre to determine what was happening. Emmeline craned her neck around to discover the source of the commotion.

Ushers suddenly materialized in the aisles. They mumbled apologies for the inconvenience, saying that because of an unexpected incident the rest of the evening's performance would have to be canceled. The ushers advised everyone to hold onto their tickets and they would be exchanged for another night. They kindly asked audience members to calmly proceed to the exits because the theatre had to be evacuated. This elicited a nervous murmur accompanied by an exchange of worried glances.

Gregory jumped to his feet, extending a hand to help Emmeline up. He nodded at Maggie and Philip. "Come on. Let's go."

People were already streaming past them. They had to wait a few seconds to squeeze into the aisle.

As she hurriedly shrugged into her coat, Emmeline's gaze happened to stray to Verena's box. Her eyes widened in disbelief. Verena was still sitting in her seat, her hand resting on the railing as it had earlier. What was the woman waiting for? A personal escort? Did she think she was the Queen?

Emmeline shook her head as she stuck close to Gregory, one hand lightly holding onto his arm. Maggie and Philip got stuck behind two older couples and were shuffling several feet behind. Emmeline signaled that she and Gregory would wait for them on the pavement outside the theatre.

The human herd had only managed to inch forward a few steps. Emmeline stood on tiptoe to see what was holding things up. Apparently, the woman directly to her right had the same idea, but she lost her footing and stumbled into Emmeline.

"I'm terribly sorry."

Emmeline gave her a weak smile, after righting herself. "No harm done."

"Oh, good," the woman said, relieved. She shook her head and one shoulder twitched in a shrug. "This gives new meaning to a captive audience. However, one thing we British are good at is queuing up." They shared a chuckle. "Except for that woman up there."

Emmeline's gaze followed to where she was pointing. It was Verena's box. She frowned. "Verena hasn't moved a muscle," she muttered. "You'd have to be blind or drunk not to have noticed all the hubbub."

Something was wrong.

She made a split-second decision and plunged down the row to get to the other side of the theatre faster.

Gregory's head whipped around. "Emmy, where are you going?"

She tossed over her shoulder. "To Verena's box." She needlessly pointed toward the ceiling, without stopping.

"For Heaven's sake why," he called, his tone tinged with exasperation. Nevertheless, he followed her.

They elbowed their way through the crowd in the aisle and managed to reach the stairs that led up to the box. A lanky man with ginger hair burst out from behind the curtain and barreled toward them. Emmeline flattened herself against the wall. She locked eyes with the fellow for the length of a heartbeat before he gave Gregory a rough shove and bounded down the steps. Emmeline was torn about whether to pursue him. She threw her hands up and sighed. She decided it would be rather pointless. He had already been swallowed up by the sea of people. They would never find him. Best to discover what the devil was amiss with Verena. Although the woman didn't deserve an ounce of concern.

The minute they pushed aside the curtain and entered the box, it was patently obvious why Verena hadn't deigned to join the masses evacuating the theatre.

Her head drooped limply to one side as if its weight was too much for her shoulders to bear. Her neck was twisted at an unnatural angle.

Therefore, it was not a leap of faith on their part to surmise that Verena Penrose was no longer among the living.

Chapter 4

Emmeline and Gregory were careful not to touch anything. As fast as their feet could carry them, they slunk out of the box and grabbed the first usher that crossed their path. In whispered tones, they conveyed to him the gravity of the situation. With each word that tumbled from their lips, more blood drained from his cheeks until his complexion took on an ashen hue. He swore under his breath and told them to remain there on the spot. He was going to alert the theatre manager. Fortunately, no one even gave them a second glance. Everyone was too intent on exiting the premises.

In the interim, Gregory drew out his mobile from the inside pocket of his jacket and started punching in a number.

"Darling, can't you make your call later?"

He pressed a finger to his lips, as he listened. After a few seconds, a smile quivered upon his lips. She shot him a quizzical look, until he said, "Oliver, I hope you weren't tucked up in bed."

She touched her husband's arm. "Don't antagonize him," she hissed. "Superintendent Burnell will be upset enough, when he finds he has a dead body on his hands."

Gregory covered the mobile. "Nonsense, Emmy. Old Oliver misses me when I'm not around. I can sense it already. I've brightened his evening."

Emmeline rolled her eyes toward the ceiling and sighed. *The game begins again. Poor Superintendent Burnell.*

Gregory held the mobile away from his ear, as Burnell's voice boomed down the line.

"Now, Oliver, why are you getting so tetchy?"

"You're like a plague," Burnell snarled. "Always hanging about contaminating everything you touch. It's bad enough that you bother me at the station. If you don't get off the line, I will have you arrested for hounding me at home."

Gregory chuckled. "Come now, you'll never make it stick and you know it. No self-respecting judge would even hear the case." He thought he heard a whimper at the other end and bit back a smile.

"Don't you have anything better to do? Is Emmeline out of town on a story and you're at loose ends? Is that why you're harassing me?"

Gregory clucked his tongue. "Oliver, I consider you a dear friend. You wound me with your harsh, unfeeling words."

"I wish you'd skulk off somewhere far away and never come back. You have thirty seconds to tell me what you want, otherwise, I'm going to ring off and try to salvage what's left of the evening."

Gregory's demeanor sobered. The time for levity was over.

"Emmy and I are St. Martin's Theatre. The theatre's being evacuated for some unknown reason, but that's not why I called. We thought you might be interested to know that a woman—her name's Verena Penrose, by the way—has been murdered."

"What?" the superintendent exploded. "This isn't one of your little jokes, is it?"

Gregory sniffed. "Oliver, you should know me better

than that by now. I never jest about anything as serious as murder. Emmy and I found the body. If you'd like corroboration, you can ask my wife."

Burnell grumbled something unintelligible and then there was a brief pause. "Right, I'm going to ring the Boy Wonder. Finch and I will be out there with a team as soon as we can. No one is to leave the theatre. No one."

"We'll pass on your instructions to the theatre manager, but there's a bit of a problem."

"Aside from a corpse, you mean."

"Touché, Oliver. You always have such a witty turn of phrase. But as I mentioned a few minutes ago, the theatre is being evacuated." He flicked a glance at the crowd on the pavement. "There are dozens of people everywhere and most likely some have already wandered off."

"Damn and blast. This is turning out to be the evening from hell. Tell the theatre manager to do everything in his power to keep those who are still around, there until we arrive. And don't you and Emmeline dare leave. Finch and I will meet you at the theatre entrance."

"Leave? And miss basking in the glow of your sunny disposition? We wouldn't dream of it. We're just going to try and find Maggie and Acheson."

"Are they there too?" The superintendent groaned in his ear. "Wonderful."

"Indeed, they are. They'll be jolly well pleased when we tell them that you and Finch are on the way. The four of us will be your welcoming committee."

"Stuff it, Longdon," Burnell retorted and rang off without waiting for a response.

෬෨෬

Burnell and Sergeant Finch drove up half an hour later. A van with a forensics team arrived virtually at the same time. It was utter chaos. Rescue units sent by the London Fire Brigade, as well as emergency services, were on the scene. The roads around the theatre had been closed.

Burnell and Finch discovered on their way to the theatre that the reason the play had been halted was because a huge chunk of plasterboard from the ceiling had collapsed into the auditorium. A group of constables was heroically trying to hold back the crowd, which looked as if it was over a thousand people.

Burnell turned up the collar of his coat against the rain and walked over and had a word with the fire brigade to apprise them of the situation. He told them that they would be allowed inside to assess the damage, once the forensics team had completed its work. He also spoke to the head of the emergency services. The paramedics had treated four people with serious injuries and an ambulance was just whisking them off to hospital.

The superintendent then took a deep breath, thrust his hands in his pockets, ambled over to sort out the mob of theatergoers, who were wet and cold, and hostile because the performance had been abruptly terminated. They demanded to know why they were being prevented from leaving. The superintendent put a hand in the air and raised his voice, which had the immediate effect of silencing everyone. He apologized for the inconvenience and informed the crowd that they would be allowed to go home as soon as they gave their statements to the constables. And not a second sooner. This elicited a few invectives, which Burnell ignored. He'd heard worse over the years from criminals he'd arrested. After a bit of grousing, the theatergoers saw the wisdom of cooperating with the police. During this lull, Mr. Hayward, a tall, slim fellow in his late fifties with thinning gray hair who was wringing his hands because he had the misfortune to be the theatre manager, sidled up to Burnell to express his horror at a murder being committed in his venerated venue. The superintendent did his best to reassure the man that the police would do their utmost to ensure that their investigation would be conducted with as little disturbance as possible.

Once Hayward scurried off, his face still pinched with worry, Burnell steeled himself for his next task. He pursued his lips and fixed a hard, blue stare on the two couples hovering under the canopy, off to one side out of the wind. Finch, pen poised over his open notebook, already was questioning Emmeline and Gregory. Maggie and Philip interjected a word from time to time.

Gregory broke off, when he saw Burnell approach. "Ah, Oliver. All hail the conquering hero."

The detective scowled at him. "When are you going to get it into that thick skull of yours? It's *Superintendent* Burnell."

Gregory offered him a crooked smile and clapped an arm around his shoulders. "Yes, yes. Such a fuss over nothing, Superintendent Burnell. There, does that make you feel better?"

Burnell's lips compressed into a thin line. He shook off Gregory's arm. "If you don't tread carefully, Longdon, there will be a second body at the theatre tonight. And it will be justified homicide."

Gregory clucked his tongue, as he smoothed out the lapels of Burnell's raincoat. "Poor *Oliver*, is your ulcer troubling you again?"

The superintendent swatted his hands away. "You're the only one on this entire planet who gives me trouble." Then his eye fell on Emmeline. "And your tiresome insistence on being in the wrong place at the wrong time has rubbed off on your wife." Although his words were stern, his tone had softened.

Emmeline extended one of her small hands and gave

him a sheepish grin. "Good evening, Superintendent Burnell. As always, it's a pleasure to see you." She inclined her head at Finch. "And you, Sergeant Finch."

Well, that was it. Burnell sighed inwardly. He could never remain upset with Emmeline for long, no matter how impetuous she could be when pursuing a story. He flicked another glance at Gregory, who was beaming at him. That was not the case when it came to her husband. The superintendent was quite certain that the man had fallen off the wagon—had he ever been on it?—and was back stealing jewels again. Reports of the seemingly stellar job Longdon was doing as chief investigator at the insurance firm Symington's did nothing to dispel the detective's suspicions that the man would always be a thief. If he could just catch him red-handed.

Ah, a man was entitled to his dreams, wasn't he? Burnell lamented to himself. He shook his head, as if physically ridding his mind of these thoughts. He cleared his throat and became officious. "Now then," he said. "Tell me how you two" —he pointed his index finger at Emmeline and Gregory—"became embroiled in another murder."

"I hate to burst your bubble, Oliver," Gregory replied pleasantly. "But Emmy and I didn't come to the theatre with the intention of stumbling upon a murder. Only to be entertained by it on the stage."

"Time will tell, but for the moment I'm inclined to give you the benefit of the doubt." He paused for a beat. "At least in Emmeline's case."

Gregory sniffed. "That smacks of discrimination on your part."

Burnell ignored this comment as he turned to Finch. "What's the victim's name?"

"Verena Penrose. She was a journalist."

Emmeline snorted. "Verena and journalist were a

contradiction in terms. She was a blackmailer, who wielded her pen as a weapon."

Burnell folded one arm over his chest, resting it on his protruding stomach, and stroked his neatly trimmed beard with his other hand. "Blackmailer? Ms. Penrose sounds as if she was charm personified."

"Hmph," Maggie grunted. "I met her tonight for the first time and once was more than enough. She was a nasty, bigoted bitch who enjoyed getting in a dig wherever she could. If you ask me, she got exactly what she deserved. Superintendent, her murderer did the world a great favor."

She and Emmeline exchanged a crisp nod of agreement on this last point.

"I see," Burnell murmured. "Obviously, the woman made a strong first impression. While that gives me a general character sketch, you still haven't told me about the events that preceded her death and how you two, of all the people in the theatre tonight, came to discover her body."

Finch began scribbling furiously in his notebook as Emmeline gave the two detectives a detailed overview of how the evening unfolded from the moment they set foot in the lobby, to their disagreeable encounter with Verena during the interval, the evacuation of the theatre, and Emmeline's decision to find out why Verena had not stirred from her box.

"After the fellow with the ginger hair and pale blue eyes nearly collided into us," she concluded, "we rushed up to the box and found Verena. It was obvious she was dead. We then informed an usher—"

Gregory cut her off and picked up the thread. "And I performed my civic duty and promptly rang you, Oliver." He punctuated this statement with a broad smile.

"Hmph," Burnell scoffed. "You don't have a civic bone in your body. You were put on this earth to harass hard-working policemen. No." He put up a hand to prevent the beginning of another verbal joust. "I'm going to have another word with the fire brigade commander, and then Finch and I and the forensics team are going inside. You will remain here, should any other questions arise."

Maggie glanced at her watch. "Superintendent, does that apply to Philip and me? The only reason I ask is that it's getting late and I'd like to get home to the boys."

Burnell nodded. "Yes, of course. I understand. For the moment, only your cohorts"—he jerked a thumb in Gregory and Emmeline's direction—"as usual appear to be in the thick of things. You and Philip may go home. Finch will prepare your statements. If you could drop by the station tomorrow to sign them, I'd appreciate it."

Maggie gave him a warm smile. "I always knew you had a heart of gold, Superintendent Burnell. Thank you." A distinct flush appeared beneath Burnell's beard. He was not one for effusive displays.

She looped her arm through Philip's, while he extended a hand toward Burnell and Finch in turn. "Good night. If we can provide any assistance, we will."

They watched as Maggie and Philip, huddled together beneath their huge black umbrella, rushed down the pavement carefully darting between large puddles, in the hopes of finding a taxi on one of the roads that had not been blocked off.

Gregory slipped an arm around Emmeline's waist and drew her close to his side, as Burnell and Finch drifted off to speak with the fire brigade's inspecting officer. A shiver slithered down her spine, a reaction to the damp chill in the air and the realization that they could have brushed shoulders with a killer.

She bit her lip. Could it have been the man who had come bounding out of Verena's box? That would be the easy solution. However, Verena was a complicated woman and she held many secrets in the palm of her hand.

Emmeline's instincts screamed that there was much more to the woman's murder than was apparent to the naked eye at the moment. She had to find out the truth.

Burnell, Finch, and the forensics team headed straight toward them now. Gregory pulled the superintendent aside, before he entered the theatre. "Oliver, if you insist on us hanging about, for Emmy's sake won't you allow us to wait inside? She's been standing in the wind for well over an hour and now it's bucketing down. She'll catch her death of cold."

She patted his arm. "I'm fine." She was only half-listening. Her gaze was intently scouring the crowd to determine if she could waylay one of the firefighters or a constable.

"Nonsense, Emmy," Gregory insisted.

"Really, I'm perfectly willing to wait here. We don't want to get in the way." She was judging which of the two younger constables would be more susceptible to flattery and therefore willing to talk.

Burnell frowned at this remark and followed her gaze. Then he flicked a glance at Finch, who was waiting for him in the lobby. He sighed and held the door open. "Inside both of you," he ordered.

"Superintendent, really I'll be perfectly all right," she protested. "Gregory's exaggerating."

Burnell pointed with his index finger. "I don't want you out here on the loose asking millions of questions before we've had a chance to examine the scene."

Emmeline shot him a wounded look and reluctantly trudged into the lobby.

Gregory patted his arm as they stepped across the threshold. "You're a prince among men, Oliver."

"And you're a king among thieves," Burnell muttered as he swept past.

ℓↄℓↄ

While the forensics team was going over Verena's box taking photos, dusting for fingerprints, and bagging any evidence they found, Burnell and Finch stepped away for a bit to escort several of the firefighters to the Upper Circle.

Finch let out a low whistle when he saw a foot-long crack in the ceiling. "Bloody hell. It's a miracle no one was killed."

"It looks to me as if the plasterboard fell as a result of a localized leak," the fire safety inspector suggested. "Of course, we'd have to conduct an investigation before I can give a definitive cause. One thing I *can* tell you is that the ceiling collapse had nothing to do with your dead victim. The debris fell here in the Upper Circle. It could never have reached that box in the Dress Circle, which you can see is off to the right."

Burnell thrust out a hand. "Thank you. I suspected as much, but I simply wanted confirmation from you."

"So, it's all right for my chaps to carry on here?" the fire safety inspector asked.

"Yes, we'll get out of your way. Our job awaits over there." The superintendent pointed in the direction of the Dress Circle.

The fire safety inspector grimaced. "I don't envy you. I don't know how you chaps do it day in and day out."

"I ask myself the same thing every time I wake up in the morning," Burnell replied. "Come along, Finch."

They made their way down the stairs to the Dress Circle and over to Verena's box, where they were each handed a pair of latex gloves. "Hello, John," the superintendent greeted Dr. Meadows, the medical examiner.

Dr. Meadows tore his attention away from Verena's dead body and lifted his slate-gray eyes to meet Burnell's probing look. "Hello, Oliver. I had a feeling that Assistant Commissioner Cruickshank would send you out to this deadly performance. It's a filthy night. Why does that man have it in for you?"

Burnell snorted, walking over to him and clapping his friend of twenty years on the shoulder. "Don't even get me started. You of all people know the Boy Wonder is a sore subject. His problems are infinite." He wagged a finger at Finch. "You didn't hear that from my lips."

"Hear what, sir? I was intent on using my power of observation to scan the scene for clues. Powers that I may add, I honed over the years in your shadow," the sergeant replied. The hint of a smile tugging at the corners of his mouth belied the seeming innocence of this comment. Finch shared his boss's opinion of Cruickshank. Supercilious prat would not be too strong a term to describe the assistant commissioner. Although Cruickshank did prove that he could be reasonable, when it came to the Jardine case. Finch wondered if that was a one-off. They would have to wait and see.

Meadows chortled. "I see that you have him well-trained, Oliver." To the sergeant, he said, "You'll go far."

"Hmph," Burnell grunted. "Don't encourage him, John. It will only make Finch think that he's clever."

"No one could be cleverer than you, sir."

"That's quite enough of that. Longdon is beginning to rub off on you."

"Lord, I hope not." A look of mock horror crept upon the sergeant's face.

"Longdon? Is he somehow mixed up in this?" Meadows asked, waving a hand at Verena.

"Unfortunately, yes. He rang me to report the murder. He and Emmeline and their friends, Philip Acheson and his wife, Maggie Roth, happened to be here tonight watching the performance before everything went to hell in a handbasket."

"Hmm. Yes, I heard about a piece of the ceiling coming down."

"Do you think that the murder was planned, or did the killer act on the spur of the moment?" Finch quizzed Meadows.

"It would be premature to offer an opinion at this point. He or she certainly took advantage of the confusion to melt away among the crowd fleeing the theatre. What I can tell you was that the victim's neck was snapped." He demonstrated with his hands. "One quick wrench and it was all over."

"That tends to suggest more a man than a woman," Burnell offered.

"A woman could have done this, if she was angry enough. That's why I recommend staying well clear of our friend Miss Kirby...Sorry, Mrs. Longdon, when she loses her temper. Petite and well-spoken, she may be, but she can be fierce."

The three men chuckled at this observation. Emmeline did indeed have a temper and she was impatient. A lethal combination that had gotten her into trouble more often than they could count. This was in addition to her tendency to dig into matters that would have been better left alone.

"Yes, well," Burnell mumbled, a faint smile still upon his lips. "Thankfully we know Emmeline is not the murderer. But it's still a nuisance that she was here tonight. It only makes her more curious and determined to find the answers. As you can imagine, she's already sniffing around."

"Par for the course, I would have thought," Meadows mused.

"That means we have to get to the bottom of this crime, before Emmeline throws herself in harm's way yet again to get the story on the front page of *The Clarion*."

"Thankfully, Oliver, you're the one who has to deal with that tenacious young woman. Delightful though she can be." After a moment's pause, he said, "An idea just struck me. Mrs. Longdon would make a model detective constable." He bit back a smile as Burnell's wispy white brows shot up and his eyes widened in surprise. "She's inquisitive and highly observant. The Met should seriously consider hiring her. I have no doubt that she'll have all of London's villains trembling in their boots within a day."

"You're crackers, John," Burnell declared dismissively, while Finch chuckled at the idea of Emmeline roaming around Scotland Yard driving everyone mad. The sergeant's mirth evaporated the instant his boss cast a frosty glance at him.

Meadows sniffed. "Ah, well. It was merely a suggestion. I almost feel sorry for the killer, almost. He or she picked the wrong night to snuff out Ms. Penrose's life."

Unbidden, their eyes were drawn to the victim, who was as cold in death as she had been in life.

"Right. Let's get cracking, Finch, so that John can take away the body."

While the sergeant made a tour of the box looking for anything that might give a hint as to the murderer's identity, Burnell started with Verena. One couldn't help but notice the awkward angle of her neck. His detective's practiced eye studied the high cheek bones of her slender face. He guessed she was perhaps thirty-five, no more than forty. The woman had been rather attractive. However, her long, straight nose was slightly turned up at the end and her mouth, camouflaged by a thick crimson coating of lipstick, had a cruel twist to it that only served to enhance the air of arrogance that clung to her even now. He stroked his beard meditatively. Was he making an objective assessment of the victim? Or had he been influenced by Emmeline and Maggie's opinions?

His eyes narrowed as he focused on Verena again. No, there was definitely something hard and unsettling about the woman.

Finch broke into his thoughts. "Sir, you have to see this."

"Mmm." The superintendent swung round and crossed over to where Finch was in the midst of examining Ms. Penrose's belongings. "What is it?"

"I found this in a zippered pocket in the victim's handbag." He handed over a small red leather notebook that came with a thin gold pen tucked in a slot on the side. "It seems she jotted down her story ideas in it."

"Did you come across anything unusual?"

"You could say that. It's certainly unexpected and raises questions. But I'll let you be the judge, sir."

Burnell frowned at this cryptic comment. He began flipping through the notebook. Nothing struck him as particularly interesting or odd, until he reached a page in the middle.

The last entry Verena Penrose had scrawled in a rather spiky and angular hand was a name followed by a note: *Amsterdam. Brussels. Barcelona. Madrid. Make him pay.*

The name was quite familiar to the two detectives. It was *Toby Crenshaw*.

Chapter 5

Gregory, hands in his pockets, arms crossed over his chest, and one shoulder leaning against the wall, watched in amusement as Emmeline chatted away with a uniformed constable and two firefighters at the other end of the lobby. Her three companions had failed to notice that she had surreptitiously taken her notebook out of her handbag and was taking down anything they let slip about the murder or the collapsed ceiling. Gregory knew that from his wife's point of view the two events made for an even more intriguing story.

"Longdon," Burnell growled from behind him.

Emmeline and her companions ceased talking, the superintendent's voice immediately capturing their attention. She quickly stuffed her notebook into her handbag, before Burnell took her to task for trying to wheedle out information from unsuspecting victims. From the set of his jaw, the superintendent appeared to be in a foul mood. Her pulse started to race. She wondered what he and Finch had discovered. She hastily crossed the lobby to find out.

Gregory slowly turned around and found himself staring into Burnell's scowling face. "You bellowed, Oliver."

Burnell slid a sideways glance at the constables hovering in the lobby like stray deer caught in the headlamps. "What are you lot gawping at?"

A chorus of "Nothing, sir" floated on the air.

"Well, don't you think you should get back to work? This is a crime scene."

Some nodded wordlessly, while others avoided making eye contact with the superintendent. But all dispersed forthwith.

Burnell rounded on Gregory again. "*Superintendent* Burnell. Remember that."

Gregory's mouth curled into an impish grin, as he sketched a cheeky salute. "Aye, aye. Anything to make you feel better. Murder is a nasty business, but you seem particularly out of sorts all of a sudden."

"Your mere presence is enough to make a sane man go gaga."

Gregory reached out and smoothed down the lapels of Burnell's suit jacket. "I know you don't mean that." He leaned his head closer. "Come now, don't be embarrassed. We're old friends. Tell me what's bothering you. It's always best to get things off your chest."

A primitive gurgling sound rumbled in the back of the superintendent's throat and his nostrils flared.

Finch stepped in to prevent another murder at the theatre that evening. "Sir, Mr. Hayward has made his office available. We could speak to Longdon there." He lowered his voice. "Less public."

"What?" Burnell snapped. Then he seemed to recollect himself. "Right." His stony blue stare impaled Gregory. "We have a number of questions for you."

"Indeed? How jolly. I can't wait."

Emmeline frowned and stepped forward. "Gregory had absolutely nothing to do with Verena's murder. What kind of questions?" she demanded.

Burnell gritted his teeth and glared at her. "Ones that I want answers to." He paused and took a breath. "I'm only going to say this once. Everything is off the record." He wagged a finger at her in warning, before the protest rising to her lips could burst forth. "Ah, ah. I don't want an argument. Otherwise, you stay right here and I will have a constable stand guard over you."

Her eyes narrowed, fire kindling in their dark depths. But she gave a curt nod.

"I agree to your terms." She sniffed. "Unfair and unwarranted, as they are."

Burnell's anger had finally petered out. He felt the corners of his mouth twitching but fought back a smile. He knew there was no way Emmeline would have docilely acquiesced to wait in the lobby while they interviewed Longdon. She would have died of curiosity.

His eye fell on her husband again and his jaw tightened. Some would describe the placid smile that graced Longdon's features as charming. Burnell's ulcer detested that infernal smile.

Damn him. How could one man harbor so many secrets? the superintendent wondered.

"Finch, take us to the office," he ordered gruffly. Then to the uniformed PCs loitering in the lobby, he said, "No one comes in, unless it is the fire brigade." The constables nodded silently in unison. "Good." He shot a look at Emmeline. "If any members of the press present their compliments, the official reply is *No Comment.* Do I make myself clear?" Another mute nod.

He waved a hand at the crowd still cluttering up the pavement. "If we've gotten their addresses and phone numbers, let them go. Dr. Meadows and his team are going to remove the body. I'd rather not have an audience."

"Yes, sir," an anonymous voice said.

The lobby became a flurry of activity in their wake. Emmeline and Gregory followed the two detectives down the corridor, their footfalls muffled by the carpeting. She gave her husband's rib cage a gentle nudge with her elbow. When he glanced down at her, she raised an eyebrow in askance. Gregory shook his head and shrugged his shoulders nonchalantly. He patted her arm lightly and mouthed, "Everything will be all right"

A flutter in the pit of her stomach told her otherwise. Her gaze settled on Superintendent Burnell's back. His movements were heavy, his shoulders taut with tension. No, everything definitely was not all right.

What had they found? she speculated. *And what could it possibly have to do with Gregory?*

Hayward's office was cramped and sparsely furnished. His desk took up most of the space. A small filing cabinet was tucked into a corner behind the door. A potted green plant, whose leaves were drooping with thirst, stood sentinel atop it.

Burnell impatiently shrugged out of his raincoat and dropped into the theatre manager's swivel chair. He steepled his fingers over his ample stomach and jerked his chin at one of the chairs across from him. Without preamble, he commanded, "Sit, Longdon."

Finch inclined his head and with a polite smile at Emmeline waved at the chair next to her husband. He flipped open his notebook and remained standing slightly to the right of the desk. As was his wont, he seemed to blend into the wall, making himself invisible. Watching and listening to see if suspects would betray themselves.

But Gregory won't, Emmeline's mind asserted loftily. *Because he hasn't committed any crime.*

She slid a sideways glance at her husband, who crossed one leg over the other and settled back in the uncomfortable chair. He offered Burnell one of his most engaging smiles. "I'm yours to command, Oliver," he murmured. "Fire away."

"Don't tempt me," Burnell muttered under his breath.

Then in a louder voice, he began his grilling. "What was your relationship with Ms. Penrose?"

"You appear to be under some misapprehension, Oliver, I—"

Burnell snapped, "*Superintendent* Burnell. I want none of your lip. If you don't answer my questions, you can become a guest of Her Majesty's prison system. The choice is entirely up to you."

The superintendent saw Emmeline open her mouth to defend her husband. He held up a hand. "No. I don't want to hear it. You are biased when it comes to your husband. You're here out of courtesy. Finch can escort you out at any time."

Burnell regretted his words as soon as they tumbled from his mouth. He never intended to take his perpetual irritation with Longdon out on her.

He pinched the bridge of his nose. "Forgive me, Emmeline. I'm just tired." Then to Gregory, he said, "Just answer my questions and we can all go home to our beds."

Gregory smoothed down the corners of his mustache. "It's my civic duty to cooperate with the police."

Burnell exhaled a weary sigh. "Right. What was your relationship with Ms. Penrose?"

"My dear, *Superintendent* Burnell." Longdon had the audacity to smile. "I never laid eyes on the woman before tonight."

Burnell exchanged a glance with Finch and then turned back to Gregory. "You're certain you want to stick to that story?"

"It's the truth," Gregory said without a trace of mockery in his tone.

"I see." The superintendent leaned back in his chair. "Then explain why the victim had the name Toby Crenshaw written in her notebook?"

Emmeline's head snapped round to gape at her

husband's profile.

Gregory reached out and squeezed her hand. However, his gaze remained on Burnell. "It's a common name."

"It isn't," the superintendent shot back. "Care to have another try?"

"I hate to disappoint you. But it's quite useless fixing your gorgon stare on me. It won't change the fact that I didn't know the late Ms. Penrose."

"I've always hated coincidences. I find it more than a bit curious that you and the victim, a woman you claim not to have known, both happened to be in the theatre tonight. And yet, she had your name—"

Gregory interrupted, "Ah, ah. You seem to forget my name's Gregory Longdon. Toby Crenshaw doesn't exist anymore. He's a ghost of the past."

"—Your name in her notebook," Burnell went on undeterred. "You're a living ghost. You haunt my days and nights."

Gregory offered him a lopsided smile. "Do I, Oliver? How touching to see that you miss me so much that you conjure up my spirit when I'm not around." He rubbed a hand in a circular motion over his chest. "It gives me a warm glow right here."

Burnell dropped his head between his hands and groaned. "Why do you insist on making things difficult all the time?" He lifted his head and wagged a finger at Gregory. "I could arrest you this instant on suspicion of murder."

This was too much for Emmeline. "You can't seriously mean that?" she asked, outraged.

"Then use your influence and tell your husband to stop wasting police time."

"There's no need to get tetchy and throw your weight about"—Gregory's glance fell upon Burnell's rounded stomach and he made a face—"Sorry, no pun intended.

I've been perfectly honest with you."

"Hmph," Burnell grunted. "You don't have an honest bone in your body. Your lies are layered in lies."

Gregory pressed a hand to his chest. "My heart is pure, Oliver."

The superintendent's gaze skewered him, but Gregory remained unfazed.

"This is not getting us anywhere, sir," Finch observed.

Taking advantage of this opening, Emmeline offered, "I think Verena came here tonight with the sole purpose of blackmailing her murderer." She had captured the attention of the three men. Good. "It surprised me that she was at the performance. Agatha Christie was definitely not her cup of tea. No, she knew her quarry would be here and she came to rattle his cage. She issued her final ultimatum in plain sight during the interval when she was hurling her insults at me and Maggie." She paused, her eyes narrowing as her mind drifted back to the ugly scene. "Yes," she murmured, nodding her head. "It was overt and subtle at the same time." She flicked a glance at Gregory. "She vowed to find out Gregory's secrets, but she was really talking to her killer. And he felt the sting of her threat."

"Why *he*? What makes you suspect it was a man?" Finch asked.

"Well as I told you earlier, after the interval when we returned to our seats I happened to glance up at Verena's box and I saw a man there with her. I didn't get a look at his face. I only saw his arm. Of course, both you and Superintendent Burnell"—she flashed a smile at the latter, hoping to get back in his good graces—"are the professionals, but I don't believe breaking someone's neck would be a woman's first method of choice when it comes to murder. Then there is the chap who burst out of the box when Gregory and I went to investigate why Verena remained there when everyone else was evacuating the theatre."

Burnell cleared his throat. "Your observations are duly noted. But I want to make something clear. From now on, there will be no more *investigating* on either of your parts."

"You can't prevent me from pursuing this story. The public has a right to know—"

Burnell cut across her. "At this stage, the public has a right to know *nothing* but the basic facts about what occurred tonight. I don't want any speculation on your part to try to lure the murderer out into the open."

Emmeline tossed her chin in the air and sniffed. "As if I would."

"You would," Burnell and Finch said in unison.

She opened her mouth to fire off an acerbic rejoinder, but then snapped it shut. It was useless. They knew her too well.

"Just the basic facts," the superintendent repeated. "I don't want another body on my hands, Emmeline. My job is to keep you and the rest of London's citizens safe."

"Truce. But will you promise to keep me apprised of any developments in the case?"

"As long as it doesn't jeopardize our investigation, I will. Don't I always?" Burnell countered.

She gave a curt nod. "Yes. I'm grateful."

"Good. Now that we've cleared the air, let's get back to business." Burnell's gaze imprisoned Gregory once again. "If you thought I had forgotten about you, you were mistaken."

A smile spread over Gregory's face. "You and I are kindred spirits, Oliver. We can never forget each other."

Finch rolled his eyes at the ceiling, while Burnell curled his fist into a tight ball.

Through gritted teeth, Burnell demanded, "What was your connection to Ms. Penrose?"

Gregory gave an exasperated sigh. "Oliver, your

faculties must be going. If you'll recall, I told you only five short minutes ago that I never met Verena Penrose before this evening."

Burnell began drumming a tattoo on the desk. "I don't believe you."

One of Gregory's shoulders twitched up in a shrug, as he eased back in his chair. "It's a free country. You're entitled to your opinion. Wrong, though it may be."

"This is a murder inquiry. Therefore, I'm entitled to answers. You can either give them to me here or down at the station." He inclined his head, his mouth stretched into a tight smile. "As you said, it's a free country and the choice is entirely up to you."

"Much as I enjoy chatting with you chaps"—Gregory's smile encompassed Finch too—"I can't tell you more than I already have because it would be a lie. Lies are pesky things that tend to wreak a good deal of havoc. And I have too much respect for you to allow one to slip from my lips because I know how much you hate them."

"Not as much as I hate you at this moment," Burnell muttered under his breath.

"I beg your pardon," Gregory prompted, but the expression on his face revealed that he had heard every word.

"Never mind. If there is such a thing as divine justice, a lightning bolt would strike you one of these days to punish you for your lifetime of sins."

"I'm as innocent as a newborn lamb."

Finch choked back an incredulous laugh. "Longdon, you were born guilty."

"Not of this murder. Or any other," Gregory asserted firmly.

"Respectfully, Superintendent Burnell," Emmeline intervened. "You're wasting your time grilling Gregory. He was never alone for an instant. You can ask Maggie and

Philip if you don't trust my word. The only time Gregory left my side was in the bar when he went to get a glass of wine for me. But he went with Philip. When the theatre was being evacuated, we got separated from Maggie and Philip. However, Gregory was with me. Therefore, I suggest that you begin looking elsewhere for your killer."

"To be brutally honest, Longdon, I never considered you the prime suspect," Burnell offered grudgingly. He scraped a hand over his beard. "But it's a devil of a coincidence that you were at the play tonight and Ms. Penrose had your name in her notebook. Why?"

Gregory stiffened and brushed off an imaginary piece of lint from his immaculately tailored trousers. "It's not my name."

"You can't deny that Toby Crenshaw was the name you were born with." When Gregory remained silent, the superintendent pressed on, "There aren't two Toby Crenshaws running around London."

Emmeline drew in a ragged breath and sat bolt upright. "But there are."

The three men stared at her perplexed.

She turned to Gregory and took his hand between both of hers. She swallowed hard. "Toby Crenshaw was Laurence Villiers's code name when he was a young MI5 agent."

Burnell's eyes widened and he shook his head. "Bloody hell. Not Villiers. If the deputy director of MI5 is mixed up in all of this, then it's far more complicated than I first thought."

"Oh, yes," Gregory replied phlegmatically. The only thing that betrayed his outward calm demeanor was a muscle pulsing along his jaw. "That makes perfect sense. I can quite see dear, old papa as your killer."

Chapter 6

I can't believe it," Finch declared. "Sir, don't you think murdering Ms. Penrose in plain sight is a bit melodramatic for Villiers? Mind you, I'm not saying the man *couldn't* kill. It's just that he's more comfortable manipulating things from the shadows. That way, his hands appear lily-white if anyone comes sniffing around to check."

"I wouldn't put anything past Villiers," Burnell griped.

Gregory lifted his hand in the air in a virtual toast. "On that point, we are in full agreement, Oliver."

Emmeline heard the bitterness in her husband's voice and ached for him. She knew that he was still reeling from the discovery a few weeks ago that Laurence Villiers was his father. Gregory didn't remember his father, the man he had been named after. All he knew was that Toby Crenshaw had abandoned his mother Clarissa when he was three years old. Clarissa had been devastated. She had no choice but to turn to her brother, Max Sanborn, for help. Sanborn, a brute of a man who Emmeline had the misfortune of crossing paths with earlier in the year, never allowed a day to go by without making sure that Clarissa and Gregory knew that they were under his roof on sufferance. Tragically, Clarissa died of cancer when Gregory was sixteen. His aunt and his two cousins did their best to console him, but Max made life even more unbearable—if that were possible. Gregory ran away at seventeen and changed his name, so no one would ever find him. He never looked back. It was a confluence of unexpected circumstances that led him to the family fold again earlier in the year.

Emmeline shook her head as she remembered those turbulent events that took place in June. She knew it was a horrible thing to think because no one deserves to be murdered. But she was glad Max was dead. The one positive outcome of all that distastefulness was that it led to a rapprochement between Gregory and his cousins Brian and Nigel, the managing director and corporate counsel of Sanborn Enterprises, the company that owned *The Clarion*. Brian and Nigel had become dear friends. She was particularly close to Nigel.

She cast a critical eye at her husband. She hadn't wanted to broach the subject of Villiers since their return from Malta, but inevitably he would be forced to confront it. Apparently, that time was thrust upon him now—whether he was ready for it or not.

"Darling" —she touched his arm lightly— "you know that you'll have to go and speak to Villiers eventually."

"He doesn't actually," Burnell interjected. "Not about the murder, at least. That's our job and I'd thank you both not to involve yourselves any further."

Emmeline threw her hands up in the air in exasperation. "That's all well and good, Superintendent. But we were here tonight." She tapped one finger on the desk. "*In locus quo*, as the police jargon goes. We can bring valuable insight to your investigation."

"Emmeline, have you heard anything I've said thus far?"

She offered him a broad smile. "I always listen to every word."

Burnell exchanged a look with Finch and then his gaze shot to Gregory. "Married only a month and a half, and you've already managed to corrupt your wife."

The corners of Gregory's mouth twitched with amusement. "I don't know what you mean." He gave Emmeline a cheeky wink. "Emmy is admired throughout the Fourth Estate for her integrity."

She beamed at him. "Thank you, darling. That's kind of you."

"However, more and more lately, a devious recklessness has led to a distinct lack of hearing when it comes to obeying authority figures—who know what's best." Burnell gave her a pointed look. "This seems to have displaced any natural integrity."

Emmeline lowered her gaze and had the good grace to look abashed. "It's not quite as bad as all that." She threw him a glance from under her dark lashes. Lifting her hand, she squeezed her forefinger and thumb together until there was only a tiny space between them. "I admit to a teeny bit. But that's only because the wheels of justice need prodding from time to time. You must admit that justice is sometimes too blind. No disrespect intended."

Laughter bubbled up in Burnell's throat. He couldn't help it. Emmeline could be utterly disarming, leaving him off balance on occasion. "Let us worry about the wheels of justice."

"Of course," she said as she rose to her feet. "If there's nothing else, we'll leave you to get on with your inquiries."

Gregory stood and helped Emmeline on with her coat, before shrugging into his own.

Burnell heaved himself out of the chair and gave a curt nod. "Thank you. The Metropolitan Police appreciates your assistance." He paused for a breath. "It ends here, though. No haring off after killers on your own. You're a journalist, not a trained police officer."

"But I *am* trained to ask questions. With the right question, you can find out all sorts of things. Eventually, all the bits and pieces lead to the truth. And I promise you, I will find out the answers." She nodded at each detective in turn. "Good night, gentlemen."

Gregory merely grinned and sketched a salute at Burnell and Finch.

And then, husband and wife swept out of the office.

The superintendent slumped back down into his chair and exhaled a long, weary breath. "I'm getting old, Finch. I don't have the stamina anymore to deal with them. I don't know which one is worse."

Finch chuckled and lowered himself into the chair Emmeline had just vacated. "The pair of them do tend to suck out all the oxygen from the air when they gang up together, don't they?"

"Hmph," Burnell grunted. "That's putting it mildly."

In a more serious tone, the sergeant asked, "Do you think Longdon was lying?"

"It's second nature for him to lie. But I was watching him. He was genuinely surprised when I told him that the victim had the name Toby Crenshaw in her notebook."

"Then that means Emmeline was right. It must refer to Villiers."

"That will be our secret. Her curiosity is already aroused. No need to fan the flames."

"Of course not. But as we both know, she has an uncanny knack for ferreting out the truth." A pensive expression flickered across Finch's face. "For the life of me, sir, I can't see what the connection is between Villiers and a muckraking journalist, who fattened her bank account with the proceeds of blackmail. You'd think he'd go out of his way to avoid her."

Burnell shrugged. "At this stage, it's only conjecture on our part—albeit educated conjecture—that the Toby

Crenshaw is Villiers. Don't forget that even we policemen have to deal with all sorts of people. Some are quite unsavory. Villiers is no saint. The spy game is a dirty business. It leaves a stain on the soul."

"Yes, sir."

Burnell placed his palms on the desk and pushed himself to his feet. "Right. I'd like to have another look at the crime scene. Then we'll call it a night. Villiers can wait until the morning. After I've had a few hours of sleep. I need my head clear to deal with the master of deception."

ഗദ്ധ

Consummate professional though he was, Burnell forgot that the early bird always catches the worm. And, in this instance, a head start on the investigation into Verena Penrose's murder. Therefore the next morning, it was Emmeline, not one of Scotland Yard's finest detectives, who was waiting in the antechamber of Laurence Villiers's office at Thames House, MI5's headquarters on the north bank of the river near Lambeth Bridge.

His secretary had done her imperious best to send Emmeline packing. Alas, Emmeline had not been impressed one iota and refused to budge from the office, until she had spoken to Villiers. The secretary knew that Emmeline was more than capable of making a scene and writing something equally unsuitable in her paper. Consequently, they tacitly called a truce, a hostile one, but a truce nevertheless. The secretary retreated to the battlement behind her desk, while Emmeline settled on the edge of the camel-colored Chesterfield leather sofa across the room, looking as if she would spring to her feet at the least provocation. From time to time, the secretary's disapproving stare fixed upon Emmeline, who did her best to ignore it. Instead, she was mentally preparing her list of questions.

A half an hour later, Villiers swept into the antechamber, a copy of *The Times* was tucked under his arm and he held his briefcase in his other hand. His features were pinched in a preoccupied expression. He hadn't noticed Emmeline's presence.

"Good morning, Dorothy," he murmured perfunctorily.

"Good morning, Mr. Villiers." She cleared her throat. "Ahem. You have an unexpected visitor."

"I don't have time for visitors, unexpected or otherwise," he snapped. "Who the devil is it?"

Dorothy gestured with her chin at Emmeline, who rose slowly.

Villiers stiffened and his jaw tightened. "Oh, it's you. I don't have time for any of your usual nonsense. I have a very busy day, so you had best be on your way."

Emmeline crossed over to him. She would not be put off. "Good morning, Mr. Villiers," she said pleasantly. "I assure you my questions will only take a few moments of your time. If you cooperate. Otherwise, I will be forced to return every day until you do speak to me. "

He stared down his nose at her. "And if I don't choose to do so?" he challenged, his gaze ablaze with annoyance.

"My journalistic instincts will begin wondering why you are being evasive. And then, I will simply have to find out what you are hiding." She smiled to dilute the hardness in her tone.

The air between them crackled with tension. Villiers glared at her for several long seconds. She couldn't read the thoughts racing behind those cinnamon eyes that were so like Gregory's. She met his gaze without flinching. By now, Villiers should know that he could not intimidate her.

In the end, Villiers relented. "Ten minutes. That's all I can spare."

He stalked toward his office and gave the doorknob an

angry flick of his wrist. He stood aside to allow Emmeline to enter first and softly pressed the door closed behind him.

He waved impatiently at a chair. "Sit," he ordered tersely, as he came around the desk and dropped his briefcase on the floor. The plush carpeting muted the *thud*.

Emmeline settled in the chair opposite and took her notebook and pen out of her handbag, as she waited until Villiers was seated.

"Well, what do you want?" he asked churlishly as he shot his cuff and pointedly glanced at his watch. Clearly, he was in no mood to extend the social niceties.

That was fine by her. The faster she was out of his presence, the better.

She gave a curt nod and launched her first volley. "Verena Penrose was murdered last night at St. Martin's Theatre. What was your connection to Verena?"

He snorted. "We didn't run in the same circles."

Pen hovering over a clean page, she persisted, "So you're denying that you knew her?"

"If you hadn't noticed, I do not count members of the press among my intimate friends. They tend to have an insatiable desire to blurt out things that are best kept out of the public realm."

"Why?"

His brow puckered in confusion. "Why what?"

"Why are you against the public knowing the truth?"

A lupine smile curled around Villiers's mouth. "There are truths and there are truths. Not everything should see the light of day."

"That's merely political double talk," she countered irritably.

"I answered your question. If you were dissatisfied with my response, that's your problem." He gave her a tight smile and stretched out a hand for a file to his right that Dorothy no doubt had prepared for his review. "If that was all you wanted to know, I—"

Emmeline leaned forward slightly. "It was not."

Villiers exhaled a bored sigh. "No, of course not. With you, it never is just one question."

She ignored the sarcasm. "If, as you *claim*, you didn't know Verena, why did the police find the name Toby Crenshaw written in a notebook that was in her handbag along with Amsterdam, Brussels, Barcelona, and Madrid scrawled next to it?"

She could see his cunning mind was attempting to gauge how much she knew. Unfortunately, it was nothing. That was why she was here, hoping to tease something out of him. She squared her shoulders and sat up straighter in her chair, arranging her features in a confident expression.

"Shall I repeat the question?" she pressed, when he remained silent.

"My faculties are still intact, despite what you may think, Miss Kirby."

"I'm delighted to hear it. Then perhaps you could provide an answer."

"I actually don't have to cooperate with you at all."

"Thus far, you haven't."

He tapped his forefinger on the desk. "Fine. How should I know why the woman had the name written in her notebook?"

"You've answered my question with a question. As a tactic, it's a failure. I'm not easily distracted."

"More's the pity," he muttered under his breath.

"Toby Crenshaw was your field name, when you were a young agent."

"It's also the name your husband was born with," he snarled.

"Yes, he was named after his father," she hurled back at him. "A father who abandoned him and his mother. Is it any wonder that he decided to change it?"

She drew in a sharp breath. She hadn't intended to bring up that particularly painful issue. It was just that Villiers was so insufferable that she had lost her temper.

"Is that what this charade is all about? Toby sits at home licking his wounds, while he sends his nosy, interfering little wife to fight his battles for him."

Emmeline surged to her feet. Her pulse was racing and blood was thundering in her ears. "How dare you? My husband's name is *Gregory*. And he's worth a thousand of you. He's more than capable of standing up to you—"

Villiers interrupted her tirade. "From this moment on, this conversation is off the record. Agreed?" By now, he was on his feet too. His nostrils flared with anger.

Emmeline gave a curt nod. She didn't trust her voice.

"You like twisting Toby around your finger so that he doesn't know whether he's coming or going. You're a loose cannon with your exaggerated sense of right and wrong. The world is not etched in black and white. Your husband is a jewel thief. That will never change. Accept it. You will get him killed if you attempt to mold him into your image of the ideal husband."

Her chest clenched and the air escaped from her lungs. Emmeline felt the full force of his poisonous words as if her head had been held underwater and she was fighting for breath.

"I never—" She cursed herself for the tremor in her voice. Damn the man. She cleared her throat and tried again. "I have never attempted to change Gregory."

Villiers snorted. "Haven't you? Who was the one who issued an ultimatum about his choice of career?"

She gaped at him in astonishment. "I find it a bit hypocritical that you, a man in the highest echelons of the country's law enforcement circles, are reproaching me for asking Gregory—"

"Asking? Ha."

She drew herself to her full height, although Villiers's six-foot frame still dwarfed her. She gritted her teeth and persevered. "Yes, *asking* Gregory to find another career path. You can't seriously tell me that you want your son to go on breaking the law. Sooner or later he would be caught."

With a smirk on his lips, he hitched a hip on the corner of his desk. "I very much doubt it. Toby is far too clever. But he loves you beyond reason and that's what worries me."

Emmeline absorbed these last words in silence. At last, she ventured, "Do you doubt my love for Gregory?"

"No, any fool can see it." It must have taken a lot for him to admit that much, she thought. Then his gaze locked on her face. "But sometimes love is not enough. And you, Miss Kirby, are dangerous. You don't even realize the damage that you do with your indiscreet questions."

She curled her fist at her side. "I'm doing my job. The truth matters."

He sighed. "Yes, yes. I know. It's all very tiresome."

She cocked her head to one side and studied him. "What are you hiding about your relationship with Verena Penrose?"

He rolled his eyes toward the ceiling, mumbled something unintelligible, and looked her in the eye again. "I told you before. I didn't know the woman. Why are you so interested in her anyway? Was she a friend of yours?"

"Hardly," she grunted. "Verena was vile and unscrupulous. She was a hack. I loathed everything about her."

"Well then? What's the big interest in her? It's a police matter."

"You're right. It is. But Verena was quite a notorious celebrity. That makes it news. I'm particularly intrigued because Gregory and I found her body."

"You were at the theatre?"

"Yes, we even had words with Verena in the bar during the intermission."

His eyes narrowed. "Words about what?" he asked suspiciously

"Nothing in particular. It was just the usual viciousness Verena tended to spout."

"If the two of you didn't get on, what the devil were you and Toby doing in her box?"

Emmeline leveled a steady stare at him and tried to keep the triumph from seeping into her voice. "How do you know Verena had a box at the theatre? I didn't mention it."

Without missing a beat, Villiers waved his hand at the door. "Your ten minutes are up, Miss Kirby."

Emmeline pursed her lips. She had no choice but to leave. Villiers was more than capable of having her escorted out of the building and that was the last thing she wanted. She closed her notebook, slipped into her coat, and hitched her handbag over her shoulder as she wished him a good day.

She turned on her heel and crossed to the door. As her fingers touched the knob, Villiers's voice called, "I'm certain that I don't have to remind you that our entire conversation was off the record."

Chapter 7

When Emmeline entered her office at *The Clarion* nearly an hour later, she found Jeremy Padgett, the editor-in-chief, and Nigel Sanborn, the corporate counsel for Sanborn Enterprises, the paper's parent company, waiting for her. They were chatting, apparently amiably, but broke off when she stepped across the threshold.

She nodded at each man in turn as she pressed the door closed behind her. "Jeremy, Nigel. To what do I owe this ambush?"

Both men rose. Nigel walked over to her and bent down to give her a peck on the cheek. "A cousinly kiss to prove that we are here in the spirit of goodwill."

She eyed him skeptically, but reached up and returned the kiss. "I very much doubt it."

"Really, Emmeline. We only wanted to have a friendly chat."

She chortled. "I'll bet you did."

She slipped out of her coat and hung it up on the hanger on the back of her door. Then, she walked over to the desk and lowered herself into her chair. She waited until Jeremy and Nigel had resumed their seats opposite her.

"Let me guess. I have Villiers to thank for this little visit." She gave an angry shake of her head and held out her wrists. "Well, go on. I'm waiting for the formal rap on the knuckles."

"Don't be silly, Emmeline," Jeremy implored.

She leaned forward and propped her elbows on the desk. "You can forget it if you think I'm dropping the story." She flicked a challenging glance at Nigel. "I need not point out that under my contract I have full editorial control without any interference from management."

"We're not here to haul you before the Royal Courts of Justice," Nigel countered quietly. "We're on your side. So if you've quite finished with your speech, perhaps you'll listen."

"Oh," she mumbled, chastened.

"Yes," Jeremy picked up the thread. "You correctly surmised that Villiers rang me up the instant you left his office. He politely, but quite firmly, made it clear that any reporting about Verena Penrose's murder would be frowned upon. I pointed out to him that it would attract even more negative attention were the *Clarion* to do a story on the government's attempt to muzzle the press."

Emmeline chuckled. "Bravo, Jeremy. I'll wager that didn't go down well."

Jeremy sighed. "No, it didn't. But Villiers realized that it was useless to force the matter. For the time being. I'm under no illusions that he has given up. That's why I consulted Nigel."

Nigel nodded. "There's nothing Villiers can do. Unless he can make the case that the country's security is at risk. Which he can't without tipping his hand. And he certainly doesn't want to do that. Therefore, we advise that you tread carefully."

Her mouth curved into a Cheshire cat grin. "I'm an expert at tiptoeing."

"Just see to it that you don't tiptoe into a minefield," Nigel offered with lawyerly caution.

ʚϡɞ

Villiers slapped the file closed. It had been his third attempt to read it. But he had no idea of its substance. The words had started to blur on the page.

He snatched his spectacles off his nose and tossed them on the desk. "Damn that woman," he cursed aloud to his office. "Why did she always have to stick her nose in where it didn't belong?"

Her curiosity was only going to stir up trouble—as usual—just when he was hoping to keep things quiet.

Oh, Toby, he lamented. *Why did you have to marry her?* It was his fault. He knew it. If he hadn't left Clarissa and Toby, his son would have turned out to be a very different man. And he would have found a wife who was less intent on disrupting the grand scheme of things. But would Toby have been happy?

The peal of his telephone jarred him from these recriminations and questions for which he had no answers.

He sighed before reluctantly picking up the receiver. "Yes, Dorothy?"

"Mr. Villiers, a Superintendent Burnell and Sergeant Finch of the Metropolitan Police are here to see you."

Villiers's dropped his chin to his chest and shook his head. "Am I going to be plagued by unwanted visitors all day long?"

"I did inform the gentlemen that you were extremely busy, sir," his loyal gatekeeper replied, "but they insist it's official business."

Villiers pursed his lips and was silent for a long moment. "Send them in."

Otherwise, they would only clutter up the antechamber making a nuisance of themselves—they had that trait in common with Miss Kirby.

He rose wearily and was on his feet, when the door swung open. Dorothy stepped aside to allow the two detectives to enter.

"Ah, Superintendent Burnell, Sergeant Finch." He waved at the two chairs before his desk.

When they were all seated, Dorothy inquired, "Shall I bring some tea?"

"No" was Villiers's brusque response. Then he sought to soften the curtness of his tone with a smile. "We wouldn't want to keep these gentlemen from their duty a minute longer than is necessary, do we?"

Dorothy nodded. "No, sir," she murmured and slipped from the room, closing the door behind her.

Villiers rubbed his hands together. "If you've come about Verena Penrose's murder, I'm afraid you've wasted a trip. As I told Miss Kirby—"

"What?" Burnell bristled. "Emmeline...I mean Miss Kirby was here this morning?"

Villiers experienced a small stab of glee at the sight of the flush spreading beneath the superintendent's beard. "Indeed." He glanced at his watch. "She left not more than an hour ago."

Burnell and Finch exchanged a wary look.

The superintendent swallowed down his annoyance and proceeded with his task. "Nevertheless, Mr. Villiers, you'll appreciate that we have a job to do."

Villiers eased back in his chair and propped his elbows on the armrests. "Naturally. And if I may say, you do it admirably. The public can sleep safe in their beds when there are men like you out there every day."

"Thank you, sir. I'm glad that you feel that way. Therefore, I'm sure you'll understand that we have to follow every lead."

"That's what any police officer worth his salt would

do."

"Yes." Burnell offered him a wan smile. "Of course, we're all on the same side."

"In a manner of speaking," Villiers hedged.

One of Burnell's eyebrows quirked upward. "I beg your pardon."

Villiers leaned forward and folded his hands on his desk. "Well, I don't have to tell you"—he lowered his voice conspiratorially—"that my assistance can only go so far. I can't comprise ongoing cases."

"We would never ask you to do so," Burnell balked, clearly incensed by the mere suggestion.

Villiers slapped the desk. "Good. I'm glad we cleared the air on that point." He reached for his spectacles. "Now, I really must get back to these files." He gestured at the stack to his right.

"But, Mr. Villiers, we haven't asked you any questions yet."

Villiers frowned. "Sorry, we seem to be speaking at cross-purposes. I did say when you first walked in that I couldn't help you with the Penrose murder in any way. As far as I'm concerned, it's strictly a police matter." He offered them a tight smile. "I wouldn't want to stick in my nose where it's not wanted. As one professional to another, I recommend that you and—" He flicked a questioning glance at Finch.

"Finch," the sergeant offered.

Villiers snapped his fingers. "That's right. Finch." His gaze returned to Burnell. "I recommend that you and Finch get out there. You wouldn't want the trail to go cold, would you?"

A muscle pulsed along Burnell's jaw. He pushed himself to his feet. Finch followed suit.

Through clenched teeth, the superintendent affirmed tersely, "Certainly not." He extended a hand toward the deputy director of MI5. "Thank you for sparing us these *very* brief moments of your time."

Villiers rose too and gave the detective's hand a brisk shake. "Think nothing of it. We're on the same side after all."

Burnell's eyes bulged and he choked back a cough. Finch tugged on his sleeve. "Come along, sir. Don't forget that meeting."

The superintendent's head whipped around. "Meeting? What meeting?"

"Oh, you know, sir. The meeting. We must be off or we'll be late."

Burnell shrugged and allowed himself to be dragged toward the door. He didn't utter a word until they were outside on the pavement.

"What bloody meeting?" he demanded.

"Sorry, sir. Bit of a white lie. I thought it best to get you out of Villiers's office before you throttled him." His face creased into a boyish grin. "It wouldn't do to have you suspended on murder charges again."

Burnell clapped him on the shoulder, his mouth twisting into a half-smile. "I nearly gave him what-for."

"I recognized the tell-tale signs. You and Emmeline could compete against each other for who has the hottest temper."

"Hey." Burnell wagged an accusatory finger at him. "Watch your step, my lad. Remember that you're addressing a senior officer."

Finch exhaled a martyred sigh. "How could I forget. At least it's not Assistant Commissioner Cruickshank."

Burnell groaned. "It's too early in the day to mention the Boy Wonder. It's bad enough that Emmeline has gotten a jump on us."

As they walked toward their car, Finch observed, "Her visit explains why Villiers was already on his guard when we arrived. Do you think that she was able to wheedle anything out of him?"

Burnell pursed his lips and thrust his hands deep into his coat pockets. "She gets under one's skin and doesn't let go." He halted and looked Finch directly in the eye. "We'll just have to ask her. After I give her a stern lecture—yet again—on the perils of investigating on her own. If anyone is an expert at rattling people, it's Emmeline."

"There's Longdon, of course," Finch pointed out.

Burnell rolled his eyes toward the charcoal clouds above their heads, which threatened another round of showers. "Don't remind me. My ulcer only allows me to deal with one of them at a time. Even if it's only in thought."

Finch chuckled as Burnell's mobile began ringing. The superintendent drew it out of his inner pocket and swore under his breath when he saw the number.

"That's all I need." He glared at the sergeant. "You tempted Providence. It's the Boy Wonder." He took a deep breath, steeling his nerves before he answered it. "Good morning, sir." To his own ears, his voice dripped with saccharine insincerity.

Forgoing a polite greeting in return, the assistant commissioner plunged in, "Burnell, I want to see you immediately. I've just had a call from MI5 Deputy Director Laurence Villiers."

"Someone wasted no time," Burnell grumbled to himself. Then aloud to Cruickshank, he said, "Indeed, sir?"

"He tells me that you and Finch have been making a nuisance of yourselves."

Burnell gripped the mobile harder and pressed it against his ear. He cleared his throat. "We were following up on a lead. Mr. Villiers's name came up in connection with the Verena Penrose murder."

"Oh, don't be ridiculous. What could Villiers possibly have to do with the victim?"

"That's what we were trying to ascertain," Burnell replied as patiently as he could. "Finch and I took up barely five minutes of Mr. Villiers's precious time. He didn't have more to spare."

"Did you really expect him to clear his diary merely because the two of you appeared? He's an extremely busy man. I can't continue this conversation over the phone. Come to my office and give me a full report the instant you set foot in the station."

No, of course, you don't have time now, the superintendent reflected to himself. *You like nothing better than a face-to-face dressing down to bolster your ego.*

"Yes, sir," he answered respectfully, while he secretly wished all the plagues in Christendom to come crashing down upon the Boy Wonder's head.

Chapter 8

By ten-thirty, Gregory already had finished writing the report on his last case. He had managed to recover a Monet that had been stolen from the Belgravia mansion of a well-connected crony of a cabinet minister. This added yet another notch in his list of successes since he joined Symington's over the summer and elevated the company's prestige in the insurance world. And his professional stature. It wouldn't cross anyone's mind that he was anything other than a law-abiding member of the society. This allowed him to indulge in his true *métier*, the vocation to which he was born: *stealing jewels*. Except for Emmy—the only woman who had captured his heart and soul—there was nothing more stimulating for his mind than planning and executing the perfect heist. His conscience wasn't terribly bothered about the owners of the coveted baubles. They were drowning in money. In all likelihood, after the momentary shock of the theft, they gleeful accepted the insurance payment. This gave them an excuse to go out and purchase an even more extravagant piece to replace the one that had been stolen. Therefore, he reasoned, no one was ultimately hurt and he should be commended for keeping the wheels of British commerce spinning at a brisk pace.

He frowned. However, he had to admit that two of his

most recent capers had nearly cost him and Emmy their lives. And yet, would he have thought twice about stealing the gems if he could have seen into the future?

Hmm. He leaned back in his chair as images of the gems danced before his eyes. The Blue Angel, a flawless twelve-carat blue diamond, and the cheeky Pink Courtesan, a fifteen-carat, oval-shaped fancy vivid pink diamond ring. His frowned deepened. He had become reacquainted with the pink vixen quite unexpectedly through his old friend Roger Delahunt, who actually stole it *twice* culminating in all that trouble in Malta.

Gregory sighed and shook his head. Beautiful, but deadly as sin. Both diamonds no longer held the same cachet as when they first came into his possession. That was because they would forever be tainted by their association with Alastair Swanbeck, the ruthless entrepreneur with underworld connections who had made it his mission to seek revenge on Gregory for interfering in his nefarious business ventures. By extension, Emmy became a target too when her probing questions came too close to home.

For the millionth time since they had returned from Malta, Gregory asked himself, "Is Swanbeck truly dead?"

The rational part of his brain told him that Swanbeck was twenty fathoms below sea level. No one could have survived the explosion. But without a body, a niggling voice told him they would be left to wonder for the rest of their lives.

He shook his head, as if to physically rid his mind of these disturbing ruminations. He was not inherently morose. Emmy tended to be the one who worried. It was rather a specialty of hers. That and placing herself in harm's way for the sake of a bloody story. For Emmy's sake and their marriage, he had to banish Swanbeck to the darkest corner of the past. And never look back.

Perhaps it was time to divest himself of the Blue Angel and the Pink Courtesan? After all, he still had the Tarasova ruby-and-diamond necklace. For a change of pace, and to exercise his skills, he could turn his attention to other precious gems. Emeralds, sapphires, and more luscious rubies. A smile tugged at the corners of his mouth. Yes. Rubies were fetching the highest prices these days.

Time to do a spot of research to find a suitable candidate to purloin. The blood began thrumming through his veins, as it always did, when he was planning another heist. The thrill would never pall. In fact, these days it was even more exhilarating because he had to be doubly careful since he was now a married man and Emmy's antennae were adept at detecting the merest hint of something suspicious.

He chuckled to himself. What she didn't know wouldn't hurt her. It was kinder, really. The truth would only upset her.

Speaking of the truth, they would have to get to the bottom of Verena Penrose's murder and her connection to Villiers. His lips pressed into a thin line, when he thought of the secretive man who had turned out to be his long-lost papa. His fingers tightened on the armrests of his chair. Gregory had no doubt that the odious woman's demise was a direct result of her ties to Villiers.

He closed his eyes and pinched the bridge of his nose. His brain told him that he would have to go and see Villiers. But he didn't relish the forthcoming encounter.

※※※

Gregory decided to make a detour before visiting Villiers. As Symington's chief investigator, no one would question his presence in the environs of Hatton Garden, which had been at the center of the diamond and jewelry trade for over a hundred years. Wedged between the lively West End and fashionable East End, "The Garden," as it was affectionately called by those who worked in the area, was located in the Holborn district of the borough of Camden. Eighty-seven different independent jewelry retailers and 300 jewel-related businesses could be found there.

The London Diamond Bourse at 100 Hatton Garden is the only place in the UK that houses a live diamond trading floor. The Bourse was started back in the 1940s by a group of Jewish *diamantiers*, or merchants, who fled from Nazi-occupied Antwerp. Several had managed to smuggle out their diamonds by sewing them into the clothes on their backs. Today, traders, manufacturers, wholesalers, craftsmen, gemologists, and merchants have offices in the building, while Hammond Bank is ensconced on the ground floor with its safe deposit unit, a vast underground network of vaults, tunnels, and workshops, located in the basement.

Gregory stood on the pavement for a moment, smiling to himself as he indulged in a bit of nostalgia. After he had run away as a teenager from his miserable existence under his Uncle Max's roof, he had found himself at the Garden. He desperately needed a job to feed himself. Although he knew absolutely nothing about the diamond industry, Howard Nussbaum, a kind-hearted man with warm brown eyes and a neatly trimmed mustache, took pity on him. He hired Gregory at Nussbaum Ltd., the family's well-established wholesale jewelry company, as an apprentice to a lapidary, the person who cuts, polishes, or engraves gems. And that's how Gregory's love affair with jewels began. He gained invaluable knowledge about every facet of the industry in the three years he had worked at Nussbaum's.

Gregory sighed. Those were happy days indeed. In the

intervening years, he had kept in touch with the Nussbaums, although not as often as he should have. He pushed open the door and stepped into the lobby of the Bourse, making a mental note to change this state of affairs. It would start today with his visit to David Nussbaum, Howard's son who was a specialist in the sorting and grading of polished diamonds of all shapes and sizes. David was the director of business.

He crossed the lobby, his heels clicking against the marble floor. At the reception desk, he flashed a broad smile at the gentleman on duty and gave his name as he handed over one of his business cards.

The sulky older man hunched his shoulders forward, providing Gregory with a view of his gleaming bald crown as he gave the card a cursory glance. This was followed by a growl, which Gregory assumed was good morning, but he couldn't be sure.

In a polite tone, Gregory said, "I'd like to see David Nussbaum."

The man's watery brown eyes narrowed suspiciously. "Mr. Nussbaum is a busy man. Do you have an appointment?"

"I'm afraid I don't, but I'm certain he will see me."

The man smirked, as his hand reached out for the phone. "Are you now? I wouldn't hold my breath."

"Why don't we allow Mr. Nussbaum to decide, shall we?"

"Hmph" was the man's response as he punched in a number.

There was a brief silence before someone on the other end of the line answered.

Gregory heard a pleasant female voice. "Hello, Ben. How can I help you?"

"There's a chap down here who wants to see Mr. Nussbaum, but he doesn't have an appointment." He looked up at Gregory, a malicious grin on his face. "Shall I send him packing?"

"What does this gentleman want?"

"How should I know what he wants?" Ben demanded with more than a touch of asperity. "He *said* he's the chief investigator at Symington's. I assume he's investigating something."

Gregory bit back a smile at the exasperated grunt emitted by the woman. "Oh, Ben. I despair of you sometimes. We haven't had a robbery in the Garden. Why would this Symington's fellow be sniffing around?"

"It's nothing to do with me. Do you think I have time to waste inquiring what every Tom, Dick, and Harry is up to?"

"Can you at least tell me the gentleman's name?"

Ben held the card aloft and squinted at it. "His card says he's a Gregory Longdon. Now, I must be getting on. Time waits for no man. Will Mr. Nussbaum see him or not?"

The woman released a heavy sigh. "Thank you for that bit of wisdom. Yes, send Mr. Longdon up. I'll sort it out."

Ben slammed the receiver back into the cradle. He sniffed. Clearly, he was disappointed to be denied the pleasure of telling Gregory to shove off. He scribbled out a pass and thrust it and the business card at Gregory. "Here. Mr. Nussbaum will see you. Fifth floor. Suite 502." He jerked his head to the left. "The lift is over there."

Gregory inclined his head in thanks and bid him good day.

Happily, Nussbaum secretary's, an attractive woman in her forties wearing a soft gray, belted wool dress with elbow-length sleeves and a white collar, greeted him with a smile as he entered the office. "Good morning, Mr. Longdon. I must apologize for Ben. He seems to become more churlish with each passing day. I will speak with the management about his behavior."

Gregory waved a hand dismissively. "Please don't do so on my account. The poor chap is probably having a bad day. It happens to all of us."

Her caramel eyes twinkled with amusement. "As you wish. Now, how can Nussbaum Limited assist Symington's?"

"I'm afraid it's rather a delicate matter. And confidential." He favored her with an apologetic smile. "I can only discuss it with Mr. Nussbaum."

She held up a hand. "You need say no more. I understand. Mr. Nussbaum stepped down the hall to speak to a colleague." She rose and walked around the desk. "He should be back momentarily. You can wait in his office."

She saw him settled in the chair opposite her boss's desk. Since he politely declined her offer of a cup of tea, she explained that she would get back to her work. The door barely creaked on its hinges as it closed behind her.

Gregory took a turn around the room, his hands clasped behind his back. Barely five minutes had elapsed when he cocked an ear at the murmur of voices in the outer office.

The next instant, the door swung open and a tall, slim man in his late fifties with a head of thick, wavy salt-and-pepper hair bustled into the room. His round face was lightly scored by lines, which hinted at his genial nature and quickness to smile and laugh heartily. "I'm sorry to have kept you waiting—"

Nussbaum broke off and stopped short. A spark of delight was reflected in his onyx eyes when he caught sight of Gregory.

"Well, as I live and breathe. Sharon said a Mr. Longdon from Symington's was waiting to see me. I didn't think it was you." A smile spread across his face. "Is it a mirage?"

Gregory grinned and extended a hand, which the other man clasped between both his. "Hello, David. It's good to see you."

"It's been far too long," Nussbaum countered, as he pumped Gregory's hand up and down vigorously. "I can't believe it, Greg. Hold up a minute. This is some sort of a joke. *You* can't be Symington's chief investigator."

"I assure you. It's perfectly true." He drew out his silver card case from his inner jacket pocket with a flourish and handed a buff card to his friend. "Here's my business card, if you don't believe me."

Nussbaum glanced down at the bold lettering and then he lifted his gaze to Gregory's face again. He cleared his throat. "I'd heard rumors that you retired from the game. Frankly, I was relieved to hear it. But this"—he tapped the card against his palm—"is rather at the other end of the spectrum, isn't it? How did you land the job with your colorful CV?"

"It's a long story. Maybe I'll tell you someday."

"You probably shouldn't. Why are you here? Obviously, it's not a social call, if you're waving your Symington's credentials about."

Gregory gestured to the desk. "Why don't we sit down?"

Nussbaum strode to his chair, while Gregory lowered himself into the one across from him.

"I thought it would be less likely to arouse curiosity," Gregory told him, "if I dropped by under the Symington's flag. I need your help, David."

The other man spread his hands wide. "Anything. You name it."

Gregory cleared his throat. "I'm married again—"

Nussbaum's eyes bulged in surprise. "Married? You?" He shook his head in astonishment. "After all that chaos with Ronnie, I never thought you'd get married again. Don't get me wrong. You certainly deserve happiness. I merely thought it was a case of once burned, twice shy. Forgive me for saying so, but Ronnie...well, she scorched everything in her path."

Silence filled the space between them as their thoughts strayed to Veronica, or more familiarly Ronnie, Gregory's tempestuous first wife. A breathtakingly beautiful woman with a mercenary black heart. In the end, all her conniving and scheming had caught up with her and she had been murdered.

At last, Gregory said, "Emmy is nothing like Ronnie. She's warm, loving, and loyal to a fault. Mind you, she has a temper. But then, none of us is perfect."

A laugh exploded from Nussbaum. "Your Emmy sounds like a treasure. How long have you been married?"

"Actually, we're still technically newlyweds. We were married at the end of October."

"Goodness. Nearly two months. So, you'd like a nice piece for your bride?" He rubbed his hands together. His eyes sparkling with glee. "You came to the right man. I have some lovely diamonds to show you and I'll get our best designer to create something really special. You won't be disappointed."

He started to get up, but Gregory placed a restraining hand on his arm. "Perhaps another time." Nussbaum sank back down.

"Today, I came to you for advice. I want to sell something. Two items, actually." Gregory paused and moistened his lips with the tip of his tongue. "One is blue and the other is pink."

Nussbaum's spine stiffened. "You don't mean...You couldn't possibly." He fixed his onyx stare on Gregory's face. His voice dropped to a rasping whisper. "The Blue Angel and the Pink Courtesan?"

Gregory smoothed down the corners of his mustache and gave a slow nod.

Nussbaum slumped back. After a long pause, he asserted, "You know Nussbaum's is a *legitimate* business.

I can't stress that strongly enough. We always have been. That's why my father and I were extremely shocked to hear of your career choice when you left us." He paused for a beat. "You said you've gone straight."

"Actually, I didn't. You inferred it. I still dabble from time to time."

"I wouldn't call the Blue Angel and Pink Courtesan dabbling," Nussbaum replied tartly. "It's more like the premier league."

Gregory smiled. "I'm not here for a lesson in semantics or a lecture on my wicked ways. I want to sell the diamonds as quickly as possible. I know it's asking a great deal, but can you help me?"

Nussbaum gasped and gave a curt shake of his head. "Absolutely out of the question. I haven't even touched the stones and I feel as if my fingers have been scalded. Greg, you know this is dangerous. The diamond industry is a small world. Everyone knows everybody else. If word gets out—"

Gregory interrupted him before he gave full vent to his outrage and disapproval. "Please, David. It's because you know everybody that I came to you. All I need is a name. Someone who is discreet and won't ask any questions. You don't have to be involved at all. Just a name."

Nussbaum pursed his lips. He propped his elbows on his armrests and steepled his hands over his stomach. He fell into a brooding silence, as he swiveled back and forth. A thousand thoughts chased themselves across his features.

"All right," he finally declared. The words were infused with a deep reluctance. "Only this once. *Never* ask me again."

Gregory crossed his fingers over his heart and held them in the air. "I promise."

"You're a good man and a friend. I would never turn you in, Greg. But why? You risk losing everything. Don't you realize that? You're a married man. Focus on your wife and your life together."

Gregory reached across the desk and gave the other man's arm a squeeze. "I am. That's why I have to get rid of the Blue Angel and Pink Courtesan. To keep Emmy safe."

Nussbaum's brow puckered. "Safe? Is *she* involved in your capers?" he demanded incredulously. His eyes narrowed. "I thought you said that she was different from Ronnie."

Gregory threw his head back and laughed. The mere idea of Emmy as his accomplice was too amusing to contemplate. "Put your mind at rest. Emmy is not, and never has been, in the game. She's a journalist."

Nussbaum gave a low whistle. "Journalist? Then you're more of a lunatic than I believed. Does she know about your life of crime?"

Gregory clucked his tongue. "Crime is an ugly word. It has such negative connotations. You're beginning to sound like my friend Oliver. His mind tends to run to the same odd notions."

The other man dismissed this comment with a wave of his hand. "Never mind. What about your wife?"

Gregory chose his words carefully. "As a journalist, Emmy is naturally inquisitive. About virtually everything. She has been able to discover certain things, but she has yet to delve into all the minute details about my past. I'd like to keep it that way."

Nussbaum snorted and nodded sagely. "I'll bet you would." He pushed himself to his feet. "Right. Give me a couple of days. I'll have a name for you."

Gregory rose too and proffered his hand. "Thanks, David. I knew I could count on you."

"I don't need gratitude. It's the pure male instinct for survival. Somebody has to save you from yourself. You've had a damn good run and more luck than one man deserves." He came around the desk and halted in front of Gregory. "Take a word of advice from someone who wishes you only the best. You're no longer a boy. Settle down with your Emmy. Be a good husband. Have a couple of children."

Gregory grinned and clapped him on the shoulder. "Who says a man can't have it all?"

Chapter 9

Nussbaum was determined to make Gregory see the error of his ways. He rode down with him in the lift. Gregory listened to him with a mixture of bemusement and affection. He was touched that his friend cared about his welfare. However, David would never understand that he couldn't give up the game, not entirely.

A soft *ding* signaled that they had arrived at the lobby. The doors slid open and they stepped out of the car. Nussbaum extended a hand to Gregory. "Don't think you've fooled me. I know you're going to ignore everything I've just said."

Gregory clasped his hand and flashed one of his most engaging smiles. "I took every word to heart."

Nussbaum shook his head. "One of these days your charm won't save you. You must promise to bring your Emmy over to the house for dinner. She sounds quite intriguing. Marjorie will be delighted when I tell her that you're married again. You know she worries about you."

Gregory laughed. "I'm flattered, but she must have better things to occupy her mind."

Nussbaum shrugged. "You know how women are. They're not happy unless they're worrying about something. You happen to be my wife's particular project."

They lingered there in the lobby for a few more minutes,

speaking about desultory things and mutual acquaintances.

Gregory's attention was diverted by a flicker of movement out of the corner of his eye. He glanced round to see a gentleman of perhaps fifty in a camel-colored wool coat enter the lobby. His features were pinched with strain and his brown eyes held a dazed expression. The fellow was so preoccupied that he hadn't registered that another man had called out to him as they had crossed paths. He spun around on his heel, clearly surprised.

Gregory frowned as he watched the brief exchange. He turned to Nussbaum and nodded with his chin. "David, who's that chap over there in the camel coat?"

Nussbaum followed the direction of Gregory's gaze. "Ah, that's Craig Sheldrake." He sighed and pursed his lips. "Frankly, I'm surprised to see him here today. Poor devil."

Gregory kept staring at Sheldrake. He was sure that he had seen the fellow somewhere before. He just couldn't place where precisely it had been.

"Why poor devil? Has he gone bankrupt? He does appear to be a bit harried."

"It's far more tragic. His wife was murdered last night." Nussbaum's voice was full of sympathy.

Gregory's head whirled round to face his friend again. "Murdered? How?"

Nussbaum threw his hands up in the air. "I don't know the details. The police are investigating. I heard that she was killed at the theatre of all places." He gave a sad shake of his head. "I can't even begin to imagine what Craig is feeling. He should be at home."

Now, Gregory remembered where he had seen Sheldrake. "His wife wasn't Verena Penrose by any chance, was it?"

"You've heard the news, I see." Nussbaum pulled a face. "I know one shouldn't speak ill of the dead, but

Verena was a thoroughly nasty woman. She was a journalist. You must know who I mean. She wrote all those salacious stories. Each was more lurid than the previous one." His shoulders shrugged in disgust. "I suppose that's what sells papers these days. I met her a couple of times when she popped by the Bourse to meet Craig. She never said anything overtly—I don't think she dared in front of him—but I got the distinct impression she was anti-Semitic."

Gregory's jaw clenched as the memory of Verena's confrontation with Emmy the previous evening flashed into his mind. "Your instincts were spot on. She cornered Emmy in the bar during the intermission and started spewing her vile rubbish. Emmy showed tremendous restraint. They had worked together at *The Times* for a short time. Emmy said that Verena was always trying to make trouble and never missed an opportunity to get a dig in."

Nussbaum's eyes widened in disbelief. "Your wife is Jewish?" Gregory nodded. "Even more reason to bring her to the house. Wait until I tell Marjorie. She'll be thrilled that you found a nice Jewish girl. *Mazel tov.*"

Gregory chuckled at this Yiddish expression for congratulations, as his gaze strayed once again to Sheldrake. "Has Sheldrake ever spoken to you about Verena?"

"He's a pleasant sort of fellow. But I'm afraid we don't really discuss our personal lives, apart from the usual sorts of things. Most of the time, our conversations focus on the diamond industry."

"So, what's his business?"

"I believe he has a degree in law, though I don't think he has ever practiced. I'm not certain about that. What I can tell you is that he's an independent dealer of polished and rough diamonds. He started out as a precious stone sorter in South Africa. He's traveled all over the world buying and selling stones. Craig lived and worked in both Antwerp and Moscow for several years. He's garnered a lot of respect here at the Bourse and in the industry." He lowered his voice and darted a glance to his left and right. "This is confidential. The Bourse's board is considering inviting Craig to become a member. I recommended another chap with superb business acumen. The latter is the son of an industrialist, who was highly respected in the Jewish community and the business world. It's early in the vetting process, so keep this under your hat."

"Mmm, of course. Interesting fellow. I wonder how he met Verena," Gregory mused.

"I have no idea. Their characters were completely different. Mind you, they made an attractive couple. However, there must be more to a marriage than mere physical attraction."

"Yes," Gregory mumbled, as images of Ronnie assailed him once again and he reproached his younger self in hindsight for being an utter fool.

He turned away from his scrutiny of Verena's husband and clapped Nussbaum on the shoulder. "Tell me, David. Do you know if Sheldrake has any enemies?"

Nussbaum's eyebrows knit together. "Enemies? We all have rivals and it's inevitable that jealousies arise. Surely that's true in any business."

"Diamonds are not any business," Gregory pointed out. "Some men have been known to kill to possess them."

His friend's face clouded. "That's true. Diamonds can be like a drug." He paused for a beat. "What are you saying? And what's this sudden fascination with Craig Sheldrake?"

"Let's just say that I find my fellow man intriguing."

Nussbaum snorted. "Pull the other one. You forget that I've known you for ages. There's more to it than simple curiosity. Spit it out."

Gregory sighed. He supposed he owed his friend that much. "Emmy and I were at St. Martin's Theatre last night. *We* discovered Verena's body."

Nussbaum blinked at him and was lost for words for several seconds. He swallowed hard. "How horrid. That must have been quite a shock."

"It was, when the only murder we expected to see was on stage."

"Your wife must have been dreadfully upset."

Emmy upset? The answer would have to be yes and no. But how could he explain this to his friend?

Gregory opened his mouth to respond, when a female voice floated to their ears.

"Mr. Sheldrake, my condolences about your wife. But can you spare a moment? I'd like to ask you a few questions."

Nussbaum clucked his tongue in disgust. "Will you look at that?" He flapped a hand in Sheldrake's direction. "The vultures are already circling. Can't they leave the poor fellow alone?" He shook his head. "The press has no respect."

Gregory slowly pivoted on his heel. A smile quivered on his lips. "You shouldn't paint all journalists with same brush." He gestured with his chin. "At least not in the case of that one."

"You know her?" Nussbaum asked incredulously.

"I should. That's Emmy. My wife."

His friend's Adam's apple worked up and down furiously. At last, he offered contritely, "I'm sorry. I didn't know...I didn't mean—"

Gregory chortled. "No offense taken. How about if you introduce me to Sheldrake, and I'll return the favor and introduce you to Emmy?"

Nussbaum agreed and they casually strolled over to where Emmeline was attempting to cajole Sheldrake into granting her an interview.

They heard Sheldrake say, "I'm sorry, Miss Kirby. It's rather inconvenient just now."

"Perhaps I could arrange to speak to you later on this afternoon?"

Neither she nor Sheldrake had heard Gregory and his friend approach. Nussbaum cleared his throat. "Excuse me, Craig. Forgive me for interrupting."

Sheldrake and Emmeline glanced round in the same instant. Her dark eyes widened in surprise and her mouth formed an "O" when she saw Gregory. He gave her a sly wink but allowed Nussbaum to do the talking.

Sheldrake's brows knit together and a spark of annoyance flashed in his brown eyes. "What? Oh, David, hello. Did you need me? Because as I was trying to explain to Miss Kirby"—he waved a hand in Emmeline's direction—"I was up half the night with the police and I have rather a lot on my plate at the moment."

Nussbaum clasped his hands together as if pleading for forgiveness. "Yes, of course you do," he replied, his tone soothing. "I heard the news about Verena. I know the words are inadequate, but I'm terribly sorry. You should be at home. If there's anything I can do…" He let his sentence trail off.

Sheldrake dipped his chin to his chest and took a deep shuddering breath. Once he had mastered himself, he lifted his gaze to Nussbaum's face. "Thank you. You're very kind. I just…I'm not staying long. I have to take care of one thing and then I'm returning home. I'll be out the rest of the week, I think."

"This will only take a moment. I wanted to introduce you to Gregory Longdon." He gestured at Gregory. "He's an old fr—"

Gregory proffered a hand and cut across him. "I'm the chief investigator for Symington's." Nussbaum frowned but held his tongue.

Sheldrake's hand was cool and dry, and his grip was firm. "Symington's. I see. I suppose you're here about my wife's jewels since they're insured with your firm."

Gregory lifted an eyebrow. "Yes," he murmured. "That and an unrelated case. I thought I'd deal with both matters at the same time. Mr. Nussbaum has been tremendously helpful."

Sheldrake's eyes strayed to Nussbaum. "David, has there been a heist here at the Bourse?" A tremor of concern rippled through his voice.

"No, no. Nothing like that." Nussbaum sought to reassure him. He threw a quelling look at Gregory, before turning to Sheldrake again. "It was a routine matter."

"I was merely consulting Mr. Nussbaum," Gregory explained, his mouth curling into a smile. "No need for any alarm."

"I see." Sheldrake reluctantly dragged his attention back to Emmeline. "You've wasted a trip, Miss Kirby. I don't intend to give any interviews. I hope you will respect my privacy."

"Naturally your privacy is sacrosanct, Mr. Sheldrake. However"—the man visibly cringed—"you must realize that your wife was a celebrity and her murder, unfortunately, is news. I'm afraid you will have to give a statement at some point. I assure you I'm not looking for a sensational headline. I'm simply trying to find the truth so that Verena's killer is caught. Surely you want that as well."

Sheldrake, who was a head taller than she was, stared down at her. Although revulsion was etched in every plane and angle of his long face, Emmeline was not intimidated. In fact, her intensity of purpose filled the space between and made her appear more than her five feet two inches. She merely waited for him to speak.

"What I *want* is to have my wife alive," he snapped, "rather than talk to a nosy reporter, who didn't know her at all."

"But I did know Verena," she countered quietly. "We worked together for a short time, when we were at *The Times*." His brows shot up. Clearly, he hadn't expected this. "Our careers took us in different directions. I'm now the editorial director of investigative features at *The Clarion*, which is a well-respected paper. I assure you the story will be handled with sensitivity."

A range of emotions chased themselves across his features. He opened his mouth to reply, but seemed to change his mind. His shoulders hunched forward and he threw his hands in the air in capitulation. "Fine. I'll speak with you." His voice was thick with misery.

Gregory interjected, "I have matters to discuss with you as well. So that you're not put out too much at this difficult time, perhaps I could sit in on your interview with Miss Kirby and then we could talk?"

Sheldrake was focused on Gregory. Therefore, he didn't notice Emmeline mouthing "No" at her husband.

"All right." The two words came out on a long, weary breath. "I suppose that would save time. Could you both come to my flat later on this afternoon. Say around three?"

"I don't have anything pressing this afternoon. Three o'clock would work for me. How about you, Miss Kirby?" Gregory asked solicitously for all the world as if they were strangers. "I could fetch you at the paper."

Emmeline's eyes shot daggers at him, but her mouth curved into a smile when Sheldrake glanced down at her. "That would be fine. Thank you, Mr. Longdon." She extended a small hand toward Sheldrake. "Again, my condolences about Verena. She was"—she struggled to find the right words—"a unique woman."

The grieving husband pressed her hand between both of

his and held her gaze. "Thank you." His voice was hoarse with pain. "I'll see you both this afternoon." His grip slackened and he slipped a hand into the inside pocket of his suit jacket. He drew out a pen and a business card and scrawled something on the back. "Here's my address."

Emmeline accepted the card and tucked it into her handbag. Sheldrake bid the other two men goodbye and strode off toward the lift.

They watched him in silence as he stepped into the first car that arrived. Once the doors slid closed, Emmeline rounded on her husband. "What the devil are you playing at? What are you doing here?"

Gregory took her by the elbow and pressed a kiss against her cheek. "Hello, darling. Love of my life." He offered her a dazzling smile, as he cupped her chin. "Can't an adoring husband miss his wife and wish to see her?"

Emmeline smiled and took his fingertips between her own. "No." The smile vanished, as she dropped his hand. "Now, what are you up to?" She wagged a finger at him in warning. "And don't tell me that you came to discuss Verena's jewels with Sheldrake. You didn't even know that Symington's was insuring them. It came as a complete surprise when he mentioned it. There's no use denying it. It was written all over your face."

Nussbaum threw his head back and laughed. He clapped Gregory on the shoulder. "Greg, this young woman is precisely the one to keep you in line. She's absolutely priceless."

Emmeline felt her cheeks flaming. She gave a sheepish grin, as she proffered her hand. "I'm Emmeline Longdon. You must forgive my rudeness. I didn't expect to see Gregory here." She cast a sideways glance at her husband.

He slid his arm around her waist and drew her to his side. "Now be honest, Emmy. The instant you laid eyes on me, you felt a warm glow all over and your day brightened in a flash."

She cocked her head to one side and tried to school her features into a stern expression, but it was rather difficult with laughter bubbling up her throat. She gave him a gentle shove. "You're incorrigible."

He kissed the top of her head and addressed his remarks to Nussbaum. "That's her way of saying that she loves me passionately. Since we've cleared up that little matter, I believe proper introductions are in order. Emmy, this is my dear friend David Nussbaum. He's the director of business for Nussbaum Limited, his family's wholesale jewelry company."

"Nice to meet you," she murmured.

"I assure you the pleasure is entirely mine. I was delighted when Greg told me that he had remarried. He needs a good woman to keep him out of mischief." He threw a significant look at Gregory. "I insisted that he bring you to the house for dinner one night. Marjorie, my wife, will be dying to meet you."

"That's terribly kind. I don't really know Gregory's friends. I would love to hear more about his past."

"Darling, you know everything that is important. There's nothing left to tell."

She tossed her chin in the air. "Ha. I very much doubt it."

"I'd like to learn more about you," Nussbaum said. "I heard you introduce yourself to Craig as Emmeline Kirby."

"I still use my maiden name professionally. It's easier that way."

"I see. Gregory told me that you're Jewish. Is it possible that you're related to Simon Kirby the QC?"

Her mouth broke into a broad grin. "Yes, he was my grandfather. Did you know him?" she asked eagerly.

"I met him, when I was a young man. He was a friend of my father's. Your grandfather was a great barrister.

There was no one more honorable than him." He pursued his lips for a moment. "That means you must be Aaron's daughter."

A frown creased her brow. Yes, she was Aaron Kirby's daughter. He was the man she had called Daddy and whom she had loved with all her heart, until he and her mother were murdered. Only a few months ago, she found out that they had been killed by a hired assassin. Someone full of hatred had wanted to make her parents disappear—well, primarily her mother Jacqueline—all because of her mother's affair with industrialist Victor Royce. What this person didn't know was that Emmeline was the result of that ill-fated liaison. Aaron Kirby married her mother knowing she was carrying another man's child. Royce himself had only discovered the truth about Emmeline over the summer, after she had interviewed him for *The Clarion*. That's when all the trouble began.

Emmeline sighed. Poor Victor Royce. She had known him for only a few short weeks. She was stunned when he left the bulk of his fortune to her. However, no amount of money could have made up for the lost years.

She suddenly recalled where she was. She blinked rapidly. "Yes," she told Nussbaum. "Aaron was my father."

"He and I became friends. We were very close for a time. Then, we drifted apart as his assignments took him more and more out of the country. The last time I saw him was at his wedding. Aaron and Jacqueline were so much in love." He gave a sad shake of his head. "Marjorie and I were shocked when we heard about the death of your parents. Such a tragic loss."

"Yes," she replied, her voice barely above a whisper. "I was only five at the time. My whole world collapsed in the blink of an eye." Tears pricked her eyelids as her memories dragged her back to that painful period. But life had gone on, all because of Gran.

The mere thought of her grandmother brought a smile to her lips. "However, I was very lucky because my maternal grandmother swooped in to take care of me. She had discussed the matter with my father's side of the family and, in the end, everyone came to the conclusion it would be best if I went with Gran down to Kent. No one could have had a more idyllic childhood. My parents' townhouse in Holland Park became mine, but the Kirbys took care of it for me until I was of age. It's where Gregory and I live today."

"Your grandmother sounds like a wonderful woman. She must be so proud of you and what you have accomplished in your career. Editorial director of investigative features at *The Clarion* is extremely impressive."

"Gran is the one who deserves all the credit. She is a warm, generous, intelligent woman. And resilient. My grandfather died when my mother was only eight months old. He had a congenital heart condition. Gran had to raise my mother on her own. Then she had to do it all over again with me." She beamed at him. "Gran is my hero."

"Helen is a marvel," Gregory concurred, a mischievous glint in his eye. "I tell you, if Emmy hadn't taken my heart prisoner, I would have been mesmerized by Helen."

Emmeline swatted his arm playfully. "He's got Gran eating out of the palm of his hand. In her eyes, Gregory can do no wrong. His charm is lethal. Gran and my best friend Maggie are always taking his side."

"As it should be, my darling. Helen and Maggie are women of discriminating taste. They can immediately see my stellar qualities." He sniffed and one of his eyebrows arched upward. "I must say you're a bit deficient in that regard. Perhaps they can give you a lesson or two?"

She rolled her eyes toward the ceiling. "Remind me

again why I married you?"

Nussbaum chuckled, but he glanced at his watch. "I'd like to chat with you all afternoon, Emmeline, but I'm afraid I have to dash. I have a meeting." He gripped her by the shoulders and brushed each cheek with a kiss. "I know the two of you will have a happy life together."

"Thank you, Mr. Nussbaum."

His brow puckered in a frown. "What's this nonsense? It's David. You're part of the *mishpucha* now."

Emmeline pressed a hand to her chest and smiled. "We've only just met. I feel honored that you consider me one of the family."

He spread his hands wide. "Naturally." He clapped Gregory on the shoulder. "This one became a member a long time ago."

Gregory dipped his head. "It's been good to see you, David."

"I will have Marjorie arrange a dinner soon." He turned to Emmeline. "I insist that you bring your grandmother."

"She likes nothing more than meeting new people."

Nussbaum left them standing there and started to walk away. After a few steps, he turned on his heel as if recollecting something. He jerked his chin. "Greg."

Gregory met his friend halfway. Nussbaum dropped his voice. "I'll give you a ring in a couple of days about the matter we discussed. Never ask me this again. Now that I've met Emmeline, I beg you for her sake to stop this insanity. She needs a husband by her side, not to peer at him once a week through the bars of a jail cell."

"Your advice is duly noted," Gregory replied circumspectly.

Nussbaum gave an exasperated sigh. "That's all well and good, but I would feel better if you actually followed it."

Gregory thrust out his hand. "There's no need to worry."

After Nussbaum shook it briskly, he added, "I never get caught."

Chapter 10

W hat was all that whispering about?" Emmeline demanded suspiciously as they were walking out of the Bourse.

He threw his arm around her shoulders. "There's no need to give me the evil eye. It's nothing nefarious. David said I was a lucky man and I should hold onto you. Which I intend to do."

She smiled up at him. "I like David. He seems like a very nice man. It's lovely to meet someone who knew both my grandfather and my father. That's why I don't think that you should involve him in an underhand scheme." She stopped and impaled him with her gaze. "You have a legitimate job now. You're well-respected by Symington's. If you've gone back to stealing"—she drew in a ragged breath—"I will leave you, even though I love you more than life itself."

Gregory gently caressed her curls. "You're being melodramatic, darling."

She pressed his hand against her cheek. "I hope so. After what we went through in Malta, I couldn't bear to lose you. Not a second time. But if you're stealing…" She choked on this last word.

He pressed a kiss to her forehead. "I promise I haven't stolen any jewels." It was true. He hadn't stolen anything since Tarasova's ruby-and-diamond necklace. His friend Roger Delahunt had *given* the Pink Courtesan to him and he was planning to divest himself of that bauble as soon as possible. Therefore, he could state with a clear conscience that he hadn't stolen anything…recently. It didn't count that he was *contemplating* a heist in the near future. That was another matter altogether.

Emmy swallowed hard and nodded, seeming to accept his declaration. "Right. I will trust your word. I *want* to trust you. You're my husband."

"As a good wife should. I promise to show you how much I love and adore you tonight." He lowered his head, his warm breath brushing her cheek, as he whispered in her ear. "In the privacy of our bedroom, where you will be left in doubt about my sincerity on the subject."

He had the pleasure of seeing a pink flush suffuse her cheeks.

"You are a thorough reprobate."

He flashed a roguish grin. "But you must admit that I'm a lovable reprobate."

A throaty chuckle escaped from her lips. "Isn't that a contradiction in terms?"

"Certainly not." He tucked her arm through his elbow. "Now, why don't I take my beautiful wife for a spot of lunch before our meeting with Sheldrake this afternoon?"

"How about a quick cappuccino instead? I was planning to drop by the Yard to see Superintendent Burnell."

The gleam in her dark eyes told him that she was trying to contain her excitement. He arched an eyebrow upward. "You've discovered something about Verena's murder?" She nodded. "I have a theory too. But I can see that you're bursting to share your news."

"A double espresso for you first. You're going to need fortification because you're not going to like what I have to say."

"Emmy, unless you're a psychopath, no one likes murder. But I will defer to my wife's wisdom on the subject." He squeezed her arm. "Besides, you know I can never refuse an espresso."

A short walk away from the Bourse, they found a spotlessly clean café on Leather Lane. The two baristas behind the counter greeted them with a smile as they entered. The café was small and stark with brick walls painted white, an oak hardwood floor, and modern tables and chairs. A few customers were scattered around the tables and booths.

Emmeline and Gregory perused the chalkboard menu on the wall behind the counter. She ordered a cappuccino, while he opted for a double espresso. The delicious aromas assailing their nostrils made them both feel a bit peckish. Neither was in the mood for a big meal, so they decided to share an almond croissant. They slipped into a booth in a corner. It had plain beige banquettes and a faux wood table. It afforded them the privacy they wanted to exchange notes.

By tacit agreement, they waited until their coffees arrived and the barista had placed the plate with the croissant on the table between them, before broaching the subject of the late Verena Penrose.

Emmeline was not looking forward to telling him about her tense interview with Villiers that morning. She stalled by ripping off a piece of the croissant and popping the morsel into her mouth. Gregory watched her over the rim of his cup, from which thin curls of steam wafted into the air.

He replaced the demitasse cup on the saucer and smoothed down the corners of his mustache. "Right. What happened this morning?"

She took a deep breath and plunged in. "I went to see

Villiers."

He leaned back against the banquette, his shoulders stiffening. His steady gaze held hers. "I should have guessed. You were being highly evasive before you left the house. You gave me a quick kiss and dashed off without breakfast."

"Sorry. I knew you would make a fuss, if I told you where I was going."

"I couldn't have stopped you. You never listen, Boadicea of the Fourth Estate."

She made a moue at him. "That's categorically untrue. I'm willing to entertain reasonable advice. However, you have a limited vocabulary. The only word you're intimately familiar with is *no*."

Gregory snorted and reached out for his espresso, but otherwise refrained from commenting.

"Anyway" —Emmeline spun her cup of cappuccino round and round on the saucer— "I needn't have to remind you that I have to do my job."

"Let's not get into that old argument again. You *know* I respect your job. So, what did dear old papa have to say for himself?"

That he despises me and thinks I will ruin your life, Emmeline thought, as a traitorous tear stung her eyelid. But she couldn't tell Gregory this. If it hurt her, it would only serve to fan the flames of anger burning inside her husband. Besides, Gregory loved her and they were married now. Villiers couldn't do anything about it. Or could he? She bit her lip and pushed this unsettling thought to a dark recess at the back of her mind. Where she was going to make certain it would remain locked away forever.

She waved a hand in the air. "After his usual nonsense, I confronted Villiers with the fact that Verena had written the name Toby Crenshaw in her notebook. He tried to fob me off with some vague explanation. He even had the nerve to point out that it was your name too."

Gregory gave her a tight smile. "That comes as no surprise. Villiers is a master of deflection. Smoke and mirrors are his forte."

She reached for his hand across the table. He interlaced his fingers with hers. "I'm all right, darling. Go on. I know there's more because with Villiers it's never simple."

She flashed him a grin. "I kept pressing him and naturally he got annoyed. He asked why I was so interested in the case. In terms of newsworthiness, I told him that last night was doubly eventful not only because of the murder, but the ceiling had collapsed as well. He was apathetic until I mentioned that we were the ones who had found Verena's body. That threw the great Laurence Villiers off balance."

"Impossible," Gregory scoffed as he tossed down the rest of his espresso.

She propped her elbows on the table and leaned toward him. "Oh, but it did. He was stunned that we were at the theatre and demanded to know what we were doing in Verena's box." She paused for a beat. "I never said Verena's seat was in a box. He couldn't have known, unless—"

His eyes narrowed and he picked up this thread. "Unless he was at the theatre last night."

"Precisely. Why is he going out of his way to hide the fact that he knew Verena? Villiers doesn't strike me as being among the legion of men, who were captivated by her feminine charms. Do you think that Verena could have been blackmailing Villiers and he killed her?" She sucked in her breath as a thought struck her. "Could this somehow be connected to Swanbeck? He threatened to destroy all of us."

He squeezed her fingers. "Emmy, Swanbeck is dead. He can't hurt us anymore."

She nodded. "Of course, you're right. He's dead," she

asserted, trying to banish the lingering doubts from her mind. But she silently cursed the uncertainty she heard thrumming through her voice. "What if Swanbeck sent Verena something about Villiers being your father before we left for Malta?"

"We've been back from Malta for several weeks. If Verena had a juicy story, she would have splashed it all over the papers at the drop of a hat. She wouldn't have waited."

"Mmm," she murmured. "That's true. And yet, as I think back to last night, I can't help feeling that Verena confronted me for a reason." Her eyes narrowed. "What if she was trying to tell me something?"

"If you'll recall, she was intent on insulting you, not sharing a cozy *tête-à-tête*."

Emmeline tore off another piece of croissant and chewed on it meditatively. "I don't deny that, but my instincts are screaming that there was more to it. She said something odd. I paid no attention to it at the time because I was focused on the vitriol. What was it?" She frowned, replaying the conversation in her head. Then she nodded. "Yes. She mentioned ravens."

"Ravens? Rather a non sequitur in the middle of a rant."

She met his gaze. "Indeed. I suppose that's why it stuck in my head. She brought up the old superstition that if the ravens in the Tower of London fly away, the Crown and Britain will fall. Verena said that she was the one who sets the ravens free like secrets locked away in a box."

"How very sinister," he replied skeptically. "Are you certain she wasn't quoting something out of a Hitchcock film?"

Emmeline shrugged. "Mind you, it could have been a case of Verena seeking to inflate her own importance. But it can't be a coincidence that she was murdered less than an hour later." She reached out and clutched his arm.

"What if she saw her killer in the bar? What if her altercation with me was merely a cover? Unless she was drunk, and I'm certain that she wasn't, she was speaking unnecessarily loudly. More than a few disapproving stares were directed at us. What if it was Verena's way of tossing down the gauntlet and warning the murderer that if he didn't pay up, she would spill all she knew?"

"It's possible," he conceded. "Rather a roundabout way of giving an ultimatum, though. Why involve you, Emmy? Clearly, she harbored professional and personal resentment against you. Wouldn't it have made more sense for her to turn to an ally like Ian Newland?"

"As you pointed out, we are not bosom friends. She couldn't have taken the direct approach. I would have been extremely suspicious. Maybe she realized that her machinations had gone too far this time and she was in danger. It was sheer bravado. She felt safe in the crowded bar. It was too public. The murderer didn't dare make a move against her there. Verena was trying to hedge her bets when she deliberately cornered me. I think she was goading me because she desperately wanted someone to pick up the story, if anything happened to her. She may have considered me a rival, but she knew I wouldn't let it go."

"Well, she was spot on. There's nothing that you enjoy more than fitting the pieces of a puzzle together. It's a solid theory. However, for all his faults, I still don't think Villiers murdered her. The killer took a great risk. It was sheer luck that the ceiling collapsed and he got lost among the people evacuating the theatre. Villiers is far too cunning and cautious. He must always have a plan, and several contingencies waiting in the wings, if it goes wrong."

She sighed. "I never seriously entertained the idea that he was the murderer. As usual, though, he knows far more than he's telling."

"That will never change. In Villiers's world, you can't

trust anyone. Now then, drink up your cappuccino before it gets cold. I have another theory."

She lifted the cup to her lips and regarded him eagerly. "Go on. I'm all ears. Does it have anything to do with your visit to David?"

"Indirectly. Perhaps Verena is collateral damage. What if the murderer wanted to settle a score with Craig Sheldrake?"

"By killing Verena in retribution?"

He nodded. "Yes, David told me that Sheldrake is an independent dealer of polished and rough diamonds. He started his career as a precious stone sorter in South Africa. He lived and worked in Antwerp and Moscow for several years. He travels all over the world to buy and sell stones. David said that Sheldrake has built up a good reputation in the industry and at the Bourse. In confidence, David revealed that the board of the Bourse wants to invite Sheldrake to become a member. There's another potential candidate under consideration as well. The vetting process is underway."

"Well, that puts a different complexion on things. An enemy could have gotten wind of this and wants to sabotage Sheldrake's chances." She shook her head. "But how would Verena's murder prevent any of that?"

"The killer may have calculated that Sheldrake will be shattered by Verena's death to such an extent that he will neglect his business, providing an opportunity for someone to sweep in and take it over. Or they may want to keep him in place to provide a legitimate front, while they maneuver behind the scenes. It would be a coup, if he were to become a board member."

"I hate to be cynical, but that's quite plausible, although whoever it was couldn't be certain that Sheldrake could be manipulated." She was silent for a moment, allowing these disturbing theories to marinate in her mind. "I suppose diamonds could seduce a man's soul to the point where he becomes obsessed and baser instincts take control. The competition must be fierce." She shuddered. "Could it be so cutthroat that murder becomes an acceptable option?"

"Darling, greed eats away at a man bit by bit, corrupting judgment and sanity. Nothing is ever enough. Diamonds are a highly portable currency. At the Garden, it's all informal dealings and large amounts of cash. Since the Bourse is technically a club, it is outside the jurisdiction of the Financial Services Authority. A member of the London Bourse can use any one of the other twenty-one diamond bourses worldwide."

"In other words, it could become a paradise for an ambitious money launderer, arms dealer, or drug trafficker," Emmeline observed, "if he's able to get his foot in the door."

"Got it in one."

She exhaled a weary sigh. "Well, that certainly adds a new twist." She leaned back and shook her head. "You make a valid point. That's a likely reason Villiers could be involved. But it still bothers me. Unless Verena got wind of this sort of scandal, she wouldn't have given her husband's business or the diamond industry a second thought. All she would care about is that he continued to make pots and pots of money. And another thing, I wouldn't have thought that an arms dealer or drug trafficker would have chosen such a public place as a theatre to dispatch Verena. Too many things could go wrong. It was a fluke that the ceiling collapsed, causing enough confusion for him to get away."

"Why don't we leave all that for dear old Oliver to decide?" Gregory's mouth curved into a mischievous grin. "We wouldn't want the poor chap to think that we're trying to muscle in on his patch. His feelings might be hurt."

She couldn't help smiling. "You really must stop

harassing Superintendent Burnell."

He put a hand to his chest. "Heaven forbid. I'm much too fond of Oliver. If there's any harassing to be done, I leave it to that fool Cruickshank. He's the expert."

Chapter 11

Burnell let loose a fluent stream of curses under his breath as he flung open the door to his office. All the invectives were directed at the assistant commissioner and Sally, his pretentious secretary. His ears were still ringing with the rambling lecture the assistant commissioner had just given him about interagency cooperation and not bothering important men like Laurence Villiers.

"Restraint, decorum, professionalism is the motto to live by, Burnell. Once you take those words to heart, you can hold your head up high," Cruickshank had concluded with a self-satisfied smile. "

Blah, blah, blah. The superintendent supposed the Boy Wonder thought he was bestowing a dollop of wisdom. *Wisdom*, the superintendent snorted. *What does a babe barely out of nappies know about wisdom?*

Burnell's brain was still fuming on the subject of his boss's many character defects, but he stopped short just inside the door.

"Ah, the man of the hour," Gregory declared heartily. "We've been waiting patiently to have an audience."

The *we* in question encompassed Emmeline and Finch as well. The latter hastily vacated Burnell's chair. "Sir—"

Without turning around, the superintendent reached

behind him and slammed the door. The rattling of the hinges telegraphed his displeasure.

"Out. All of you," he roared as he stalked over to his desk and dropped heavily into his chair. "Especially you, Longdon." His mood softened only fractionally as his eyes met Emmeline's dark gaze. "Sorry, Emmeline. Even you."

While Gregory remained nonplussed and comfortably ensconced in his chair, she had leaped to her feet at the superintendent's entrance. She offered him a sympathetic smile. "We know that you're extremely busy." He snorted, as he rested his head against the chair and squeezed his eyes shut to blot out her pretty face. "However," she went on in a cajoling tone, "we discovered some facts this morning that are pertinent to the case. We felt we had to inform you straight away."

She waited expectantly for a reaction, but Burnell didn't stir. She flicked a questioning glance at Finch, who gave a shrug.

Gregory decided to take matters in hand. "What Emmy is trying to say is that we knew you missed us terribly and we came to brighten your day."

Burnell's eyes flew open and he scowled at Gregory's beaming face. "You're like an eclipse that blocks out the sun."

"Come now, Oliver. No need to be embarrassed. You can admit that something is missing when we're not around."

Burnell's feet came down on the carpeted floor with a *thud*. He leaned forward, propping his elbows on his desk. "Yes. You know what's missing?" he snarled. "Trouble. It blows in on the wind whenever you're in the vicinity." He gave Emmeline an apologetic look. "You to a lesser extent than your silver-tongued crook of a husband, but you're guilty too. Take your morning outing to see Villiers, for instance."

"Ah," she mumbled and lowered herself back down into the chair. "You heard about that."

"Oh, yes." His mouth curved into a smile that did not touch his eyes. "Villiers told us that you dropped by for a chat. By the time we arrived, he was in a stiff-upper-lip lather and on his guard. He went into full obstructionist mode when we attempted to interview him. But that wasn't the best part of my day. Can you guess what it was?" Emmeline gave a mute shake of her head, while Gregory merely returned his stare, an impish gleam in his eyes. "I've just spent the last half hour being lectured by the Boy Wonder about not disturbing the great Laurence Villiers."

"I'm truly sorry." Emmeline's voice was low and full of contrition. "It was not my intention to cause—"

"Trouble?" A pink flush crept up her cheeks. "No, it never is. But you manage to do it effortlessly. I suppose you're to be pitied. It can't be easy when your husband is a bad influence." He glared at Gregory.

"Oliver, you have such a way with words. It brings tears to one's eyes."

Burnell's hands curled into tight fists, the skin stretched taut and white across his knuckles. "*Superintendent Burnell*," he snarled.

Gregory raised an admonishing finger in the air. "Temper, temper. Remember your ulcer." He punctuated this suggestion with a smile.

"I would not be at the mercy of my ulcer," the superintendent griped, "if you had not embarked on a life of crime."

Gregory clucked his tongue in disapproval. "You are particularly overwrought today. Shall I nip up to Cruickshank's office and have a quiet word with him? He's working you far too hard if you've decided to lash out at your closest friends who only have your well-being at heart."

"Gregory," Emmeline hissed out of the corner of her mouth.

"What, darling?" he asked in mock innocence. "You know our only concern is for dear Oliver's happiness in life."

Burnell's eyes grew wide. Their blue depths held a mixture of disbelief and fury. He opened his mouth to fire off a retort, but Finch intervened to douse water on the blaze. "Sir, it wouldn't hurt to listen to what they have to say. We wouldn't have to follow up on it, unless *you* determined there was any merit in it. You must concede that in the past Emmeline and Longdon have been able to discover information that has been helpful in our investigations."

The superintendent cast a sidelong glance at Finch and pursed his lips. Then, his gaze trailed back to the husband and wife sitting opposite him. Emmeline leaned forward in her chair, an expectant smile playing about her lips.

Gregory dipped his head with an air of deference. "*Superintendent Burnell*." He winked at the detective, as he raised his head again. "If only to jolly your mood."

Burnell threw his hands up in resignation. "I give up. What have you two managed to ferret out?"

Emmeline smiled. She knew the storm had passed and they were back on solid ground. "I can tell you why Villiers was vexed when you and Sergeant Finch visited him."

The superintendent propped his elbow on the desk and rested his chin on his hand. "I'm listening."

"As in your case, he refused to answer my questions about his connection to Verena and the fact that she had Toby Crenshaw written in her notebook. But I kept pressing and he became more and more irritated. He thought if he turned the tables and started interrogating me, I would become distracted. He was wrong."

A genuine smile broke out across Burnell's face. "He'll

never learn. Go on."

She went on to describe how the entire tenor of the conversation changed the instant she mentioned that she and Gregory had been the ones who discovered Verena's body. "Villiers's practiced cool demeanor cracked and he demanded to know what we were doing in Verena's box. I never said that we went to her box. He could only have known it if he had been at the theatre meeting her for Lord knows what cloak-and-dagger purposes."

Burnell chortled. "I suppose even the mighty can be undone by a slip of the tongue." Then he sobered again. "Although that's interesting, we suspected as much last night. It doesn't really bring us any closer to finding Ms. Penrose's killer. Having been caught out, you can be certain that Villiers at this moment is intent on erasing the merest cobweb strand that links the two of them together."

"With Villiers, you won't even find links to his own shadow. The man is scrupulously careful, bordering on the obsessive," Gregory offered drily, as he crossed one leg over the other.

The superintendent straightened up and stroked his beard. "He'll deny he even spoke to you, Emmeline."

"Granted, Villiers is far too intelligent and wily to have committed such a public murder, but he knows something," she insisted.

"Whatever *it* is, we've hit a brick wall at this stage. We'll have to try to pursue other lines of inquiry."

"I'm glad you said that, Ol—Superintendent Burnell," Gregory quickly corrected himself at a fierce look from the detective, "Emmy is not the only brilliant member of the Longdon family."

Burnell folded his arms over his broad chest and raised a skeptical eyebrow. "Right, I suppose you'd better get on with it."

The superintendent listened as Gregory explained about

his visit to the London Bourse and his discussion with David Nussbaum about Craig Sheldrake's background as an independent dealer of polished and rough diamonds, who travels all over the world. Then he speculated that Verena's murder may have been part of an elaborate scheme by an underworld figure to gain a lucrative foothold in the diamond trade.

"If I were of the criminal persuasion," Gregory asserted loftily, "which I am not—"

"A psychiatrist would hold you up as a classic example of a man who was detached from reality."

Gregory sniffed. "That doesn't even merit a response. I'll put it down to the lingering aftereffects of your encounter with that prat Cruickshank. One minute in his presence is enough to sour anyone's mood." Burnell smirked at this comment. "As I was saying, think about a criminal's excitement. With diamonds accepted in every corner of the globe, new financial avenues would open at his fingertips. Diamonds are an unregulated form of investment. Brokers are not required to be registered with the Financial Services Authority, or FSA. A lot of trading is negotiated privately. All our boy would have to do would be to target a well-respected company. CS Gems Limited would be a prize indeed, especially being a member of the London Bourse, an exclusive institution that does not fall under the jurisdiction of the FSA. Not only that, David told me confidentially that Sheldrake is one of two candidates being vetted for a seat on the Bourse board, which would elevate his prestige and exposure."

"I'm curious how you know so much about diamonds, illicit trading, money laundering, et cetera, if, as you claim, you are not a member of the criminal classes."

Gregory smiled knowingly. "I worked for Nussbaum Limited when I was a young man and gained a good deal of insight into the industry. And, of course, I'm

Symington's chief investigator. I have to keep up-to-date on what today's con men are doing."

"Hmph" was Burnell's only comment. He pursed his lips and fixed his stare on Gregory, who didn't flinch under the scrutiny. At last, the superintendent said, "Much as I hate to admit it, you make a convincing argument about Sheldrake."

An impish smile danced on Gregory's lips. "I always knew we were sympatico, Oliver."

Burnell tilted his head toward the ceiling and implored the Almighty, "Why me? I know I'm not perfect, but what did I ever do to be cursed with that for eternity?" He flapped a hand in Gregory's general direction.

Yet again, the Lord chose not to communicate his intentions to a mere detective. The superintendent gave a weary sigh. Working in mysterious ways was all well and good, but when it came to himself it was not quite sporting of the divine being.

Emmeline took advantage of the brief lull to venture, "I don't deny that Sheldrake's company would be a golden goose for an underworld figure. However, something still bothers me about your theory, darling." She turned and looked her husband directly in the eye. "Now that Verena has been murdered, what incentive does Sheldrake have to sell his company or act as a frontman? Surely, *threatening* to harm her would have been a more effective form of pressure. It would have gotten the criminal everything that he wanted. With Verena dead, that leverage is gone."

"Perhaps things got out of hand at the theatre," Gregory suggested. "If I may be morbid for a moment, we all agree that the murder lacked finesse. With that serpent's tongue of hers, Verena probably provoked her killer and he lashed out before he knew what he was doing. She was dead in an instant and he had to beat a hasty retreat."

"Well, that young man who careened into us as we were

making our way to Verena's box was certainly in a hurry." Her eyes narrowed as she recalled the incident. "And yet, he appeared terrified rather than cold and vicious. His complexion was gray and he looked as if he was about to be sick."

"In the pandemonium going on around us, you had time to register all that?" Gregory marveled at her observation.

She flashed a smile at him. "As a journalist, I'm trained to notice details." She flicked a glance that encompassed Burnell and Finch. "Of course, my skills pale in comparison to your and Sergeant Finch's professional eye. However, I'd be happy to sit down with a police sketch artist."

Burnell wagged a finger at her, but she had managed to coax a smile from him. "Flattery will get you nowhere. Don't think I've forgotten your ill-advised foray to Villiers's office this morning so that you could get a scoop."

"No, I didn't think you would," she replied contritely. "But I was *hoping*"—the arch of her eyebrow was mildly flirtatious. After all she was a married woman, but she was determined to get in the detective's good graces again. A journalist's job is much easier when the law is on one's side—"your generosity of spirit saw fit to forgive me since we've brought you some solid leads."

Burnell sighed. "You are infuriatingly stubborn and have selective hearing upon occasion." Some of his earlier bluster had dissipated and there was a gleam in his eyes.

Emmeline bowed her head. "*Mea culpa*," she murmured as she cast a look at him from beneath her lashes. "On the other hand, like you, I'm only interested in finding the truth."

"Try to be a bit more circumspect from now on. Finch and I don't want to be called out to a crime scene, where your body plays the starring role."

"Certainly not. I can assure you I'm not too keen on that scenario. All sins forgiven then?"

Burnell's chair groaned as he leaned back. "Was there ever any doubt?"

She inclined her head and returned his smile.

"Does that apply to me too?" Gregory chimed in, fluttering his eyelashes at the detective. "Are my sins forgiven? I do hope so."

Burnell tore his eyes from Emmeline. A scowl chased away his smile, as his gaze impaled Gregory. "Your sins are too numerous and wide-ranging to count. You are a lost cause."

"Oh, Oliver, don't say that." He pressed a hand to his heart melodramatically. "I'll have a deep emotional scar for the rest of my life."

The superintendent grunted. "Then we're even. I have you to thank for my ulcer."

"Aren't you concerned for my soul?" The corners of Gregory's mouth were quivering.

Finch rolled his eyes. "Don't you ever stop?"

Emmeline touched her husband's arm lightly. "Darling, perhaps we should go. We don't want to wear out our welcome."

"You're right, Emmy." He shot his cuff and glanced at his Patek Phillippe watch. "Is that the time? Come along." He took her by the elbow and drew her to her feet. "We wouldn't want to be late for our interview with Sheldrake."

Burnell slammed his open palm on the desk and exploded, "Your what?"

"Didn't we mention it earlier?" Gregory asked. The superintendent stared at him stone-faced. "Sorry. In the excitement of seeing you, it must have slipped our minds. You'll be delighted to hear that we've arranged to interview Sheldrake at three-thirty. Well, Emmy's doing the formal interview. I'm tagging along to ask him some questions about Verena's jewelry as Symington's is insuring them."

"Have you two heard anything I've just said about obstructing a police investigation?"

Ignoring the detective's question, Gregory propelled Emmeline toward the door and with a flick of the wrist turned the knob to open it. Over his shoulder, he tossed, "Don't worry. Emmy is frightfully good at taking notes. She doesn't miss a thing. We'll tell you all about it later. Cheery-bye for now."

He blew a kiss to Burnell, waggled his fingers at Finch, and then they were gone.

Chapter 12

Gregory drew his sleek blue-gray Jaguar to the curb along Albemarle Street in Mayfair's fashionable Artisan Quarter. He came round the car and opened the door for Emmeline. It was a five-minute walk down the block to the Excelsior, an Edwardian property that had a magnificent Beaux-Arts façade that stretched eighty feet along the street. The building had been constructed in 1905 and was originally a luxury motorcar showroom. Two years earlier, a developer had converted it into a sumptuous residence that now boasted a grand duplex penthouse and three enormous lateral apartments. The property was two streets away from the Ritz hotel in the heart of London.

Gregory gave a low whistle as they came to a halt outside the Excelsior. He shaded his eyes from the sun as he tilted his head back to appraise the elegant structure from roof to pavement. "*This* is where Verena and Sheldrake lived?" he asked incredulously as his gaze trailed back to Emmeline's face. He rubbed his thumb and forefinger together. "They must have serious money. One of these apartments must be a fortune."

"I don't know about Sheldrake's wealth, but Verena is rumored to have extracted hefty settlements out of her three ex-husbands. Very hefty settlements."

"Having met the odious woman, the poor sods probably

were willing to pay anything to see the back of her."

Emmeline chuckled. "What's money compared to a nice peaceful life."

He nodded and offered her his elbow. "Shall we go see if Sheldrake can shed any light on his wife's murder?"

They stepped into a sedate, modern foyer, where a twenty-four-hour concierge desk was located. They gave their names to the concierge, who rang Sheldrake. "Very good, sir." He replaced the receiver. "Mr. Sheldrake is expecting you. He says you can go straight up. Each apartment has its own private lift." He waved a hand to his right. "That one will take you to Mr. Sheldrake."

They murmured their thanks and bid him a good afternoon. The lift carried them up to the first floor. Sheldrake was standing there to meet them when the doors slid open directly onto the main drawing room.

He had purple smudges under his eyes and looked more haunted than he had that morning, but he greeted them with a watery smile. "Hello again. Welcome." He extended a hand toward Emmeline and then shook Gregory's. "Thank you for accommodating me and coming to my humble abode. As you can imagine, today has been total chaos. The phone hasn't stopped ringing. Everyone's heard about Verena..." His baritone voice trailed off.

They hovered there, awkwardly staring at one another. "Well." The word came out on a sigh. "Where are my manners? I thought we could talk in here." He gestured to his left. "I've always found it the more comfortable of the two living rooms. I thought you two might like some tea. The housekeeper is preparing it. She'll bring it in shortly."

Emmeline wasn't surprised that the apartment had two living rooms. She felt as if she had been swallowed up into a gaping cavern. Surely, one needed a map—or at least a good supply of breadcrumbs—to navigate one's way around. The apartment occupied in excess of 333.33 square meters and had ceilings that were three and a half meters high. The last golden strands of afternoon sunlight flooded in through the eight, twenty-five-meter windows overlooking Albemarle Street and glissaded across the highly-polished, oak parquet floors. At the southern end of the open-plan drawing room, she glimpsed a library with floor-to-ceiling bookcases and a reading nook.

As she followed their host, a shiver slithered down her spine. The apartment may have been filled with natural light, but the modern décor drained it of warmth. The walls were either beige or eggshell white. The contemporary furniture with crisp lines and rugs with geometrical patterns were strategically positioned to enhance the impression of space. Combined with the abstract expressionist paintings and oddly-shaped lampshades, they provided the only splashes of color. She supposed the interior designer had sought to make a bold artistic statement. However, Emmeline's aesthetic sensibilities silently revolted. Of course, it was a matter of personal taste. She preferred color, the graceful lines of Queen Anne-style furniture, and rich wood tones. Things that were inviting and cheerful. This modern tripe was sterile, thoroughly depressing, and left her with a sense of loneliness. She couldn't wait to escape this mausoleum that paraded as a home. On the other hand, she had no trouble imagining Verena roaming around this cold and unfeeling domicile. Had Verena and Sheldrake ever been happy? As she had last night at the theatre, she felt a stab of pity for Sheldrake. It couldn't have been easy to love a woman like Verena.

Sheldrake showed them into a rectangular room where a U-shaped, apple-green sofa took pride of place in the center. A low, black octagonal block that masqueraded as a coffee table stood before it. The sofa faced a flat-screen television, next to which was a black lacquer table with three coffee-table books on modern art.

"Please make yourselves comfortable." Sheldrake motioned toward the sofa.

Comfortable? You must be joking, Emmeline thought. *I can't wait to get out of here.*

She pasted a smile on her lips, as she lowered herself onto the sofa. Perching herself on the edge, she discreetly drew her notebook and pen out of her handbag. "Thank you for agreeing to speak with me, Mr. Sheldrake. Again, my condolences. I realize you must be under a tremendous strain. But it's important to get your side of the story out there."

Gregory settled himself next to her. "I echo Miss Kirby's sentiments. At a time like this though, Symington's feels it's imperative to ensure that everything is in order."

Sheldrake nodded and dropped heavily into a stiff-backed chair without armrests that was covered in café au lait velour. His long limbs spilled out from the chair, but he didn't seem bothered. "I realize that you're both right. I must apologize for my behavior this morning at the Bourse. I felt as if I was being attacked from all sides at the same time. It's just"—he choked back a sob—"I can't believe Verena's gone. She was so vibrant and exciting."

"Indeed." She flicked a sideways glance at Gregory, who managed to arrange his features into a bland expression. He was leaning forward slightly with his clasped hands dangling between his knees.

After Sheldrake had regained his composure, Emmeline cleared her throat and gently began to probe. "Do you know of any reason why someone would want to…to harm Verena?"

Sheldrake's gaze scoured her face. It hurt to look at the pain reflected in the brown depths of his eyes. "She was a wonderful woman."

You poor deluded man. Your wife was a blackmailing

viper, her brain screamed.

"Of course, she must have had at least one enemy. Her articles tended to spark a good deal of…controversy. Perhaps someone didn't like the story she was currently working on."

Sheldrake's shoulders shuddered and he shook his head pathetically. "Verena never discussed her work with me. Therefore, I can't help you in that regard. We actually didn't talk about work at all. She never exhibited any interest in my company, even when we first met."

I'll wager Verena made it her business to know exactly how much money you have in your bank account, Emmeline mused. *Money was Verena's favorite topic.*

"I see," she mumbled as she pushed aside her cynicism and jotted down this note. "Do you know if anything was troubling her? Was Verena anxious about anything lately?"

"I think—" Sheldrake stared down at his hands in his lap. A range of emotions chased themselves across his features, as he nervously twisted the signet ring back and forth on his pinky. He appeared to be having an internal debate. Finally, he lifted his eyes to meet her gaze, and swallowing down his misery, answered, "Verena was…She changed over the last three months. She shut me out. I barely saw her. She was gone before I woke in the morning. She wouldn't come home until well past midnight. Some evenings she never came home at all. I tried to find out if anything was bothering her, but she refused to talk to me."

They were interrupted when the housekeeper came in with the tea tray. As the cups and saucers were handed around, Emmeline's mind flew to the tense conversation between husband and wife that she had overheard at the theatre.

"I…I'm ashamed to admit," the distraught husband continued, once the three of them were alone again, "that I became so concerned that I"—he took a ragged breath—"hired a private investigator to follow her." Emmeline's ears perked up at this revelation.

"Perfectly normal reaction," Gregory murmured soothingly, as he shot a pointed look at her.

"Is it?" Sheldrake took a distracted sip of tea. "I've been second-guessing myself. What kind of a husband does that? I should have trusted her. Maybe in time…eventually…she would have come to me with her problem. Now, I'll never know."

"You can't think like that, Mr. Sheldrake," Emmeline entreated. "You loved your wife and naturally you were concerned." She paused to let these words sink in. "Did…What did the private investigator find out?" She tried to make her tone as casual as possible.

Sheldrake set his cup down on the so-called coffee table. "I have no idea." He began fiddling with his signet ring again. She concluded that it must be a nervous habit. She had seen him do it at the theatre. "He was supposed to send me his report tomorrow. I don't care anymore. I'll pay him for his services, of course. But it doesn't matter what, if anything, he discovered."

The blood started to race through her veins. She moistened her lips with the tip of her tongue. "You're not the least bit curious?"

He threw his hands up in the air. "What's the point? Verena's dead."

"Forgive me for being blunt," she pressed, "but that's precisely why the report is important. It could provide a clue as to who her killer might be."

He closed his eyes and squeezed the bridge of his nose with his thumb and forefinger. "I'm not thinking straight." His eyes flew open. "Of course, you're right. It's just…I can't…" He broke off.

"That's your grief speaking. There is another alternative

to consider."

His brow furrowed. "Is there?"

"Yes. Since it is too painful," she suggested, "perhaps you might authorize me and Mr. Longdon, if it puts your mind more at ease, to meet with the private investigator and read the report. It goes without saying that we would inform you and the police of its findings." She held her breath and waited for his answer.

Sheldrake was silent for so long that her heart began to sink. Oh, well, nothing ventured, nothing gained. It was worth a try.

"All right," he said at last. "I agree. It would be foolish to ignore it. His name is Michael Underwood and the firm is Foster Reeves Investigations. Their office is a stone's throw from here in Regent Street. I'll give Underwood a ring and tell him to expect you tomorrow morning."

Emmeline wanted to leap in the air, but she restrained herself. "Thank you. That would be helpful."

Gregory cleared his throat. "Yes, Symington's would be most interested to hear what Underwood found out. It would help with my own report."

Sheldrake's attention shifted to him. "Forgive me, Mr. Longdon." His eyes narrowed. "I don't see why Symington's has sent you. Verena's jewels haven't been stolen. I don't intend to make any sort of claim."

Gregory's mouth curved into a benign smile. "I assure you it's routine. In a case such as this when a client has died suddenly and in suspicious circumstances, the company likes to satisfy itself that an attempt will not be made to steal the insured's property."

Emmeline marveled at how the words rolled so smoothly off her husband's tongue. He exuded supreme confidence, which belied the fact that Symington's was not concerned in the least about Verena's jewels. As long Sheldrake continued to pay the premiums, the company was perfectly content to allow things to stand as they were.

Sheldrake shrugged and appeared to accept Gregory's explanation at face value. "It seems silly, but I suppose you have procedures to follow."

Gregory inclined his head and spread his hands apologetically. "I'm afraid so. Symington's prides itself on protecting its clients as if it was protecting its own family members."

Emmeline rolled her eyes. *Ugh. What utter drivel.* Gregory's charm was lethal. As intended, Sheldrake was lapping up every word and looking more relaxed by the second.

"I have the list of Verena's jewels in the safe. Shall I fetch it so that we can go over it?"

"If you would," Gregory replied. "It shouldn't take long. Best to get it over with, so that you can focus on other matters."

Sheldrake nodded and rose to his feet. "I'll be back in a tick. I'll have Mrs. Fairchild bring in some more tea, while you're waiting."

Gregory held up a hand. "No, thank you. I'm fine."

"Emmeline, what about you?" Sheldrake asked. "Sorry, may I call you Emmeline?"

"Of course. And please don't trouble your housekeeper." She reached out and lifted the pot. "There's plenty of tea left and it's still warm."

"Right. Excuse me for a moment."

As soon as he was gone, Emmeline scooted toward Gregory and whispered in his ear, "A private investigator. And we'll have access to his report. What a stroke of luck." She glanced up, but Sheldrake was still out of sight. "The poor man is in for a shock, though. Do you think he has any inkling that Verena was having an affair?"

"Darling, he's in denial if he doesn't. He's just putting up a brave front. All those late nights and Verena's cold attitude." He smirked. "He knows something was amiss, otherwise why hire a private investigator. I'm wondering what *else* the investigator found out."

Her eyes widened. "Do you think he could have stumbled across the killer and doesn't even know it?"

"It's quite possible. If, as I suspect, a criminal is after Sheldrake's company as an entrée into the diamond industry, the investigator could very well be in danger. As could Sheldrake himself."

Chapter 13

A damp, chilly breeze followed them into their Holland Park townhouse. Gregory bolted the door, shutting out the gloomy December evening. It was only five-thirty, but it felt more like ten o'clock. *Oh, how I hate when it gets dark early*, Emmeline thought half-consciously, as she shrugged out of her coat and hung it on one of the pegs along the wall. Her mind was still on their interview with Sheldrake. She was eagerly anticipating their meeting with Underwood, especially getting her hands on his report.

First things first, though. "I'll run upstairs to change and then I'll get dinner ready," she told him. "I made a spinach quiche yesterday. All I have to do is pop it in the oven and I'll make a salad. It won't take long."

"Sounds wonderful. But before you rush off"—he gently backed her up toward the wall and braced his hands on either side, trapping her in his embrace—"don't you think your adoring husband deserves a kiss?"

Emmeline tilted her head and threw him a saucy look. "It depends on your level of adoration."

One brow rose, but there was a bemused gleam in his eyes. He bent his face close to hers and brushed her lips with a kiss that left her in no doubt of his ardor. A delicious tingling sent a warm shock to every nerve in her body.

The taste of his kiss lingered on her lips, when they broke apart. "Well," she said, her voice slightly hoarse, "I'll give you high marks for enthusiasm."

He leaned in closer and pressed his mouth to a sensitive spot behind her ear. "I have an idea. Why don't we skip dinner and go upstairs? I assure you I can refine my zeal."

Her breath caught in her throat and her cheeks flamed. She took his face between her hands. "What a scandalous suggestion."

"Is that a yes, Mrs. Longdon?" He kissed the hollow at the base of her throat.

"That's not fair," she murmured as she twined her arms around his neck.

He chuckled in her ear and whispered, "My darling Emmy, everything is fair in love and war."

She placed both hands on his chest and pushed him away. "And which is this?"

His mouth twisted into a crooked smile. "Whichever you like. I'm willing to debate the matter at length"—he pointed to the ceiling—"upstairs, in our bed, where we'll be far more comfortable."

Emmeline opened her mouth, but her flirtatious rejoinder died on her tongue. A clattering of pots rumbled from the kitchen.

Her startled expression must have mirrored the one in his eyes. "Someone's in the house," she hissed out of the corner of her mouth.

"Stay here," Gregory ordered and began to make his way down the hall on the balls of his feet.

"I will not," she declared in a defiant whisper and hurried after him.

He halted unexpectedly on the threshold to the kitchen, causing her to collide into the solid bulk of his muscular back. "Oof." The word flew unbidden from her lips. Really, he could have given her some warning.

Gregory leaned against the doorframe and crossed his arms over his chest. He cleared his throat. "Ahem. Is your new hobby housebreaking?"

Who the devil was the intruder? Emmeline poked her head round her husband. The tension left her body, when she saw her grandmother standing in the middle of the kitchen with an apron tied around her waist.

Gran flapped a hand at Gregory. "You silly boy. You know I have a key. Now, come here and greet me properly."

He crossed to her and bent down to give her a peck on the cheek. "You're a heavenly vision, as always, Helen."

"What utter piffle." She tittered merrily. "But when you get to be my age, you enjoy the silver-tongued flattery all the more."

He lifted her hand to his lips and gallantly grazed her knuckles with a kiss. "Your age? Have you glanced in the looking glass lately? At seventy-eight, you're more vibrant and alive than women half your age. If Emmy hadn't taken my heart prisoner, I would have been your slave." He flashed one of those smiles that set female hearts aflutter.

Helen wagged a finger at him. "That's quite enough of that." She sniffed. "Slave indeed."

Emmeline nudged her husband out of the way and gave Helen a hug. "Why didn't you tell us that you were coming up to London? We could have fetched you from Charing Cross."

"Nonsense. You're both busy with work. I wanted to surprise you."

"Surprise? You nearly gave me a heart attack."

"Don't exaggerate, Emmy." Then Helen's eyes narrowed, as she held her granddaughter at arm's length and appraised her from head to toe. "Your face looks thinner. You've lost weight."

Emmeline rolled her eyes toward the ceiling and

exhaled a weary sigh at this familiar refrain. "No, Gran. I haven't lost weight."

Helen surveyed her critically. "Are you sure?"

"Quite sure."

"Good. Are you pregnant yet?" Helen asked point-blank.

Emmeline groaned and sank into one of the chairs at the kitchen table. She shook her head. "No, I'm not pregnant."

Gregory snorted. He leaned against the counter, arms folded over his chest, entertained by the proceedings.

Emmeline shot him a withering look. "You are not helping matters." He merely spread his hands wide and winked at her.

"Why?" Helen continued her interrogation.

"Gran, it's too soon. We have to get used to being together."

Her grandmother threw her hands up in exasperation. "Don't give me that rubbish. You've been married nearly two months and you've known each other for three years. And I'd like to point out that in between you've wasted quite a bit of effort being foolish. It's high time my great-grandchild made an appearance in this world." She rounded on Gregory, who coughed to muffle the laughter threatening to burst from his throat. "You're just as much at fault. What do you have to say for yourself?"

He tried to school his features into a sober expression. "I assure you, my dear Helen, that I'm doing my best."

She cocked her head to one side and considered him for a moment, before reaching up and patting him on the shoulder. "Yes, of course you are. That means someone else is the stumbling block." Her brown gaze locked on Emmeline again.

"Why do you always take his side?" Emmeline demanded.

"Because, my precious girl"—she crossed over to the

table and cupped Emmeline's chin in her hand—"you think too much and get peculiar ideas into your head." Her tone softened. "There's nothing to be afraid of. It's perfectly natural. You two love each other."

"What if—" Emmeline broke off. Tears stung her eyelids and a lump rose in her throat.

"Hush," Helen cooed and took her face between her hands. "You won't lose this baby."

"You don't know that, Gran. No one knows." Emmeline cursed the tremor she heard in her own voice. "I can't go through it again. The emptiness is unbearable. It doesn't go away."

"Everything is different now," Gregory said tenderly as he crouched down at her side.

"Of course, it is," Helen agreed, her mouth curving into a loving smile.

Emmeline threw her arms around Gregory and buried her face against his neck.

"I'm never going to leave you again," he murmured against her hair. "Never." He waited a beat. "I wouldn't dare. Helen would hunt me down, if I did."

This broke the tension and made them all laugh.

Helen shook her head. "Ooh, you. Now then, I want the two of you to work *much* harder to remedy this situation in the very near future. My great-grandchild takes priority over everything else. Do I make myself clear?"

Gregory rose, clicked his heels, and sketched a little salute. "*Message received and understood.*"

"And don't you forget it. I will be extremely cross, if you two disobey orders." She rubbed her hands together. "Right. Make yourselves useful and set the table. Dinner will be burnt to a crisp if we continue chuntering on all night."

Emmeline rose and kissed Helen's cheek. "That was sweet. You didn't have to make dinner. Thank you."

"It was my pleasure. Besides, I want to discuss something with the two of you. That's the reason I came up to London."

Emmeline frowned. "Nothing's wrong, is it? You're not ill, are you?"

"There you go worrying again, as you if you have nothing better to do. I'm rude with health, as the old saying goes. I simply need some advice." She flapped her hands at Emmeline. "Set the table." Then to Gregory, she said, "Instead of standing there looking gorgeous, go get a bottle of wine."

Helen waited until after dinner, when they were settled in the living room with coffee, to broach the subject she wanted to discuss. "A nice young man rang last week with what sounds like a wonderful investment opportunity."

Gregory set his cup and saucer down on the coffee table. One brow rose skeptically. "Oh, yes? Who was this fellow and what kind of investment?"

"I was coming to that. Honestly, you're becoming as impatient as Emmy."

Emmy eyed her grandmother over the rim of her cup. She felt a flutter in the pit of her stomach.

"His name was Christopher Morton. He's a salesman for a company called Stonecrest Commodities Limited. They sell colored diamonds, which he assured me would increase in value tremendously in a short time. He guaranteed that I could make a fifteen to twenty-five percent profit on the investment. He said that if I do decide to invest, I'll be sent reports that provide details to indicate the authenticity of the specific diamond purchased."

Although Gran became more animated with every word, the anxious butterfly in Emmeline's stomach twisted into a tight knot. She traded a worried glance with her husband.

"He sent me some glossy brochures that explained

everything. I brought them with me." Helen jumped to her feet. "I'll just go get them."

She hurried out of the room and returned a moment later. She deposited the material into Gregory's hands. Emmeline came to stand behind the wingback chair and peered over his shoulder as he leafed through the pages.

Helen looked at him expectantly and gestured toward the brochure. "As you can see, Stonecrest has received glowing testimonials from its clients."

Gregory remained silent as he closed the brochure facedown in his lap. He smoothed down the corners of his mustache, before propping his elbows on the armrests and steepling his fingers over his stomach. "How much did he ask you to invest?"

"He was extremely nice about the whole matter. He said that while I would reap returns, if it were his granny he'd advise her to invest a modest four thousand pounds in the beginning, in view of the fact that I was a novice to the diamond market. He also told me that they have a buy-back guarantee, in case I change my mind."

He gave her a tight smile. "Did he? How very civilized."

"I thought so. Now, the poor chap is getting rather anxious. I don't really blame him. He deserves an answer. He's rung me every day this week."

"Give me his number and I'll tell him to go to the devil," Gregory retorted with icy disdain. He waved the brochure in the air before tossing it onto the coffee table. "If there are any diamonds, which I doubt, they're nowhere near the value this chap purports. It's a bloody boiler room scam."

Emmeline hitched a hip on the armrest and slipped an arm around his neck. "What's a boiler room scheme?"

He tilted his head back and rested it against the chair. "A group of con men get together and rent out an office, where they likely install a bank of telephones. The 'salesmen' start making cold calls to scores of victims, enticing them with the deal of their lives. They print up informative brochures like that one"—he gestured with his chin in disgust at the table—"and provide certificates for the diamonds, proper invoices, et cetera."

Helen placed her hands on her knees, her face crumpling into a crestfallen expression. "I see. I trust you implicitly, but I must admit I got a teeny bit excited by the whole idea. Imagine me owning diamonds." She clucked her tongue. "I should have known it was too good to be true."

"I'm sorry, Helen."

"Don't be." She reached across and he clasped her hand. "That's why I came to you. I know you have my best interests at heart and would steer me in the right direction."

"Ooh." Emmeline leaped to her feet and hugged herself as she stalked around the room. "It makes my blood boil—"

"I always knew you were a hot-blooded woman," Gregory muttered under his breath.

He and Helen exchanged a smile, but Emmeline was having none of it. "It's all well and good. You were able to prevent Gran from parting with what could have been her life's savings, but think of the millions out there"—she flung an arm in a vague arc toward the window overlooking the street—"who aren't as lucky. I'm going to do a series on these types of crimes—what did you call them?—boiler house schemes."

"No, Emmy," he asserted quietly.

She halted in her perambulations and pinned him with her gaze. "What do you mean no? These criminals can't be allowed to get away with it."

"I agree. But if you start a crusade in black and white, they are going to go underground in the blink of an eye. They'll just reinvent themselves in another endeavor that could be far worse. You wouldn't want that, would you?"

"No." The word came out on a frustrated sigh, as she plopped down heavily on the sofa next to Helen. "We have to do something."

"*We* don't have to do anything. It's a matter for the Fraud Squad." He held up a hand to forestall the protest leaping to her lips, which she snapped shut. "I'm glad we are of one mind on that score. However, I would like to have a word with the nice Christopher Morton." He snatched up the offending brochure again. "Ah. Here it is. The address."

"What are you going to do?" Helen eyed him nervously. "You won't hurt him, will you?"

Gregory's mouth curved into one of his most engaging smiles. "No, nothing so crass. I'm simply going to scare the living daylights out of him."

"Oh, well, if that's all." Helen leaned back and took Emmeline's hand in hers. "If it were Emmy, she would have gone there and killed him with her bare hands."

Emmeline sniffed. "Really, Gran. You're as bad as Gregory. You make me sound like an unhinged murderer."

"No, just someone who has a killer instinct for unearthing nasty truths," Gregory offered as a way to placate her. "Besides, I would have thought that one murder was more than enough crime to be getting on with?"

Helen sat up straight and scooted to the edge of the sofa. "Murder? Do tell? You know I love a good mystery. I'm waiting. Enlighten me." She fixed her gaze on Emmeline.

Over another pot of coffee, Emmeline and Gregory told her about their eventful night at the theatre, which culminated in the discovery of Verena Penrose's body and a slew of questions.

Chapter 14

At nine-thirty the next morning, Emmeline and Gregory were taking the lift up to the fifth floor in 207 Regent Street.

The doors slid open to reveal an immaculately clean corridor with eggshell white walls and dove gray carpeting. Just beyond a staircase to the left was a solid oak door with a gold plaque that proclaimed that they had arrived at the office of Foster Reeves Investigations. Gregory rapped on the door with his knuckles and then pushed it open.

The office was small, not quite square, and free of any columns. Its open-plan design gave the impression of space. The walls and carpeting echoed the color scheme of the corridor. The wall overlooking the center of Regent Street sloped at a slight angle toward the two windows. Four desks faced the center of the room and were positioned in a loose semi-circle. The owners of two of the desks were absent. At a third, a fellow with sandy hair who had to be in his mid-thirties, sat with his phone pinned between his ear and shoulder, while he scribbled down notes. He was silent for the most part, interrupting only to ask an occasional question.

A gentleman in his fifties dressed in a crisp white shirt and silver tie took off his spectacles and rose from behind the last desk. "How do you do? I'm Michael Underwood."

His round face creased into a smile as he walked around and thrust out a hand. "You must be Miss Kirby and Mr. Longdon."

Once they had exchanged social niceties, Underwood motioned to the two chairs before his desk as he lowered himself into his own. "Would you like some coffee or tea?" He waved a hand toward a mini kitchen area that could be cleverly hidden behind a pair of folding doors. It featured a counter with a sink, a coffee machine, a stack of cups, and a tin of biscuits.

Emmeline and Gregory politely declined the offer. "Well then," Underwood said as he slipped his spectacles back onto his nose and opened a file in front of him. "Down to business."

He was silent for a few seconds as he leafed through the neatly typed pages. Emmeline supposed that he was refreshing his memory on the salient points of the case. She noted that the file also contained a number of black-and-white photos. She craned her neck as unobtrusively as possible, but she couldn't see any of the photos from this angle.

Underwood closed the file and folded his hands atop it. Steely intelligence vied with curiosity, as his gray gaze assessed each of them in turn. "Now then," he said in an even tone, "Mr. Sheldrake directed me to be completely candid with both of you. Of course, I will do as my client wishes. However, before I disclose what I and my associates have discovered about the late Ms. Penrose, I would like to know what is your interest in her. I assure you it is purely to tick boxes off in my own mind. I like to know where I stand with people."

"A perfectly reasonable request," Gregory replied with self-assurance. "I'm the chief investigator for Symington's. The firm insured Ms. Penrose's jewels."

Underwood's brow creased into a frown, as his thick

dark brows drew together. "Were any of them stolen?" he asked in confusion. "Mr. Sheldrake neglected to mention that fact."

"No, nothing was stolen. It's merely routine procedure when one of our clients dies unexpectedly, especially in such violent circumstances."

"I see," the private detective muttered, not fully satisfied. He turned his attention to Emmeline. "And you, Miss Kirby, naturally I know who you are. I find it surprising that Mr. Sheldrake would allow a member of the press to have full access to this file" —he tapped it with his forefinger— "even before he has seen it. I hope you are not here looking for salacious gossip. I will not be party to some sort of smear campaign. Foster Reeves Investigations is a respectable agency."

Emmeline sat up straighter in her chair. "I assure you, Mr. Underwood, I'm only after the truth to ensure that Verena's killer is caught."

"Verena? Did you know Ms. Penrose?"

"We were...colleagues"—she nearly choked on the word—"for a short while at *The Times*."

"Is that so? I had no idea."

"No reason you should. What's really driving me to pursue this story more than any other issue at the moment is the fact that my husband and I were at the play that night. When the evening started out, we hadn't bargained on the ceiling coming crashing down and finding a dead body."

His brows shot up. "Good Lord. You discovered her?"

"Yes," Gregory murmured. "It's not a sight we will soon forget."

Underwood pointed at the two of them. "Do you mean that the two of you are married?"

Gregory bit back a smile at the man's surprise. "Yes. Is it a problem?"

The detective shook his head as he gaped at Emmeline.

"No, no problem at all. It's just that Mr. Sheldrake hadn't mentioned it. Not that it would have made any difference if he had."

"That's probably because it never came up yesterday, when we spoke to him," she explained. "Gregory and I are following up the matter from different angles."

"Right, of course."

"I hope we've allayed your concerns about our intentions," Gregory prompted, "and you can perhaps now share what you've learned about Verena Penrose."

Underwood hesitated. "Yes, I will. But I find your involvement together highly…unusual, to say the least."

One of Gregory's shoulders shrugged nonchalantly. "We're a team in every sense of the word." Emmeline nodded and returned his grin.

"Indeed. I can see that." Underwood cleared his throat. "Well, I don't want to waste any more of your time." He leaned back in his chair and pursed his lips. He seemed to be searching carefully for his words. "I've seen all manner of lies, betrayal, and depravity in this business. One never gets used to it, but it helps to preserve your sanity if you develop a sort of numbness. I must confess, though, it came as quite a shock when I heard about Ms. Penrose."

"Why? Because of the cold, calculated nature of the crime?" Emmeline probed, as she drew out her notebook.

"Frankly, I expected to hear that Mr. Sheldrake was the one who was dead."

"What?" She and Gregory exchanged a stunned glance.

Underwood nodded his head gravely. "In the course of my investigation," he explained, "I learned that Ms. Penrose and her lover—well, one of them anyway—were planning to kill her husband.

"I immediately contacted a friend of mine at the Metropolitan Police, Inspector Paul Wheeler. I had arranged to go down to Scotland Yard yesterday morning to bring him what little evidence I had. And then came the news about her murder. I can tell you, it fair threw me for a loop."

"Verena was always devious and vicious," Emmeline muttered *sotto voce*. "It shouldn't surprise me that she would cross the line and contemplate murder. And yet...it does."

She couldn't reconcile this revelation with the confrontation she had with Verena at the theatre. Emmeline was certain that her instincts were correct and the woman was obliquely asking for help. But help with what? Surely Verena was astute enough to realize that she would never condone murder.

She frowned. *Secrets and the lies people tell to cover them up*, she reflected. *Verena lived and breathed secrets, and, ultimately, they were her undoing.* Emmeline was convinced on that score. Secrets and ravens. The latter gnawed at her. What did ravens have to do with this sordid mess?

These frustrating questions rattled around her mind in ever-widening circles. However, the answers eluded her. She cast a sideways glance at Gregory. He was staring at some invisible point on the opposite wall. His face was pinched in a pensive expression as his brain digested this disturbing new twist.

Underwood had the file open again and threw her a questioning look. "Pardon me, I didn't catch what you said, Miss Kirby. Or rather, I should say Mrs. Longdon?"

"Nothing important. Kirby is fine. I use my maiden name professionally. You can call me Emmeline, if you like. Please go on."

The detective nodded. "As you wish. Mr. Sheldrake, the poor sod, loved his wife desperately." He exhaled a long sigh. "I'm afraid it was the old story. He suspected she was cheating on him. He didn't want to believe it. He was embarrassed to unburden himself to a stranger and yet he needed to know. That's why he came to Foster Reeves. While the agency has a reputation for being discreet, Ms. Penrose was not."

Emmeline snorted. She could have saved him a great deal of aggravation and told him that.

"Within a week," Underwood continued, "my colleagues and I had discovered the flat in Kensington where she and her boyfriend met. Ms. Penrose owned the flat. They met there regularly every Monday and Tuesday for two months. She often spent the night there and only returned to her home at the Excelsior the following morning. As you can see, the boyfriend is a good-looking chap."

He slid a photo across the desk. Emmeline picked it up and cocked her head to one side as she studied Verena's paramour. He was indeed attractive. He was tall with an athletic build. His wavy dark hair framed a lean face with a strong, square jaw. Although she couldn't determine their color since the photo was black-and-white, his most arresting feature were his eyes. They seemed to suck the air from one's lungs. Yes, she could see how Verena would fall for this chap. He radiated sex appeal and danger.

She passed the photo over to Gregory. "Have you been able to find out anything about him?" she asked Underwood.

"His name is Scott McCallister. He has a duplex in Fitzrovia. A hefty bank account. He drives a top of the range BMW. And, as far as I've been able to determine, he has no visible means of support."

"Hmm," Gregory murmured as he stared at the photo of McCallister. "It sets one's mind to wondering, doesn't it?"

"It certainly does. Of course, McCallister could have been born with a silver spoon in his mouth and doesn't have to work."

Gregory lifted his gaze to meet the detective's eye. "True," he concurred. "But neither of us believes that, do we?"

Underwood gave an emphatic shake of his head. "No. McCallister is too smooth. The way I see it, he's either an underworld criminal or a gigolo, or both. I just haven't been able to determine which. That's one of the reasons I wanted to meet with Mr. Sheldrake. I needed guidance on how he wanted me to proceed." He slumped back in his chair. "I suppose the point is moot now that Ms. Penrose is dead. Mr. Sheldrake likely will want me to halt my investigation."

Emmeline scooted to the edge of her chair. "That seems a reasonable assumption. However, we could continue to look into McCallister. As you've indicated, he's highly suspicious. Who knows? He may be involved in Verena's murder." She ignored the warning look Gregory shot at her and pressed on, "After all, Mr. Sheldrake did say that we could have full access to your report."

Underwood drummed his fingers on his armrest. "Yes," he answered slowly. "Normally, I would hesitate to turn over the report to a member of the press. But this case bothers me. I wouldn't want a murderer to go free."

"Exactly. We absolutely can't have that." Tentatively, she reached out a hand. Her fingers were itching to delve deeper into the report's details.

Underwood sat up straight, closed the file, and gave it to her. "I hope you can find the truth."

Emmeline snatched it from him as graciously as possible. "I assure you I will leave no stone unturned."

She placed the file in her lap and started scanning the report as Gregory asked the detective a few more questions. She barely registered what they were discussing. Underwood's observations were meticulous. The file was going to be a great help as she chased down the story. She began flipping through the rest of the photos. Most of them were of Verena and McCallister in different locations. However, her hand froze in mid-air when she came to the sixth photo. She gaped at it. A tendril of cold dread curled around her heart. It couldn't be. She squeezed her eyes shut. It had to be the light here in the office. She opened her eyes again. But the same image stared back at her.

"Mr. Underwood." Her voice came out as a hoarse croak. She cleared her throat and tried again. "Mr. Underwood, who…who is this with Verena?"

Her hand trembled as she relinquished the photo to the detective. She could feel Gregory's eyes on her, but she didn't dare look at him.

"Oh, that's the other boyfriend. He appeared on the scene in the last month. Ms. Penrose was quite enamored. If she hadn't been killed, I think McCallister would have been shown the door in the not-too-distant-future."

Her stomach sank with every word.

Underwood tapped the photo. "His name is Adam Royce. He's a big industrialist. He now runs the family company, Royce Global Holdings Group. As a journalist, you must have heard of him."

Yes, I've heard of him, Emmeline thought ironically. *He's my brother.*

Chapter 15

Emmeline's legs felt like water. Still, she managed to put one foot in front of the other as she and Gregory took their leave and walked out of the office.

She clutched the file to her chest as they waited for the lift. *Adam and Verena?* she silently ruminated. Adam must have gone stark, raving mad. Couldn't he see that Verena was a conniving schemer only out for herself? Apparently, not. Like most men—she thanked the Lord that Gregory and Philip were more discerning—Adam had allowed himself to be swayed by a part of his anatomy that was disconnected from his brain. She shook her head. He was more like his twin Sabrina than she cared to admit.

Her teeth clenched as the lift doors slid open. Adam deserved better than Verena. Her fingers tingled. Damn and blast. She was going to throttle him.

Suddenly, she felt Gregory take her hand and uncurl each finger until they no longer formed a tight fist. He gave her hand a squeeze. "I needn't have to point out that fratricide is not an option."

She tilted her head to look up at him. His eyes were full of sympathy, which helped to ease the tension in her taut muscles. "Who says so? The law according to men," she responded mulishly. "Oh, Gregory." She leaned into him and rested her head against him. "Why?"

He slipped his arm around her shoulders. "Adam is a grown man. It's none of our business."

Her head snapped up. "None of our business?" Her voice rose an octave. "He was having an affair with a blackmailer. A *married* blackmailer at that, who was involved with another man at the same time. Oh, my God." A hand flew to her mouth as a thought struck her. "No matter what Underwood believes, Verena was not in the throes of a grand passion. She was just using Adam to wheedle out the gory details about everything that happened over the summer with his father. At the theatre, Verena taunted me about becoming Victor Royce's heiress. She suggested that I had insinuated myself into the family by blackmail. The hypocrite." Her temples throbbed with fury. "Bloody, stupid Adam."

Gregory took her hand once more and rubbed his thumb along the web of skin between her thumb and forefinger. "Emmy, you are not the guardian of the world. Don't put Adam on a pedestal. He won't thank you for it. No one is perfect. Everyone makes choices in life."

"Well, Adam made the worst possible one," she shot back.

Gregory huffed a sigh as the car arrived in the lobby and she stormed out. "Darling, you're upsetting yourself for no reason. You should be happy. Adam is safe from Verena's clutches. Her death saw to that."

"Yes, but she addled his brain—if he had one, which I very much doubt after this episode. Someone has to prevent him from making the same mistake again."

Gregory took her by the shoulders and spun her around to face him. "No, someone doesn't. Especially not you."

Her eyes narrowed to dark slits. "I'm sure Gran would agree with me."

He groaned and threw his hands up in the air. "It's a good thing Helen went back to Swaley. Don't get her involved. Or Maggie for that matter."

"Men," she grunted.

"Yes, darling. We are inferior creatures. And you"—he kissed the top of her head—"take things far too much to heart. This revelation about Adam is a distraction."

"Because of the intimate nature of their relationship," she declared with a shudder, "he could know what story she was working on or if she had received any threats recently. I'll go see him."

Gregory raised an eyebrow. "Emmy."

"A good journalist must follow all leads," she responded primly. "That's why I'm also going to look into Scott McCallister. To find out both sides of the story."

She reached up and kissed his cheek. "Thank you, darling. I feel much better. It's always good to talk things out."

"Talking works both ways." He gave her a pointed look. "The problem is you're stubborn and don't listen to sound advice."

She sniffed and hitched her handbag higher on her shoulder. "Everyone is entitled to his opinion. I'm going to drop by Royce Global Holdings and surprise Adam."

He snorted. "You mean ambush him so that he doesn't have a place to run?"

She made a moue at him. "Ha. Ha. Don't you have something more constructive to do than to cross-question your wife?"

"Even though I'm a mere male, I think it would be a good idea if someone told dear, old Oliver what we have discovered."

"Ah," she mumbled.

"Oliver would be terribly hurt, if you didn't keep our promise. The spirit of cooperation and all that."

She poked him in the chest. "Me. Why do I have to be the one to inform him?"

A smile spread across his handsome features. "Because, my darling, Oliver can be a bit tetchy and you know how to smooth out all of his rough edges."

"Hmph. What are you going to be doing?"

"Many, many things. Starting with tracking down Christopher Morton and making sure that he never comes near Helen again." He exhaled a weary sigh and grimaced. "Then, I'm going to see Villiers. I've put it off long enough."

She reached up and lightly caressed his cheek. "Thank you for Gran. It makes me so angry that she could have become another victim. As for Villiers, don't let him get under your skin." She stood on tiptoe and pressed a gentle kiss against his lips. "Give me a ring after you've seen him."

"I'll probably need a stiff Scotch first."

She chuckled and snatched up the lapels of his coat in her fists. "I have a better idea. Why don't we send Gran to have a word with him? She'll set him straight. He'd think twice about interfering in our lives again." She heard the catch in her voice.

If wishes were horses…

Gregory smirked. "Villiers would run for his life, if he knew what was good for him. But why put Helen through all that strife?" He kissed her forehead. "Give my best to Oliver. Tell him not to cry. I'll pop by again very soon."

She swatted his arm. "He'll be thrilled."

He grinned. "Of course, he will. He leads a dull life. Now, be gentle with Adam. He doesn't deserve the third degree. And mind how you go with your questions in general. I don't want the killer casting a lethal eye in my wife's direction."

∽∾∽

Superintendent Burnell, a cup of coffee in one hand and the postmortem report from Dr. Meadows tucked under his arm, lumbered down the corridor toward his office. His mind sifted through the evidence they had uncovered thus far in the Penrose murder, which was precious little. The motive was likely to put an end to Verena's blackmailing and to prevent her from spilling the killer's secrets. Her malicious articles had destroyed so many people. Therefore, it was unsurprising that her victims were reluctant to speak to the police, making their job that much more difficult.

"Ah, there you are, Superintendent Burnell," a woman called from behind him.

The detective stiffened. "The voice of doom," he muttered under his breath. He quickened his pace.

"Superintendent, I know you can hear me," she intoned with asperity. "I need to have a word."

Burnell swore silently and came to a halt in the middle of the corridor. His shoulders slumped forward. He let out a long, exasperated breath as he pivoted on his heel to face Sally Harper, Cruickshank's secretary. There she loomed, the Amazon of the Metropolitan Police. Nostrils flaring like a bull being chased by a toreador, her brown eyes alight with the devil's fire, and her mouth twisted into a permanent scowl of disapproval. She instilled fear in the hearts of mere mortals. For Burnell, she was a constant, caustic irritation. Like a rash that never went away.

She would be an attractive woman, he mused, if she didn't make it her mission in life to make everyone around her utterly miserable. Her husband had all his sympathy.

"At last. I've been trying to hunt you down all morning."

I'm not surprised. I always suspected you were a predator at heart.

He pasted a smile on his face and spread his arms wide.

"Lucky you. You've found me."

She tossed her chin in the air. "Lucky? You must be joking," she scoffed. "Every minute I have to spend in your presence is a curse. You are the most insufferable man I know. I don't understand why you weren't booted off the force years ago."

He gritted his teeth and inhaled deeply. She was *not* going to goad him into losing his temper. "Perhaps it's because I'm a damn good detective and I put the baddies behind bars. My record speaks for itself."

She made a dismissive gesture with her hand. "That's debatable."

He'd had enough. "What do you want, Sally?" he asked, his tone sharp as shards of broken glass.

"Assistant Commissioner Cruickshank wants to know where you stand with the Penrose murder. He was expecting an update first thing this morning, but you've been rather elusive. He's an extremely busy man. He doesn't have time to chase down his subordinates."

Oh, yes, the Boy Wonder is busy making a nuisance of himself every chance he gets, Burnell griped bitterly. *That's his area of expertise.*

"Well, you can tell his Excellency that I'm hard at work following up on leads and he should let me get on with my job instead of sending his lapdog to harass me."

His blood sluicing through his veins, he started to walk away. Her outraged gasp brought a smile to his lips. Let her stew, the harpy.

He had only taken a few steps, when Sally retorted crisply, "Assistant Commissioner Cruickshank, the poor man, knows how disagreeable and uncooperative you tend to be so he wanted me to reiterate that you are not to go near Laurence Villiers again." She paused and raised her voice to draw the attention of anyone who happened to be nearby. "If you disobey his direct order, the assistant commissioner will be left with no choice but to discipline you."

The superintendent wanted to wipe the spiteful grin off her face. He opened his mouth to fire off a barbed rejoinder, but he was forestalled.

"Superintendent Burnell," a familiar voice drifted to his ears.

He and Sally peered round to see Emmeline walking toward them at a brisk pace.

She offered them a smile and inclined her head in greeting at Sally, as she drew level with them. Her gaze flitted between them. "I apologize if I'm interrupting something."

"No, we were quite finished," Burnell responded gruffly.

Sally sniffed. "Indeed. Superintendent Burnell now knows the importance of proceeding with discretion." Then her demeanor became all sweetness. "It's a pleasure to see you again, Miss Kirby."

Like Dr. Jekyll and Mr. Hyde, Burnell marveled. *I wouldn't have believed it, if I didn't see it with my own eyes.* He squinted. *Is that an actual smile? I didn't know Sally's face could do that.*

"I'm afraid Assistant Commissioner Cruickshank is tied up at the moment. You really should have made an appointment," Sally chided gently.

Emmeline darted a look at the superintendent. "Actually, I've come to see Superintendent Burnell."

Sally's spine stiffened and she drew her shoulders back. "Have you really?" She glared at the detective with a mixture of disgust and bafflement, while he beamed back at her. "How odd. I really don't see what the superintendent could possibly have to tell you. But that's your business."

Burnell clucked his tongue. "Isn't it time for you to go back to your lord and master, Sally? Otherwise, he'll send out a search party to find you. We wouldn't want that."

She turned her back on him. "Goodbye, Miss Kirby. I pity you," she murmured before she swept off, her heels clicking an angry tattoo.

Emmeline and Burnell shared a giggle at Sally's expense.

He sniffed the air. "You smell that?" She shook her head in confusion. "It's the foul wind that always lingers when Sally is around," he grumbled. Then, he added more cheerfully. "Thank heavens you appeared when you did. Now, how can I help you?"

Emmeline darted a glance to her left and right. "I came directly from the meeting that Gregory and I had with Michael Underwood, the private detective Sheldrake hired."

The superintendent raised an eyebrow in askance and she responded with a significant look.

"I see," he said as he took her elbow. "We can talk in my office." He spied Finch by the lift and called out, "Finch, my office now."

"Yes, sir." The sergeant caught Emmeline's eye and inclined his head as he hurried toward them.

Finch closed the door just as Burnell was lowering himself into his chair. The sergeant took the chair next to Emmeline.

"Before you start, where's your other half?" Burnell asked. "It makes me nervous when Longdon is on walkabout alone."

"Gregory has to…take care of something for Gran." She didn't meet his eye as she prevaricated. She felt guilty for not telling the superintendent about the boiler room scam that nearly snared Helen, but she promised Gregory that she would let him handle it. Then on more solid ground, she continued, "Afterward, he was going to see Villiers."

Burnell snorted. "Good luck with that one. Villiers is as

slippery as a wet bar of soap." Finch nodded grimly in agreement.

"What did you find out?" the sergeant inquired.

"Verena was indeed having an affair. Two actually." She swallowed down the bile that rose in her throat, when she thought of Adam.

"From what I've discovered about Ms. Penrose, she always had a man warming her bed," Finch replied with derision.

Emmeline curled her fists as Adam's face danced before her eyes again. "Yes, well, Verena was becoming indiscreet. Her husband suspected that she was being unfaithful." She leaned forward. "However if anyone was going to be murdered, Underwood feared it was going to be Sheldrake because Verena and one of her boyfriends were plotting to kill him."

Burnell slammed his open palm against his desk and exploded, "What? And the man didn't inform the police? It's criminal. I'll have his license revoked."

"Please, don't do that, Superintendent Burnell. Underwood had arranged to bring the evidence he had to Inspector Paul Wheeler yesterday morning. But of course, it was too late. Apparently, Wheeler is an old friend. Do you know him?"

Burnell slumped back in his chair, his muscles slackening. "Yes, Wheeler's a good detective." He stroked his beard meditatively.

"This is an unexpected turn of events," Finch muttered. "Who's the boyfriend?"

Emmeline took Underwood's file from her lap and placed it on the desk. "This is Underwood's report." She tapped it with her finger. "It's all in there. Photos, dates, et cetera. Verena's partner in crime is Scott McCallister. He has a hefty bank account and lives the high life, but Underwood hasn't been able to find out how he makes his money." The sergeant reached out to take the file, but she placed her hand on top of it. "I'd like it back, so that I can follow up on that angle."

"Emmeline, this is a murder investigation. I can't have this splashed all over the front page of *The Clarion*."

"I came here in the spirit of cooperation. You promised to share what you find out."

"And I will. Within reason."

Her gaze flitted between the two detectives. "I'm not going to drop the story."

"You think that we're not aware of that," the superintendent acknowledged grudgingly. "We know you're only doing your job, but I can't have your reporting prejudicing the case or jeopardizing public safety, especially yours."

"That goes without saying and I would never do so intentionally."

"It's the *unintentional* part that worries us," Finch chimed in, but his crooked smile blunted the sternness of his words.

She felt a flush rise to her cheeks. "Fine. Then we understand each other."

"Finch, go make a copy of the file for Emmeline," Burnell ordered. She inclined her head in thanks. "Then I want you to start digging up everything you can about Scott McCallister. I'll have a team watch Sheldrake. He may still be in danger."

While Finch stepped away for a few minutes to make the copy, she grilled Burnell, "As we're on the subject of Sheldrake, have you had a chance to explore Gregory's theory that an underworld figure may be targeting him and his company?"

"Thus far, Finch and I haven't heard anything through our usual sources." Frustration clouded her face. "Don't worry. We're still looking into that angle."

"All done," Finch said as he returned a few minutes later and shot a pointed look at Emmeline. "Sir, there's something in Underwood's report I think you need to see."

She felt her cheeks drain of blood. Her gaze met Burnell's for an instant and then dropped to her hands in her lap.

"Oh, yes?" The superintendent waggled his hand impatiently in the air for the file. "Anything you care tell me, Emmeline?"

"It's Adam." The name came out on a whisper. "Adam was Verena's other...lover."

"Not the bloody Royces again," Burnell cursed. When her eyes flew to his face, he quickly apologized but the irritation lingered in his tone. "Until now, I have had nothing against Adam. He's a personable chap. But look at it from my point of view. That family attracts trouble like the scent of blood to a shark."

"You can't possibly believe that Adam would ever be involved in a murder," she insisted, a note of defiance in her voice.

"It does run in the family," he countered matter-of-factly.

She leaped to her feet. "You're wrong. It's McCallister. Or a crime lord. Adam had nothing whatever do with Verena's death. The only thing he can be accused of is *extremely* poor taste in women."

The two detectives exchanged an amused grin.

"I'm not accusing Adam of anything. Yet." This drew a thunderous look from her. "We need to interview him. He had an intimate relationship with the victim."

She rolled her eyes at the ceiling. "Don't remind me," she griped. "I'm going to pop by his office before I go back to the paper."

"No, you won't," Burnell commanded. "This is a police matter."

He didn't like the smile curling around her lips, as she gathered up her handbag and coat. "There's no law against visiting my brother."

Burnell surged out of his chair, pressed his palms on the desk, and leaned toward her. "Emmeline, I could detain you for twenty-four hours."

Her eyes widened for an instant, but then she shook her head. "We both know you wouldn't do that." She calmly shrugged her arms into her coat. "You can't justify it. I haven't broken any laws."

She was quite right. The thought of throwing her in jail, even for one night, was utterly ridiculous. But how else could he prevent her unswerving loyalty, albeit an admirable quality, from sending her straight into danger?

She scooped up the file, hugged it to her chest, and crossed to the door. The dark embers of a challenge kindled in her eyes.

"You're walking a thin line, Emmeline. Make sure you don't cross it," Burnell cautioned. "I have to question Adam."

"I'll be sure to mention it to him. He'll be happy to assist the police in any way he can. He has *nothing* to hide."

"In my experience, everyone has something to hide," he observed. "Just ask your husband."

Chapter 16

The dome of St. Paul's Cathedral loomed over Paternoster Square, the colonnaded urban development near Ludgate Hill, the highest part of the City. The square derived its name from Paternoster Row, a medieval street on the site. The area had been devastated by night bombing raids during the Blitz in the Second World War. The centerpiece of the plaza is a Corinthian column of Portland stone topped by an urn of golden flames, which commemorates both the Great Fire of 1666 and the one that destroyed the area in December 1940. The square was once the heart of the publishing industry. However, the London Stock Exchange relocated there in 2004. A number of investment banks and fund managers now had their offices in the square.

Gregory leaned his shoulder against one of the columns. His eyes roamed around the plaza. It was nearing the lunch hour and office workers were starting to emerge from their lairs for a break before tackling the demands of the afternoon. The cafés, restaurants, bars, and shops were preparing to accommodate the onslaught.

His attention was concentrated on Juxon House at 100 St. Paul's Churchyard, the prestigious address of Stonecrest Commodities Ltd. It was a gleaming, modern building that was intended to impress and overwhelm. His jaw clenched when he thought of the lengths that Christopher Morton and his cohorts were willing to go to dupe vulnerable people out of their life savings.

He pushed away from the column and strode across the plaza. When he stepped from the revolving door and into the lobby, the attractive young woman with wavy golden tresses behind the reception desk glanced up and threw him a frosty look. Ah, not the typical reaction he received, but he wasn't fazed. He was certain things would change once he engaged her in conversation. He flashed a charming smile, even before he reached the desk. However, her expression remained stubbornly stone-faced and her manner brusque as she inquired in clipped tones whom he was there to see. His honeyed compliments failed to make even a tiny chink in her armor.

Hmm. Decidedly unfriendly. He sighed inwardly. He had always found it more pleasant to conduct things with a smile and perhaps a bit of harmless flirting. Alas, it was not to be the case today. Pity.

He cleared his throat and mirrored her stiff demeanor as he handed her one of his cards. "I'm Gregory Longdon, chief investigator at Symington's. I'm here to see Christopher Morton of Stonecrest Commodities Limited."

She gave the card a cursory glance, and reached out to pick up the telephone. Holding the receiver in the air halfway to her ear, she asked, "Do you have an appointment?"

He tried another smile. "I'm afraid I don't."

"I see." She sniffed and replaced the receiver in the cradle. "Then you can't see Mr. Morton. You'll have to come back another day."

He left the smile on his lips, as his mind tried to assess whether she was part of Morton's scheme. As he held her hard hazel gaze, he thought not. It was more likely that she derived a sense of power as a gatekeeper. No one trespassed into Juxon House's inner sanctum without being vetted by her first.

Darting a glance to his right and left, he leaned one elbow on the desk and lowered his voice. "I think not. You see, miss, I'm working on a case with Detective Superintendent Oliver Burnell of Scotland Yard. It has come to our attention that Mr. Morton has vital information, but he has been reluctant to speak with us. He's perilously close to being charged with obstruction of justice." His smile broadened. "Between you and me, I believe you are only doing your job. But Superintendent Burnell might not view your behavior in quite the same light. Knowing how a policeman's mind works, he might even come to the conclusion that you were aiding and abetting Mr. Morton." He paused to allow his words to sink in. "You can ring the superintendent to verify my story, if you like."

If you dare, he mused as he watched her complexion become ashen. The haughtiness of only moments ago was replaced by uncertainty mingled with worry.

She held up a hand. "No, no. No need to bother the superintendent."

How considerate of you, he quipped to himself. *Somehow, I thought that you would come to that determination.*

"Naturally, I wouldn't want to stand in the way of a police investigation." She cleared her throat, as her hand hovered over the phone. "Shall I ring Mr. Morton to let him know that you're on your way up?"

He gave her a wry wink. "Why don't I just surprise him?"

A watery smile quivered upon her lips. "As you wish. Stonecrest is on the fourth floor. Suite 407."

He nodded his thanks and started to head toward the bank of lifts. But she called out to him, "Mr. Longdon."

He spun round. "Yes?"

"You will be sure to mention to Superintendent Burnell that I was of assistance."

"You can rely upon it," he intoned seriously.

She lowered herself into her chair, a pink flush of relief spreading across her face. "Well, that's all right then. If I can help the police in any other way, I'll be more than happy to do so."

He merely inclined his head and chuckled silently. *I'll bet you would.*

The glass door with Stonecrest Commodities Limited stenciled upon it in bold white letters glided back and forth with a soft *whoosh*. From the corridor, one glimpsed a spacious, ultramodern office suite decorated in muted shades of gray and white. No doubt, the color scheme was intended to convey a sense that this was a staid place of business.

Gregory grimaced as the doors slid open and beckoned him inside. He took in the empty waiting area to his left, which featured dove gray wall-to-wall carpeting, groupings of rectangular glass coffee tables, and wide, square armchairs. His footsteps echoed off the caramel parquet floor as he approached the tall, U-shaped oak reception desk. Lining the tiled-floor corridors to the left and right were cubes of glass-walled offices and what seemed to be meeting rooms beyond them. The only odd thing was that there was no sign of human life in this sterile microcosm of business, aside from the middle-aged receptionist. Her slate-gray eyes widened in surprise at his unexpected appearance. Then almost the next second, they crinkled at the corners as she rose and offered him a courteous smile. She was the epitome of professionalism in her well-tailored eggplant suit. A string of pearls of the highest quality, he noted, caressed her throat, while a slim gold band and a marquise-cut diamond ring graced her left hand. She was the perfect window dressing to give this scam a patina of legitimacy.

"Good afternoon, sir," she greeted him in plummy tones. "How may I help you?"

He returned her smile. "Hello. I'm Arthur Davis and I'd like to see Christopher Morton. He's been in touch with my grandmother, Helen Davis, recently about investing in some diamonds. As I hold Granny's power of attorney, I have a number of questions that I need answered."

Her smile slipped slightly and two vertical lines formed between her brows, but she recovered quickly. She was a pro all right. "I'm sorry, Mr. Davis, but I'm sure you can appreciate that Mr. Morton has a great many demands on his time. I can personally attest that his diary is booked with meetings from morning until evening for the next month. You simply can't turn up here unannounced and expect to see him. My suggestion is that you ring Mr. Morton with any issues you may have. He will return your call promptly."

"Forgive me, madam," he sneered, "but I don't believe a word that has just come out of your mouth."

She put a hand to her throat and feigned shock. "Well, really, Mr. Davis, there's no reason to be rude or to lose your temper. I'm at a loss of what else to tell you."

His laugh was devoid of mirth. "Madam, don't say anything. I'll find Morton myself."

He brushed past the desk and left her staring after him with her jaw gaping open. He plunged down the first corridor. The offices on either side were empty.

The woman became sensible again. Her agitated voice floated to his ears. "You can't go there, Mr. Davis. I'll call the police."

He ignored her because he knew that the last thing she wanted was the police making a grand entrance. He continued his search for his elusive quarry, throwing open doors as he went along.

Gregory vaguely registered that the receptionist was fumbling for the telephone. "Tell Chris to make himself scarce" was her panicked plea. "Mrs. Davis's grandson is out for blood."

"Morton, you coward, I know you're here," he bellowed. "Show your face or I'll rip this place apart."

Muffled voices, a sudden of shuffling feet and the sound of laptops being banged shut came from a meeting room directly in front of him. He rushed forward, just as the door burst open.

A tall, slim man in his mid-thirties with chestnut hair and brown eyes clouded with terror barred his way. "Look, Mr. Davis, there's nothing to get upset about," he babbled. "We can discuss this calmly, like gentlemen, and"—his eyes bulged—"Bloody hell. I don't believe it. Greg?"

"Well, well, well, if it isn't Mick Walcott," Gregory said as he came to a halt before the man. "So, you're the infamous Christopher Morton. I should have guessed. Since when did boiler room scams become part of your CV?"

No response. "Hmm, Mick," he prodded, as he poked the other man in the chest, forcing his back against the solid bulk of the door.

Mick gave a nervous laugh. "Listen, Greg, I can explain everything."

The smile that curved around Gregory's mouth did not touch his eyes. "I bet you can. And you will." He reached around Mick and gave the doorknob a violent twist. "Aren't you going to introduce me to your friends?" He clucked his tongue. "Where are your manners?"

A group of startled faces gaped when Gregory shoved Mick into the room and kicked the door closed with his foot. The other man stumbled forward and clutched at the nearest chair. He collapsed into it, his gaze fixed on Gregory's face.

Gregory took a half-step backward and leaned against the door his arms folded over his chest, effectively barring anyone from leaving the room.

He flicked a glance at the dozen or so men hovering around a conference table scattered with laptops and headsets. They were frozen like deer caught in the headlamps of a car.

"Now then, chaps, tell me about your lucrative business swindling widows and pensioners out of their savings."

Walcott gave a sheepish shrug of his shoulders, an obsequious smile trembled upon his lips. "You know how it is. A man has to find creative ways to get by in this cruel world we live in."

A muscle in Gregory's jaw pulsed. It was taking all his willpower not to knock the man flat on his back. "It's a dirty game."

"What happened to you?" Walcott shook his head in disgust. "You've gone soft. There was a time when you wouldn't have batted an eye."

"Never," he hissed through gritted teeth. He only stole from those who could afford the loss of their jewels.

Walcott threw his head back and laughed. "Oh, come off it, you hypocrite." He spat this word. "You're a bloody thief."

Gregory ignored this jab. "Scams like this hurt people."

"Since when did you become part of the moral police?" Walcott demanded incredulously.

"I'm not going to discuss morality with you. Just stay away from Helen Davis."

"Oi. Who is she to you? And why pretend to be her grandson?"

"Let's just say she's a friend."

Walcott leaped to his feet. Clearly, his initial shock and

fear were ebbing. "That's not good enough, mate. You muscle your way in here and threaten my private enterprise, and you expect me to retreat quietly with my tail between my legs. Think again."

"How did you come to target her in the first place?" Gregory countered.

"That's none of your concern. It's a trade secret."

Gregory lunged and snatched up a fistful of the other man's lapels. "Your trade secrets will land you in the nick, if I whisper a few sweet-nothings in a certain detective superintendent's ear."

"I don't think you've changed that much," Walcott declared smugly. "You wouldn't grass to the coppers."

Gregory glared at him for several seconds and then let him go.

"You're not clever enough to come up with all this"— he waved an arm in an arc that encompassed the entire room—"who are you working for?"

The other man sniffed and tossed his chin in the air. "I resent your insinuations about my mental prowess."

"Mental prowess," Gregory sneered. "You must be joking. You have the IQ of a flea. Who's behind the scam?"

Walcott twitched his fingers in front of his mouth, as if he were turning a key in a lock. "It's against the code. My lips are sealed."

Gregory's hands clenched into fists at his sides, but Walcott adroitly scurried around the table to place himself out of reach.

"Since I've always liked you—"

Gregory cut across him. "The feeling is far from mutual."

Walcott went on as if he hadn't spoken. "—I'll make a deal with you. If I promise to forget that I ever heard the name Helen Davis, will you walk out that door straight away and pretend that you never set eyes on this place?"

The corners of Gregory's mouth quirked into a grin. "That depends."

Walcott's eyes narrowed suspiciously. "On what?"

"On whether you give me the name of the bloke who came up with this—how did you term it?—*private enterprise.*"

Walcott pressed a hand to his heart and replied solemnly, "A debt of honor prevents me from doing so. As one gentleman to another, surely you must understand that."

"You don't know the meaning of the word honor. You're a weasel, Mick. You'll be one to your dying day. And if you don't want your demise to come in the next sixty seconds, you'll tell me who you're working for."

The air crackled with tension. None of Walcott's associates had dared to utter a word during this entire exchange. They could see the lay of the land. If Walcott antagonized Gregory any further, they would all be spending the rest of their lives in prison.

Walcott moistened his lips with a quick flick of his tongue. Gregory could read it in the man's eyes that he was carefully weighing his options.

Walcott threw his hands up in resignation. "All right. I'll tell you. For old times' sake—"

"There was nothing good about the old days," Gregory grumbled.

"—We've had a recent change in...management. A hostile takeover really. Old Sid's daughter didn't really give us much choice."

"What? You mean Sid Cranbrook. The one who had his finger in everything from racketeering to drugs and prostitution, before he died of a stroke a few years ago."

The other man nodded.

"I didn't know he had a daughter. I wasn't even aware he was married."

"No one did." Walcott sighed. "His wife, a very cultured woman by all counts, died when their daughter was born. Sid raised the girl on his own. To protect her against any retaliation from his enemies, she went by her mother's maiden name. Sid had pots of money, so he lavished her with everything. He sent her to the best boarding schools in Switzerland. After obtaining her degree at the Sorbonne, she came back home and made her own mark on London. Granted, in a different way than old Sid. All legal. Until now, that is."

Gregory ran a hand through his hair. He was certain that Walcott was telling the truth. He just couldn't fathom what it all meant. A piece was missing.

"If she was clean in the law's eyes, why jeopardize everything with a boiler room scam?"

"She wanted to divorce her husband and she was angling to get everything. She cooked up the boiler house and told us to list her husband's company as the wholesaler of record to make it all smell legitimate. She wanted us to bilk a dozen or so people and stressed that everything should be organized in such a way that it pointed to her husband. She said that if he were convicted of a crime, under the law, as his spouse, all his assets would automatically be transferred to her. Once that happened, she was going to divorce him without having to go through a messy court battle. And he would be disgraced and rot in jail without a penny to his name. 'Out of sight, out of mind' were her words."

"Charming," Gregory grunted. It sounded quite bizarre and highly improbable.

"None of it made any sense to me. Sid left her his fortune and his empire is thriving. He made sure she received what toffs call an annuity from all his ventures."

Gregory rolled his eyes at this last comment.

"Of course, I wasn't going to say anything to her face.

But I think she was lying to me," he confided.

Gregory's brows shot up and his eyes widened. "No," he remarked, his tone laced with sarcasm. "Absolutely shocking. Imagine that. Someone actually lying to a pillar of society like you."

Walcott drew his shoulders back and scowled. "There you go again with the personal insults. I'm only telling you what you wanted to know. In my opinion, this was a matter of pure revenge. I think she wanted to hurt our former boss by creating competition. She kept asking all sorts of odd questions about him. Questions we couldn't answer because we never set eyes on the bloke. Everything was conducted by phone or e-mail.

"She certainly acted like a woman with a score to settle." He shrugged and shook his head. "Well, it doesn't matter anymore. She's dead. We were planning to wind down the scam in a few days. Things were getting a bit too hot. The former boss might come after us." He chuffed a nervous giggle. "Typical. Nobody cares about the poor working man these days. We're merely pawns and considered expendable."

Gregory ignored this bit of self-pity. His mind was fixated on only one thing that Walcott had uttered. "What do you mean she's dead?"

"It's been all over the papers. She was murdered the other night."

A cool whisper of apprehension tickled the nape of Gregory's neck. "You mean *Verena Penrose* was Sid Cranbrook's daughter?"

"That's right."

The missing piece fell into place. The problem was the puzzle had shifted out of focus.

Chapter 17

An occasional gust of wind stirred the bare branches of the trees as Emmeline crossed St. James's Square and entered the lobby of Royce Global Holdings Group. Ned, the receptionist on duty, glanced up and his face immediately creased into a broad smile when he saw her. He offered her a hearty greeting as he handed her a visitor's pass. They exchanged a few pleasantries before she headed to the lift. She had become a familiar face around the office since the summer. She could come and go as she liked now that she was an acknowledged member of the family. She was still adjusting to that fact. And she was not looking forward to her forthcoming conversation with Adam about his relationship with Verena.

Fool, bloody stupid fool, she cursed her newfound brother, as the lift rose. Far too soon, she found herself stepping out of the car. By rote, she headed down the corridor to her left. Her footsteps were muted by the plush, cream-colored wall-to-wall carpeting. She came to a halt outside the antechamber to Adam's office, which had formerly been his father's.

Best to get it over with. She drew in a deep breath, before she gave the knob a twist and pushed the door open.

"How lovely to see you," declared Delia, Adam's

secretary. She always had a smile for Emmeline. This helped to unwind the knot in the pit of her stomach.

The two women had gotten on well ever since that first time Emmeline had come to the office to interview Victor Royce.

Delia rose and came around her desk. "You're just the person to brighten Adam's spirit. He's been in a bit of a mood the past couple of days."

"Has he?" Emmeline frowned. *Damn Verena.*

"It wasn't my place to pry, but perhaps you can get him to talk." She winked as she turned to the desk and picked up her telephone. She pressed a button. "I'll let Adam know you're here." She murmured a few words and then replaced the receiver. "You can go straight in. I'll be back shortly with some tea."

Yes, tea, Emmeline thought. *Tea was* definitely *needed. If anything could soothe tempers, it was tea.*

She pasted a smile on her lips and opened the door. Adam was sitting on the caramel leather sofa, but he stood as soon as she stepped over the threshold. His smoldering good looks were marred by the pain reflected in the dark depths of his eyes. He must have sensed her scrutiny because he averted his gaze as he gathered her into his embrace.

He pressed a kiss to her cheek when they broke apart. "This is a nice surprise. I haven't seen you since you returned from Malta. I admit it's been entirely my fault. I've been busy with work and the situation with Jason—"

The pit of her stomach fluttered with unease.

Jason. Adam's older brother, her half-brother. Jason, who with his red-gold hair and blue eyes, was the spitting image of his remote and frosty mother, Lily.

Jason was arrogant and spoiled. He believed everything should be handed to him on a silver platter. He had always been jealous of Adam, who had been their father's favorite.

He conveniently ignored the fact that Adam's business acumen was far superior. Jason had become involved with Alastair Swanbeck several months ago in a bid to take over the reins of Royce Global Holdings. However, he got more than he bargained for when Pavel Melnikov ended up impaled on the iron railings after being thrown from the balcony of his Mayfair duplex.

"Jason?" she demanded, her voice rising. "What situation? He's in jail awaiting trial."

Adam heaved a weary sigh. "I'm afraid his lawyer has painted him as an unwitting victim."

"That's insane. Jason tried to steal the company. He colluded with Swanbeck for heaven's sake."

"We both know that, but his lawyer is a shrewd bastard and has all sorts of tricks up his sleeve. He's trying to negotiate a deal with the Crown Prosecution Service. Jason may be set free in the near future."

"He's guilty as sin," Emmeline fumed.

Adam rubbed the back of his neck. "Yes, well. I'm on the phone with our lawyers practically every day. They're monitoring developments. That's why I've been a bit out of touch lately. That and…other things." The lost look reappeared in his eyes.

He shook his head as if to physically free the worries from his consciousness. "Never mind. How's life in the Longdon household?" he asked politely as he motioned for her to sit. She chose one of the two matching high-back armchairs clustered around the low coffee table. He resumed his place on the sofa, his hands clasped and hanging loosely between his knees.

She cast a glance around the office. The magnificently carved mahogany antique desk still stood in the center, while a bookcase with glass doors and the same exquisite craftmanship took up most of the nearby wall. She was glad Adam hadn't changed anything. It was tasteful and understated. It would have been a terrible shame to redecorate the room.

"How's Gregory?" Adam's voice drew her back to the present.

She couldn't repress a wide grin. "Incorrigible, but wonderful."

Adam chuckled. "Ah, there speaks a woman in love. It warms my heart to see you both happy. You and Gregory were meant for each other."

She gave a rueful grimace. "There was a point not so long ago that I wasn't sure we would make it."

"But you did. Some people don't get a second chance or even a first..." His voice trailed off and a pensive expression shadowed his face.

"Adam," she ventured tentatively. "I need to speak to you about something...someone actually."

"Hmm." His brow furrowed. "Why so glum all of a sudden? Surely you know by now that we can discuss any subject."

She nodded and leaned forward, unable to relax and settle back in her chair. "Of course. I'm glad that you feel the same way. This is rather...delicate." She paused and leveled a direct gaze at him. "I want to ask you about your affair with Verena Penrose."

She held her breath and watched as his thick brows knit together. "How?" he rasped. He cleared his throat and then in a stronger voice continued, "There's no use denying it." He eased back on the sofa. "Why do you want to know?"

"I'm working on the story about her murder."

"Right. Of course, you are. Always in the thick of things."

Was that a trace of irritation she heard in his tone? If he found her questions annoying, it was only a precursor of what was in store when Superintendent Burnell interviewed him. Therefore, he had better buck up.

"Gregory and I were at the theatre that night. We found...her." She almost said the body.

A spasm of surprise shot across his haggard features. "What?"

"Yes," she replied cautiously. "It was chaos that night. The ceiling had collapsed as well."

"I read about that. Why didn't you tell me straightaway?" His eyes held an accusation.

"I didn't know that you and Verena were...close. We discovered that subsequently. Did you know she was married?"

He nodded. "It was complicated, but she was planning to get a divorce. I was...going to ask her to marry me."

She drew air into her lungs and tried to calm her racing mind. "I can't believe what I'm hearing. How long had you been seeing her?"

"Not that it's any of your business, but we'd been going out for a little over a month."

"And you wanted to marry her?" she demanded, her voice trembling with outrage. "Do you know what she was like?" She jabbed a thumb against her chest. "I can tell you. We both worked at *The Times* for a short time. Verena was a vicious witch who took pleasure in ruining people's lives with her exposés. She was a blackmailer. She was anti-Semitic. She—"

Adam leaped to his feet. "That's enough," he roared. "I don't want to hear another word against her."

She jumped up too. "You can't bury your head in the sand, Adam. It hurts me beyond words to tell you, but she didn't care for you at all. She was using you to get all the details about—" She faltered for a moment. "—about everything that happened with your father...our father and how I came to be his heiress."

"You're lying," he snarled.

She took a half-step backward, stunned by his

vehemence. She felt tears sting her eyelids, but she blinked them back.

"I would never do that." She was surprised by how calm her voice sounded to her own ears. "I care about you too much. I thought we'd become close over these past few months. I thought we could be honest with one another."

The minutes ticked by, as an uncomfortable silence sucked the oxygen from the air.

"My apologies for the delay," Delia prattled on as she entered the office with a tray of tea and a plate of biscuits.

She stopped short when she saw Adam and Emmeline glaring at one another. "Ah. Not to worry. A new pot of tea can be brewed later."

The door closed with a soft click behind her and they were alone once more.

"Adam, I'm—"

He held up a hand to forestall her. "No, I'm sorry. I shouldn't have said that. Let's sit down and discuss this like the adults we're supposed to be."

She inclined her head and lowered herself onto the chair, perched as if she were sitting on hot coals.

For a moment, neither uttered a word as they eyed each other warily across the coffee table. Emmeline folded her hands in her lap. Well, someone had to start.

"I believe Verena became involved with you," she remarked carefully, "as part of her ongoing attacks against me. I'm not saying this to give myself airs. She never liked me. I did my best to ignore her, but things deteriorated when I was assigned a story that she wanted. Ever since that day, I think she's been looking for a spectacular way to get her own back at me."

She released a long breath. "Unfortunately, you became an integral part of her machinations. I'm terribly sorry. I know the words are inadequate. But I'm being utterly sincere. Adam, you're a wonderful, caring man. You didn't deserve to be treated in this manner."

He huffed a laugh that was robbed of any joy. She reached out a hand, which he clasped. He squeezed her fingers before dropping her hand and settling back against the sofa.

"I won't deny that it hurts. I never met a woman who got under my skin like Verena." He lapsed into silence and she wished that she hadn't shattered his illusions. But she couldn't have left him in ignorance, could she? Not with a murderer on the loose.

"I'll survive, though," he asserted bitterly, doing his best to rally himself from his brooding.

"Of course, you will," she concurred.

She watched him to gauge whether to proceed. Yes, he was strong. He could handle it. The only way to move on was to get everything out in the open. "I'm afraid there's a bit more unpleasantness."

He waggled a hand in the air. "Go on. Tell me all of it."

"Verena was having an affair with another man at the same time." The color drained from his cheeks, but she went on in a rush. "Her husband hired a private investigator. That's how we know. During his surveillance, the investigator also learned that Verena and her lover were plotting to kill her husband."

Adam's dark eyes, which mirrored her own, widened in disbelief. "I don't understand it. This is becoming more bizarre by the minute. It's sheer insanity."

"Murder generally is." She paused for a beat. "You should expect a visit from Superintendent Burnell. He wants to question you."

"It goes without saying that I'll cooperate. Surely he doesn't think that I had anything to do with Verena's death?"

One of her shoulders lifted in a helpless shrug. "To Superintendent Burnell, everyone is a suspect until he can prove otherwise."

Adam gave a grim nod. He stared off at a point somewhere over her left shoulder. Likely this stirred up memories of the investigation into his father's murder. "Burnell is only doing his job according to the law."

She smiled. "I've always found him to be fair." She pulled a face. "Unlike Sabrina who took against him from the outset."

He laughed, a genuine laugh this time. "Well, you know our dear sister. She's thoroughly spoiled. However, she's not a bad sort deep down."

"If you say so," she murmured. "I've tried to get close to her. Really I have. But she goes out of her way to make things difficult. Especially the way she continues to eye Gregory like a ripe strawberry."

"You have absolutely nothing to worry about on the score. Gregory is your slave and you know it. He ignores her antics, which irks her. As for Sabrina, I admit she's an acquired taste."

"Hmph. Obviously, I haven't acquired the taste," she groused. "If she continues to put up roadblocks, I wonder if I ever will."

"Don't give up. To get back to Burnell, though, I suppose he's already spoken to Craig about Verena. I've been trying to work up the courage to ring him. I've picked up the phone a dozen times in the last two days, but at the last minute the words failed me."

She frowned. "You know Craig Sheldrake?"

"Yes, he made an appointment to see me about two months ago. Craig is trying to persuade me to invest in his company. Dad was a well-known collector of jewels. I advised him on a few acquisitions. When he died, you very generously allowed the collection to come to me although it was yours by right under Dad's will." She waved off this comment, still uncomfortable with the notion that she inherited a fortune. "Anyway, Craig suggested that I put up the collection as collateral in his new venture. We've had a few lunches together. I'm still mulling it over, but I'm inclined to go ahead. The idea is sound." He fell silent for a moment and gave a rueful grimace. "I'm ashamed to admit that I met Verena through him."

"I see." She slumped back trying to digest this nugget of information. "Does Sheldrake need money? I was under the impression CS Gems is a flourishing business."

"It is. Craig wants to expand. He's considering acquiring other firms. For that, he needs liquidity."

This made her recall Gregory's theory about a criminal gang potentially seeking to muscle in on Sheldrake's company by force.

"Did Sheldrake ever mention any threats against himself or his company? A jealous competitor or anyone else?"

Adam's brows furrowed in confusion. "No, not at all. What are you getting at?"

"Before we discovered that Verena had been contemplating murdering her husband—and at this stage we don't know how serious or far that effort went—we had a theory that an underworld figure may have been trying to pressure Sheldrake into selling his company or becoming a front for some sort of money-laundering operation. Perhaps this person thought Sheldrake would be attending the play with her and wanted to frighten them to get what he wanted. The situation probably spiraled out of control, when he found Verena all alone."

"That means Craig could still be a target."

Chapter 18

Gregory's head was still spinning as he bounded up the marble steps of the gleaming white building in Pall Mall. Rather than go inside, he took up a position in the shadows of one of the sturdy Doric columns. He shot his cuff and checked his watch. He knew the other man would arrive any minute now. It was Wednesday, after all.

Just as Big Ben stuck noon, a sleek black Mercedes drew to a halt at the curb. The driver walked around the car to hold the rear door open. The next second, Villiers alighted from the back seat, all crisp and impeccable in a navy Burberry wool trench coat. He flipped up his collar against the wind. The driver shut the door and scurried round to the other side of the car. Villiers murmured something to the driver over the roof. The driver nodded and then slid behind the wheel. The car merged into traffic and was gone almost immediately.

Villiers lingered on the pavement and turned his face up to the sky. To the casual observer, he appeared to be soaking up the anemic warmth of the sun, which had steadfastly remained out of sight for nearly a week. However, Gregory knew better. The master was checking to see whether he had any unwanted admirers. He watched as Villiers lowered his gaze to cast a subtle glance up and down the block, before pivoting on his heel. The man's footsteps were measured as he climbed the wide marble stairs.

Villiers must have sensed some movement out of the corner of his eye because he came to standstill two steps from the entrance. His brow puckered into a frown when Gregory came out into the open. "What the devil are you doing here?" he hissed.

Gregory, hands thrust in the pockets of his coat, ambled forward. He had the advantage, looming over the other man because he was on the top step. The smile that curved around his mouth did not reach his eyes. "Aren't you happy to see me, *Papa*?"

"No" was Villiers's terse rejoinder.

"On that point, if nothing else, we are in agreement," Gregory quipped.

"What do you want?" the other man demanded as he stepped up so that they could be on the same level.

"We need to talk."

"Why did you come *here*? We could have met at Hatchard's." The venerable bookshop was their usual meeting place, when something urgent arose.

Gregory peered through the door of the club and glimpsed the black-and-white tiled marble floor of the foyer. "I thought you could offer me lunch."

Villiers shot a sideways glance at the door. "You know that's out of the question."

"Is it? Don't tell me that you're embarrassed, *Papa*."

"Stop calling me that," Villiers barked.

"I agree, the unfamiliar term does leave a bitter taste on the tongue. Unfortunately, there's nothing either of us can do to change the familial tie that binds us together."

Villiers rolled his eyes skyward and groaned. "This is your wife's doing, isn't it? She pushed her way into my office yesterday to interrogate me. You married a bulldog, not a woman. The only reason that I didn't have her removed from the building was because it would have caused an even bigger scene."

The muscle along Gregory's jaw pulsed. He balled his hands into tight fists in his pockets. "I know you said something to upset her. I could see it in her eyes. It wasn't merely the fact that you had refused to answer her questions."

"That woman is far too temperamental for her own good. Or yours," Villiers sneered. He fixed a hard stare on Gregory's face. "She's always poking and probing, where she doesn't belong. One of these days she's going to get you killed."

Gregory took a step closer. "I am never leaving Emmy again. We're married and we're going to stay married. I don't care whether you approve or not. It's none of your concern. If anything happens to her because of your machinations, you will live to regret it."

The older man laughed and clapped his hands. "How touching. That was said with the bravado of a knight in shining armor." His expression sobered. "It doesn't suit you, Toby."

"Now that I know the truth about you," Gregory remarked tartly, "I'm even happier that I changed my name to Gregory Longdon all those years ago. I don't have to walk around with the stigma of a father's name that was an alias from the outset."

Villiers noticed that the concierge, his face pinched with apprehension, was hovering in the vestibule. "We're attracting attention."

"I'm not leaving until I speak with you—"

"And here I was under the impression we were doing precisely that for the last few excruciating minutes." He glanced at his watch. "I don't intend to drag this out any further. I'm late for my lunch. The subject of your wife will ruin my appetite."

Gregory blocked his path. He clucked his tongue. "We couldn't have the great Laurence Villiers fainting from hunger on the threshold to his club. London would be in an uproar. I'm perfectly willing to continue our conversation in the dining room. Shall we?" He waved an arm toward the door.

Villiers pushed past him. "Come on," he said without turning back to look at Gregory. "You'll only hang about here making a nuisance of yourself otherwise. Your wife has been giving you lessons in that respect."

In one stride, Gregory caught up with him. "I must say that I've never received a more gracious invitation in my life."

A porter materialized to whisk away their coats, while the concierge courteously hailed the two men. Villiers introduced Gregory and signed him in as his guest. Villiers barely heard the concierge wishing them a hearty lunch and a good afternoon. He gave a curt wave of his hand and jerked his chin at Gregory.

Villiers waited until they were out of earshot and halted halfway up the carpeted staircase. He drew near Gregory, his voice barely above a whisper. "This is the first and *last* time that you ever set foot inside the club. Do I make myself clear?"

Gregory smoothed down the corners of his mustache. "Clear as the crystalline waters of a Scottish loch." He smiled and couldn't resist adding, "*Papa*."

A spark of irritation flared in Villiers's eyes before he turned his back on Gregory and stalked up the remaining steps.

At Villiers's request, they were shown to a table in a far corner of the dining room. A handful of the other members caught his eye and nodded a greeting, as he lowered himself into his chair.

With a flick of his wrist, Gregory snapped open the pristine linen napkin and draped it across his lap. As he began to peruse the menu, he murmured, "I didn't know you were such a popular fellow. I could have sworn you didn't have any friends."

"Friends," Villiers scoffed as he leaned across the table. "Not one of those fools is a friend. They want to stay on my good side to prevent me from looking into their dirty little secrets."

Gregory cast a glance over the top of the menu. "Ah, of course. That makes much more sense. I should have smelled the stench of fear in the air. What a jolly way you have about you."

Villiers leaned back in his chair. "Mock all you like. Fear has its advantages."

Their verbal tussle was interrupted by the appearance of the sommelier, who tempted them with several French and German wines. Gregory was ultimately persuaded to choose a Sancerre, while Villiers opted for a Riesling. Only a few minutes had passed before a cheerful waiter came to take their order. With a deferential nod of his head, he was soon off to the kitchen and they were at last left alone.

Villiers folded his hands on the table. "What do you want?" he asked without preamble.

"Verena Penrose."

Villiers gave an exaggerated sigh. "I never heard of the woman. I tried to tell your wife that yesterday. However, she has a nasty habit of not listening."

"You lied, as usual," Gregory shot back. He dropped his voice. "The only way you could have known Verena had seats in a box is if you were at the theatre that night."

Although Villiers knew he was caught out, his face was as still as the glassy surface of a lake on a day without a breath of wind. Seemingly transparent but hiding things beneath the surface. Gregory knew the man's mind must be racing to come up with a plausible answer, but he barely even blinked.

"What could you possibly have in a common with what was essentially a glorified gossip columnist who dabbled in blackmail on the side? You have many flaws, but I can't believe you were careless enough to become one of her victims."

Villiers chuckled at this comment, as the sommelier appeared with their wine. They remained quiet as he went through the motions of pouring a tiny bit of the Riesling into a glass. Villiers lifted it by the stem and held it up to the light. Then, he swirled the golden liquid around, inhaling its aroma, before taking a sip. After allowing it to dance on his tongue, he nodded and allowed his glass to be filled. The sommelier didn't leave until he had repeated the same ritual with Gregory.

"I'm waiting," Gregory pressed.

Villiers twirled the stem of the glass between his fingers. "None of this is your concern. Or your wife's."

"This would be far less tedious for both of us, if you stopped deflecting. You know we're not going to let this go."

"More's the pity," Villiers murmured under his breath, his tone crisp. "Why do you want to know?"

"Emmy and I found the body—"

"I would think a newly married couple would have better things to do than to go chasing after dead bodies."

Gregory went on as if he hadn't spoken. "—Then the police found your name in Verena's notebook—"

Villiers's jaw clenched. "I needn't have to remind you it was the name you were born with."

Gregory took a long swallow of his wine. "Not sporting, Papa. We both know Toby Crenshaw was your code name as a young agent." He arched one eyebrow. "Therefore, one inevitably draws the conclusion that your connection with

Verena Penrose has something to do with your vaunted position as deputy director of MI5."

Villiers pressed his tongue against his cheek and fixed his stare on Gregory, who didn't flinch under the scrutiny. They dueled in silence as the clink of glasses and the tinkle of cutlery against plates mingled with the hushed ripple of conversation around them.

Villiers relented at last. "Oh, very well. I better tell you, if only to maintain the peace in London." He shook his head. "Why have you and your wife made it your mission in life to stir up trouble?"

A crooked smile tugged at Gregory's mouth and one shoulder gave a nonchalant shrug. "Everyone needs a hobby."

"That sort of hobby can get you killed."

Gregory's jaw clenched and the hand that rested on the table curled into a fist. "Then start talking so that I can protect Emmy and make sure a murderer pays for his crime."

"Yes, I knew Verena Penrose," Villiers snarled. "We had an arrangement."

"You mean she was an agent?" Gregory asked incredulously.

"Don't be silly," Villiers sneered. "Verena didn't have the proper temperament to be an agent. She was too indiscreet and her ego was over-inflated."

"Then I'm at a loss to see what your 'arrangement' was."

Villiers twirled his glass again. "My job is to protect this country from all sorts of threats, whether they're foreign terrorists or homegrown loonies." He paused. "To that end, I need to gather as much information as possible. And I must deal with all sorts of people. Civil servants, politicians, petty criminals, and journalists."

The truth dawned on Gregory. "Ah, you vetted all of

Verena's tittle-tattle to see if it would yield fruit against the baddies of the world."

Villiers gave an airy wave of his hand. "In a manner of speaking. She moved in so many different circles. No one would suspect her of passing on whispers to MI5."

"I'm astonished. I very much doubt appealing to her sense of queen and country stirred her to action."

A derisive sneer escaped from Villiers. "It didn't. Patriotism was not one of Verena's admirable qualities—"

"Did she have any? Thankfully I only met her once, but the only thing she seemed to have in abundance was arrogance and a vicious streak."

Villiers folded his hands on the table. "That was certainly true. In the end, she said that she would only help me if I gave her something in return."

Gregory's eyes bulged. "I can't believe it," he hissed. "*You* fed her all the gossip she put in her columns. You helped her to destroy people's lives all in the name of Her Majesty's government." He took a gulp of wine, barely even tasting it. "That's despicable, even for you."

"You're the last person who should be taking the moral high ground. That's more the domain of your inquisitive little wife."

"Leave Emmy out of this."

"I would love nothing better, but she's like a bee incessantly buzzing in one's ear. Always ready to sting."

"If anyone wielded a stinger, it was Verena," Gregory fired back.

"I could care less what you think about me. I will not apologize for keeping the country safe."

Gregory gripped the edge of the table with both hands, the skin across his knuckles stretched taut. "Fine. Why did you meet Verena at the theatre? It had to have been something urgent, if you took the risk of being seen together in public."

They were forced to break off their tense exchange because the waiter arrived with their lunch. Gregory's stomach roiled as he stared down at his steaming sole. He pushed his plate away. When he lifted his gaze again, Villiers had his fork and knife in hand and had already taken a bite of his trout.

He gestured with his chin. "Go on, eat. It's a pity to let it go cold."

"I've lost my appetite," Gregory muttered. "You were about to tell me why you met Verena that fateful night."

Villiers speared another morsel of trout with his fork and chewed it meditatively. "Was I?" he asked innocently.

"You're not going to get around me that easily. Or Emmy for that matter."

Villiers rolled his eyes at the ceiling and set down his knife and fork. He dabbed at the corners of his mouth with his napkin. "How is it that your wife, petite though she is, looms large even when she's not in the room?"

Unbidden, a smile flew to Gregory's lips. "It's her strength of character."

"Hmph." Villiers leaned back in his chair. He lowered his voice. "I want to remind you in the strictest possible terms that you and your wife signed the Officials Secrets Act." He put up a hand to forestall any protest formulating on Gregory's tongue. "Therefore, I had better not see what I'm about to tell you on the front page of tomorrow's *Clarion*. I assure you that I will not hesitate to have the two of you arrested."

A scowl etched itself onto Gregory's features. "You would," he complained. "Stop stalling. You know very well that we don't pose a threat to the security of the realm."

Villiers darted a glance around the room. "Verena found out the identity of the Raven. But she reverted to a tease and didn't tell me his name."

Chapter 19

Raven?" The word was snatched from Gregory's lips on a harsh breath.

Villiers's antennae were immediately alert. He dropped his napkin and leaned across the table. "What do you know?" he demanded in a crisp tone.

"Nothing. Only that when Verena cornered Emmy at the theatre, in the middle of her spiteful tirade, she rattled off the old legend about when the ravens in the Tower of London fly away, the Crown and Britain will fall. Then she rambled on about the ravens being like secrets locked away in a box and she was the only one with the power to set them free."

Villiers pounded his fist on the table, making their plates jump and sloshing some of his wine onto the pristine white cloth. "Damn the bloody woman and her games," he declared hotly.

Startled by the disturbance, their waiter hustled over to the table. "Is everything all right, Mr. Villiers?" he asked, an anxious spasm flitting across his features.

Villiers shooed him away with a brusque wave of his hand. He also silenced the curious stares he attracted from the other tables with a single frosty look.

"Damn and blast," he swore again.

"Emmy suspects," Gregory went on, "that Verena was

seeking her help in a rather oblique manner. She also thinks that Verena's speech was a warning to her killer that she intended to reveal all she knew. I'd say Emmy's instincts were spot on. Now, tell me about this Raven."

Villiers shook his head, his fingers drumming an angry tattoo on the table. "Of all the people," he grumbled. "Verena decided to turn to the bulldog of the Fourth Estate, rather than MI5. I find it rather ironic."

"Never mind that. Who is the Raven?"

"We don't know. He's a chameleon. He enjoys nothing better than playing a role. His mind is razor-sharp. He can become anything he likes. A lawyer, a financier, a doctor, an engineer, a professor. Lord knows what else. He has a Midas touch and appears to make money hand over fist."

"That's impossible. He would need training. Surely, someone must be able to tell that he's a fraud."

Villiers's lips pressed together in a grim line. "No one has doubted the authenticity of his chosen guises. He's flawless. But the part he returns to again and again is that of murderer. The trail of bodies that he's left behind stretches from Australia and Asia to Europe and Russia. We believe he's been operating in the UK for at least the last seven years. It could be longer. MI5 and the Metropolitan Police have been working to nail him. We're quite certain that a number of unsolved murders scattered about the country are his handy work. Ironically, some of the victims were in a witness protection program but they had no connections to one another. The devil of it is, the Raven doesn't have an affinity for a single method of dispatching people. We also suspect that his sympathies lie with the Russians."

Gregory's jaw tightened. "And now because of the scene Verena caused, the Raven thinks that Emmy was part of her machinations and she's carrying on the torch."

Villiers nodded bleakly. "As I said, your wife is a

magnet for trouble."

✲✲✲

Emmeline tracked down Scott McCallister to Osteria Giorgio, a favorite haunt of his in Knightsbridge. The small Italian restaurant was located next to Hyde Park. It put her in mind of a cozy *agriturismo*, a sort of farmhouse resort, that she had the pleasure of staying at in Tuscany several years earlier.

This memory brought a smile to her lips as her eyes roamed over Osteria Giorgio. The walls were a blend of ochre and saffron hues. The simple wooden flooring and furniture enhanced the sense of rustic chic. Little copper lamps hung from the wall and spilled pools of creamy light over each table, which were graced with a pot of lush basil. A wall-to-wall wine rack stood at the back of the room.

"Good afternoon, miss. Table for one?" the hostess asked solicitously, as she scooped up a menu.

"Actually, I came to meet someone. Mr. Scott McCallister." Her eyes darted around the handful of tables. "I was told he was lunching here today."

The hostess's chestnut eyes twinkled. "Oh, yes. Mr. McCallister is one of our regulars." She nodded with her chin. "He's at the table over there in the corner."

Emmeline followed the woman's gaze. Although McCallister's dark head was hunched over his plate, she immediately recognized him from the photo in Underwood's file.

"Thank you. There's no need for you to see me to the table."

"It wouldn't be a bother. It's my job after all," the hostess replied, as she cast a smoldering glance in McCallister's direction.

"Thanks all the same," Emmeline said. She could feel

the woman's jealous gaze boring into her shoulder blades as she headed toward the table.

She cleared her throat. "Mr. McCallister."

He lifted his chin and she felt her cheeks flame as his intense sea-green gaze washed over her. While his brow puckered in perplexity, there was a glimmer of amusement in his eyes. He threw his napkin on the table and rose to his feet with languid grace.

He proffered a hand. "You have the advantage of me because I'm certain that we've never met." His full, sensuous lips broke into a broad grin. "I would never have forgotten such a lovely face."

Emmeline gave him a polite smile in return as she shook his hand. His grip was firm and assured. "Forgive me for interrupting your lunch. This was the only place I was certain that I'd be able to speak to you."

His smile grew at this last remark. "I'm flattered. It's not every day that a beautiful stranger trails my movements in the hopes of making my acquaintance." He motioned at the table. "Please join me."

She inclined her head and lowered herself into the chair opposite him.

"Would you care for something to eat or perhaps a glass of wine?" He gestured with his chin at his plate. "I highly recommend the *saltimbocca alla romana* or, if you enjoy pasta the bucatini with amatriciana sauce. It's spicy and delicious."

She shuddered. She was not enamored of spicy dishes. And she certainly wasn't here to share a meal with this man.

"No, thank you," she declined politely. "Please allow me to explain." She surreptitiously drew her notebook and pen from her handbag.

He exuded the supreme confidence of a man who knows how attractive he is to the opposite sex. He didn't try to hide the fact that his eyes were boldly assessing every inch of her. He propped an elbow on the table and cupped his hand under his chin. "I'm all ears."

"I'm Emmeline Kirby. I'm the editorial director of investigative features at *The Clarion*. I would like to ask you a few questions about Verena Penrose."

Although his smile remained in place, a watchfulness clouded his eyes. She could feel his guard go up.

She sighed inwardly. This was invariably the reaction when she informed someone that she was a member of the press. Oh, well. It couldn't be helped.

"I never heard of the woman" was his curt retort.

"Come now, Mr. McCallister. Isn't it true that you and Verena were lovers?"

"Even if that were the case," he hissed, "why would I admit it to a nosy reporter? My life is a private matter."

She breezed on undeterred. "Verena was murdered. I would think if you had an intimate relationship with her, you would want to see the culprit brought to justice. Or are you concerned that the police will learn that you and she were plotting to kill her husband?"

His smile was snuffed out by the spark of anger that flared to life across the planes and angles of his face. "That's slander," he spat with contempt. "I'd tread carefully if I were you, Miss Kirby. Or else your paper will have a lawsuit on its hands."

If he thought this threat would send her scurrying out of the restaurant, he was very much mistaken. "It's only slander, if it isn't true. If I'm forced to do so, I will produce evidence in a court of law." She waited a breath to allow her words to sink in. "I assure you I'm not the only one interested in your answers. The police are eager to make your acquaintance. Therefore, it would be in your best interest to give me your side of the story."

He made a disgusted noise as he leaned back and

hooked an arm around the back of his chair. The look of lascivious playfulness was nudged aside by a flicker fear. His eyes narrowed. "I can't figure you out. What's your game? Is it money you're after? I wouldn't blame you. The newspaper business can't pay well." His words were steeped in scorn.

"Every journalist doesn't fit into Verena's mold. Blackmail was her forte. But you already seem to know that. Perhaps you even shared her exploits in that regard." His jaw tightened at this comment, but he held his tongue. "What I'm after is the truth. A concept that was completely foreign to Verena."

"I had nothing to do with her murder."

"So, you do know her after all," she observed loftily, which earned her a fierce scowl. "In any event, the police will ultimately make a determination about whether you're guilty, or not."

"Then why are you here?" Some of his bravado had returned.

"I care about the truth. Even for someone like Verena."

"Why? It wasn't as if she was a bosom mate." He gave a knowing nod. "That's right. I remember Verena mentioning you. And it wasn't in glowing terms. Far from it. She despised everything about you."

Emmeline gritted her teeth. "I could care less what her opinion of me was."

He threw his head back and a derisive laugh exploded from his throat. "Liar. You want to get a bit of your own back at Verena's expense. You want to paint her as an ogre in your article as a balm to your ego." He shook his head. "How pathetic."

She drew in a sharp breath. "From where I'm sitting, Mr. McCallister, you don't appear to be too distraught over Verena's death. And you've gone out of your way to turn this conversation around to avoid answering my questions.

That sets my mind to wondering all sorts of things."

He abandoned his pose of deliberate insouciance and hunched over the table. He pitched his voice low, his tone heavy with menace. "A wild imagination is a dangerous thing."

She held his gaze and merely smiled. "In my experience, people resort to threats when they're scared. What are you desperate to keep hidden?"

His hands curled into fists. "Leave now, before I have you arrested for harassment."

Emmeline stared at him, unblinking, for a few seconds, before pushing back her chair and rising. "As you wish," she murmured as she shrugged into her coat and gathered up her handbag. "But stand warned, I won't stop digging until I find out who killed Verena and why. Have a pleasant afternoon, Mr. McCallister."

She pivoted on her heel, leaving him to stew in his lies and secrets.

McCallister's eyes lingered on Emmeline as she passed in front of the restaurant's window. She never glanced back and then she was gone.

He silently cursed as he glared down at his now cold *saltimbocca alla romana*. He would never be able to look at the dish again without thinking of bloody Emmeline Kirby. He poured himself another glass of Amarone. He took a long swallow of the dry red wine. Its strong bold flavor burst upon his tongue, but did nothing to numb the unease that clutched at his chest. He tossed back another swig and drew out his mobile from his inside jacket pocket.

He swirled the wine round and round as he waited. "Come on, you bastard," he muttered under his breath. "Pick up the damn phone. I know you're there."

A few more seconds ticked by. "You took your sweet time," he reproached, his voice louder than he intended, when the other party deigned to answer. He dropped his voice. "I hope you're not trying to avoid me. It would be a grave error in judgment if you were." He listened for a moment. "You can save your excuses. We have a problem on our hands. I just had that nosy reporter Emmeline Kirby sniffing around. She was overly curious about Verena and me. I sincerely hope you didn't point her in my direction. I'm not taking the fall for Verena's murder alone. This is your mess. I merely stepped in to distract her because she was getting too close to the truth. Mind you, I'm not complaining. Verena was awfully good fun in the bedroom, but she was a grenade with the pin removed and any minute she was going to explode in our faces. Now, when do I get my money?"

He pressed his mobile to his ear, as he concentrated on what his associate had to say. A harsh bark that could never have been described as a laugh escaped from his lips. "Think again, mate. We *agreed* to split it evenly." He clucked his tongue in disapproval. "Frankly, I'm surprised you would try to cheat me in view of what I know. You see, I'm quite sure that MI5 and Scotland Yard would be over the moon, if I were to tell them who the elusive Raven is. I think it would be the highlight of their year. I would be hailed as a hero in law enforcement circles the length and breadth of the country." His mouth broke into a grin. "I rather like that idea. How about you?" He paused for a response, but was met with stony silence.

"What's the matter? Cat got your tongue?" He exhaled a weary sigh. "I see I'll have to sort this. I'll make a deal with you. Give me a modest down payment of ten thousand pounds *in cash* by Friday evening and you'll never have to see me again. London has become excruciatingly dull. I have a flight booked over the weekend. I'll trust you to deposit the rest into my account in Geneva by next week. But"—he dragged this syllable out, making it sound like two words—"if you try to diddle me, first I'm going to pop over to MI5's offices for a cozy chat about the bird they love to hate. Then, I'm going to inform our friends in Moscow that you've been a very naughty boy and haven't been sharing your vast wealth like a good little comrade is indoctrinated to do. You must admit that I'm being eminently fair and reasonable. Remember Friday evening. Otherwise, the Raven will become an endangered species."

He rang off abruptly. It was always better to have the last word.

Chapter 20

I wouldn't call you birds of a feather, but you and the Raven share something in common. He likes bright, shiny objects." Villiers shook his head and grunted. "For the life of me, I can't understand this fascination with jewels. You're grown men."

Villiers's parting words replayed themselves in Gregory's mind that evening as he maneuvered his blue-gray Jaguar XJ6 into the spot across from the townhouse in Holland Park. The lights were on in the living room, a sign that Emmy was home.

He clambered out of the car and stood for a moment, peering off into the distance. Strands of moonlight tumbled from the inky sky and played hide-and-seek amid the bare branches of the trees in the park in the square. His thoughts were lost in the shadows.

The Raven, Gregory mused. He was trying to conjure up a picture of this devious criminal. In the law's eyes, he was a ghost. A legend with lethal tendencies. The authorities didn't even know what the man looked like. But the Raven wasn't made of ether. He was a human being, if a killer could be deemed human. That meant, like his fellow mortals, he was riddled with flaws and weaknesses.

A smile tugged at the corners of his mouth as he crossed the road and climbed the steps. "And your Achilles heel, my dear Raven, appears to be your penchant for jewels," he said aloud as he slipped the key into the lock. "I wonder what we can do to lure you out of your nest."

The Raven had to have a certain degree of knowledge about jewels. Gregory reasoned that the man likely kept his ill-gotten fortune in jewels because they were a liquid form of currency. They could be sold at any time. A buyer could always be found no matter the state of the economy. And there was no paper trail whatsoever if they were sold on the black market.

"Hmm. I wonder," he mumbled as he shrugged out of his coat and hung it on a peg. His thoughts strayed to his encounter with Mick Walcott and his band of thieves.

Was it possible the Raven was the former mastermind of the boiler room scam and Verena found out? When her plan to draw him out by muscling in on his business failed, did she resort to what was second nature—blackmail?

He nodded to himself. Yes, that fit. But Verena was out of her league this time and paid with her life. The Raven must have been at the theatre. Once the performance had started, no one would have noticed him sneaking into her box. The ceiling collapse and the subsequent confusion was a sheer stroke of luck. Gregory's jaw clenched as he ground his teeth together. The fiend must still be laughing at how easy his escape had been.

"My goodness. You have a face like thunder." Emmeline's voice tore him away from his jarring suppositions. "I hope that doesn't mean that you've soured on married life already."

He smiled as she slipped her arms around his waist and tipped her head back to look up at him.

"Never. Life with you, darling, is a constant adventure." He drew her more deeply into his embrace. He inhaled her delicate scent of lily of the valley, as he bent his head down toward hers and their lips met in a passionate kiss.

When they drew apart, she reached up and caressed his cheek. "That's better." Then she became serious. "Do I have Villiers to thank for putting that frown on your face? Was your meeting with him that awful?" She searched his face in concern.

He snatched up her hand and kissed her fingertips. "You know dear old Papa. He was confrontational and argumentative in an understated way," he replied in an off-hand manner. "However"—he dropped his arm around her shoulders and guided her into the living room—"it also was extremely enlightening."

Her dark eyes shimmered with curiosity. "Oh, yes? Do tell."

They settled down on the sofa. Emmeline tucked her feet underneath her, looped her arm through Gregory's, and snuggled up against him. She listened intently as he recounted his discussion with Villiers. With each word her husband uttered, the excitement bubbled up inside her.

"At last, we're getting somewhere. I was right. Verena *was* issuing an ultimatum to her murderer. The Raven." She shuddered as a shiver slithered down her spine and her mind reeled. "If only"—she rested her head on Gregory's shoulder and exhaled a long breath that was infused with frustration—"I wish she hadn't been so cryptic and arrogant. What did she mean?" She bit her lip and then murmured, "'Secrets locked away in a box.' What proof did she have? Did she mean a literal box? If so, where did she hide it? Does the Raven have his hands on it now? Did she give it to McCallister? Or"—she lifted her head and her eyes held Gregory's gaze—"Could McCallister be the Raven?"

"At this stage, I think we have to consider it highly probable. McCallister is not averse to a bit of larceny. From Underwood's surveillance, we know that he and Verena had at least entertained the idea of killing her husband. A man with a clear conscience would have run a mile at the mere suggestion of murder. On the other hand, the Raven wouldn't bat an eye at another death."

She nodded. "Yes. And yet, I'm quite certain that he was rattled by my questions."

He kissed her forehead. "That's because you have an expert knack at upsetting people's sense of equilibrium. You do it with such finesse." A teasing gleam sparked in his eyes.

She wrinkled her nose at him. "Ha. Ha. I will take that as a compliment."

"It was intended as such."

"Besides," she pointed out, "if one has nothing to hide, there's absolutely no reason to be nervous about my questions."

"Here, here," he cheered. "Now that you've wrung me dry about Villiers's revelations and we've cudgeled our brains about what drove Verena, it's time for you to share your insights about McCallister's lack of candor and the overall negative impression he made."

This prodding was completely unnecessary because she had been bursting to share the details of her interview with the evasive Mr. McCallister. The fact that she had failed to loosen his tongue had only served to make her more suspicious—and determined—to discover what he knew about Verena's murder. After they mulled over potential theories about what McCallister could be hiding, Emmeline told Gregory about her visit with Adam and the unsettling revelations about Jason.

When she finished, she bit her lip and swiveled around to reach for the phone on the console table behind the sofa. "I'll ring Adam now to see whether Superintendent Burnell has contacted him about an interview. That way I can arrange to be there too."

Gregory's fingers clamped down on her wrist, forcing

her to replace the receiver. "No, Emmy, you won't."

"But—"

"No, Emmy," he said more forcefully. "Oliver may hold a tender spot in his heart for you, but there is no way he will allow a member of the press—and a family member to boot—to sit in on an interview with a suspect. And I'm certain Adam wouldn't want you there."

She leaped to her feet. "*Suspect*?" Her voice thrummed with outrage. "I can't believe my own husband considers Adam a suspect. He's not a murderer."

Gregory exhaled a pained sigh and patted the sofa. "Sit down, darling. I can feel those eyes of yours boring holes into my anatomy and it's beginning to get drafty in here." He patted the cushion next to him again. "Come on. Sit down. I assure you I'm not a traitor."

She loomed over him for several more seconds, before plopping back down mulishly.

He draped his arm around her shoulders. "That's better, isn't it?"

"Hmph," she sniffed.

He repressed a smile. At least her temper had lowered to merely simmering, rather than boiling.

He nuzzled a kiss against her neck. She half-heartedly attempted to push him away. "If you're trying to seduce me, it won't work. We were having a serious discussion. Remember."

He chuckled and continued to leave a trail of soft kisses along her throat. "You know I'm right about Adam."

"You're not," she whispered huskily, as she took his face in both of her hands.

He flashed a roguish grin. "That's because I'm part of that lowly sect known as a mere male. I need a good woman to show me the error of my ways. Are you willing to take on the job? Please say yes," he implored earnestly. "Otherwise, I'll be wandering around lost. You don't want that on your conscience, do you?"

She threw her head back and laughed. "What a load of rubbish."

He stood and pulled her to her feet, drawing her against his body in one fluid motion. "How about if we go upstairs? I think I really ought to start my lessons straightaway."

She tilted her head back to look up at him. "You have a one-track mind."

"That's because Helen left us strict instructions. And I wouldn't dare to disobey your grandmother. It's more than my life is worth."

ه‌ڡه

Burnell took a sip of his coffee, which was his third since he had arrived at the office. His brain was in need of stimulation. He had been at his desk since seven. Even he couldn't believe it. It had been dark when he left his flat in Battersea and still dark, when he had set foot in the station. His eyes felt gritty and droopy with lost sleep. And all because the Boy Wonder wanted a report on his desk.

The Boy Wonder's command echoed in his ear. "First thing in the morning, Burnell. Remember, you're a senior officer. Must set an example for the younger men."

Stuff the 'younger men,' Burnell grumbled to himself. *They should make their own mistakes in life and their careers. It builds character. Something the Boy Wonder woefully lacks.*

Yet, here he was finishing the damn report. He hit save and print. He'd have P.C. Cooper take up his *chef d'oeuvre* to the Boy Wonder later. A great, big yawn burst from his mouth. He turned away from his computer monitor and stretched his arms over his head. His neck and shoulders were knotted with strain and stiffness.

He opened his eyes wide and blinked several times. He

took another gulp of coffee, as he reached out a hand for Dr. Meadows's postmortem on Verena Penrose. He hadn't had an opportunity to read it yesterday because first Sally had assailed him; then Emmeline had dropped by with her revelations about McCallister and Adam Royce; and as a follow-up he and Finch had interviewed Adam. The interview hadn't elicited any earth-shattering information or persuaded him to consider Adam as a serious suspect. It had to be done, though. But it had been a waste of his time. All in a day's work for a weary policeman.

The superintendent sighed and shook his head. He slipped his spectacles on his nose, flipped open the postmortem, and started scanning Meadows's findings.

"What?" he exploded and then reread the first couple of paragraphs.

His head ached, but it wasn't because he was too tired. He hunched over his desk and devoured every word of the rest of the report. Meadows had been meticulous, as always. There was no doubt. It was there in black and white.

Burnell was scribbling a few notes, when there was a light tapping at his door. Finch's head popped in the next second. "Good morning, sir," he said cheerily. Too cheerily for the mood the superintendent was in at the moment. "I couldn't believe it when Cooper told me you were already here. Crack of dawn were his words."

The superintendent flapped the back of his hand in the air and pointed to the chair opposite. "Never mind that. Come in and shut the door."

Finch nodded and crossed the room in two strides. As he lowered himself into the chair, his gaze strayed to the open file on the desk. He gestured with his chin and raised an eyebrow. "New developments?"

"You could say that." He picked up the file and waved it the air. "This is John's postmortem on Verena Penrose."

Finch's brow puckered in a frown. "Was the cause of death something other than a broken neck?"

"Oh, her neck was broken all right. But read it for yourself." He tossed the report at the sergeant.

Finch mumbled aloud, "The victim's blood indicates traces of hydrocodone. A common prescription painkiller that can be used to treat moderate to severe pain, but it also causes sedation and euphoria while slowing the central nervous system." He lifted his eyes to meet Burnell's. "She was drugged."

The superintendent nodded. "Making it easier for our killer to do the nasty deed. As you can see from John's findings, she was likely unconscious and unable to put up a struggle."

"But how, sir?" Finch puzzled it out. "She wouldn't have taken the drug willingly." He tapped the report. "Dr. Meadows concludes that there is no indication that she had a history of drug abuse."

"My guess is that someone slipped it into her drink when she was in the bar during the intermission. Emmeline and Longdon said that it was crowded. The barman's attention could have been distracted. It would have taken a matter of seconds. In the crush, no one would have noticed. However, this revelation raises another more worrisome question. Are we dealing with a single person or did our killer have an accomplice?"

Finch slumped back. "That would complicate matters." He was quiet for several seconds, a pensive expression flitting across his features. "In terms of the logistics, it makes sense that there were two of them. The accomplice scuttles off when the bell rings and melts into the night. Meanwhile, the killer is waiting up in the box or in the corridor nearby ready to spring into action. After the play started again and he was certain that she was unconscious or insensible enough, he slipped inside and broke her neck with a quick twist. For an experienced killer, it would have taken mere seconds. Then the ceiling collapsed and he became a ghost." He shook his head and gave a low whistle. "But, sir, the sheer nerve of it. He must have ice in his veins."

"That's what makes him even more dangerous than we first imagined."

"Sir, do you think it could be McCallister? I'm still looking into his background. I haven't been able to find anything incriminating yet. He doesn't have a record. At least, not here in the U.K. He's disgustingly wealthy. He appears to have made a fortune on the financial markets. He likes taking risks and living on the edge. Aside from his Fitzrovia duplex, he has a villa on the French Riviera, a townhouse in New York, and an apartment in Geneva."

"Mmm," Burnell murmured. "That explains what set the late Verena Penrose's heart aflutter. He's also an extremely good-looking chap. The combination must have been irresistible."

"By all accounts, money was the thing that aroused her most. Do you think that's why she cast her eye in Adam Royce's direction? A bigger fish to fry?"

Burnell pursed his lips and leaned back in his chair. "Most likely. However, we both know Royce. He's easy-going, not cutthroat by nature. He may have been momentarily dazzled by her, but I think their affair would have fizzled out fairly soon."

"Probably all for the best." Then Finch chuckled. "In any case, it certainly would have been over the minute Emmeline found out."

Burnell permitted himself a laugh. "You're right on that score." His amusement faded, though, as his eye fell on the postmortem. "I don't believe in the supernatural. Our murderer is flesh and blood. He's not infallible. He'll make a mistake, if he hasn't already. It's the arrogance that always does them in. He couldn't have disappeared into thin air. I want you to go down to the theatre and look over the CCTV footage again. It's a long shot because of the chaos after the ceiling collapse but do it anyway. It will ease my mind and we can tick all the boxes."

Finch pushed himself to his feet. "Right, sir. I'll ring Hayward, the theatre manager."

The superintendent nodded. "Then, we'll pay a visit to Mr. McCallister and see what he has to say for himself. In the meantime, I'm going to ring Villiers."

Finch raised an eyebrow. "Is that wise in view of Assistant Commissioner Cruickshank's order?"

"The Boy Wonder can go to the devil. As usual, Villiers is in the thick of things. I can't worry about stepping on people's toes. We have to catch a murderer before he kills again."

Chapter 21

The door had barely closed behind Finch, when Burnell snatched up his phone and punched in Villiers number. He knew it by heart because the deputy director of MI5 had become involved in several of their cases lately. And the superintendent had chafed every time. Cloak-and-dagger was an understatement when came to describing Laurence Villiers.

A female voice echoed in his ear, after the first ring. "Good morning, Mr. Villiers's office. How may I help you?"

He cleared his throat. "Good morning. This is Detective Superintendent Oliver Burnell with the Metropolitan Police. I need to speak with Mr. Villiers. It's about an ongoing investigation."

"I'm afraid that's impossible. Mr. Villiers cannot be disturbed. Matters of state. I'm certain you can appreciate that they take time and must be handled with the utmost delicacy. I'd be happy to take a message and he'll return your call within the next few days."

Burnell slammed his open palm on his desk. "I'm not some junior civil servant, who jumps at Villiers's shadow. Tell him that if he doesn't get on the line in the next sixty seconds, I'll be paying him another visit this morning."

He heard her draw in a disapproving breath. "There is

absolutely no need for rudeness."

"When it comes to murder, I don't have time for the niceties of polite society. Your boss has a choice: Either he speaks to me now or he will be staring at my face across his desk within the hour."

"Well, I never," she huffed. "What a disagreeable man you are."

"Sally Harper, the scourge of the Met, shares your opinion, for which I could care less. I must speak with Villiers."

There was a soft *click* and then a brief silence ensued as he seethed inwardly.

"Make it fast, Burnell," an irritated Villiers boomed in his ear at last.

The superintendent curled his fist into a tight ball and summoned every ounce of willpower to remain calm. It wouldn't help the case if he gave vent to his temper. "Ah, Mr. Villiers, thank you for sparing me a moment. I know that you are an ardent believer in interagency cooperation."

"Get on with it, man. I thought I made it perfectly clear to you that I did not know Verena Penrose and I can contribute nothing to your case. I feel sure that Assistant Commissioner Cruickshank reinforced that point."

Burnell clenched his teeth, but persevered, "He did indeed. But it has come to light during our inquiries that you were at the theatre in Ms. Penrose's box at some point on the night in question. Therefore, your relationship with the victim was more than meets the eye. So, let's drop the pretense, shall we? She was working for you or MI5 in some sort of capacity, wasn't she?"

"This is spiraling out of control. Toby told you about the Raven, didn't he?" Villiers demanded. "It's evident by the leader in today's *Clarion* that he told his nosy wife. When is he going to learn that one can't trust a bloody reporter with anything?"

The Raven? Mmm, you learn something every day, Burnell mused. "More to the point," he said aloud, "why didn't you or one of your underlings at MI5 inform the Met?"

"*You* didn't need to know. Above your pay grade. Surely you can see this is a highly sensitive matter. A plodding detective would only have mucked up the works."

Arrogant bastard, Burnell swore silently. "As the Raven clearly has something to do with my case, I should have been brought into the loop."

"As I reminded Toby yesterday—"

Because Villiers deserved to be needled for his condescension, Burnell interrupted, "I think you'll find he prefers Longdon. He shed the mantle of Toby Crenshaw when he was a teenager. However, the name was in Penrose's notebook." He paused for a second. "Your old code name I believe."

Villiers roared, "That's neither here nor there. As I reminded *Longdon* yesterday, all of you have signed the Official Secrets Act. I'd tread carefully, if I were in your shoes."

"I always *mind the gap,*" the superintendent responded facetiously, "because I hate not knowing what's lurking in the dark. Knowledge is power, as they say."

He chuckled as Villiers rung off abruptly without even saying goodbye.

"The Raven," Burnell muttered as he replaced the receiver. The fellow sounded rather ominous and he still didn't know a damn thing about this villain.

His chest heaved in a sigh. But as usual, Longdon and Emmeline were already a step ahead and most likely about to take a deep plunge into a cauldron of boiling hot water.

Sometimes a policeman's lot was a lonely one.

⌒∽⌒

As she wended her way across the newsroom, Emmeline's mind speculated on the Raven's identity and how his path collided with Verena. Gregory's assumption that the Raven had likely been running the boiler room scam from afar was plausible. But why embroil himself in such a scheme? If the Raven was as dangerous and cunning as Villiers claimed—and she had no reason to doubt it— the only thing that made the most sense was that he was involved in something bigger and Verena got in his way. Could McCallister be this killer? He was definitely a man of secrets.

"Emmeline," Matthew, the deputy editor, called to her.

He was hovering near a reporter's desk with some copy in his hand.

She walked over and bid them good morning with a smile. She flicked a glance at the copy. "A problem?"

Matthew shook his head. "No, not at all." He waved it in the air. "This is first-rate stuff. It should sell lots of papers. I just wanted to warn you that you have a visitor." He jerked his head. "He's waiting in your office. He *said* he had an appointment. I'm guessing he's one of your sources. But he struck me as a bit odd. If he gives you any problems, just give a shout."

Her brows knit together. Her gaze drifted toward her office, but the blinds were all drawn and she couldn't see who was waiting for her. "I have no idea who it is." She patted his arm. "Thanks, though. Even if he has wicked intentions, I don't think he'd dare try anything with an entire newsroom on the other side of the window."

Matthew smiled. "You're right. We reporters can be intimidating when we want to be. But only in the interest of the truth."

"Naturally. Well, I'd better find out what this mystery

man wants."

The man leaped from the chair the minute she flung her office door open.

Her jaw dropped. "*You*," she exclaimed as she stared at the young man who had burst from Verena's box the night of the murder.

"Yes, I'm sorry if I frightened you and that chap." He shifted from foot to foot, as if he were standing on sand that had been scorched by the desert sun. There was a slight tremor in his voice as he went on, "I didn't kill her. I swear to you, I didn't. She was already dead, when I entered the box. All I wanted to do was to talk to her. She promised to help, but she'd been avoiding my calls for over a week."

His pale blue eyes implored her to believe him. Emmeline didn't feel as if her safety were being threatened, so she quietly closed the door.

She motioned to the chair he had recently vacated. "Why don't you sit down again and tell me everything from the beginning?"

He ran a hand distractedly through his ginger hair and after a moment nodded. "Yes, of course."

She slid into her own chair and casually propped her elbows on the armrests, silently willing him to calm down sufficiently to unburden himself. She recognized that he was the type who would clam up and bolt if she pushed him. So, she waited. But she wished he would hurry up and get on with it. She offered him an encouraging smile in the hopes of loosening his tongue.

He gave her a watery smile in return. Progress, she thought.

"My name's Ted Sanderson," he began haltingly. "I'm an accountant. My dad is a pensioner and he suffers from Alzheimer's. He's seventy-seven and lives alone in Hertfordshire." His chest rose and fell on a sigh. "Over the course of three months, he was duped out of ninety thousand pounds"—his jaw clenched—"by some spineless, gutless, faceless charlatans, who sold him some colored diamonds that were marked up at seventeen times their value. Each time a transaction was planned, Dad was told to keep it a secret."

Diamonds. Emmeline's breath caught in her throat and her stomach churned with disgust. Oh, the poor man. There but for the grace of God, the same fate would have befallen Gran.

Sanderson described how the crooks made everything appear genuine by sending his father glossy brochures, invoices, and certificates for the diamonds. "The only reason I became aware of this scheme is because my father's financial adviser contacted me to ask why a large sum had been requested." His eyes impaled her. "You see, Dad was about to invest another eighty-five thousand pounds. I think he was quite frightened of them and for his safety. Since I have power of attorney over his affairs, I demanded that the diamond brokers stop ringing and hand over the gems so that they could be sold. However, every time I contacted them another problem arose that prevented them from sending the stones. Then, they became aggressive and threatened to take legal action against Dad for breach of contract. I went straight to the police. There were three of them at the center of the scam. They were found guilty of defrauding hundreds of thousands of pounds to finance their lavish lifestyles. Can you imagine?" he asked, his voice trembling with fury and bitterness. "In October, they were jailed for thirteen years but Dad lost the bulk of his life savings."

"I know the words are of very little comfort, but I'm terribly sorry. I share your indignation, Mr. Sanderson. Truly. My grandmother was nearly swindled by a similar scam. Fortunately, she asked advice from my husband and me before she invested anything."

His eyes widened. "Really?" He swallowed hard. "I'm glad your grandmother had a happy ending."

"Thank you. However, I fail to see what any of this has to do with Verena Penrose."

His shoulders tensed and his eyes blazed with ferocity. "Fool that I was, I went to her first because she had a reputation for splashy exposés. Her stories garnered attention. People are always commenting about them. She was very sympathetic to my father's plight. She took notes and asked all sorts of questions. In the end, she promised she would write a story that shamed all those in authority who had done nothing to get my father's money back.

"A week went by. Then, two. I explained it away as Ms. Penrose doing her due diligence to ensure that she had corroboration."

Ha, Emmeline laughed to herself. *If you only knew. Verena and facts didn't even have a nodding acquaintance.*

"After a month," he went on, "and no movement on her part. I tried ringing her. I left several messages at the office and on her mobile. I managed to find out her home number. The housekeeper answered and I was forced to leave another message." His gaze beseeched her. "I was getting desperate. Every day that slipped by meant it would be more difficult to get restitution for Dad. I thought if I spoke to her in person again, she might take the matter more seriously."

"So you what—? Began following her?" she probed gently.

He dropped his chin to his chest and nodded. When he lifted his eyes again, he said, "I'm not proud of it. But yes. I overheard her saying that she would be at the theatre that night. It was a neutral setting. I thought that she'd be relaxed and therefore in a more receptive mood. I couldn't get near her in the bar. It was too crowded. I decided to wait for her in her box. It was more private. Just as the bell rang and people started returning to their seats, I darted up the staircase and ducked into her box. Only it wasn't. I'd made a mistake and went into the one next to hers. A startled couple found me in there. The wife was ready to call security. It took a few minutes to convince her that I had no immoral intentions. Once the muddle was explained and I left them, the play had already started. I didn't want to frighten Ms. Penrose, so I cleared my throat. She appeared engrossed in what was going on stage and didn't turn around. I tried whispering her name, but that failed to gain her attention either. There was nothing for it. I tapped her lightly on the shoulder and"—he stared over her shoulder and back into the awful past—"and her head lolled to one side. I must have frozen because of the shock. When my wits returned, the ceiling had come crashing down and there was pandemonium everywhere. I know it was the act of a coward, but I just wanted to get as far away from that box as possible. That must have been when I ran into you. I know it sounds far-fetched. But it's the truth. Please believe me."

Emmeline offered him a reassuring smile and murmured in soothing tones, "I do, Mr. Sanderson."

He collapsed back against the chair. "Thank you. It's been eating away at me ever since that night."

"While it took courage to come here and I understand your reaction," she said carefully, "you must go to the police and tell them everything."

He leaped to his feet. "I couldn't do that. Then, Dad would be dragged into this mess and he's been through quite enough."

"It's precisely because of what happened to your father that you have to go to the police. It could be a motive. Perhaps the killer was another poor victim of the scam. Or…" She broke off before she finished her sentence.

"Or what?"

She swallowed hard. She had to be honest with him. "Or maybe you caught a glimpse of her murderer and can provide a description."

He drew in a sharp breath. There was a tremor in his voice, when he spoke. "Good Lord. I never thought of that."

"Look, I know Superintendent Burnell, the detective in charge of the case. He's highly respected." She tried to put him at ease. "I promise he will listen to you without making any judgments." Her hand hovered over her phone. "Shall I ring him now?"

She held her breath for the space of a heartbeat. At last, he broke the silence. "Yes, of course, you're right."

She nodded as she picked up the receiver. "You've made a wise decision."

He leaned forward and grabbed her wrist. "But you must promise me one thing."

She held his gaze. "If it's in my power to do so, I will."

"Please write the story about the scam and help me get Dad's money back."

Her mouth curved into a broad smile. "You didn't have to ask. There's nothing that I enjoy more than sinking my teeth into a juicy bit of corruption."

ぐろもろ

Finch burst into Burnell's office without bothering to knock.

Burnell saw the eager gleam in the sergeant's eye. "What did you find out?" he demanded.

"McCallister was at the theatre the night of the murder. The CCTV shows that he was in the bar during the intermission."

Burnell surged to his feet. "Did he speak to Verena

Penrose?"

Finch shook his head. "No, he was doing his best to avoid her seeing him. But he was watching her closely. He was lingering at one end of the bar and disappeared shortly before the intermission bell rang. I couldn't find him on any of the other footage, though."

The superintendent folded his arm over his chest and stroked his beard with his other hand. "So, McCallister clearly had the opportunity to drug her drink. But did he kill her? Or did he leave the dirty deed to the Raven?'

Finch arched an eyebrow. "Raven, sir?"

"Villiers inadvertently let that little nugget slip. Apparently, this Raven is someone MI5 is extremely interested in."

Finch's brow knit together in puzzlement. "Who is he, sir? And what does he have to do with Verena Penrose's murder?"

Burnell wagged a finger at him. "That's a very good question. Unfortunately, we 'plodding' policemen are deemed unworthy of such knowledge. We'd only 'muck up' the works."

"I see," Finch mumbled in frustrated resignation.

"However, there's no need to be upset or uneasy because it seems Longdon and Emmeline are hot on the trail of the Raven."

Finch's warm brown eyes widened in disbelief. "Bloody hell."

Burnell clapped him on the shoulder. "I would say that is a fairly accurate assessment."

"I suppose it's too much to ask, but have you heard from either Emmeline or Longdon today?"

"Emmeline actually rang a little while ago—"

"Did she? I am surprised. What did she say about the Raven?"

"Not a peep. She did tell me that a Mr. Sanderson wants

to speak with us. Apparently, he was the first person to find our victim. He was the man she and Longdon ran into in the corridor."

"What? How the devil did she manage to track him down?"

Burnell tapped the side of his nose. "Our intrepid reporter has a magic touch. The fellow came to see Emmeline." He nodded at Finch's incredulous expression. "Oh, yes. Sanderson's story is that he was spooked and fled in shock. Riveting stuff, isn't it? This case is turning out to be more interesting than we ever could have dreamed."

The sergeant rubbed the back of his neck and shook his head. "I don't understand. Why was he in Verena Penrose's box?"

"Emmeline mumbled something about his father and a boiler room scam. I've asked Sanderson to come down to the station this afternoon for a chat."

"Mmm," Finch acknowledged distractedly. "Murder, a boiler room scam, and a Raven. The more we dig, the more we seem to be running around in circles."

Burnell rolled down his sleeves and wriggled into his jacket. "The trouble with you, Finch, is that you worry too much. Emmeline and Longdon already have all the answers."

"But will they share them with us before it's too late?"

"There you go again with the negative thinking. We have to trust our fellow man—and woman—to do the right thing."

Finch snorted. "You don't believe a word of that."

Burnell crossed to the door and shrugged into his coat. "True," he conceded philosophically, "but hope springs eternal." His jaw clenched and his tone hardened. "If they don't confess all they know, I'll let them stew in a cell until they come to their senses."

"They'd probably drive the constables on duty mad."

"Most likely. One problem at a time, though." He flung open the door. "Grab your coat. Mr. McCallister has a good deal of explaining to do."

Chapter 22

Gregory was skimming through the details of a police report on the theft the previous evening at a Belgravia mansion of a priceless collection of hand-blown lamps and vases by Emile Gallé, the French artist and designer considered by many to be the pre-eminent glassmaker of the late 19th and early 20th century. The owner, the CEO of a pharmaceutical company, thankfully was away on holiday with his wife in Bermuda. But, he happened to be one of Symington's oldest clients. For this reason, the case landed on Gregory's desk and was considered a top priority.

He heaved a weary sigh at the sheer audacity of the heist, as he made some notes. The mansion had a sophisticated security system. Therefore, the thieves must have had insider help. He would have Denise, one of his top investigators, check into the lives of the entire staff to see whether anyone was not who he or she purported to be or had connections, however tenuous, to the criminal world. Or if any had been coerced into becoming involved in exchange for expunging a gambling or other debt. Denise was thorough and discreet. In that sense, she was a bit like Emmy. She didn't accept things at face value.

The thought of his wife brought a smile to his lips. Emmy never stopped until she had answers. By association, his mind strayed to the Raven and he grimaced. While he loved Emmy for her tenacity, this was one of those times when he sorely wished she practiced a different profession. Preferably, one that didn't involve dealing with individuals who relished all manner of illegal activities.

Ah, well. He couldn't change her, nor did he want to because then she wouldn't be Emmy. Therefore, his lot in life was to protect her to the best of his ability. He exhaled a long sigh. He freely admitted that it could be utterly exhausting, but exhilarating nonetheless.

His mobile purred in his pocket, dragging him away from these reflections. He frowned when he drew it out. He didn't recognize the number.

"Hello," he said guardedly and waited.

"Longdon?" asked a male voice, made gravelly and hoarse by years of smoking.

"There you have me at a disadvantage. I know for a fact that I don't know you. So, who are you and how did you get this number?"

"The name's Jasper. I heard it through the grapevine that you are acquainted with two ladies. One's blushes are a lovely shade of pink and the other is blue with cold."

Gregory sat up straighter. *Good old David. Despite his strong misgivings, he put the word out on the street that the Pink Courtesan and Blue Angel were for sale*, he thought as he listened to the stranger.

"I have it on good authority," the man went on, "that these ladies are genuine and are looking to relocate."

Gregory lowered his voice. "Your information is correct."

"Right. Let me tell you the ground rules. I will handle the entire transaction. You won't see the client. Before any money changes hands, I have to inspect the ladies. I don't know you, therefore I can't take your word for their authenticity. After I'm satisfied, I will contact the client. Once an offer is made and agreed upon, I will select the location where the transaction will take place. If you have any objections, this ends here and now."

"I agree in principle. As I'm the ladies' guardian at the moment, I feel it's my duty to obtain the best deal possible and see that they go to a home where they'll be truly cherished."

"What are you blathering on about? I just explained the rules," the stranger barked in his ear. "You're in no position to dictate terms."

"Don't worry. You'll still receive your hefty commission. I wouldn't want to deprive a man of his livelihood. But I'm only willing to relinquish the ladies to one man." He paused and heard Jasper's heavy breath infused with annoyance. "The Raven."

A stunned silence filled the air for several seconds.

"Are you still there?" Gregory prodded.

The man swallowed. "I'm here. The Raven? You're barmy."

"My psychological state is my own affair. I hear the Raven is a connoisseur and he'd be willing to pay handsomely for such feminine beauty."

"That's true," Jasper replied cautiously. "But, mate, word is he's as nasty as they come."

"I'll take my chances. Look if you're afraid, consider making an exception to the rules, just this once. Allow me to finalize the deal with Raven one on one. If, that is, you verify that the stones are genuine. What do you say?"

The other man emitted a low whistle. "I say you have a death wish. But if I allowed sentimentality to get in the way of business, I'd be bankrupt."

"A man must be pragmatic, after all," Gregory quipped, his mouth curving into a smile.

"Precisely. I'll be waiting on the promenade on the

south bank at the foot of Westminster Bridge at one o'clock. If you're even a minute late, I'm gone and you can find a buyer yourself. Since this is a special case and I'm taking a risk, I want a thousand pounds in cash for my trouble. I keep the money, whether the stones are real or not. Take it or leave it."

"I think that's eminently reasonable. I agree to your terms."

"Good. I'll be carrying a rolled-up copy of the *Daily Mail* under my arm. Remember one sharpish."

"I'll be counting the minutes, Jasper."

Gregory's restless fingers tapped a pen against his desk. His thoughts were racing. It was sheer madness. He knew it, but it was worth the risk if they could bring down the elusive Raven. Emmy would tear him to shreds, of course. Mainly because she hated not being in the heart of the action. With that in mind, and since he was a considerate husband concerned about his wife's welfare, he wouldn't tell her what he was up to until it was absolutely necessary.

A light rap on his door drew him out of these ruminations. He glanced up to find his boss hovering on the threshold, his brow puckered in a frown. "I'd like a word, Greg."

Gregory offered him a broad smile and rose to his feet. He wondered what was amiss. His boss was not one to go on walkabout. He usually stayed in his office, unless he had a meeting outside the building. "Certainly, Cecil." He motioned toward a chair. "Please sit down."

His boss gave a curt nod and ambled over to the desk. Gregory resumed his own seat and regarded the other man.

Cecil cleared his throat. "You've done an exemplary job, since you joined Symington's. Above and beyond, I'd have to say." Gregory inclined his head in thanks but remained silent. "I haven't felt the need to look over your shoulder. I've given you *carte blanche*."

"I'm grateful that you let me get on with the job at hand," Gregory replied.

"What I demand, though, is to know if there is a problem."

Gregory raised an eyebrow. "Problem? What are you getting at?"

"That's for you to say. Ron told me that you've asked to see the Verena Penrose file. Why?" His clear gray gaze anxiously searched Gregory's face. "The woman, sadly, was murdered. I wasn't aware that there was any theft involved. Is her husband filing some sort of large claim? If so, why? He rang up earlier to inquire whether it was standard procedure for our investigator to be at tomorrow's reading of the will."

Gregory made a mental note of this tidbit. He would make a point of attending. It shouldn't be too difficult to find out where it was taking place. Wills were fascinating documents that provided insight into the deceased's frame of mind and relationship with his or her loved ones. He flashed a reassuring smile at his boss. "No need for you to worry. I simply wanted to familiarize myself with the file. Not only was Verena Penrose a high-profile client, she was a celebrity. I thought it would be in Symington's best interest to be prepared for all eventualities."

Cecil leaned forward. "Are you anticipating an unpleasant surprise?"

Gregory shook his head. "Not at all," he replied smoothly. "I'm merely being thorough."

"I see." Cecil, his lips pressed in a thin line, stood up. "Well, I can't fault your initiative. Carry on." He turned on his heel and crossed to the door. Before he left the office, he tossed over his shoulder, "By the way, I told Sheldrake that you'd be attending the reading of the will. Keep me informed about anything important. I don't want Symington's to be caught off guard."

"That goes without saying. I'll give you a full report."

e/ɔe/ɔ

Fitzrovia, a quiet upmarket enclave tucked between Marylebone and Bloomsbury, derives its name from nearby Fitzroy Square. The formerly bohemian area was home to such writers as George Bernard Shaw and Virginia Woolf, as well as artists and intellectuals. The neighborhood is known for its restaurants, Georgian squares, unique galleries, and smattering of boutique and luxury hotels. The wide streets and cozy side alleys feature a mix of architectural styles, ranging from Victorian brick buildings to contemporary structures. The BT Tower, one of the city's tallest and most iconic buildings, looms over the area.

The building where Scott McCallister's duplex could be found was close to Regent's Park. The ground-floor façade was white stucco, while the upper stories were gray-brown brick. The door was painted a bright cherry red. Its nondescript exterior belied how much it must have cost.

Finch rapped on the brass door knocker that was shaped like a lion's head. A disembodied voice burst from the intercom. "Yes? How can I help you?"

Burnell pressed the button on the panel and raised his voice. "Detective Superintendent Burnell and Detective Sergeant Finch of the Metropolitan Police. We need to speak with you, Mr. Callister, about Verena Penrose."

The intercom crackled again. "It's inconvenient just now. I'm rather busy."

Burnell flicked a glance at Finch and smiled. "The poor chap." He cleared his throat and pressed the button. "That's a pity, Mr. Callister. Perhaps it would be more convenient if you came down to the station for a formal interview. Or better yet, I could get a warrant and have your premises searched."

He released the button. A minute elapsed and then they heard the bolt being eased back and the door swung open. McCallister, in an open-necked sky-blue button-down shirt and faded but designer jeans, filled the door frame. His rich brown hair was slightly tousled, as if he had run his hand through it in frustration and his sea-green eyes blazed.

"Ah, good of you to spare us a moment, Mr. Callister," Burnell remarked brightly as he and Finch stepped over the threshold.

"You didn't leave me much choice," McCallister groused under his breath. When he had turned back from slipping the bolt into place, he said with a smile that lacked sincerity, "Anything to help the police. Come in."

He waved an arm impatiently and proceeded to stomp up the wooden staircase to their left. They remained silent until they reached the first floor. McCallister showed them into an airy reception room with two large windows. The high ceiling gave the detectives the impression that the flat was even more spacious. McCallister's taste ran to crisp, clean lines. The walls were eggshell white. A fireplace took up one wall. A modern caramel leather sofa, a boxy beige leather armchair and a low oak coffee table were grouped in front of the fireplace. On one side of it stood a cherry bookcase, where books were stuffed in hodge-podge fashion. Tucked in the other corner was a television. There was a standing lamp in between the windows and a cherry console table along the opposite wall.

McCallister motioned at the sofa, as he lowered himself into the armchair. He cast a pointed glance at his watch. "Right. What is it that you want to know about Verena? I barely knew the woman."

Burnell and Finch traded a dubious look. The superintendent sighed inwardly. Why do they always lie? he wondered.

He pasted an obsequious smile on his lips, as Finch flipped open his notebook to a clean page.

"Is that so?" He fixed a puzzled stare on McCallister. "Because in the course of our inquiries thus far, we've discovered that you and Ms. Penrose were lovers?"

The planes and angles of McCallister's chiseled features contorted into a glare. "Who told you that?" He huffed a bitter laugh. "I bet it was that nosy reporter. Emmeline Kirby, wasn't it?" His hand curled into a fist on his knee. "I warned her that I would sue her and her paper for slander."

The superintendent groaned. That's Emmeline. Out ruffling feathers again. When was she going to tell them about her interview with McCallister? And everything else she and Longdon had found out?

"Actually, Mr. McCallister, Ms. Penrose's husband suspected that she was having an affair and hired a private investigator."

"I see," he murmured noncommittally.

"So please stop wasting our time."

The other man's jaw tightened. "What of it? We were two consenting adults. It was nobody's business but ours."

"You're perfectly correct. I'm not here to make moral judgments. My duty is to the law and, by extension, to finding justice for Ms. Penrose. As someone who was close to her, I would think you'd want that too."

"That goes without saying," McCallister responded loftily.

"Good. When was the last time you saw her?"

McCallister waved a hand in the air. "I don't know precisely. A week ago, perhaps a fortnight. Verena and I had a relaxed relationship. We weren't in each other's pockets."

He cast a glance at Finch, who was conscientiously scribbling away. When his eye met Burnell's, he quickly looked away and pretended to brush an invisible piece of lint from his jeans.

The superintendent repressed a smile by pursing his lips. He rubbed the back of his neck. "I must admit that I'm confused."

"I suppose that's a policeman's lot in life," McCallister quipped.

"You see, my problem is that you were caught on the CCTV at St. Martin's Theatre the night Ms. Penrose was murdered. How do you explain that discrepancy?"

McCallister laughed, but it rang hollow. "It's very simple. You've got the wrong night."

Burnell gave a sad shake of his head. "No, I'm afraid not." He was quiet for a moment. "Why are you lying?" His tone was soft and even, but it held a steely edge. "If there's one thing I can't abide, it's lies. It makes me jump to all sorts of conclusions."

Finch stopped writing and met McCallister's gaze. He jerked a thumb at the superintendent. "The guv has a vivid imagination. Very vivid. My advice is to come clean."

McCallister leaped to his feet. "Fine. I was there that night. But I never spoke to Verena. I didn't even know she was there."

Burnell shared a chuckle with Finch. "Come now. The CCTV proves that you were in the bar during the intermission. Only steps away from Ms. Penrose."

McCallister thrust his hands into his pockets and took a step toward the sofa. "You can believe what you like," he shouted. "I told you we hadn't seen each other in at least a week."

"Sit down, Mr. McCallister," the superintendent ordered, as he settled back against the sofa and folded his arms over his broad chest. "There's no reason to get excited." He gestured with his chin. "Please sit down."

The other man remained rooted to the spot, silently

warring with Burnell. At last, he threw his hands up in resignation and stalked over to the armchair.

While his back was turned, the superintendent caught Finch's eye and flicked a glance at the door. The sergeant nodded. "Excuse me, Mr. McCallister. Could I use the loo? The coffee at the station goes straight through me."

"It would be an honor," McCallister retorted facetiously. He waved a hand at the door. "Downstairs. You can use the bathroom in the guest bedroom."

Finch inclined his head and murmured his thanks to their reluctant host.

McCallister watched the sergeant leave the room and then his gaze trailed back. Burnell merely stared at him.

McCallister tried to brazen it out, but he could stand the silence for only a couple minutes. He scraped a hand over the light stubble covering his cheeks. "Well, aren't you going to say something? Or is this part of the heavy-handed psychological intimidation tactics that the police resort to these days?"

"I wonder why you feel intimidated. I'm only after the truth. I don't like the fact that a killer is roaming the streets of London, while his victim—your mistress—"

McCallister smirked. "Verena was hardly that. Mistress connotes a deeper relationship."

Burnell went on as if he hadn't spoken. "—while your *mistress* lies dead in the morgue."

McCallister casually crossed one long leg over the other. "It's very sad. Tragic, in fact. However, Verena made a lot of enemies with her articles. Rather than wasting time grilling me, I suggest that you and your minion get out there and talk to them. I'd start with that little reporter. Verena despised her and I take it the feeling was mutual." He started warming to his subject. "Did you know that Emmeline Kirby was at the theatre that night and had a heated row with Verena right in the middle of the bar?

There are dozens of witnesses. I don't want to do your job. But wouldn't my taxpayer money be better spent if you questioned them?" he suggested smugly.

The superintendent gripped his knees hard and stoked down the irritation building in his chest. How he hated arrogant chaps like McCallister, who had no respect for the law and thought they could get away with anything. Burnell chafed at the tell-tale signs. And yet, beneath that nonchalant demeanor, McCallister was nervous. Because he had a hand in Verena's murder? Or was he hiding something else entirely?

Burnell was jarred from this line of thought by Finch's reappearance.

"Ah, there you are, Sergeant," McCallister hailed. "You look more relaxed. Bladder all right now, is it?"

Finch stiffened, but he refused to be baited. He directed his attention to Burnell, giving him an infinitesimal nod. "Sir, you have that meeting at the station in an hour," he said as he shrugged into his coat.

"Right. Thank you." Burnell got to his feet and buttoned his suit jacket, before slipping on his own coat.

McCallister rose too. "Leaving already? Just as we were getting to know one another. I'm devastated." The smile tugging at the corners of his mouth showed that he was far from heartbroken. "I'm sure you clever detectives can manage to find your own way out. I'd be worried if you couldn't."

Burnell ignored the dig and followed Finch to the door. He stopped on the threshold. "We'll be speaking again."

"No, we won't," McCallister asserted and hurried across the room. He rummaged around in a drawer in the console table for a moment. "Ah, yes. My lawyer's card. Contact him if you have any other questions."

Chapter 23

Once they were in the car, Burnell pounced, "What did you discover?"

Finch's face broke into a grin, as he eased into traffic. "Our friend McCallister is going on a trip. From the number of bags already packed, he plans to be away for quite a while."

Burnell clucked his tongue. "The naughty boy." He stared out the window. "He's as cunning and slippery as an eel. We know he was at the theatre. He's involved up to his bloody neck, but it's all circumstantial at this stage. We'd be laughed out of court. Damn and blast." He slapped his thigh with his open palm. "The guilty always do a runner. In McCallister's case, he's floating in money so the world is his oyster."

"If only someone had seen McCallister and the victim together," Finch ventured, "we'd have probable cause and we could prevent him from leaving London. It would give us more time to find evidence."

"Yes," the superintendent replied distractedly. "There's no such thing as a perfect murder."

"Perhaps we should have asked McCallister about the Raven to gauge his reaction."

Burnell slid a sideways glance at Finch and jabbed his thumb against his chest. "I'd like to know who this Raven is first and what we're dealing with, *before* we go tossing his name about."

"I suppose that means you still haven't heard from Emmeline or Longdon?"

Burnell's brows knit together and he gave a negative shake of his head. "Mmm," Finch mumbled.

Each detective retreated into his own thoughts. Only Burnell's ulcer rumbled in displeasure—and concern.

ᘒᘓᘒ

Emmeline knew Villiers had been loath to reveal the *exceedingly* little he had disclosed to Gregory about the Raven. If she appeared at his office again, she was certain that Villiers would have her arrested. The cards were stacked in his favor. However, he should know by now that he couldn't intimidate her. No matter how much it would please him, she was *not* going to drop the story. She would simply have to maneuver her way around Villiers. Carefully, very carefully.

Who was the Raven? Did Verena find out his identity and try to blackmail him? Or did McCallister kill her for reasons of his own? Was McCallister the Raven? And what, if anything, did the boiler room scam have to do with Verena's murder?

Emmeline frowned, as she stared out her office window at the view of Tower Bridge and the gray-green ribbon of the Thames below. Question upon question circled around her mind.

Her brow suddenly smoothed and her mouth curved into a smile. There was one source who could give her some answers, or at least point her in the right direction.

She hurried to her desk, shoved her notebook into her handbag, and shrugged into her coat. She had her hand on the door handle, when her phone rang.

"Oh, bother," she muttered.

She was tempted to leave without answering it. *But what if it's a new lead?* a voice inside her head pointed out.

She sighed and snatched up the phone. "Hello. Emmeline Kirby."

"Hello, Miss Kirby. My name's Stuart Aldridge. I'm a partner at Aldridge and Thayer. I was Verena Penrose's personal lawyer."

Emmeline's ears perked up. "Yes, Mr. Aldridge. How can I help you?"

"I'm calling about Ms. Penrose's will. The reading will be held tomorrow at noon. I was hoping you could attend. Ms. Penrose left something for you."

She stared at the phone, not believing what she had heard. "For me? I find that quite surprising. Verena and I were hardly friends. Are you certain, Mr. Aldridge?"

"Look, I don't want to discuss the matter over the phone. Everything will be explained tomorrow. The firm's address is Ninety High Holborn. It's a five-minute walk from the Holborn Underground Station."

Emmeline was silent for a few seconds. She was riddled with curiosity. "Yes, of course I'll be there tomorrow." She tried not to sound too eager.

"Thank you, Miss Kirby." He bid her good day and rang off.

"Well, well, well," she said aloud as she replaced the receiver. "What the devil is Verena plotting from the grave?"

തൗന

Gregory strolled over Westminster Bridge, casually scanning the faces of the people he passed, as he made his way to the south bank. The only one who exhibited an interest in him was a woman with long golden hair and cornflower blue eyes. When she came level with him, she stopped, favored him with a seductive smile, slipped her arms around his waist and gave him a hug. "Hello," she murmured in a husky voice. "You just brightened my day."

Startled by this unexpected gesture, he disentangled himself from her embrace. He didn't feel threatened by this beautiful stranger. Either she was overly friendly or something else was afoot. He raised an eyebrow in askance.

She didn't say anything else, but her bold glance roamed over his features for a few seconds. Before moving on, she pressed a piece of paper into the palm of his hand.

"Call me," she tossed over her shoulder.

He threw his head back and laughed when he unfolded the paper and saw her name and phone number staring up at him. Well, that was a novel way of meeting people. He pivoted around to watch her retreating figure. She must have sensed his scrutiny because she spun on her heel to blow him a kiss, leaving him in no doubt about what she had in mind.

He chuckled to himself as he crumpled the paper and tossed it over the parapet into the Thames. He was used to the effect he had on members of the opposite sex and found the incident amusing. However, little did the woman know how lucky she was. Emmy would have scratched her eyes out. For a start. Emmy needn't worry, though. His heart belonged to her and always would.

The smile lingered on his lips as he thought of his wife. But enough distractions. Time for business.

He increased his pace and a few minutes later he was descending the steps on the south bank. A glance at his watch revealed that he had five minutes to spare before his meeting with the mysterious Jasper. The crisp December air sharpened his senses as he mentally prepared for the upcoming encounter. He leaned his forearms on the parapet and gazed out at the boat traffic on the Thames. The midday sun winked on the water's surface and caressed the golden façade of Parliament on the opposite bank.

As Big Ben struck one o'clock, Gregory reluctantly dragged his eyes away from the riparian scene and turned around. A compact, wiry man with closely-cropped salt-and-pepper hair dressed in an expensive onyx cashmere coat was heading straight toward him. Tucked under his left arm was a rolled-up newspaper. As the man neared, he could see the *Daily Mail* masthead.

The man closed the few yards between them. Before uttering a word, his gaze darted in a 360-degree circle. Satisfied, he said without preamble, "Longdon." Gregory nodded. "I've checked into your background and know you don't carry a gun. But I had my associate make certain." He gestured with his chin toward the bridge and Gregory realized that his encounter with the woman was more than met the eye. "So I can dispense with the tedious task of having to search you." He waved a hand. "Let's take a walk."

Gregory fell into step with the fellow. Neither spoke and they kept their eyes straight ahead.

"This is good enough." Jasper motioned toward a bench.

Once Gregory sat down, his companion became brisk. He waggled his fingers. "Right, let's see the ladies."

"A great lady can't be rushed. She deserves to be admired," Gregory pointed out as he dipped his hand into his inside pocket and drew out two black velvet pouches. He placed them gently in the other man's open palm.

"I'm not here for a chinwag," Jasper countered, as he pulled out a loupe and pressed it to his right eye. Gingerly, he loosened the drawstring of one pouch and the Pink Courtesan tumbled into his hand. An involuntary gasp escaped his lips. He lifted the ring to his eye and examined it in silence for the next minute. He gave a grunt and a nod, before repeating the same procedure with the Blue Angel.

Gregory could tell that he was even more impressed with the second gem. "What's the verdict?" he asked unnecessarily.

Jasper removed the loupe and handed the two pouches back to Gregory, who returned them to his pocket. "To be honest, I never doubted that they would be genuine." His clear gray eyes locked on Gregory's face. "You have a certain reputation in that regard. However, I would have been remiss in my duty to my client if I didn't do my due diligence."

"That goes without saying," Gregory conceded magnanimously. He lowered his voice, although there was no one within listening distance. "Now, as to next steps. Have you contacted the Raven?"

Jasper rubbed his chin. It was the only gesture that betrayed his nervousness about the prospective deal. "Word has reached his ear and, as you surmised, he's extremely interested in the ladies. I am authorized to offer you three million for both of them."

Gregory threw his head back and laughed. "You must be joking. You can attest to their superiority. They're flawless. I want eight million. That's a bargain."

Jasper shifted uncomfortably on the bench. He tapped his temple with a forefinger and hissed, "You're missing a gear or two. You don't want to tangle with the Raven. He'll kill you. Just take the three million. It will be the easiest money you make in your entire life."

Gregory folded his arms over his chest and gave a curt shake of his head. "Eight."

Jasper threw his hands up in the air in exasperation. "Stubborn bugger, aren't you?" he swore.

"A man must look out for his interests."

"You're just full of little witticisms," Jasper shot back

sarcastically. "All right. I'm empowered to go as high as six million. That's my client's best and *final* offer."

Gregory cocked his head to one side as if he were giving it serious consideration. Jasper's eyes became tiny slits, his gaze intense.

Gregory extended a hand. "I accept."

The other man released his breath. "Thank the Lord for that."

"When and where do I make the exchange?" He wagged his forefinger. "Remember. I will only turn over the stones to the Raven himself."

Jasper rose and thrust his hands deep in his coat pockets. "I'll contact you with the details in a day or two. Aren't you forgetting something?"

Gregory raised an eyebrow. "Am I?" he asked in mock innocence.

"My money," Jasper demanded through gritted teeth.

"Oh, yes, of course." Gregory drew out an envelope from inside his coat with the air of a conjurer and handed it to the other man, who snatched it out of his fingers and tore it open. "No need to count it. I assure you the entire thousand pounds is there."

"They say you're a gentleman. I'll take your word for it."

With business concluded, Jasper shuffled off without bidding him farewell.

Gregory waited five minutes, before rising casually and making his way toward the stairs for the trek back across the bridge.

He knew the Pink Courtesan and the Blue Angel would have the Raven salivating. Now came the tricky part. Because one thing was certain. The Raven couldn't afford to let him live once the diamonds had exchanged hands.

eɔeɔ

Emmeline flashed her press pass at the constable on duty by the wrought-iron railings. He scrutinized her *Clarion* credentials carefully, before giving a satisfied nod and opening the gate. She smiled and sauntered up Downing Street, where fellow members of the Fourth Estate had gathered in front of the gleaming black door of the modest terrace house that was at the heart of British government: Number 10, the Prime Minister's residence.

The low hum of conversation was carried by the wind, as everyone waited for the Prime Minister to step out and make a statement on the trade and defense talks he was holding with the foreign ministers of France and Germany, and a European Union delegation. She was content to hover at the fringes of the group and exchange a few words with an old friend from *The Times* and a reporter from Sky News. Owen Collins, the reporter from the *Clarion* who had been assigned to cover the press conference, caught her eye and threaded his way over to her side. She reassured him she was not here to steal his thunder nor to look over his shoulder. He shrugged and ambled off to reclaim his spot at the front of the group, where he had positioned himself initially.

Out of the corner of her eye, she could see him shooting perplexed glances in her direction. Clearly, her unexpected appearance here today did not please him. Well, he could just lump it. She knew Owen was among a small group of reporters, who had resented the fact that she had been hired as editorial director of investigative features. She jutted her chin in the air and kept her gaze straight ahead. She didn't give a fig for their opinions. She worked hard and was damn good at her job.

She was torn from these reflections, when the door burst open and the Prime Minister and the other officials spilled out onto the pavement. The group of reporters surged forward, pens, tape recorders, and cameras at the ready.

Emmeline craned her neck and stood on tiptoe. For one moment, she thought she had made a wasted trip. But she relaxed, when Philip came into view. His blond head was bent close to the ear of one of the other officials. He cupped a hand over his mouth as he whispered something. The woman nodded and offered a reply. They were deep in conversation and Philip hadn't noticed Emmeline yet. That was all for the good.

She sidled closer to the front, as the Prime Minister gave a brief overview of the agreements that had been reached during the meeting and what issues still remained to be resolved. It was only when her colleagues were firing off questions at him that Philip's gaze fell on her. His blue eyes widened for an instant and then narrowed. Emmeline flashed him a smile.

The press conference broke up a few minutes later and her colleagues either bolted to file their stories or go on air to provide an update. Emmeline, though, dashed toward Philip, who lingered on the pavement.

"Whatever you're doing here, the answer is no," he declared sternly.

"Hello, Philip. My, how well you look."

He huffed a laugh. "Flattery won't get you anywhere."

"Hmph," she sniffed. "I think hello or something equally polite is the customary form of greeting, especially when it comes to a friend."

"Hello, Emmeline," he replied grudgingly. "The answer is still no."

She tossed a glance over her shoulder and tugged him by the elbow a few steps away from the door. "Look, it's rather important. You're the only one who can help."

"It's always important *and* dangerous." He wagged an admonishing forefinger at her. "That means you shouldn't be involved."

"Who mentioned the word dangerous? I'm a reporter. I need information. I was hoping, as a friend, you would be happy to oblige. Maggie and the boys, in particular, would want you to help me."

One of his brows arched upward. "First it was flattery. Now, you're trying to make me feel guilty."

She grinned up at him. "Am I succeeding? Come on, Philip," she cajoled. "I know that you don't have a heart of stone in that chest of yours. Deep down you want justice too." She dropped her voice. "Someone like the Raven shouldn't be allowed to run around with impunity. He must be stopped."

Philip grabbed her the elbows. "The Raven?" he hissed. "How did you stumble across him? And what the devil does he have to do with Verena Penrose's murder?"

"Actually," she hedged, "Villiers might have mentioned something about the Raven, when he had lunch with Gregory yesterday."

"What? Tightlipped Villiers," he smirked. "I can't believe it."

She sighed. "It's true. However, he only relented after Gregory pressed him. Apparently, Verena was passing on information to Villiers to try to help him unmask the Raven. That's why the name Toby Crenshaw was in her notebook."

"A gossip columnist? What could the old boy have been thinking? What boggles the mind, even more, is the fact that Verena agreed."

"I assure you it wasn't out of any sense of patriotism. Villiers fed her dirt for her exposés in exchange," she sneered in disgust.

"Ah." Philip nodded. "That's the first thing that makes sense. So, I take it Verena discovered the Raven's identity and he silenced her before she could tell Villiers."

"Not exactly. Verena did learn who the Raven is and

summoned Villiers to the theatre that night, but ultimately it was a tease. She didn't tell him anything, deciding that blackmail was a more lucrative prospect."

He grunted. "Stupid, greedy woman." His brow puckered in concern and he fell silent for a moment. "That means the Raven was at the theatre that night too."

"That's what we assume. He appears to have melted into the woodwork again. We have to find him. Villiers waved the Officials Secrets Act in front of our noses to ensure that Gregory and I drop this, but we won't."

"You mean *you* won't and Longdon is scrambling to keep you from getting yourself killed. As usual."

She chose to ignore this comment. Why did men have a tendency to overexaggerate? "Anyway, I was wondering whether you could give me a lead to catch the Raven. I'd be happy with the tiniest crumb," she said hopefully.

"I can't in good conscience help you. First"—he enumerated on his fingers—"you'd be making yourself a target and second, it's a security matter. *The Clarion* would be sued if it printed a word."

"Rubbish. It's a straightforward murder investigation. Albeit, it appears that the likely culprit may be an international spy and assassin or merely an underworld criminal."

He snorted. "Oh, *merely* an underworld criminal. Emmeline, stop pretending to be naïve."

She flapped her hand dismissively. "I don't want to argue with you, nor am I asking for sensitive security material that will get you into trouble with your superiors. I don't want to quote you as a source. Just give me something and I can take it from there."

"I've wasted my breath." He shook his head. "It would be better for you and everyone else if I made a few discreet inquiries. At least, I could keep an eye on you and a modicum of control."

She opened her mouth to say something, but he put up a hand to forestall her. "I promise nothing. I will not jeopardize your safety."

She lowered her gaze and nodded dutifully. "Understood," she mumbled.

"I'm not fooled by that humble demeanor for a single instant. What else have you and Longdon found out?"

She looked him directly in the eye and took a deep breath. "A private investigator Verena's husband hired discovered that she was having an affair with a chap called Scott McCallister. The investigator told us that Verena and McCallister had discussed murdering her husband."

"What? The more I hear about that woman, the more revolting she becomes."

"Yes, well. I knew that a long time ago. In any case, aside from the fact that McCallister lacks moral fiber, I've hit a brick wall trying to find out how he has amassed his fortune. There were whispers he made it in the City. A hedge fund, perhaps. However, the money trail is cold as ice."

"Right. Anything else I should be aware of?"

"Gregory found out that Verena was the daughter of Sid Cranbrook."

Philip's eyes widened in disbelief. "The underworld figure who died a few years ago?" He shook his head in astonishment. "I can't believe it."

"It's true. Cranbrook wanted to protect her, so she went by her mother's maiden name. It seems that Verena, wielding her influence as Cranbrook's daughter, ordered some of his former underlings to carry out a boiler room scam. Gregory and I think that she was trying to lure out the Raven, but we can't determine how precisely. If you're unfamiliar with the scam, the goal is to bilk vulnerable people, especially the elderly, out of their money by persuading them that they're buying diamonds at a bargain price."

"How jolly. The Raven, diamonds, and murder. I'll say one thing for you and Longdon. You don't do things by halves."

Her mouth curved into a smile. "We are always on the side of justice," she responded virtuously.

"You are. The jury is still out on Longdon."

Her eyes narrowed and she shot a withering look at him. "That remark was uncalled for. Gregory is legitimate now."

"For your sake"—he placed his hands on her shoulders and held her gaze—"I sincerely hope that's true."

Her chin jutted in the air defiantly. "It's not a question of hope. It *is*." Then, she demanded briskly, "Now, what can you tell me about the Raven? Don't try to fob me off with any diplomatic double talk. I saw your reaction a few moments ago. You know *something*."

Philip dropped his chin to his chest and shook his blond head. When he lifted his gaze again, he couldn't help but laugh at the fierce expression on her face. "I'm not the enemy."

"That hinges on whether you provide some information."

The crowd of reporters was breaking up. "I suggest we take a walk." He took her by the elbow and guided her toward the wrought-iron gate. "It's bad enough that you know about the Raven, it would be a nightmare if your colleagues got wind of him too."

She beamed up at him. "How can I resist an exclusive?"

Chapter 24

As soon as they had returned to the station, Finch scuttled off to check with the airlines and Eurostar to try to determine when and where McCallister was planning to flee. The man reeked of guilt. Burnell had no doubt that he was going to scarper soon. Their visit, on the heels of Emmeline's questions, had clearly rattled McCallister. That was all to the good. It wouldn't take much to push him over the edge and force him to make a mistake.

If only they could find something, *anything*, to prevent McCallister from leaving London.

Burnell plopped down into his chair, which groaned in protest under his weight. He shoved his spectacles on his nose and flipped open the file on McCallister's finances. Finch already had gone through it, but a second set of eyes didn't hurt.

He was making notes on a few items that he wanted to follow up on when Finch entered his office after a brief knock.

"Sir, Mr. Sanderson is here. The gentleman Emmeline rang about."

The superintendent snatched off his spectacles. "The one who had been following Verena Penrose and ran into Emmeline and Longdon at the theatre?"

"Yes. He's a bit tense. I think he's afraid the killer may come after him. I've tried to calm him down. Cooper is fetching him a cup of coffee. Are you ready to speak with Sanderson?"

"Let's see what he has to say."

Finch gave a curt nod and disappeared. He returned almost instantly, accompanied by a tall, lanky fellow with ginger hair. The man had an angular face with pale blue eyes that darted around nervously.

Burnell rose and extended a hand. "Good afternoon, Mr. Sanderson. It was good of you to come down to the station to help us with our inquiries."

Sanderson dipped his head deferentially and mumbled, "I apologize for not coming forward sooner. I...I..."

Burnell motioned to one of the chairs across from him and resumed his seat. "It's a typical human reaction. You wanted to get away from the horror as soon as possible. It was the shock."

Finch slid into the chair beside the other man and took out his pen and notebook.

Sanderson nodded. "It was. I never"—he put a hand to his mouth and his eyes glazed over—"To see her like *that*." His voice dropped to a raspy whisper on this last word.

He lifted his eyes to the superintendent's face. "How can someone do that to another person?"

Burnell heaved a weary sigh and settled back in his chair. "We ask ourselves that every day and have never been able to come up with an answer."

They lapsed into silence for several seconds, which was broken when Cooper appeared with the coffee for Sanderson.

He wrapped his hands around the cup. After taking a grateful sip, Sanderson was ready to talk. He repeated everything he had told Emmeline about his father and the boiler room scam; how he had approached Verena Penrose about the story; and his resorting to following her when she ignored his calls, which ultimately drove him to confront her at the theatre.

Although he answered all the questions that the two detectives had posed, Sanderson was unable to shed any light on who their culprit might be. It was a case of being in the wrong place at the wrong time.

Sanderson took another swallow of coffee. "I haven't been much help, have I?"

"Mr. Sanderson, I assure you that every piece of information is useful. Consider yourself lucky. A moment earlier and you could have run straight into the murderer."

Sanderson ran a hand through his hair. He cast a sideways glance at Finch and then his gaze settled on Burnell again. "Believe me, I've been thinking of nothing else since I spoke to Miss Kirby. She insisted that I come speak to you at once."

"She was right about that," the superintendent replied.

If nothing else, he thought drily. *It would make my life infinitely easier if Emmeline and Longdon would leave the police work to the professionals. It wasn't an unreasonable request.*

Sanderson licked his lips and scooted to the edge of his chair. He propped his elbows on Burnell's desk. "Superintendent, I was wondering," he began haltingly. "As you're a senior officer, could you do anything to help get my dad's money back from those con men? It was his life's savings for God's sake." His voice cracked with shame and desperation.

His eyes beseeched Burnell for assistance. The superintendent was not unmoved by the man's story. During his thirty-year career at the Met, he had seen too many similar schemes perpetrated on the vulnerable and gullible. It angered him beyond words every time a new one came to light. But unfortunately, there was not much he could do.

He cleared his throat and looked Sanderson directly in the eye. "Believe me, Mr. Sanderson, if there were something in my power I would do it in a heartbeat. Another division handles those types of cases. I could make a few discreet inquiries. But I have to be honest, I don't hold out much hope. You must come to terms with the fact that the money is probably gone. That's how the police were able to catch the scoundrels. They went on a spending spree with their ill-gotten loot."

Sanderson gave a sad nod of acknowledgement and pushed himself to his feet. "Yes, I was just hoping." He thrust a hand out to Burnell, who rose too. "Thank you. Miss Kirby said that she would pursue the story. I'm hoping the press attention might help Dad's cause."

Burnell smiled. "It certainly can't hurt. I know Miss Kirby and she won't give up. Making the public aware of such scams may bring them to an end, once and for all. Now, if you'll follow Sergeant Finch, he'll have your statement typed up for you to sign. I assure you it won't take long."

"Yes, of course. Thank you." He thrust out his hand to the superintendent. In doing so, Sanderson inadvertently brushed a file off the desk. "How clumsy of me. I'm sorry." He bent down to scoop it up and then froze. "That's him."

Burnell and Finch traded perplexed glances. "Who is?" Finch asked.

Sanderson straightened up and tapped a photo in the file. "That man was there the night Ms. Penrose was murdered. I passed him on the stairs on the way to her box."

Burnell grabbed the file. "Are you sure?" he demanded sharply.

"Yes, I remember him distinctly. Everything about that night is imprinted in my mind."

Burnell grinned and pumped his hand up and down.

"Thank you very much, Mr. Sanderson. You've been extremely helpful after all. If you'll just step outside, P.C. Cooper will be along in a moment to type up your statement."

The minute the door closed behind Sanderson, Burnell whirled round to Finch. "Bring our friend McCallister to the station. We have some pointed questions to put to him."

Finch was already moving toward the door. "My pleasure, sir."

⅌⅌⅌

Emmeline and Philip had strolled up Whitehall to the National Gallery. After the incident in November when Special Branch agents had come to his office to arrest him, Philip had tried to keep his head down. Even though he was no longer under suspicion, it had left a bitter taste in his mouth. He was diligently concentrating on his diplomatic responsibilities, rather than his MI5 duties, while Villiers worked behind the scenes to determine who had put a target on his back and why. For this reason, Philip had decided against taking Emmeline back to the Foreign Office. The whispers would start flying the instant they crossed the threshold that he had been seen speaking with the editorial director of investigative features at *The Clarion*. It didn't matter that she was his wife's best friend. Emmeline was a well-known figure around the corridors of power. People ran for cover because they knew she was on the hunt for a story. Diplomats tended to have an innate aversion to controversy of any kind.

The museum didn't appear to be crowded today. Philip and Emmeline climbed the marble staircase in the Central Hall to Level 2. He led her to Room 38, a must for both of them whenever they had a chance to pop into the gallery.

Their footsteps echoed as they crossed the highly polished parquet floor and settled themselves onto a black leather-covered bench in the center of the room. The red damask walls featured paintings by Canaletto and Guardi, as well as Bernardo Belloto and Giovanni Panini. Emmeline cocked her head to one side and allowed her eyes to roam over Canaletto's *The Doge's Palace and the Riva degli Schiavoni*. The warm crimson of the wall only seemed to bring out the painting's bold brushstrokes and exquisite details into sharper focus.

Venice was one of her most favorite cities in the world. Canaletto made her feel as if she were wandering along the canals and narrow *calle*, or streets, once again. It also brought to mind that terrible business at the beginning of the year when she had witnessed two men trying to murder her friend and fellow journalist, Charles Latimer, in Campo San Bartolomeo. A lump rose in her throat at the thought of Charles and the chain of terrifying events that followed, as she and Gregory followed the trail of a Russian spy all the way back to London.

She exhaled a long sigh and tore her eyes from the painting.

"Villiers wasn't entirely truthful with Longdon," Philip said, breaking the silence.

She huffed a laugh and lifted her gaze to meet his. "That comes as no surprise. Villiers is probably so conditioned to lie that he does it in his dreams. What can you tell me about the Raven without compromising your position?"

Two vertical lines formed between his brows. "What I'm most concerned about is your safety and Longdon's. Emmeline, as your friend, I urge you to drop your pursuit of the Raven."

She shook her head. "That's a nonstarter and you know it."

His shoulders twitched in a resigned shrug. "It was

worth a try. I thought for once the voice of sanity would win the day.'

Her mouth curved into a smile. "Haven't you heard? Sanity is overrated. It's the lunatics that have all the fun."

A laugh rumbled from his throat. "You and Longdon certainly fall into that category."

"What did Villiers conveniently omit from his narrative?" she prodded impatiently.

"This is off the record," he asserted.

She groaned and shook her head. "I'm sick of hearing that tired refrain." Her gaze snaked back to his face. "The English language is rich. I wish you would learn a different turn of phrase."

He was not moved by this dig. He merely folded his arms over his chest and waited.

She threw her hands up in the air in resignation. "All right. Off the record. But, I'd like to remind you that I'm not the enemy. I'm just doing my job."

"You tend to be overzealous and enjoy waving the red flag in front of the bull. People, especially criminals, take exception to your tenacious poking around in their business."

"I'm not here for a philosophical discussion on the merits of journalism."

"Fair enough." He lowered his voice and darted a glance around the room, but they were alone. "What Villiers neglected to mention was that while a handful of the Raven's victims were in witness protection, they were Russians who either defected or were working as double agents and were planning to turn over damaging documents to us."

Her jaw tightened. "Why does Putin insist on using the U.K. as his personal spy playground? That means the Raven is Russian."

Philip pursed his lips and shifted his gaze to the painting

again. "Not necessarily."

She studied his profile. "You mean he's British?"

She took his silence as confirmation, as her brain sought to digest this revelation.

"The Raven has killed more than a dozen men. If MI5 knows that he's a British citizen, how is it that you haven't been able to catch him?"

Philip gave a frustrated shake of his head and looked her directly in the eye. "It's a bloody nightmare. It's as if he's a ghost. Villiers spoke the truth when he told Longdon that the Raven can assume any identity he likes, as if he's slipping on a coat. What I can't fathom is how a gossip columnist like Verena Penrose stumbled into his path."

"Verena insinuated herself into many circles. I have no doubt that her blackmailing paved the way in most instances." She pushed herself to her feet. "Well, thanks for being honest with me and filling in some of the missing pieces. It helps to give me a better focus."

Philip leaped up and grabbed her by the shoulders. "Emmeline, I told you all of this to put the fear of God into you. This is not a game. In different ways, Charles Latimer, Pavel Melnikov and Yuri Sabitov tried and failed to disrupt Putin's machinations. They're all dead. However now, you and Longdon want to play footsie with the Raven, another of Putin's creatures. You're out of your depth. You're not trained agents."

She held his gaze. "Ah, but thanks to you we're not walking into the situation blind. Knowledge is power. We'll be careful." She patted his arm reassuringly. "I promise. The bottom line is that someone has to put an end to the Raven's deadly spree."

"Bloody obstinate woman." He gave her shoulders a shake. "What I'm worried about is that he'll put an end to you."

"Impossible. Don't you know that good *always*

triumphs over evil? Gregory and I are on the side of right,"
she declared with bravado rather than conviction.

Because the more she heard about the Raven, the more
terrifying he became. But she couldn't possibly admit that
to Philip. Or anyone else.

Chapter 25

What the devil am I doing here? Is anyone out there? You have no right to treat me in this disgraceful manner. I want my lawyer." McCallister's muffled, angry cries seeped through the door of the interview room, where Finch had deposited him a quarter of an hour ago.

Burnell stood in the corridor a few feet away, one arm folded over his chest and one hand stroking his beard, listening to McCallister's increasingly incensed pleas. Soon, he'd probably start pounding with his fist on the door. Suspects invariably did so. He'd let the man stew for another five minutes. Eventually, McCallister would wear himself out when he realized that he didn't have a sympathetic audience. The reaction was similar to that of a spoiled toddler demanding his own way.

Finch walked up to the superintendent and handed him a cup of coffee. Burnell nodded his thanks and took a grateful swallow.

The sergeant gestured with his chin. "McCallister sounds as if he's ready to talk."

"Mmm. I rather doubt he's going to oblige us with a confession."

"You didn't really think he would, sir. But at least now we have a reason to upset his travel plans."

Burnell grinned. "There is that." He inclined his head and cupped a hand around his ear. "All quiet on the Western front. I do hope our friend hasn't suffocated in there." He finished the rest of his coffee and tossed the cup into the nearest rubbish bin. "Shall we find out?"

Finch gave a deferential nod and followed the superintendent into the interview room.

McCallister's head snapped up, his glare assaulting them with undisguised defiance.

"At last," he grumbled.

Burnell crossed to the table and pressed a button on the tape recorder. He identified himself and Finch as present, as well as the date and time of the interview. All the while, McCallister continued to vent his frustration.

The detectives ignored him, as they lowered themselves into the chairs opposite. Burnell folded his hands and regarded McCallister across the table.

"It makes an unfavorable impression, when you lie to the police," he observed in a clipped tone.

McCallister smirked and hooked an elbow around the back of his chair. He was trying much too hard to appear nonchalant. "I cooperated fully when you barged into my home unannounced." He tapped his finger on the table for emphasis. "At an extremely inconvenient moment, I might point out. You have no right to drag me down here and make such a spectacle." He waved a hand that took in the entire room.

Burnell slammed his open palm on the table, making McCallister flinch. "We are conducting a murder inquiry. It is our duty to follow the evidence and to question anyone who may have been involved."

"I told you I had *nothing* to do with Verena's murder. I demand to see my lawyer. It's illegal to keep me here like this."

Burnell turned to Finch. "You remember that saying

about protesting too much?" The sergeant nodded. "Our friend here seems to be doing an awful lot of protesting."

"Indeed, he does," Finch replied. "It makes one wonder what he's hiding."

McCallister leaned forward and the inevitable fist-pounding manifested itself. As a dramatic gesture, it failed. The two detectives didn't even blink.

"I want my lawyer," he bellowed, his voice bouncing off the walls.

"All in good time, Mr. McCallister. Please calm yourself. We simply would like to clarify a few discrepancies in your statement to us earlier. Surely you want us to get the facts correct?"

"What I *want* is for you to stop harassing me. Do I look like a criminal?"

"We've seen all sorts. Looks can be deceiving, after all" was the superintendent's cool rejoinder.

McCallister slumped back and retreated into a brooding silence. His nostrils flared, as it began to sink in that he was a captive audience and he wouldn't be leaving the room any time soon.

Burnell allowed him to seethe. He could almost hear the wheels of the other man's mind cranking furiously. Oh, how he enjoyed seeing suspects squirm. It was a bright spot in a policeman's otherwise vexing existence. He deliberately kept his expression neutral. It wouldn't do to rub salt in the wound.

"Now then, if you're quite finished with your little tantrum, I'd like to go back to the night Ms. Penrose was killed."

McCallister groaned and threw his hands up in resignation.

"You told us that although you were at the theatre that night, you never spoke to her, right?"

"Got it one," McCallister replied facetiously. "Verena

was in the bar having a row with Emmeline Kirby. It was pretty heated. Why don't you grill the Kirby woman? From what I saw, she could have murdered Verena with her bare hands."

Burnell steered clear of the subject of Emmeline. He merely pressed on. "You didn't see Ms. Penrose again at any time afterward?"

"No," McCallister said through gritted teeth. "I just told you." His hands curled into tight fists on the table. "Are you hard of hearing? Or do you have problems with your short-term memory? Perhaps you should have that looked at by a doctor."

"How do you explain the fact that you were seen leaving Ms. Penrose's box shortly before her body was discovered?"

McCallister scowled back at him. "Who said that I was there?" he demanded.

Burnell disregarded his question. "You do understand why I find this revelation unsettling. It gives you means and opportunity."

McCallister's lips pressed into a thin line and his features smoothed into an unreadable expression. "I refuse to say another word until my lawyer arrives."

Burnell exhaled a weary sigh. "Just when we were getting on so well."

Daggers of loathing shot from the other man's eyes. *Ah well, I can't be popular with everyone*, the superintendent thought philosophically.

"I will have to ask you to surrender your passport."

"What?" McCallister exploded. "Not bloody likely."

"I'm afraid you have no choice. You are a suspect in a murder investigation. That makes you a flight risk."

He hit the button on the tape recorder, ending the interview and beginning McCallister's legal woes.

Chapter 26

Emmeline and Philip parted ways in Trafalgar Square. Not surprisingly, his pleas to tread carefully fell on deaf ears. She sent him off with a peck on the cheek and her regards to Maggie and the boys. He swallowed down his concern because he had to rush back to the Foreign Office for a meeting. Meanwhile, Emmeline turned down Piccadilly with the intention of going straight to Scotland Yard to inform Superintendent Burnell and Sergeant Finch about everything she had learned about the Raven. She was feeling a bit guilty for having left them out of the loop until this point. However, she reasoned that now she and Gregory had more details, which was a good thing and would help the investigation. At least, she *hoped* that Burnell would see it in that light and not be cross. At least not too cross.

She decided to walk to the station, rather than take the Tube. The exercise would get her blood flowing and the wind's crisp bite would clear the cobwebs from her mind to sharpen her senses. She had to determine the best way to unmask the Raven's identity without compromising Philip or violating the Official Secrets Act, which Villiers was only too happy to wave under their noses every two seconds. She grimaced at the thought of the fine line that she must toe. She gave a mental shrug. She couldn't ignore the truth simply because it was inconvenient. That would go against all the tenets of journalism that she held dear. To say nothing of her conscience, which would never forgive her.

Her feet couldn't help but come to a halt in front of Fortnum & Mason's windows. Although she was Jewish, it didn't prevent her from appreciating the festive Christmas displays. Always an opulent confection of whimsey, humor, and joy, this year they ingeniously featured three-dimensional reproductions of six classical paintings from the National Gallery. Her gaze trailed from one window to the next in delight. But one part of her brain couldn't stop thinking about the Raven. As she mulled her next move, a soft *tap, tap, tap* drifted upon the air despite the rumble of traffic behind her and the murmur of conversation all around. A flicker of movement out of the corner of her eye sent a frisson slithering down her spine. She tore her gaze from the display. In the window, her eyes met the intense reflection of a woman, who made no attempt to disguise her brazen interest.

Who was she?

Emmeline swiveled around unexpectedly hoping to catch the stranger off guard. But the woman remained rooted to the spot near the curb, her unblinking gaze fastened on Emmeline's face.

"What do you want?" Emmeline hissed.

The woman didn't scurry off. Instead, she limped forward, weaving her way around pedestrians rushing past, to close the distance between them. When she came to stop before Emmeline, she leaned heavily on her metallic cane.

"You're Emmeline Kirby," the woman's husky voice asserted, pinning her with her smoky-blue eyes.

Emmeline frowned up at the slim woman with long, chestnut hair, which was carefully arranged but failed to completely conceal a scar that stretched from her earlobe down the right side of her neck.

"I don't know you. Why are you stalking me?"

The woman huffed a bitter laugh. "Don't flatter yourself. You're a reporter. I have information that can help you."

Emmeline hitched her handbag higher on her shoulder. "Why should I trust anything you tell me?" She sought to keep her voice even and not betray the fact that she was unnerved by the menace hovering just below the surface of the woman's calm demeanor. She surreptitiously took a step to her left, seeking to put space between herself and the stranger.

The woman shuffled forward and bent her head close. Her warm breath tickled Emmeline's ear as she whispered, "Because you want to catch the Raven so badly you can taste it."

As she drew back, her full lips curved into a Cheshire cat grin.

Emmeline released a startled gasp. "Who are you?"

The woman waved a hand dismissively in the air. "That's not important."

"It damn well is," Emmeline bristled. "For all I know, you could be a con artist seeking publicity."

The woman clutched her arm in a surprisingly strong grip. "Believe me," she said through gritted teeth, "seeing my name splashed in the pages of your newspaper is the farthest thing from my mind."

Emmeline shook off her grasp. "Lay your hand on me again and I'll scream at the top of my lungs for a constable."

She knew she should make a dash for it. And yet, she lingered there on the pavement. Damn it, she swore silently. She was forced to admit that her journalistic instincts had been aroused.

The stranger lifted one hand in surrender, while her

fingers curled tightly around the handle of her cane. "Feel better now?"

Emmeline inclined her head. "Now then, let's start with your name."

A challenge kindled in the depths of the woman's eyes. She couldn't have been more than forty, but the thin skin around her eyes was scored by a netting of fine lines making her appear twenty years older. Her gaze was at once armored and haunted by pain. She had been badly scarred, not only physically, but especially mentally. This observation made Emmeline even more curious to hear her story.

"Stephanie." The name came out on a strangled sigh. "That's all you need to know."

Emmeline pursed her lips and grunted, "Hmph." She supposed it would have to do. For the moment.

Stephanie darted an anxious glance at the passersby and flicked the tip of her tongue over her bottom lip, before turning back to Emmeline. "Come on. We need to talk in private." She jerked her chin and started to walk away.

Emmeline gave an emphatic shake of her head. "I have no intention of being alone with you anywhere. I know nothing about you."

"You're crackers. You know that," Stephanie declared, her tone laced with exasperation. "Surely you don't expect me to spill my guts *here* on the pavement?"

Emmeline folded her arms over her chest and stared back at her without responding.

"I assure you the Raven poses a greater threat to you than I do," she hissed. She craned her neck around. "Fine. St. James's Church is only a few steps away. We can talk out in the open in the forecourt, where the arts and crafts market is being held if it makes you feel safer."

Emmeline thrust her hands in her pockets and pivoted on her heel. "Let's go."

The wrought-iron gates opened onto the flagstone courtyard of the church, which had been designed by Sir Christopher Wren. Stalls selling food, gifts, and other treasures were ringed around the forecourt. As it was the Christmas season, the stalls were doing a brisk business. Tourists and London natives alike were wandering around.

"Why don't we sit on one of those benches over there?"

Emmeline nodded. They remained silent as they wound their way around the perimeter of the stalls. They climbed a curved stone double staircase nestled around a fountain featuring two cherubs riding dolphins. They settled down on a bench on the small terrace that overlooked the forecourt.

A gust of wind swirled around them, setting the bare branches of the trees to chatter nervously. Emmeline cocked an eye at the sky, as she took out her notebook and pen. A lugubrious, charcoal cloud drifted over their heads, blocking out the white-gold rays of the late afternoon sunshine and holding a threat of rain. Her fingertips tingled with cold. She curled them into her palms and dug her hands deep into her pockets. She wished Stephanie would get on with it. Only a few minutes ago, she had been desperate to unburden her soul. Now, here she sat, silent as the tomb, staring off into the distance.

"Where to begin," Stephanie murmured as if reading Emmeline's thoughts. She didn't look at her. "It's a story about wickedness and greed," she rasped. Her voice was brittle like shards of broken glass.

Emmeline's ears strained to hear her. It took all her willpower, but she held her tongue.

"He's evil, oh so evil. But I didn't see it at first." She slumped back against the bench, one hand still clutching her cane. "No, that's not right." She huffed a bitter laugh. "I think always knew. I simply didn't want to admit it to myself." She turned her tormented gaze on Emmeline and wagged an admonishing finger. "Never lie to yourself. It's the worst thing you could do."

Her gaze slithered back into the past. "He was charming and terribly handsome. I was married, but I forgot my vows the instant I met him. From the first moment, he was under my skin. My husband was in the diamond business." Emmeline's ears perked up at this little nugget. "We had just moved to Amsterdam so that my husband could expand his company. He became partners with William." The name came out on a ragged breath, as if it were a foreign word. "My husband thought it was sheer good fortune to find someone of William's experience. He was certain that they would be high-flyers in no time. But in hindsight, I see clearly that it was all part of William's calculated game. A secret agenda, where everyone is his pawn. Our affair was a means to an end. He consumes people and spits them out when they've outlived their usefulness." The hand that gripped the cane was like the talon of a bird of prey. Her voice trembled with raw emotion. "He insinuates ideas into your head"—she tapped her temple with her forefinger—"that you never would have contemplated on your own."

She dropped her chin to her chest. "I killed my husband for him."

Emmeline's pulse quickened and a knot formed in the pit of her stomach at this shocking confession. She leaped to her feet, stumbling backward in her haste. "Wh-what?"

Stephanie's head snapped up. "Yes, that's right. Don't be squeamish." Her hand flashed out and clamped around Emmeline's wrist like a vice. "Sit down," she sneered and gave a violent tug. Emmeline plopped down heavily beside her again.

Stephanie didn't release her grip, forcing Emmeline to confront the depravity that was mirrored in her gaze. "My husband would never have agreed to a divorce. I had to kill him. I was nervous at first, but it was actually easier than I imagined it would be. William obtained some poison. I didn't ask him what it was or where he got it. I didn't want to know. And then…it was all over. My husband was dead. For appearance's sake, William and I waited a month before going off to Gibraltar to get married."

Emmeline was tongue-tied. She couldn't comprehend how matter-of-factly this woman was relating the horrifying details about the crime she and the sinister William had perpetrated.

"That was the happiest day of my life." A ghost of a smile touched Stephanie's lips and the next instant her features were pinched with barely controlled anger. "It was the last time I was ever happy.

"My husband—the dead one in Amsterdam—left me his half of the company. Fool that I was, I signed it over to William on our wedding night. He had been subtly angling for that all along." She shook her head and laughed. It was a harsh sound that grated on the ears. "And I gave it to him on a silver platter. That's when I ceased to exist for William."

She swallowed hard and lapsed into silence. A sheen of unshed tears shimmered in her eyes. "He's impatient and restless by nature. Perhaps it's because he has such a brilliant intellect and the rest of us are dull-witted by comparison."

Oh, spare me. He's an erratic psychopath, who is a master at manipulation, Emmeline reflected grimly.

Stephanie's shoulders hunched forward and her muscles coiled with tension. "He chartered a small yacht and we cruised to the Costa del Sol on our honeymoon. He had a villa in Torremolinos. Villa del Nido de Cuervo. We were going to stay there for a week, before going on to Mallorca. It was a slice of heaven…until he tried to kill me."

Well, I can see how that would put a damper on things,

Emmeline quipped in silence.

"It was nearly midnight. We went up on deck to enjoy the full moon. We were quite alone. I don't know where the crew was." Stephanie's hand flew to her throat. "Suddenly William's hands were around my throat. His thumbs were pressing on my windpipe. Squeezing with all his strength. I struggled against him, but I couldn't draw in any air. I felt myself beginning to lose consciousness. I desperately scrabbled around for something, *anything*, to fight him off. We tumbled to the deck and I felt a knife between my fingers. I don't know how it got there. He must have had it on him. I didn't stop to question it. I was frantic and terrified. I raised my hand above his head. I was going to plunge the knife between his shoulder blades. I hesitated, though. In that fraction of a second, William twisted my wrist and grabbed the knife. He was about to slash my throat, but I managed to roll away." A strangled sigh escaped her lips. "I never really had a chance. The cards were stacked against me. He lunged for me." She choked back a sob. "I can still feel the knife ripping into my skin." She pulled back her hair to expose the nasty scar that Emmeline had caught a fleeting glimpse of earlier. "I was stunned and losing blood fast. William took advantage of my helpless state. He gathered me up in his arms and tossed me overboard as if I was a feather."

Emmeline drew in a sharp breath. The bitterness of bile coated her tongue. "And yet here you are. How…how did you manage to survive?"

"Frankly, I don't really know. When I came to, I was drifting in the Mediterranean. I was in sheer agony. Every part of my body hurt. At some point, the waves had flung me against some rocks. I was battered quite badly." She slapped her left thigh. "My leg was broken into two places and my ankle shattered. Three ribs were broken. The only thing I wanted to do was die. To let the sea drag me down.

Where there was no more pain. No more William.

"But the Lord, or the devil more likely, had other plans for me. Some men found me and took me to the closest hospital, Vitas Xanhit International Hospital in Benalmádena. They tell me I was there for a couple of weeks. I was in a coma. When I woke up, I was in Hospital Regional Universitario de Málaga. I don't remember being transferred. My injuries required several surgeries. The damage was extensive. The doctors didn't think I'd ever walk again. It was eight, long months before I took my first step again. To this day, I still have pain." She slapped her leg. "But pain is good. It reminds me of William. His treachery pushed me to get out of that hospital bed. I vowed to hunt him down. He ruined my life." She rounded on Emmeline. "So don't judge me about my first husband. I paid for his murder a thousand times over."

Emmeline's skin crawled. Was it her own sense of morality that rebelled? As a journalist, she knew there was ugliness in the world. But her soul felt dirty listening to this sordid tale.

She swallowed down her distaste. "I would never judge you," she said softly.

"Liar," Stephanie smirked. "I can see it in your face. But I don't care. We all have to find a way to survive."

"I don't understand why you came to me."

"I'm burnt out. I've been following his trail for seven years. *Seven.* I tracked down all the crew members who were on the boat that night. Unfortunately, each one died in 'an accident.' I'm passing on the torch. It's up to you now to destroy William."

"I will not allow you to use me to as your personal weapon of revenge," Emmeline bristled in outrage. "I'm a journalist. I deal in facts. What proof do you have that he is the Raven?"

"Facts? Proof?" The words were infused with scorn.

"Why you ungrateful woman. I just gave you a hot lead. You're the investigative journalist." She waved an arm in the air. "Get out there and do the job you're paid to do."

"With what?" The last strand of Emmeline's patience snapped. "You just said that you've been hunting William down for seven years. It's a virtual certainty that William was an alias. You haven't given me his surname. But that's another matter. He's probably changed it a dozen times since you were involved with him." She was struggling to keep her tone even and tamp down her temper. It was becoming increasingly difficult. "How do you expect me to trace him? Hmm? I don't even know what he looks like. Do you have documents? Photos?" She rose and hitched her handbag over her shoulder. "How can I trust that what you say is the truth otherwise?" She gave a curt shake of her head. "No, I'm afraid you've wasted my time."

Stephanie lumbered to her feet and gripped the cane with both hands. "So that's it? You're going to walk away in a snit. I guess you're not the bulldog they all say you are. You don't actually roll up your sleeves and do any of the hard work." She sneered with disdain. "No, you leave that to others. You're lazy. Just like that other bloody woman."

Emmeline had started walking away, but she stopped short at this last comment and retraced her steps. "Do you mean Verena Penrose?"

"Yes. I'm happy she's dead. She was a phony."

Emmeline's breath caught in her throat. Had she been wrong? Did Stephanie kill Verena?

"I don't have any of your precious proof because I gave it all to her. She was brimming with sympathy and soothing words. She sent me off with promises of a scathing exposé that would bring the law down on William's ears. In the end, she did nothing."

Adrenaline sluiced through Emmeline's veins and her brain tingled with excitement. Verena had done precisely the same thing when Ted Sanderson had come to her with the information about the boiler room scam. She tucked it away to profit from the misery of others. Stephanie's tale was confirmation that Verena had tried to blackmail the Raven and he killed her. But that still didn't bring them any closer to finding him.

"If you want me to pursue the story, you must give me something. Even a more seasoned journalist would find it a tangled nightmare."

She paused, hoping Stephanie would relent. The woman stared at her without blinking.

"Be reasonable," she implored. "My paper would never allow me to write such a story without corroboration." She pursed her lips and waited. Stephanie didn't utter a word.

"Your name," Emmeline demanded. "William's full name. The company he and your first husband owned together." Still nothing. "Fine. This conversation is at an end."

It was not the first time a potential source had proven to be unreliable. She felt no qualms about leaving Stephanie standing there. The woman had admitted to being a murderer. Emmeline should turn her in, but all she wanted to do was to get away and pretend that Stephanie had never sought her out in the first place.

"How will you live with yourself when I'm dead?" Stephanie called after her.

Emmeline froze on the bottom step. Slowly, she pivoted on her heel to look up at Stephanie. "What do you mean?"

Stephanie loomed over her. She drew in air through her nostrils. "I think… that is I'm fairly certain that William knows I'm after him. Someone has been following me the past few weeks. If" —her voice cracked—"when he catches up with me, I need to know someone else will be there to pick up the pieces and carry on." She awkwardly descended the steps and clutched Emmeline's sleeve when she came level with her. "He must be stopped." She squeezed her eyes shut. "I'm so tired. I need peace in my grave." Her eyes flew open. "Please."

Emmeline's gaze raked over her face, which was now stripped bare. Why hadn't she seen it before that fear seeped from every pore? She placed a hand on top of Stephanie's and pitched her voice to a reassuring whisper. "I agree that the Raven cannot continue to evade justice. But to keep you safe, you have to help me."

Stephanie nodded and swallowed down the lump that had lodged in her throat.

"Stonecrest," she croaked. "That was the company." Her chest swelled on a shuddering breath. "I knew him as William Faraday. But you're right, he sheds his name like a snake sheds its skin. Once I discover the latest one, he vanishes. Then, I have to start all over again to trace the new identity he's assumed and it turns out to be a blind alley." Her jaw clenched with frustration. "That's happened too many times for me to count."

Emmeline patted her arm. "Leave it with me." She rooted around her handbag and until she found her card case. She flicked it open with her thumb. "Here's one of my business cards. If you think of anything else, give me a ring. You can always reach me on my mobile." She hesitated a moment before adding, "I'm on my way to Scotland Yard to see Superintendent Burnell. Why not come with me? He can put you in protective custody or, at the very least, have you watched until the Raven is caught."

Stephanie gave a violent shake of her head. "No," she snarled. "I'd only be a bigger target. I'm better off moving about on my own." She waved Emmeline's card in the air. "I'll check in with you. If you don't hear from me in a day or two, you'll know I'm dead."

Chapter 27

Armed with the fresh details Stephanie had provided, Emmeline's mind began fleshing out a fuller sketch of the Raven.

William Faraday, Stonecrest, Spain. And he was on the Russian payroll as a killer-for-hire. Was he a spy too? That remained to be determined.

Stonecrest, Stonecrest, she repeated to herself and frowned. She had heard that name recently. Where was it?

Her feet practically flew down the pavement. She couldn't wait to dissect what she had learned with Superintendent Burnell and Sergeant Finch. She was slightly breathless by the time she burst through the Dacre Street entrance to Scotland Yard. However, she grinned upon seeing Sergeant Trimble on duty at the desk. He never made a fuss about her requests to see Burnell. She walked over to the constable and exchanged a few words. It was always the best policy to be polite and keep people on one's good side. Result: she was sauntering toward the bank of lifts within minutes, visitor's pass in hand.

When the doors slid open on the seventh floor, she bolted from the car, without a glance to her right or left. She tried not to catch anyone's eye as she headed straight to the superintendent's office.

She rapped lightly on the door with her knuckles.

"Come in," Burnell called.

"Right, Finch, I want you to go through McCallister's—"
He broke off and covered the phone's mouthpiece when he
looked up to find Emmeline hovering on the threshold.

She offered him a sheepish grin and a lifted a hand in a
wave. "Good afternoon, Superintendent Burnell."

Burnell ended his call and snatched off his spectacles
from his nose. He leaned back in his chair and steepled his
hands over his ample midsection. His eyes narrowed. "If it
isn't London's most intrepid reporter."

He waited until she had closed the door and slunk across
the room to settle herself in one of the chairs opposite his
desk. "Rumors have reached my ears that you and your
husband have been very busy digging up information on
interesting topics. For example, I hear you're a fount of
knowledge about someone called the Raven."

She beamed at him. "That's precisely why I'm here."

Burnell's lips curved into a smile, but his blue eyes held
no glimmer of amusement. "Really? What a treat." He
rubbed his hands together. "I can hardly contain my
excitement." He lifted a finger and reached for his phone.
"Hold that thought. It wouldn't be fair to leave Finch out
of all the fun, now would it?" Then into the receiver, he
said, "Finch, step into my office for a moment."

Finch's reddish-brown head popped round the door
almost instantly. "Sir?"

"Look who dropped by for a *long* overdue visit. Aren't
we lucky?"

"Ah," Finch murmured and inclined his head.
"Emmeline." His curt tone was softened by the quick smile
he flashed.

Burnell flapped an impatient hand at the empty chair
beside her. "All right. Come along."

Once Finch was seated, the superintendent folded his
hands on the desk and launched into his grilling. "The

Raven. A dangerous criminal, I assume. But that's all we know because everything about him is very hush-hush. And yet, despite all the people in law enforcement, you and Longdon are the only ones who are privileged to have been told a damn thing about him."

She cleared her throat and crossed one leg over the other. "It's not quite like that."

"How is it then?" he asked brusquely.

She tried another smile, but it failed to melt the granite wall Burnell had erected. Her gaze slid back to Finch. Some of the tension eased from her body, when she saw that she had at least one ally.

She nodded and turned back to Burnell. "It wasn't my intention to keep anything from you," she began contritely. "It's simply that so much information has come tumbling out in the last twenty-four hours that it's been a race to make sense of it all."

"Here's a novel idea," the superintendent countered. "Why not leave the investigation to the professionals? After all, that's our job."

"Not a very sporting point of view, Oliver." Gregory's voice drifted to their ears.

Their heads lifted in unison to find him leaning against the door frame, arms folded over his chest. A mischievous grin broke out over his face. He winked at Emmeline.

"All Emmy and I are trying to do is ease your daily burden," he said as he took a step into the office. "We're concerned about your health, Oliver." He wagged an admonishing finger at the detective. "You know you've been looking more than a tad peaky lately."

"Longdon," the superintendent roared. "It's about time you showed your miserable face."

Gregory clucked his tongue, as he hitched a hip on the corner of Burnell's desk. "Dear, oh dear. Someone is in a foul mood today. I put it down to that prat Cruickshank.

That's the only explanation for such a remark. I'll have you know that there is nothing repulsive about my face. Emmy happens to adore seeing it." He flicked a glance at his wife. "Don't you, darling?"

Before her tongue could formulate a response, Burnell grumbled, "Naturally. She's your partner in crime. She's the only one on this earth who can stand seeing you."

"Isn't that a bit harsh?" The superintendent scowled, but Gregory cheerfully prattled on, "We're fine, upstanding citizens, who have no connection whatsoever to the criminal underworld." Burnell rolled his eyes at the ceiling. "And to correct you on another point, there are a great *many* people who blossom in my presence. I have a knack for bringing out the best in people."

A disbelieving grunt rumbled from Burnell's throat. "You're delusional. Only women fawn all over you."

"Feeling a bit jealous, are you?"

"Hardly," Burnell sniffed.

"I'll have you know women are the more discerning of the human species. They're highly perceptive and attuned to the nuances that we inferior males are wont to miss."

A pink flush began spreading beneath the superintendent's beard like lava oozing down the sides of a volcano. He jerked his thumb at Gregory and rounded on Emmeline. "How can you stand this rubbish day in and day out?"

She shrugged her shoulders and gave him a sheepish smile.

Gregory reached for one of her hands and twined his fingers through hers. "It's called love, Oliver."

Burnell slammed his open palm against the desk, making his spectacles, files, pens, pencils and any other loose objects jump. "Enough. The two of you have just wasted an eternity of our precious time without telling us a blasted thing. Start spilling what you know about the Raven or I swear I'll throw you both in a cell."

Gregory sketched a cheeky salute. "*Oui, mon général*."

He proceeded to recount his discussion with Villiers about the Raven. However, he kept mum about his dealings with Jasper and his arrangement to sell the Pink Courtesan and Blue Angel. He was certain that the two detectives would disapprove of his taking such initiative to flush the Raven out into the open. Besides, it wouldn't do for them to know that he was in possession of two stolen diamonds. Meanwhile, Emmy would be none too pleased, to say the least. As an eminently considerate man, he justified this omission as not wanting to burden any of them with the knowledge.

"Is that it?" Burnell demanded.

"You have squeezed the well dry, Oliver." In a dramatic gesture, Gregory placed his wrist against his forehead and exhaled a sigh. "I feel mentally drained."

The superintendent smirked. "If only that were true. Your tongue has a life of its own. It runs on and on and on." He stroked his beard as he peered at Gregory suspiciously. "Why do I get the feeling that you're concealing something?"

Gregory's eyes widened, his countenance a portrait of innocence. "Me? I wouldn't dare withhold information from a distinguished member of the police force. It would be unconscionable." He paused, his gaze darting around the office. "Do you happen to have a Bible handy? I'll swear on it, if you like."

"Not only is that sacrilegious," Burnell scoffed, "it would be an exercise in futility. You'd probably have your fingers crossed behind your back."

"I'm rather curious. Were you born jaded? Or is it a trait you developed over the years?"

"Stuff it, Longdon."

Emmeline rapped her knuckles on the desk to draw the

men's attention. "I can add a few more details that Gregory is unaware of because this is the first opportunity we've had to exchange notes."

"I must say I've felt the void, darling." Gregory playfully blew her a kiss.

"All right, you lovebirds," the superintendent intoned irritably. "My office is not the place for saccharine displays of marital affection."

Gregory cast a pitying glance at him. "I despair of you. I really do. You have no romance in your soul."

"There's no room for romance in a murder investigation," Finch interjected bluntly.

Emmeline squeezed her husband's knee to prevent a snippy rejoinder escaping from his lips. He smiled and inclined his head deferentially.

She picked up the thread by passing on what Philip had revealed in confidence about the Raven's victims being Russian defectors or having the misfortune to have crossed Putin in one way or another. Then, she related Stephanie's harrowing story. By the time, she finished all three men were scowling in concern. They did not like the fact that Stephanie, a confessed murderer, had tracked Emmeline down.

"The minute Villiers reared his head in this case, I knew there would be complications," Burnell groused. "After what you've just told us"—his intense stare latched onto Emmeline's face—"I like it even less now."

She made a dismissive gesture with her hand. "My instincts are screaming that she's telling the truth."

Burnell leaned forward and propped his forearms on his desk. "That only increases my anxiety."

Finch nodded in grim agreement. "If she's right, and the Raven is having her followed," he pointed out, "that means he *knows* she met with you. The last person Stephanie approached was Verena Penrose and now she's dead."

Emmeline avoided looking Gregory in the eye and instead went on as if Finch hadn't made his unsettling, and unwanted, observation. "We have three leads: William Faraday, Stonecrest, and Spain. Isn't that wonderful?"

Burnell folded his arms over his chest, Finch raised a reddish-brown eyebrow in exasperation, while Gregory, lips pursed in disapproval, gave a curt shake of his head.

"No," her husband pronounced with finality.

Deliberately misunderstanding him, she remarked, "I find that rather surprising. Here we were with *nothing* and now we're overwhelmed with a deluge of information. I, for one, can't wait to get cracking." She cocked her head to one side and pressed a finger to her cheek. "Hmm. I think the best place to start is with William Faraday, although he's probably changed his identity a dozen times by now. Still, we're better off than we were this morning."

Her brows knit together. "Stonecrest," she murmured. "Why does that sound familiar?"

Gregory smiled and cupped her chin with one hand, as she pondered. "Emmy, you've gone above and beyond. Leave it in Oliver and Finch's capable hands."

"That's the first sensible thing you've uttered today," Burnell commented.

Emmeline grasped her husband's hand and detached his fingers, dropping them as if they were hot coals. "I don't interfere with your work—"

"You do with ours," Burnell muttered under his breath.

Gregory's eyes glinted in amusement, but Emmeline's gaze narrowed, lashing the superintendent with fury.

She opened her mouth to unleash a steady stream of aggrieved objections, but Burnell held up a hand. "Don't take that the wrong way." Her lips parted again, but he gave a crisp shake of his head. "And don't spout that drivel at me about the public having a right to know. It does *not*. The public will have the facts, all the facts, when we apprehend the murderer. Not before. We don't want to tip our hand to the Raven, if he's the culprit, or anyone else who may be involved. My greatest concern by far is ensuring your safety"—he shot a glance at Gregory—"and your husband's."

Gregory pressed a hand to his heart. "I'm touched, Oliver."

Burnell arched an eyebrow. "*Superintendent Burnell*," Gregory corrected quickly.

"We're not the enemy," Finch added quietly.

She pressed her tongue against her cheek and surveyed each man in turn, as she chose her words carefully. "I see your point, of course, and appreciate the fine line you must toe."

The superintendent settled back in his chair and favored her with a smile. "Good. I'm glad you're being sensible"

She returned his smile. "I'd like to point out that Villiers's threats couldn't persuade me to drop the story. So, what makes you think I will do so at your request?" She tapped the desk with her forefinger. "My job is to report the news, good, bad, or indifferent. Verena's murder and the Raven are news." She tossed her chin in the air defiantly. "I haven't broken any laws."

Burnell scowled at her. "Only if you count sheer pigheadedness as a crime."

"There's no reason this should be a battle. I came here in a spirit of cooperation. We can pool our resources. You know I'd never print anything without corroboration, nor do I disclose sensitive security information."

Although Burnell and Finch were exasperated, they couldn't argue with this statement.

Emmeline suddenly sat up straight and her eyes widened. "How stupid of me. I know why Stonecrest rang a bell." She turned to Gregory. "That's the name of the phony company Verena had Mick Walcott establish for her boiler room scam. She *was* taunting the Raven, aka William Faraday." She paused, before pointing out, "Scott McCallister was in the bar at the theatre. The CCTV caught him. It could be him."

Emmeline glimpsed the guarded look that passed between the two detectives. "You've discovered something else about McCallister, haven't you?" Her gaze shot from one to the other, as excitement swelled in her chest. She leaned forward in her chair. "I'm right." When they remained silent, she persisted. "It's no good trying to fob me off. You know I'll find out in the end anyway. Why not save yourself the fuss?"

Burnell stroked his beard. "Yes," he conceded reluctantly. He raised a warning finger. "I will tell you on the condition that it doesn't appear in tomorrow's paper. I don't want our case to be jeopardized."

Emmeline nodded eagerly, offering a smile for good measure. "You have my word."

The superintendent regarded her thoughtfully. "Hmph. I'll hold you to that. Right, then. We interviewed Mr. Sanderson this afternoon and he told us that McCallister passed him on the stairs, when he was on the way to Verena Penrose's box. In his initial statement, McCallister said that he never spoke with her that night."

"Ha," Emmeline said with undisguised relish. "However, I suspect there's more."

Burnell silently swore. Oh, how he wished that she wasn't so astute.

Gregory tucked his chin to his chest and chuckled. "I did tell you that women were more perceptive. Emmy is the *crème de la crème.*"

The superintendent glared at him. "You are here on sufferance. Just remember that."

"Ah, no need to feel embarrassed. You miss me terribly when I'm not around. It's all right to admit it, Oliver. We're bosom mates for life. Nothing will tear us asunder." He fluttered his eyelashes coquettishly.

Burnell tilted his head back and implored the ceiling. "Lord, a man can only stand so much torture. One day I'll crack."

The Almighty was unimpressed and once again refrained from offering him an ounce of pity.

Finch cleared his throat and intervened, while Burnell and Gregory engaged in a silent duel of wills. The sergeant addressed Emmeline. "McCallister was not pleased when we popped by his flat this morning. It was patently obvious that he wanted to see the back of us but didn't want to arouse our suspicions by refusing to answer our questions. He failed on that score. On the pretense of needing the loo, I had a putter around his bedroom. You can learn a lot about a man in the room where he sleeps. The things that stood out immediately were McCallister's packed bags. After we returned to the station, I did some checking and discovered that he's booked on a Saturday night flight to Geneva."

Emmeline's dark eyes sparkled with smugness. "McCallister was a fool to lie. We already knew he was at the theatre that night. He should have admitted that he had met with Verena. It was only a matter of time before you found out."

"He was probably counting on the ceiling collapse to obscure his movements," Finch suggested.

Emmeline turned to him. "Yes, but at the outset of the evening, he couldn't have known that the ceiling would cave in. If everything had gone according to his plan, McCallister would have slipped away unnoticed. With everyone streaming out of their seats into the corridor and squeezing down the staircase, he was trapped in the crush and ran a greater risk of being seen." She bit her lip and her brows knit together. "Clearly, McCallister is the murderer. What bothers me, though, is how he did it. He couldn't have taken Verena by surprise. From my seat, I saw her turn around and speak to someone."

She closed her eyes, replaying the scene in her mind. Verena smiling. A man's hand caressing her cheek. "Verena would have screamed her head off and thrashed about if he had tried to wrap his hands around her throat."

Her eyes flew open. "I keep asking myself why she didn't scream. Why didn't Verena run?"

"She didn't view McCallister as a threat," Gregory suggested.

"Even so, she would have fought back once she realized that he wasn't there for an amorous rendezvous. The human instinct for survival takes over." She gave a dissatisfied shake of her head. "It doesn't make sense."

"Ahem." Burnell cleared his throat and her gaze shot to his face. "This is off the record."

She rolled her eyes toward the ceiling. "You and Philip are becoming far too fond of that phrase lately," she complained. "At this rate, the *Clarion* will sack me because I can't get an attribution from my sources."

"Emmeline." The superintendent's tone held a warning note.

A martyred sigh escaped her lips. "Fine. If it means I get a tiny crumb of information."

The superintendent gave a curt nod. He knew she would keep her word. "The postmortem found that the victim had traces of hydrocodone in her system. According to Meadows, it's a common prescription painkiller that can be used to treat moderate to severe pain. However, it also causes sedation and euphoria while slowing the central nervous system."

"Charming," Gregory spat in disgust. "McCallister smiled and flirted, as he waited for Verena to pass out."

Emmeline shivered involuntarily. "How utterly cold and calculating."

"The toxicology report indicates that the drug was ingested about half an hour to forty-five minutes before she died."

She frowned. "But that would mean it happened right under our noses in the bar during the intermission."

"Although McCallister denied speaking with the victim," Finch pointed out, "he could easily have slipped something into her drink when the barman and everyone else was momentarily distracted by your argument. It would have been easy for McCallister to melt into the crowd. Perhaps he loitered about in the loo, until the bell rang for the audience to return to its seats. Or..." He broke off, when he caught Burnell's eye.

"Or?" Emmeline prodded, her ears perking up.

"What I think our friends are trying to say, darling," Gregory interjected, "is that McCallister had an accomplice who put the drug in her drink, ensuring that she would have passed out by the time he nipped up to her box or he wouldn't have to wait too long. Am I right, Oliver?"

"That's the working theory," Burnell responded gruffly. "It stays in this room."

"Understood. We wouldn't want to jeopardize the case. However," Emmeline broached cautiously, "it is only natural for me to ask whether you have questioned McCallister again in light of this new evidence about the drug and the fact that Mr. Sanderson saw him."

"No comment," was the superintendent's terse reply

Emmeline propped one elbow on his desk and rested her chin on her hand. "I appreciate the delicate situation, but you must give me something."

His brow puckered in stubbornness, he folded his arms across his chest.

His sullen silence failed to make an impression and she continued to press her point. "Oh, come now, Superintendent. You do realize that the public will begin shouting cover-up, if you don't issue some sort of statement about the investigation's progress." She offered him her sweetest smile.

His gaze flitted from her face to Gregory, who raised an eyebrow. Burnell exhaled a long breath and wagged an accusatory finger at him. "Longdon, you are a corruptive influence on your wife."

A faint smile tugged at the corners of Gregory's mouth. "Emmy is her own person. She makes her own decisions. It's more than my life is worth to try to sway her one way or another."

She gave a curt nod of confirmation of the deadly consequences in store should he contemplate such foolish behavior.

Burnell grunted, while Finch mumbled, "Two peas in a pod."

She drew circles on the desk with her finger. "You do know that it is far better to give a statement to a friendly journalist like me"—a cajoling smile danced on her lips as she lifted her eyes to meet the superintendent's—"than to have one of my aggressive colleagues banging on your door and hounding your every step. I'm on your side. The side of the truth."

"Hmph," Burnell sneered. "The only difference between you and your colleagues is that you attack with velvet gloves. The bruises appear only after you've gone."

Her smile broadened. "Does that mean you'll make an official statement?" She was already digging in her handbag for her notebook and pen.

The superintendent threw his hands up in the air in mock surrender. "All right." He gave a gusty sigh. "If only to get rid of you and your husband."

"For the record," Gregory piped up, unhelpfully, "I must point out that not half an hour ago, you were chomping at the bit to see us. Demanding a report on our movements."

Burnell made a dismissive gesture with his hand. "I never want to see *you*, Longdon. But the problem is that somehow you and your wife always seem to be in the middle of *my* investigations. Sticking your noses in where they don't belong. It's uncanny. I can't get away from you."

Gregory clapped him on the shoulder. "But, Oliver, you wouldn't want to. Your day would be terribly empty without us. I hate to think of you sitting locked up in your office, your brain turning to mush, because you lack the stimulation that only we can provide."

Burnell shook off his grasp and focused his attention on Emmeline. "You can tell your readers that the Metropolitan Police is following up on several lines of inquiry and hope to make an arrest soon. That will let the public know that we're actively working on the case."

Emmeline shook her head. "I'm afraid that won't satisfy anyone. I need more details. How about if I say the postmortem revealed that Verena Penrose had been drugged?" Two vertical lines etched themselves between the superintendent's brows. "This prompted the police to question a person of interest, who had been planning to flee the country this weekend. Definitely dodgy behavior and highly newsworthy."

"Emmeline." Her name rumbled off Burnell's tongue, as his fingers curled into fists.

"What? It's the truth. I haven't compromised your investigation. I didn't mention your theory about an accomplice. I'm certain anyone on the police beat already knows that you've interviewed a suspect. Mind you, it would be far more authoritative if I were allowed to name McCallister." One eyebrow quirked upward.

"No," the superintendent snapped.

She pressed her lips together, but she didn't argue further. With her pen poised over her notebook, she asked,

"Has McCallister turned over his passport? That much you can tell me."

"We requested that he do so," Finch answered for his boss. "He was livid and demanded to see his lawyer. In the meantime, I'm taking another look at his finances."

Something in his tone made her take particular notice. "What is it?"

"They only go back five years. It's as if McCallister didn't exist before he turned up in London."

She scribbled in her notebook. "Hmm, interesting," she murmured. "That seems to support the theory that he's the Raven."

"We can't make that assumption at this stage," Burnell pointed out. "We simply don't have the proof."

She inclined her head. "Fair enough. But since the subject of the Raven has been raised, I'd like to write that while details remain sketchy, one of the theories that the police are exploring is that Verena Penrose could have been killed because she was working on a story about an international assassin."

The superintendent thumped his fist on the desk. "You are pushing your luck."

"All right. How about Verena was working on a story about an elusive, international crime figure?"

"I don't like it," Burnell groused. "But I can live with that."

"Good." She closed her notebook and tucked it safely into her handbag. "One last thing." He eyed her warily as she rose. "Can I quote you, Superintendent?"

"Very well," he replied reluctantly. "But from this moment on" —he leaned forward and fixed his glacial stare on husband and wife— "I want the two of you to keep me informed of what you're up to *at all times*. Finch and I have far too much work to do as it is. We don't want to find your bodies in an alley."

Gregory chuckled as he held Emmeline's coat for her to put it on. "Your wish is our command. As a demonstration of good faith, I am officially informing you that I will be at the reading of Verena Penrose's will tomorrow at her solicitor's office. I will be there as Symington's representative since Verena insured her jewels with the firm. Meanwhile, I can double as your secret spy and report all the juicy details."

Burnell opened his mouth, but Emmeline cut across him. "Make that two spies. Stuart Aldridge, one of the partners at Aldridge and Thayer, rang this morning and asked me to attend. He said that Verena left something for me."

The superintendent's eyes bulged in disbelief, as they stood before him beaming like two children up to mischief.

Gregory gave him a cheeky wink. "This is your lucky day, Oliver. You couldn't have asked for two more reliable sources. Well, until tomorrow. Cheerio."

He hustled Emmeline out of the office before Burnell surged out of his chair.

"*Lucky*?" the superintendent bellowed. "I was cursed at birth."

Chapter 28

Home for Aldridge & Thayer was a modern building with a curved glass façade. The law firm's offices were a five-minute walk from the Holborn Underground station. Emmeline and Gregory stepped off the lift on the fourth floor and into a cavernous communal space painted in subdued tones of beige and cream. The noonday sun cascaded through the wall of windows overlooking the traffic below on High Holborn.

They gave their names to the receptionist, who smiled and put a call through to the senior partner's secretary to announce their arrival. They had barely settled down on one of the cream-colored sofas when a compact woman in her mid-thirties dressed in an elegantly tailored café au lait suit strode toward them. Her chestnut hair was pulled back from her oval face and fastened at the back of her head with a mother of pearl clip.

"Good afternoon, Miss Kirby and Mr. Longdon. I'm Daphne, Mr. Aldridge's secretary," she said with a smile. She waited for them to rise, before thrusting out her hand. "He asked me to show you to the conference room. Please follow me. The others are already waiting."

Gregory glanced at his watch. "We're sorry to have delayed the proceedings. We were told the meeting was at noon."

He offered her an apologetic smile. Emmeline couldn't fail to notice the pink flush that suffused the secretary's cheeks and the appreciative glint in her gray eyes, as she lapped up every ounce of Gregory's charms.

The woman waved a hand in the air, but continued walking. "You're not late." She dropped her voice and whispered out of the corner of her mouth, "The others arrived early. It's a phenomenon known as the vulture instinct." She sighed and gave a resigned shake of her head. "I should be used to it, but I still find greed distasteful."

"Well, here we are," Daphne said without expecting an opinion on the subject. They stopped in front of a door to a rectangular conference room with glass walls, which failed to muffle the sound of male voices raised in heated argument.

"Oh, dear" the secretary mouthed and rapped her knuckles once on the door. All conversation came to an abrupt end, as she opened it and stepped aside for Emmeline and Gregory to enter.

Emmeline's eyes widened when she saw Sheldrake *and* McCallister seated opposite one another at the long table, virtually foaming at the mouth liked two caged dogs. McCallister had half-moon purple smudges beneath his bloodshot eyes. A faint shadow of stubble covered his cheeks. Obviously, his little interlude at the police station had him tossing and turning all night. *Guilty conscience?* her mind posited as she repressed a smile. His hands were clasped in front of him, skin chalk-white and taut over his knuckles.

"*You,*" he hissed, his voice trembling with undisguised rage. He pushed himself to his feet. "It's all your fault. You sent the police to poke their noses into my business."

Emmeline squared her shoulders. She was not going to be cowed by this outburst. "Mr. McCallister, the *only* thing that attracted the police's scrutiny was your actions," she replied tartly. "I'm more than happy to give you an opportunity to tell your side of the story, *if* you agree to an interview. For the record, I'd like to point out that you refused to do so when I spoke to you yesterday. Perhaps you've had a change of heart now."

He took a step toward her and snarled, "It will be a dark day in hell, before I let you twist my words around to make a name for yourself."

She shrugged. "Ah, well, if that's your attitude. You can't have it both ways."

"Why you, scheming little…"

Gregory pressed a hand against the other man's chest and gave him a not-so-gentle shove backward. "I suggest you sit down, mate, before you embarrass yourself any further." His eyes dared the other man to do otherwise.

McCallister's nostrils flared. "Who the devil are you?"

"I'll tell you." Sheldrake leaped up from his chair. "He's her bloody husband." His gaze shot from Gregory to Emmeline. "That's right. I found out. You didn't think I would, did you? I'd like to know the game the two of you are playing." He slowly circled around the table. "You came into my home, during a very difficult time, under false pretenses, giving two different names. And here you are again." He tapped the table with his forefinger. "This is a private matter. The press was not invited, nor is it wanted."

"I assure you, Mr. Sheldrake," Emmeline offered in earnest, "we did not misrepresent ourselves in any way. I use my maiden name professionally. There was nothing underhand about our visit the other day. Verena's murder simply has our respective jobs working toward the same goal. That's the long and short of it."

Sheldrake scoffed, "I don't believe a word that comes out of your mouth. You abused my trust." He flicked a disgusted glance at Gregory. "Both of you."

"I'm sorry you feel that way, but—"

He held up a hand. "I've had enough of your sniveling excuses. Get out or I'll have your removed."

Ugly crimson stains flamed beneath his beard. Emmeline drew in a sharp breath. She was used to the public's negative view of the press. However, his vehemence was unjustified.

"Ahem." A man cleared his throat.

They turned in unison in the direction of the voice. It belonged to a tall gentleman with a head of thick silver hair who was dressed in an impeccably tailored charcoal double-breasted suit, pristine white shirt, and navy tie. His shrewd blue eyes regarded them calmly. Emmeline assumed that he must be the senior partner, Stuart Aldridge. She hadn't noticed him until that moment.

He strode toward a chair at the head of the table, where several closed files had been placed in two piles. "I suggest that we sit down and proceed to the matter at hand." His tone was even, but it held a firm command that discouraged further acrimonious bickering.

Sheldrake grumbled to himself as he returned to his seat, while McCallister plunked down heavily in the closest chair. Emmeline and Gregory settled into chairs side by side at a safe distance from the two men.

Aldridge slipped his spectacles over the bridge of his nose and opened a file before him. He skimmed the top page, although Emmeline was certain he probably knew its contents word for word. Most likely, the action was intended to give the flaring tempers time to cool.

It failed.

"I find this situation intolerable," Sheldrake blurted out.

Aldridge sighed and removed his spectacles. The planes and angles of his long face were pinched with annoyance.

"It was a distasteful shock," Sheldrake went on, "to discover my wife's lover here, but" —he jerked his thumb at Emmeline and Gregory— "to have those two intruding is too much."

Ah, so he was aware Verena was having an affair with McCallister, Emmeline commented to herself. *Well, that's not surprising. He appears to be an intelligent man.* She frowned, as she studied his profile. *I wonder if he knew about Adam.*

Aldridge gave a curt nod and slipped his spectacles back on. "Right, duly noted. I appreciate your position, Mr. Sheldrake. The reading of a will is always a delicate and stressful matter for everyone involved. But on the topic of Miss Kirby and Mr. Longdon's presence, they are here legitimately. And they will remain as long as I deem necessary."

Sheldrake's lips parted to protest further, but the lawyer ignored him and breezed ahead. "I'm glad we've cleared that up. One small matter before we proceed. One of Ms. Penrose's beneficiaries could not attend this meeting because of a scheduling conflict. I went over the details with him over the phone."

The aggrieved husband lapsed into surly silence. His lips were pressed in a tight line and his brown gaze simmered with loathing. Surely, the volley of daggers flying from his eyes had perforated McCallister's torso a hundred times over, Emmeline thought.

The lawyer's voice dragged her from these observations. "I want to make it perfectly clear from the outset"—he tapped the file with his forefinger—"that Ms. Penrose's will is airtight from a legal standpoint." He paused, as his gaze roamed over the faces of his captive audience. "Despite the fact that she changed it completely a week ago."

McCallister's sensuous mouth curved into a reptilian leer, while the smug gleam in his eyes telegraphed the fact that he was already aware of this fact. "Do go on, Mr.

Aldridge," he entreated solicitously. "I'm fascinated by the law."

Emmeline's brows shot up at this brash display of greed, arrogance, and poor taste. She noted that across the table Sheldrake was twisting his signet ring around his pinky and gnashing his teeth.

Seeing the lay of the land, Aldridge didn't mince words and moved to get through the proceedings as swiftly as possible. He cleared his throat. "I, Verena Jane Penrose, being of sound mind," he read, "at the time this will was written would like to recognize two important men in my life. My husband, Craig Sheldrake, and my friend, Scott McCallister."

The lawyer fell silent and everyone held his or her breath.

"First dear Craig, you are not the man I thought you were. My biggest regret is that I married you." Emmeline put a hand to her mouth to stifle a gasp. She shouldn't be surprised at Verena's lack of shame or tact, even at the end. "Still, I'm not a hypocrite. Life wasn't all bitter disillusionment. I took my pleasure where I could," Aldridge continued without emotion. "The secrets I uncovered will pay hefty dividends. I'm just sorry I won't be around to see the results of what I set in motion. I've had to leave the details in someone else's hands. But enough of that. Down to business as my wise dad would have said. I'm a woman of considerable means and you are my next of kin. Therefore, I want to leave you something priceless."

Sheldrake straightened his spine and his nervous fingers stilled.

The lawyer lifted his eyes and fixed his stare on Sheldrake. "I leave you my favorite photo of me. The one taken in Cannes last year. I've had a silver frame engraved especially. I know you'll treasure it always."

Sheldrake blinked several times and slumped back in his

chair. His jaw slackened and his complexion took on an ashen hue beneath his beard. It appeared the air had been knocked from his lungs. Clearly, he deemed Verena's action as incomprehensible. A double betrayal of their marriage.

McCallister answered his hostile glare with a mocking smile. "No hard feelings, mate. It's only money after all." Then to Aldridge, he said, "Do go on." He shot his cuff and glanced at his watch. "I hope to catch my financial advisor this afternoon, so that he can start making arrangements for my money. But first, I'll have to know how large of an inheritance I can expect."

Emmeline's sensibilities churned with revulsion. She raised an eyebrow at Gregory, silently asking "Did the man forget that the police suspect him of Verena's murder?"

If Burnell and Finch prove their case, McCallister wouldn't be able to touch a penny of the money.

She could see the same thoughts were running through Gregory's mind. They both focused their attention on the lawyer again. If the last few minutes were a barometer and knowing Verena's penchant for vindictiveness, more fireworks were sure to be in store this afternoon. Emmeline was impatient to learn what the woman could possibly have left her. She had no illusions that it was money.

Aldridge's forehead furrowed in puzzlement. "Mr. McCallister, I'm afraid you are under some misconception."

The smile lingered on McCallister's lips, but a wary expression had clouded his eyes. "What do you mean?" he demanded guardedly.

"All will be made clear in a moment, if you'll just allow me to continue." He found the point where he had left off and resumed reading, "Now for Scott McCallister, my devastatingly handsome lover. Darling, what can I say? I appreciated your enthusiasm between the sheets. You're a true master of the sensual arts." McCallister preened, while nausea roiled Emmeline's stomach. "However when I was thirteen, my dad had a talk with me about your type—"

McCallister cut across him. "Type? What does she mean?"

The lawyer went on as if he hadn't spoken. "—You're nothing more than a gigolo. It was never going to last and you were never going to become my next husband. I did like you, though. So, to help you remember all our stolen hours of pleasure, I'm leaving you that naughty photo you took of me during our little jaunt in Bermuda. I've had a silver frame engraved for it."

McCallister thumped his fist against the table. "The lying, conniving witch. She played me for a fool."

Emmeline dipped her head and bit back a smile. She didn't dare cast a glance at Gregory because she knew she would start laughing at McCallister's well-deserved comeuppance. From beneath her eyelashes, she could see Sheldrake lapping up with relish his rival's outraged disbelief.

McCallister surged to his feet. "I'll sue. She promised—"

Aldridge shook his head. "I wouldn't advise it. If you'll recall, I did warn you that the will is sound." His tone was clipped. "There are no loopholes. I saw to that. Now, please sit down."

"But, but," McCallister stammered. "She told me…." His sentence trailed off as he sank back into his chair, deflated and outmaneuvered probably for the first time in his life.

The lawyer's gaze skimmed over each of their faces. "I'd appreciate it if there were no more interruptions." He gave a crisp nod. "Right. For Emmeline Kirby, editorial director of investigative features at *The Clarion*, I leave an envelope. Although I have always despised her, and I know the feeling is mutual, she is the only person I can trust to see this thing through."

Aldridge opened another folder and took out the envelope in question. He wordlessly slid it across the table to Emmeline.

She stared down at it. Her name was scrawled across the front in Verena's spiky hand. She flipped it over, stuck her finger under one corner, and proceeded to tear it open. When she drew the letter out, a tiny key tumbled out. She frowned at it as she turned it over in her palm.

She shook her head in bafflement. Hopefully, this wasn't some sort of twisted game. Her lips moved silently, as she skimmed the page.

Emmeline,

I overplayed my hand. However, the Raven is not as clever as he thinks. This is a key to a safety deposit box at the Cottingham branch in Berkeley Street. It contains a treasure trove of his dirty secrets. Go to the bank and ask for the manager, Howard Chivers. I've arranged everything. Show him your identification and the key. He will take you to the box. Under no *circumstances are you to deal with anyone else.*

I want you to destroy the Raven. My father may not have gone to Eton and Oxford, but he had a first-class brain. He was the one who conceived the diamond scheme. The Raven killed him and stole the idea. I only recently discovered this. However, the silver-tongued government bastard named Toby Crenshaw knew it. All those months I was helping him, he never breathed a word. For that he has to pay.

I've never liked you and always found your crusades excruciatingly tiresome. Now, though, I've come to understand what drives you. You're the only one I can turn to. Please do this. Not for me, but for something you prize above all else: justice.

Verena

Emmeline blew out a long breath and slumped back in her chair. It came as no shock that Villiers knew more than he had told them. That was the nature of the beast. Gregory caught her eye and raised an eyebrow. In answer to his mute question, she slid the letter across to him.

When he looked up, she tapped the paper and pitched her voice low. "The safety deposit box must be what Verena was babbling on about at the theatre." He gave a grim nod of agreement, while both Sheldrake and McCallister regarded her intently.

She tossed her chin in the air, tearing her gaze from their hostile speculation. Thoughts chased themselves round her mind. She was only half-listening to Aldridge. However, she sat bolt upright when he concluded, "And so, I leave my entire fortune to Adam Royce."

Her mouth went dry. Blindly, her fingers clutched at Gregory's sleeve. She couldn't have heard the lawyer properly.

"*Adam Royce?*" Sheldrake exploded, before she could make her tongue form any coherent words. He placed his palms on the table and gave a violent shake of his head. His shoulders began to convulse with hysterical, bitter laughter. "Royce and my wife. The joke's on me. I wonder what other nasty surprises are in store today." A tremor of wounded fury echoed in his voice.

McCallister, his face flushed, leaped out of his chair again. "This is a bloody farce."

He stalked to the door and wrenched it open. Whirling round, his black look scorched the three men and Emmeline to the bone. "You're not getting away with this conspiracy. Any of you. That's a promise," he declared savagely.

The door rattled on its hinges behind him like the macabre chattering of a corpse's teeth.

Emmeline's gaze fell upon Verena's letter again, the words blurring before her eyes. *Why*, she asked herself, *would Verena leave all her money to Adam? Was it part of her game to draw out the Raven? But how?* Her head was reeling. It didn't make any sense.

A tendril of cold dread clutched at her chest, choking the breath from her lungs. What if this unexpected turn of events makes Burnell jump to the conclusion that Adam knew about Verena's new will and killed her for her money? She ran a hand distractedly through her curls. Or worse yet, what if the superintendent reckons that Adam was one the who *persuaded* Verena to change it in his favor?

No, no, no. Burnell was too open-minded, she reasoned. Wasn't he?

She stuffed the letter back in the envelope and leaned over to whisper in Gregory's ear. "I have to get out of here." She pushed her chair back and waved the letter in the air. "I'm going to Cottingham. The sooner I get Verena's damning evidence out of that deposit box, the sooner I can clear the cloud hanging over Adam."

He rose too and touched her arm lightly. "Emmy, I know you're worried about how this looks for him. But everything will get sorted."

She slid a sideways glance to her left. Aldridge was gathering up his files and Sheldrake had his ear pressed to his mobile. His lips were moving rapidly in a heated, hushed conversation.

She turned back to Gregory and hissed out of the corner of her mouth, "You don't know that. Appearances, even false ones, have a way of making a strong impression that is hard to ignore."

"Darling, you're—Blast." He broke off when his mobile began purring. He drew it out of his pocket. His brows knit together when he saw the number. "Sorry. I have to take this."

She stood on tiptoe and gave him a peck on the cheek. "Go ahead. I'm going to the bank. I'll see you tonight at home."

"No, wait." He tried to snatch her arm, but she stepped just out of reach and dashed out of the conference room without a backward glance.

She was standing on the pavement debating whether to take a cab or hop on the Tube, when bony fingers dug into her shoulder and spun her around.

She gasped because she thought she was being mugged. Fear quickly turned into antagonism, when she found herself staring up into McCallister's seething face.

"How dare you, Mr. McCallister. Remove your hand before I scream for a constable." She spat the words at him.

His hand fell away, but his expression remained fierce. "You would just to spite me, wouldn't you?" He made a dismissive gesture in the air. "Never mind. I want—"

He was interrupted, when a familiar female voice called out, "Emmeline, thank goodness I've caught you."

Emmeline shook her head in disbelief, pivoting on her heel to see Stephanie clomping toward them. Her limp seemed more pronounced than it had yesterday. Her bad leg was dragging behind her, slowing her progress.

Stephanie was slightly breathless by the time she reached their side. She took a deep gulp of air. Her hand clamped around Emmeline's upper arm. "Thank goodness," she repeated. She shot a suspicious look at McCallister, suddenly becoming aware of his looming presence. "Who are you?"

"None of your business," he snarled.

Her brow furrowed and she drew Emmeline a few feet away from him. There was barely a hairsbreadth of space between their bodies.

"What are you doing here?" Emmeline demanded, shaking off her grasp. She took a pace backward.

"I rang the paper. They told me where to find you."

"I don't like the fact that you keep following me," she replied with a touch of asperity. "I gave you my card. You should have called first."

Stephanie bit her lip. "Sorry. I need to talk to you. *Now*. I have more information." Her tone was edged with desperation.

"Terrific. It's not a good time. I have an…important appointment. Pop by the *Clarion* this afternoon."

Emmeline left Stephanie standing there gaping. She wanted to put distance between them. This was the second time the woman had tracked her down. She shivered as Sergeant Finch's ominous words replayed themselves in her head. *The last person Stephanie approached was Verena Penrose and now she's dead.* And the woman had admitted to killing her first husband.

Yes, well. That was not a fact that she wanted to dwell on for the moment. She raised her hand and a cab drew up to the curb almost immediately. She clambered in and was telling the driver her destination, when Sheldrake ran up to the cab. Gregory was close on his heels.

"Wait," Sheldrake implored, as he banged on the window.

"Oi," the driver yelled. His gaze flicked to the rearview mirror. His eyes held a question as he watched Emmeline.

She sighed. "It's all right. If you could just wait a moment, please." She offered him a smile and rolled down the window.

Sheldrake bent down. He had one hand on the window and one foot on the curb. "As I was telling your husband"

—he waved a hand vaguely behind him— "I wanted to apologize for my behavior. It was inexcusable. The only thing I can offer in my defense is that these past few days have been one surprise after another. Apparently, I didn't know my wife as well as I thought I did. I didn't mean to take it out on you or your husband."

"Of course, I understand, Mr. Sheldrake. I, we"—she saw Gregory hovering at the distraught husband's side— "can't begin to imagine what you're going through. I want you to know that I will follow this story until Verena's murderer is caught. I realize that is cold comfort and can't bring her back." He gave a mute nod. "But I promise you that I will do my utmost not to intrude on your grief."

Sheldrake tapped the window with his palm and straightened up. When he spoke, his voice was hoarse. "Thank you. I suppose that's all I have a right to ask."

"No," she corrected. "You have a right to find a measure of peace. That can only come if justice is served." Out of the corner of her eye, she saw the driver drumming his fingers on the steering wheel impatiently. "I'm afraid I must go now."

"Yes, right. Of course." He stepped back onto the pavement.

She leaned her head out the window and told Gregory, "I'll ring you after I've been to the bank."

"I wish you'd let me come with you, darling."

"No, it's better if I go alone. The bank manager might be leery if I turn up with you in tow."

He couldn't argue with that reasoning and banged the top of the cab to let the driver know he could go.

As the cab trundled down High Holborn toward Kingsway, the driver kept up a running patter of conversation. Fortunately, he enjoyed the sound of his own voice so it was only necessary for Emmeline to offer a comment now and then. This gave her time to process everything that had come to light. She cursed the midday traffic. At this rate, the bank would be closed by the time she got there.

Stewing in frustration, she craned her neck to survey the situation on the road ahead of them. The driver let loose a string of invectives at a gleaming black Audi that cut in front of them.

Emmeline shared his dismay, but for an entirely different reason. She had caught a flash of Stephanie's face and couldn't believe who was in the car with her.

Chapter 29

The sharp gust of wind felt good against Stephanie's flaming cheeks, as she stepped onto the pavement leaving behind the cloying warmth of the Novikov restaurant and bar. Her head was spinning slightly and her legs felt a bit wobbly. Perhaps, it hadn't been wise to have that third cocktail on an empty stomach. On the other hand, it was a celebration. And oh, how she needed a stiffner to lift her spirit. She slapped her crippled leg. For once, the near-constant pain didn't bother her. Laughter erupted from deep within her belly and burst upon the cold air in a plume of wispy vapor. Finally after all these years, she could taste victory. She felt emboldened, alive, *free*. Her revenge would be sweet and so justly deserved.

Humming softly, she hitched her handbag higher on her shoulder and started to make her unsteady way toward Piccadilly. She lost her footing once, but she managed to right herself before she fell flat on her face. Whether it was the alcohol or sheer recklessness, she halted her shambling trek and pulled out her mobile. She blinked a few times, opening her eyes wide because the numbers blurred. In the end, she managed to punch the correct buttons.

She chuckled as the ringing echoed in her ear. The fog evaporated from her brain all of sudden and she demanded, "William? I'll always think of you as William. How strange it is to hear your voice. It's Stephanie, in case you hadn't guessed." She paused, a range of conflicting emotions choking the speech from her throat. She took a deep breath, her tone hardening with malice. "I'm back from the watery grave and here in London. Do you ever think about me?" No response. "Because I think about you." She ground her back teeth and hissed, "Every second of every minute of every day since that night. At last, I've caught up with you. Start looking over your shoulder. In a few days, your world is going to explode. Everyone is going to know that you're the Raven. It's time to pay for your crimes. Verena Penrose compiled a hefty dossier on you and I've just sold it to a very interested party. Now, I'm going to sit back and watch you go down in flames."

She severed the connection. She threw back her shoulders and tossed her head high. At last, she had exorcised him from her life forever.

ഐഐ

McCallister sat hunched in caramel leather armchair in the lounge bar. He was thankful for the anonymity of this shadowy corner. He rolled his whiskey tumbler between his hands, staring into its amber depths. He had merely moistened his lips. He couldn't manage even a single sip because his stomach was coiled in angry knots. Snippets of different conversations floated in the air around him, as he sat cursing Verena for outmaneuvering him. He slammed his glass down, sloshing some of the whiskey on the low table in front of him. He grunted and slumped back, stretching his long legs and crossing them at the ankles. His ego was irked at how easily she had deceived him. She was dead, but there was no way he was simply going to walk away. Someone had to pay.

He sat up straight and snatched up his mobile from the

smoothly polished table. He pressed it to his ear. It barely
rang once.

"A bit on edge, are we?" he spat acidly. "Good. Now,
listen. We agreed to split Verena's fortune fifty-fifty. It's
in your interest to get me my money. You owe me. If you
even think of crossing me, you'll regret it. Or should I say
the Raven will regret it?"

His mouth curved into a sinister smile as he patted a
leather satchel resting against his chair leg. "You're in no
position to bargain. I hold all the cards. I'm not going down
for Verena's murder, no matter how much you manipulate
the situation. You'll be relieved to hear that I still intend to
leave London. However, the bloody police have frozen my
bank account here. Therefore, the price has gone up. I want
one hundred thousand pounds in cash by this evening. That
should be enough to tide me over for a few days. I still
expect half of Verena's money. When it's transferred to my
Geneva account, then we can enter into negotiations for the
papers she had locked away in the bank." His fingers
caressed the satchel. "It makes for colorful reading. Verena
was extremely thorough. There are tidbits that I didn't
know. A certain nosy journalist would find it fascinating."

He propped one elbow on the armrest and listened for
several seconds. "Stop stalling. You're a clever chap. If
you weren't, the Raven wouldn't have survived this long.
And don't even think of fleeing to Spain or anywhere else
you fancy, before the money is in my hands. I don't care if
it's difficult to gather such a large sum in a few hours. Just
do it. You have until six-thirty. I'll be waiting in the main
section of the Victoria Embankment Gardens. It will
already be dark. Perfect for the exchange, but it's also a
public place. And remember," he added ominously,
"silence is golden. I'm not too proud to have my silence
bought. Money makes the world go round."

He gave a gusty laugh, as he ended the call. He took a

long swallow of whiskey, welcoming the burn as it traveled down his throat. After the fiasco at the lawyer's office, he felt as if he was back in control of the situation. He turned over in his mind the best, the most *lucrative*, way to make use of the papers in the satchel. They were far too precious to waste. Besides, it was high time the Raven's reign came to a close.

⌀⌀⌀

Emmeline pushed open the glass door, which was protected by a wrought-iron grill. She gritted her teeth as she stepped into the bank. She was not in the best of moods. The cab ride had taken twenty-five minutes because of the traffic. She clenched her fists. All that time wasted. She chided herself for not taking the Tube.

She set aside her irritability, pasted a smile on her lips, and politely asked the security guard where she could find the bank manager. He directed her to a young man seated at a desk in a cubicle with glass walls. "Check with Mark, the assistant manager, he'll be able to help you."

She thanked him and crossed to Mark's desk. She hovered outside his cubicle because he was on the phone. He flicked a glance at her and held one finger in the air. She nodded. Within a minute, he had concluded his conversation. He smiled and rose to his feet.

"Good afternoon, madam. How may I assist you?"

She drew out her press pass from her handbag and showed it to him. "I'm Emmeline Kirby, the editorial director of investigative features at *The Clarion*. Verena Penrose sent me a letter and told me to speak with Mr. Chivers. Apparently, she left me the contents of her safety deposit box."

Mark's brown eyes clouded with confusion as he scanned her press pass. "Ah, I see."

Emmeline frowned. "Is there a problem?"

He shook his head. "No, no. No problem. Let me see if Mr. Chivers is free." He snatched up his phone. His gaze kept snaking to her face, as he spoke into the mouthpiece. "Yes, Mr. Chivers, a Miss Kirby from *The Clarion* is here to see you." He lowered his voice. "It's about Ms. Penrose's safety deposit box." He was silent for a moment. "Right, I understand." He returned the receiver to its cradle and flashed a smile at her. "Mr. Chivers apologizes, but he has to resolve an issue. It shouldn't take long. He asked me to show you to his office." He extended an arm to his left. "If you'll follow me, please."

Mark made sure she was comfortably ensconced in one of the chairs in the bank manager's office and then excused himself, pleading pressures of work. He wished her a pleasant afternoon and was gone.

Ten minutes later, the door swung open and a tall, balding man in a charcoal suit, the jacket of which was a bit snug because of his paunch, strode into the room. His features were creased in a severe expression.

"Miss Kirby, is it?" he demanded in a clipped tone.

She smiled. "Yes. I believe Verena Penrose arranged for me to collect the contents of her safety deposit box."

He held up a hand. "Just a moment." He turned and opened the door. "Owen, please come in."

"Yes, Mr. Chivers."

Emmeline found herself staring up at the security guard she had spoken to earlier. He pressed the door closed behind him and planted himself in front of it.

Chivers gave him a curt nod and focused on Emmeline once more. "Now, tell me again. Who you are?"

Emmeline's back stiffened and the hairs on the back of her neck prickled. "As I told the other gentleman, I'm Emmeline Kirby, the editorial director of investigative features at *The Clarion*. Here's my press pass." She waved it at him.

He took her identification and studied it, before showing it to Owen, who examined it between his plump fingers.

"Look, I sense that there's a problem."

Chivers returned her press pass and replied in a lugubrious tone, "The problem is that Emmeline Kirby was here not more than fifteen minutes ago."

Emmeline's jaw went slack. "That's impossible."

The bank manager shook his head. "I'm afraid it's quite true. She had a letter from Ms. Penrose. Which leads me to ask again, who are you?"

"The woman was an impostor."

Chivers and the security guard traded a dubious look.

"I have proof. *I* have Verena's letter," she declared triumphantly. "It explains everything."

She opened her handbag and fumbled around in the inner pocket, where she had tucked the letter. But it was empty.

Without asking, she dumped the contents of her handbag on the desk. "I don't understand," she muttered under her breath, as her fingers picked through the jumbled heap.

"Unfortunately, I do," Chivers sneered. "You were trying to defraud this bank—"

Her head snapped up. "I was *not*. I'm a journalist. Ring the *Clarion*. The paper will vouch for me. Better yet, call Nigel Sanborn, the paper's corporate counsel. I'll give you his direct number." She hastily scribbled it down and thrust it at the bank manager. "He will set you straight. You've been duped by a criminal."

"That, young lady, is a matter for the police to decide." Then to the security guard, he said, "Owen, Mrs. Bartholomew is away on maternity leave. Put"—Chivers cast a withering glance at Emmeline—"whoever *she* is in her office. Here's the key."

"Please, miss," Owen implored as his hand gripped her elbow and gently lifted her to her feet.

"You've got the wrong end of the stick," Emmeline continued to protest.

Chivers's nose wrinkled in abject disapproval. He sniffed and turned his back on her.

⁊⊃℘⊃

Emmeline rattled the door handle violently, but it held fast. Just like all the other times she had tried.

Ooh, she fumed, as she stalked round and round Mrs. Bartholomew's desk. She wanted to wrap her hands around Stephanie's long neck and squeeze, until the woman begged for mercy and admitted what she had done. There was absolutely no doubt in Emmeline's mind that Stephanie had stolen the letter from her handbag when she had waylaid her outside the lawyer's office.

She now saw that it was all part of an elaborate ruse. McCallister must have called Stephanie the instant he stormed out of the conference room to make sure she was ready to pounce when Emmeline set foot on the pavement. Their little argument was all for Emmeline's benefit.

How had she missed the signs that they were conspiring together? she reprimanded herself. *Was McCallister's affair with Verena part of the scheme? Or did he and Stephanie cross paths later and come to an arrangement?*

Too many questions needed answers. Emmeline threw her hands up in the air in frustration. It was useless to scour her brain. What's past was past. She had to concentrate on how to stop Stephanie and McCallister. Justice was a foreign concept to them. They were both consumed by greed and supreme arrogance. Therefore, their next logical move would be to wave the incriminating papers under the

Raven's nose and demand a hefty sum.

Fools, Emmeline observed with contempt. Verena's ill-advised attempt at blackmail came to a dead end. Did Stephanie and McCallister really imagine they would escape the same fate?

She glanced at her watch. Where were Gregory and Superintendent Burnell? She had rung them as soon as she had been thrown into this office nearly an hour ago. She rubbed her throbbing temples with her fingertips. They were losing ground.

The jangling of a key in the lock and the murmur of male voices on the other side of the door made her halt her restless perambulations.

The door swung open. The knot of irritation in the pit of her stomach uncoiled, when she saw Nigel step into the office.

"These accusations are utterly ridiculous," Nigel reproached Chivers, who hovered close on his heels. "Miss Kirby is a well-respected journalist. That your bank would treat her in such a manner is unconscionable."

With barely a pause, his gaze shifted to Emmeline. "Are you all right?"

She gathered up her coat and handbag, and crossed over to him. "I'm fine. Merely annoyed." She threw an affronted glance at the bank manager.

"Please accept the bank's apologies." Chivers's tongue tripped over itself, as he sought to smooth things out. "But you must try to see the situation from my point of view."

Nigel gallantly held her coat as she slipped her arms into the sleeves. He then took her elbow. "Come on, Emmeline. You've had quite enough of this shoddy treatment." He propelled her out the door, but tossed over his shoulder. "Expect to hear from me again, Mr. Chivers."

It was mean-spirited she knew, but she experienced a stab of triumph as the bank manager's gasp floated to their ears. Let Chivers have a sleepless night or two worrying whether the bank was going to be the subject of a lawsuit. Nigel was scrupulously professional and would never even contemplate such action. He'd consider it a complete waste of time and effort. But perhaps it would teach Chivers a lesson not to jump to conclusions the next time.

As she and Nigel swept past the tellers, she glimpsed Sergeant Finch speaking to the assistant bank manager. She raised a finger to catch his attention, but Nigel shook his head. "Let Finch do his job. We don't want to give them another excuse to detain you."

She inclined her head. He wasn't being overbearing, merely cautious like any good lawyer. It was still vexing because she was bubbling over with newfound knowledge and she was being forced to keep it bottled up. Her frustration evaporated, though, when her eye alighted on Gregory and Burnell loitering on the pavement.

"It's about time," Burnell grumbled. "If Nigel didn't come back out in the next five minutes, I was preparing to go inside myself."

"Thankfully it was unnecessary to make a scene, Superintendent. But I appreciate you and Sergeant Finch dropping everything to come down to the bank. I'm certain Assistant Commissioner Cruickshank won't be pleased, when hears about it."

Burnell grunted. "Stuff the Boy Wonder. I can handle him."

She went to Gregory's side and slipped her arm through his. He kissed the top of her head and teased, "This is what happens when I let you out of my sight for a minute. If I had known you were a master criminal, I would never have married you." He gave her a cheeky wink.

She swatted his arm. "Ha. Ha." Then to Nigel, she said, "I'm sorry you were dragged into this mess too."

He made a dismissive gesture with his hand. "Nonsense.

Sanborn Enterprises values its employees. But more importantly, you're family now. On the other hand, had it been my disreputable cousin"—he flicked a glance at Gregory—"I would have thought long and hard about whether to stir myself out of my chair."

"Oh, how I know the feeling," Burnell muttered under his breath.

Gregory arched an eyebrow. "What was that, Oliver?"

The superintendent glared at him.

Emmeline nudged Gregory in the ribs with her elbow. "That's quite enough of that. We have bigger fish to fry," she asserted.

First, she proceeded to inform them about the dramatic revelations at the reading of Verena's will, doing her best to gloss over the part about Adam being left her fortune. Then, she went on to recount how she wound up as the bank's temporary captive.

She explained that Stephanie must have been the woman who impersonated her by stealing Verena's letter. The three men trusted her instincts and were unsurprised by the fact that she had seen Stephanie with McCallister.

"I can't be sure how long they've been working together," Emmeline concluded, "but it means that he can't be the Raven. What I'm confused about is whether Stephanie's story was true about turning over all the proof she had to Verena. It bothered me because Stephanie didn't strike me as a woman who trusts her own shadow. I can't blame her after the way William, aka the Raven, betrayed her. Her hatred was definitely genuine. She couldn't have faked her injuries. Therefore, the more likely scenario is that Verena is the one who gathered all the dirt. Stephanie somehow discovered it and saw her chance at last to punish the Raven. I'm more certain than ever McCallister killed Verena, but I think he's an opportunist of the worst kind and is playing all sides against the middle. He must know who the Raven is."

"We suspected as much from the beginning," Burnell conceded. "The man is as slippery as they come. I've had Finch digging into his background." He shook his head in frustration. "The lad's had a devil of a time. McCallister doesn't seem to have existed before 2005."

The adrenaline raced through Emmeline's veins. She drew out her notebook and pen. Pitching her voice low, she speculated, "Could he be a spy?"

Burnell's thin white brows knit together. "Emmeline," he admonished in a stern tone. "Don't let that fertile imagination of yours run away with you." He scowled at her notebook. "And put that away. I'm not saying anything for attribution."

"It's not a far-fetched theory," she argued. "Remember Philip divulged that some of the Raven's suspected victims were Russian defectors, who were in witness protection."

"That sort of protection doesn't inspire much confidence," Gregory quipped. "The poor sods would have fared better if they had stayed in the wind."

"Mmm," Burnell murmured. "Bureaucracy and incompetence. Absolutely no excuse for them." He drew out his mobile from the inner pocket of his coat and hit a number he had on speed dial. "I'm going to have an all-ports warning issued for Stephanie and McCallister. The cordon will be so tight, even Houdini would be trawled in the net." He squinted at the window and saw that Finch was preparing to exit the bank. "Hopefully those fools in there were able to provide some information about Stephanie." He turned back, his gaze locking on Emmeline's face. "As a reasonable and intelligent woman, you do realize that I have to question Adam again in light of the victim's will."

Emmeline felt the blood drain from her face. She cleared her throat. "Adam is wealthy in his own right. He doesn't *need* Verena's money."

"Nevertheless, I can't ignore it. It is my duty under the law."

She drew her shoulders back and declared with renewed purpose, "Right. I won't stand in the way. I, too, have work to do. I'm going back to the paper."

"I don't have to remind you that this is an ongoing investigation," Burnell stressed.

She offered him a broad smile. "Of course not. However, as editorial director of investigative features, I would be remiss if I didn't follow up on all leads. In fact, I would be quite negligent if I didn't."

The superintendent groaned and shook his head. He shot a glance full of suspicion at Gregory. "And you? What are you up to?"

Gregory pressed a hand to his chest. "Me? As a devoted husband, I rushed to my wife's side to make certain she was all right. Now that everything has been sorted as a result of the prompt intervention of you and Nigel, I'm going to return to the office. As you are aware, I'm a dedicated employee of Symington's."

"Hmph," Burnell grunted. "Why does that answer fill me with unease?"

Gregory clapped him on the shoulder and flashed one of his most engaging smiles. "The workings of a policeman's mind remain a mystery to a humble man like me. I'm afraid only a psychiatrist would be able to explain your deep-rooted mistrust of your fellow man."

Chapter 30

A cream-colored halo glowed against the evening sky from the string of lamps set at intervals along the curving pathway in the Victoria Embankment Gardens. The velvety darkness muted the sound of the traffic rumbling past along the Thames. The air was infused with the wind's damp breath forcing McCallister to quicken his pace as he wandered toward the York House Water Gate, the Italianate-style archway. The gate, which looks like a folly stranded in the middle of the park, was conceived by the architect Inigo Jones in 1626 as an extension to the palace built by the first Duke of Buckingham. Although the Portland stone was smudged with grime, the structure was impressive. McCallister stood for a moment before it and blew on his gloveless hands. His fingertips were icy. He stamped his feet to get the blood circulating. The cold was beginning to seep into his bones. This was the third time he'd passed along this stretch.

He glanced at his watch. Seven o'clock. "Where the devil is the bastard?" he fumed aloud. The Raven was playing with fire.

Muttering to himself, McCallister pivoted on his heel and stalked off. He decided to go to the Savoy Grill and enjoy a lavish steak dinner, while he plotted his next move.

He had to get out of London tonight or tomorrow morning at the latest.

His brain had rejected two alternatives when his mobile vibrated in his inside breast pocket. He smirked when he saw the number.

"Get lost, did you?" he scoffed. "With the things I know, that was a grave miscalculation. I'd even say reckless. But that's none of my concern. You'll have plenty of time in jail to regret the choice you made. Meanwhile, I'll become the hero of the piece when I drop everything into Emmeline Kirby's lap and begin whispering sweet-nothings in Superintendent Burnell's ear."

He fell silent for several seconds. "Is this some kind of a joke? What do you mean the money is here in the gardens?" He paused to listen, his back stiffening. "Taped to the underside of a bench? Pull the other one, mate. I don't believe it. Fine. I'll check."

He hurried past the Imperial Camel Corps memorial, the bronze statue of a mounted infantryman on a camel atop a Portland stone pedestal with bronze panels. It commemorated the men of the corps who died in Egypt, Sinai, and Palestine between 1916 and 1918.

He stopped short, his eyes widening in disbelief, when he saw the outline of a package strapped to the bottom of a bench a few feet from the statue. He spun around in a circle, his gaze searching the shadows cast by the bare branches of the London plane trees. No one. He flicked the tip of his tongue over his lips and crossed to the bench. His steps were slow and tentative.

He bent down and awkwardly freed the bulky package from its hiding place with one hand. "I've got it," he mumbled into the mobile.

He plopped down onto the bench, pinning his mobile between his ear and his shoulder. His fingers clawed at the thick tape and tore the package open. He slumped back, stunned. Despite the gloom, he could see that there were dozens of neat bundles of money inside. He huffed an astonished laugh. It was incredible. He was the only man to bring the Raven to his knees.

"All in all, you must admit that wasn't such a bad bargain to keep your secrets safe." He tried to keep the smug triumph from creeping into his voice. "Remember this was the down payment. I want the rest of the money transferred into my Swiss account by next week. The *early* part of the week, mind you."

He couldn't help chuckling, as he rang off.

He set his mobile on the bench and plunged his hand into the package. He drew out one of the packets and held it close to his ear as he feathered the bills with his thumb. He tingled with childlike glee as the bills whispered as they fell back into place. He had expected the Raven to put up a greater fight. His capitulation demonstrated that the man was desperate to keep the truth from leaking out at any cost. And McCallister was the beneficiary of that fear.

A laugh tickled his throat. It turned into a cough, as the biting wind carried in the dampness off the river. The first droplet of rain kissed his cheek. Another cough rumbled through his chest. He couldn't afford to get sick. Not now. He stuffed the money back into the package and leaped to his feet.

His head began swimming and he collapsed back onto the bench, as a fit of coughing paralyzed him for several seconds. He clutched the package to his heaving chest, as he waited for it to subside. He opened his mouth wide to gulp air, but he was having trouble drawing air into his lungs.

Water streamed from the corners of his eyes, after another bout of coughing. He was trembling with the effort. Beads of perspiration had broken out on his forehead. He squeezed his eyes shut. His vision was blurred.

How could he have gotten ill in the space of a few minutes?

And then, realization infused with cold dread sharpened everything into focus. He was going to die here on this bench. The Raven had killed him.

The bloody money, McCallister swore. The Raven had poisoned the money.

He probably only had a few minutes to live. With a supreme effort, he opened his eyes and fumbled for his mobile. His hands were trembling violently. It took two attempts to punch in the number.

The call was answered on the second ring. However, a vicious bout of coughing stole his voice and he had to wait until it passed.

"Hello" he heard a woman say. Her voice was muffled, as if she were speaking at the end of a long tunnel.

"Look, I know someone is on the line," Emmeline asserted, her tone laced with irritation. "I'm going to hang up in five seconds."

His throat was constricting, but he swallowed hard. "*Raven*," he rasped.

"Mr. McCallister, is that you?" Emmeline demanded.

He was gasping for air, but he had to hold on. "*Ro-yce… Raven…watch—*"

"What…what do you mean?"

He tried again. "Raven…ki-killed…me—" He took a final gulp of air. "Royce…Raven…watch…Devarest… Spain."

His mobile slipped from his fingers. McCallister was already dead by the time it shattered into a thousand pieces on the pavement.

∽∾∽

Stephanie's head was throbbing. The drinks she had

consumed earlier were attacking with a vengeance. All she wanted to do was to crawl into bed and sleep for twenty-four hours uninterrupted. She could dream about how she was going to spend all that lovely money. The adjustment to becoming a lady of leisure would pose no problem whatsoever. She deserved every last penny.

She chuckled to herself and then wished she hadn't. She rubbed her fingertips against her temple. Bed, she told herself. She had all the time in the world to make plans.

A frigid gust of wind reached down from the evening sky like a giant hand and pushed her along the Regent's Canal towpath. She had wound her way from Paddington Tube station to the houseboat in Little Venice, where McCallister had offered to let her stay. She didn't know whether the boat belonged to him, and neither did she care. She had almost refused. But it was quiet and anonymous, and she reasoned that William would never think to look for her here. Thus, necessity forced her to tamp down her aversion to boats.

Her toe caught on an icy patch on the pavement and she stumbled forward but managed to steady herself at the last second. Her boots echoed hollowly upon the air. The bare branches of the trees to her right cast strange, distorted shadows onto the benches set at intervals on the path. Stephanie shrugged deeper into her coat and listened to the nocturnal hiss of the water lapping against the boats. It had a hypnotic, soothing effect on her nerves.

Until a sudden, irrational, paralyzing panic clutched at her chest.

Her pulse began to race. She was not alone. She could feel invisible eyes boring into her shoulder blades. Her fingers tightened around her cane, ready to lash out.

How did he find me? her terrorized brain screamed.

Her eyes darted around wildly. The shadows taunted her. The nearby boats were cloaked in forbidding darkness.

No one would hear her cry out. She tried to quicken her pace, but her crippled leg refused to cooperate.

She felt his warm breath against her cheek a second before his strong hand clamped over her mouth. He jerked her body against his own, bringing her footsteps to a jarring halt.

"Naughty, Stephanie," he murmured. "We've come full circle. You should have done the decent thing and drowned." He gave an exaggerated sigh. "Now, I'll just have to finish what I started all those years ago. Ah, well, better late than never."

Chapter 31

"Mr. McCallister?" Emmeline shouted into her mobile. Rising unease clawed at her throat.

A heavy, menacing silence echoed in her ear. She wanted to throw her mobile across the kitchen.

He said *Royce*. She didn't imagine it. He couldn't possibly mean that Adam was the Raven, could he? That was ludicrous.

The man was clearly deranged. *No*, she corrected, *not deranged. It was the confession of a dead man, who had nothing to lose.*

Her hands began trembling. She knew in her heart that Adam couldn't be the Raven. But a malicious voice in the back of her mind hissed, *Can any of us truly know another human being?*

"Yes," she spat aloud through clenched teeth. "I know Adam. And I *won't* believe it."

"What's going on, Emmy? Won't believe what?" Gregory's voice rippled across the air, making her jump.

She whirled around and flung herself into his arms, as he stood in the doorway. "Oh, Gregory."

He rested his chin on top of her head, smoothing back her curls before pressing a kiss to her temple. They stood there for a few seconds not speaking. Then, he held her away from him, his cinnamon gaze full of concern.

"Darling, what's happened?"

She gathered up fistfuls of his sweater in her hands and pulled him closer. "I just had a disturbing call from McCallister."

His jaw tightened. "Did he threaten you?"

She shook her head. "I…I think." She drew in air through her nostrils and started again. "That is, I'm quite sure he's dead."

Gregory's eyes widened in disbelief. "He was attacked? How? Where *is* he?" He fired off the questions, barely pausing for breath.

Emmeline gave a helpless shrug. "I don't know. All he said was"—she felt the sting of salty tears prick her eyelids and her tongue felt heavy with the burden—"Royce, Raven, watch, Devarest, and Spain. Then he sounded as if he was choking."

Her husband's lips pressed into a grim line and a sober expression creased his features. "Mmm."

She wanted to shake him. "Is that all you have to say?"

"No." He crossed to the telephone on the wall. "I'm going to ring Oliver. Leave it to the police to track down McCallister."

She nodded mutely. Yes, that was the wisest course of action. She had been taken off guard and wasn't thinking clearly. Her gaze strayed to the kitchen table. Their dinner lay cold and forgotten. She should pop it into the oven. But she couldn't bring herself to make a fuss over something so mundane. Not when her mind was fixated on Adam and McCallister's terrible, horrifying accusation.

It was *not* true.

She hugged her elbows and hovered by Gregory's side, as he tersely informed the superintendent of the virtual certainty that he had another murder on his hands.

Two hours later, the doorbell rang and Gregory ushered

in a solemn-faced Burnell and Finch into the living room. Since an all-ports alert had already been issued, the police had found McCallister fairly quickly. Burnell said that the forensics team was still processing the scene at the Victoria Embankment Gardens, but Dr. Meadows's preliminary diagnosis was that McCallister had been poisoned, possibly some sort of nerve agent.

"Nerve agent," Gregory exploded. "Bloody marvelous. It can only be the Russians up to their usual tricks. Both Villiers and Acheson said that MI5 suspected the Raven of having Russian ties."

He shot a concerned glance at Emmeline, whose legs felt like water. "Yes," she mumbled. She motioned toward the sofa. "Please sit down, Superintendent and Sergeant Finch. I'll go make some coffee. I think we're all going to need it."

Burnell inclined his head gratefully, but he frowned as he sank down on the sofa beside Finch. Emmeline scurried out of the room far too quickly. He wondered what she was up to, as he watched Gregory stalking back and forth in front of the fireplace. In the interlude, only the sound of Emmeline gathering cups and saucers in the kitchen floated to their ears.

When she returned a few moments later, Gregory took the tray from her and set it down on the coffee table. Her complexion had turned ashen with strain. He knew she was dreading what she had to impart. That was why she was studiously concentrating on handing round the cups. He sighed inwardly. It was best to get it over with. Oliver was a sensible chap. He flicked a glance at the superintendent over the rim of his cup. For the most part.

After taking a sip of his coffee, Burnell got down to business. "Now then, Emmeline, what precisely did McCallister say?"

Emmeline reluctantly dragged her gaze from the depths

of her cup and stared directly at the superintendent. Her lips parted, but no words rose to her tongue. Her throat felt parched. Stalling, she took a long swallow of coffee.

Burnell and Finch shared a perplexed look. This behavior was out of character for her.

"Emmy," Gregory prodded. "You have to tell them."

Her dark eyes confronted the question reflected in Burnell's intense blue gaze.

"I want you to remember that McCallister was a criminal. You can't put any stock in what he said. He lived, and died, to deceive." Her voice trailed off.

The superintendent set his cup down on the table and perched on the edge of the sofa. His hands were loosely clasped together and dangled between his knees. "Let us be the judge of that."

She nodded mutely. "McCallister said…Ro-Royce,"— she stumbled over the name and swallowed the lump that lodged in her throat—"Raven, watch, Devarest, and Spain."

She saw Burnell stiffen. Then in a rush, she implored, "Adam is *not* the Raven. You can't think…"

His face was a blank canvas, all trace of emotion was gone.

She leaped to her feet. "McCallister was simply making trouble. It was a distraction."

"Why would he do that?" Burnell asked quietly. "He was dying. It makes more sense that with his last breath he would want to make sure that his killer was caught."

She gave a violent shake of her head. "No. You're wrong. If it was Jason, I'd agree in a heartbeat. But this is Adam we're talking about. He's not an evil mastermind, who roams the globe murdering people for hire. Jason was the one who threw in his lot with Swanbeck and the Russians."

"The apple doesn't fall from the tree," the detective

pointed out impassively.

Emmeline shot a pleading glance at Gregory, who chimed in, "Oliver, you must admit that the idea stretches the bounds of credulity."

"We'll see where the evidence takes us," he replied briskly.

Finch looked up from his notebook and said, "We found an envelope bursting with money beside McCallister. It appears to be some sort of pay-off. Once the forensics team finishes dusting everything for prints, we'll trace the serial numbers on the notes."

"Good. Follow the money to its source and you'll find the murderer," Emmeline declared. "And I assure you, it won't be Adam. I can't believe you're seriously entertaining the idea."

Burnell brushed aside this last comment. "It's something to be getting on with. Meanwhile, I had a couple of PCs track McCallister's movements after he left Aldridge & Thayer's offices this afternoon. Witnesses saw him with a woman fitting Stephanie's description in the lounge bar of the Novikov restaurant, which is—"

"Which is directly around the corner from Cottingham Bank," Emmeline finished for him.

Burnell gave a curt nod. "The barman said that they sat at a table in a corner and looked very cozy. He had his hands full with other customers, but he described McCallister and Stephanie as all smiles and laughter. He thought perhaps they had just gotten engaged and were celebrating the happy occasion."

Emmeline huffed a bitter laugh. "Ha. They were engaged all right. Engaged in patting themselves on the back for pulling off such a coup." Her fingers drummed an angry tattoo on the armrest. "All they had to do was to bide their time and everything they needed to bring the Raven to his knees fell into their laps."

"Blackmail is greed driven by supreme arrogance," Burnell observed soberly. "It is an egregious miscalculation on the perpetrators' part because they *think* they'll be able to bleed the poor victim dry."

"Again, I'd like to underscore that Adam would never even contemplate such a despicable scheme."

Burnell sighed. "Emmeline, your loyalty to those you care about does you credit. But in my many years in this job, I've learned that people tend to let you down most of the time because they are only out for themselves."

She leaped to her feet. "Not Adam. McCallister is…was a pathological liar and most likely a killer."

"I hate to point out the obvious," Finch interjected, "but he's dead and Adam is—"

She whirled on him. "Adam is nothing. He's not guilty of this or any other crime."

"Emmy, you're too close to the situation. You're not being your usual objective self."

She drew in a sharp breath, her hot gaze sweeping over her husband and the two detectives.

"Verena Penrose was having an affair with Adam and McCallister at the same time," Burnell remarked. "And now two of that trio are lying in the morgue. It raises a great many questions."

She clenched her fists at her sides and challenged, "What good is evidence when accusations suffice? Is that what we've come to?"

A pink flush spread beneath Burnell's beard and his Adam's apple worked up and down.

Gregory crossed to Emmeline and took her by the arms, pressing her back down into the chair. "Steady on, Emmy. You don't know what you're saying," he reproached.

She gripped the armrests and glared up at him for an instant. Then, the fire in her chest burned out. She slumped back and drew in a ragged breath. Salty tears stung her eyelids.

Her gaze snaked over to Burnell, who sat there in stunned and angry silence.

A lump of regret rose to her throat. "That was unforgivable. I didn't mean it. Truly." The superintendent inclined his head, accepting her apology. "I know that you and Sergeant Finch are the most diligent detectives on the force. It's just that..." Her voice cracked. "Not long ago I was accused of a murder I didn't commit, as were you. Our innocence was proved in the end, but the stigma sticks. The mere whisper of another scandal could do untold damage to Adam. He's worked so hard these past few months to restore the family's good name and maintain Royce Global Holdings' standing in the industry. To have all of that come tumbling down around his ears because of vicious innuendo"—her dark gaze raked the superintendent's face—"because that's what this is and we all know it would be more than a tragedy."

Burnell cleared his throat. "I can't play favorites." His gentle tone held a note of sadness. "Justice is blind. I must, and *will*, follow the law. No matter where it leads me. It does no good at this stage to upset yourself with wild speculation. We will interview Adam again." She gave a resigned nod. "Of course, we have to wait for Meadows's postmortem."

"Meanwhile, I can look into whoever Devarest is and find out how he's involved. Spain appears to be important too." She was talking more to herself than the three men. It gave her brain something constructive on which to focus. "It's the second time that it has come up in connection with the Raven. He nearly murdered Stephanie off the Costa del Sol." She sat bolt upright. "Stephanie said that he had a villa in Torremolinos. Oh, what was the name of it?" She tilted her head back and stared up at the ceiling, as if the name was painted there. Her fingers drummed on the armrests. "It was some Spanish name. Villa del…" She snapped her fingers and flashed a triumphant smile at them. "Villa del Nido Cuervo."

"Nothing escapes you, does it? But leave it to us," Burnell commanded. "Finch and I will follow up. On all of it. Unfortunately, Stephanie is still in the wind. But we'll find her. I'll give Philip a ring in the morning. He might be able to provide some more insights."

"Respectfully, Superintendent, you can't prevent me from pursuing any of these angles. McCallister's murder is a legitimate story. I could uncover something that will help you catch the Raven."

Burnell grimaced and placed his hands on his knees to push himself wearily to his feet. Finch tucked his notebook in his inside jacket pocket and stood as well.

"I wish you wouldn't, but I'm too tired to argue," the superintendent responded. "We have to get back to the station. All I ask is that you tread lightly."

Emmeline rose too and pressed a hand to Burnell's arm. "On tiptoes, I promise." She paused before adding, "Please don't think too badly about my outburst earlier."

The superintendent's mouth quirked into a crooked smile. "Never." He flicked a glance at Gregory. "Your husband is an entirely different matter, though. I believe the worst until he demonstrates otherwise."

Gregory placed a hand over his heart and rubbed it in a circular motion. "You've torn a hole right here, Oliver." He sniffed theatrically. "I'm going to cry myself to sleep tonight."

Burnell rolled his eyes. "That's our cue to leave." Then to Emmeline, he said seriously, "You can't right all of the world's sins alone. It will wear you down."

Chapter 32

Emmeline's fingers hammered at her keyboard the next morning. She muttered under her breath as if she were still carrying on the argument she'd had with Gregory before she left the house.

"Darling," she heard his mellifluous, cajoling voice inside her head, "Be reasonable. McCallister's murder and the subsequent visit from the Met's finest pushed it straight from my mind."

"Really?" she had challenged. "We'd been home for an hour, *before* McCallister rang and set the evening's events in motion. You didn't utter a word, not one, about having to leave town. And for Spain no less. I find that rather curious."

Gregory's shoulder lifted in a nonchalant shrug. "Curiosity is a sign of an intelligent mind. I'm a lucky man that my wife is not only sharp as a whip, but a vision of loveliness to boot."

"Huh. Your honeyed phrases will not work. What business could Symington's possibly have in Spain?" she demanded. "I thought it was solely based in the UK."

On it went as she trailed after him from the kitchen to the living room. To her frustration, he silenced her with a passionate kiss that left her breathless. In the few seconds it took to gather her wits again, he grabbed his coat off the peg, unbolted the door, and had one foot over the threshold. The last thing she glimpsed was his sensuous mouth curved into a smile, while she was left standing in the hall without being any the wiser.

She finished typing her last sentence and exhaled a long sigh. Whatever Gregory was going to do in Spain, it was connected to the Raven. She *knew* it. She was both hurt and angry that he was keeping her in the dark. Yet again. She thought he had outgrown the inclination to keep secrets. She was his wife, after all, not some stranger he bumped into at the pub.

Her fists curled into tight balls. Why couldn't he trust her? His impulse to coddle and protect her, although gallant, only caused her to worry because it meant that he was walking into Lord-knows-what danger alone.

To make matters worse, he was counting on the fact that she wouldn't dare leave London now. Not with McCallister's murder and the scurrilous accusations he cast upon Adam.

Bloody men, she swore. Gregory would pay for his treachery.

Well, she was simply wasting time by marinating in her grievances. So, she pushed her errant husband from her mind and got back to the task at hand: catching the Raven before he killed again. Her only lead was tenuous at best.

Villa del Nido de Cuervo, Torremolinos. The Raven's hideaway.

But that was seven or eight years ago. Most likely he had sold it by now. What if…She sat up straighter in her chair, as a thought struck her. If that's case, there must be a public record of the sale. Perhaps she could find the estate agent who handled the transaction.

After half an hour and several false starts that left her cross-eyed, she wanted to leap for joy. She had come across a French property listing service, which featured a real

A MIND TO MURDER

estate agency run by a British expatriate that specialized in properties in the Costa del Sol area from Malaga to Estepona. The firm catered to a British clientele, who yearned to leave behind England's damp winters.

She jotted down the number and reached for her phone. Her fingers tingled. The excitement of the hunt never dulled. However, she also didn't want to get her hopes up too high. She knew only too well that to get to the truth, it was often a torturous slog through the mire.

Still, she hummed to herself as she willed someone to pick up her call.

"Good morning, Colthurst Real Estate Agency," a woman with a Spanish accent answered in fluent English, "How may I help you?"

"Hello, my name is Emmeline Kirby. I'm the editorial director of investigative features at *The Clarion* in London. I'm doing research on a story about the owner of a villa in Torremolinos. I was wondering whether the property was or is on your books. I believe the owner is British. That's why I'm ringing."

The woman had listened to her without interrupting. "I see. I can't provide any information, especially over the phone. But please hold the line and I'll see if Mr. Colthurst, the boss, will speak to you."

"Hello, Miss Kirby," a rich baritone voice boomed in her ear after only a minute. "I'm Ken Colthurst. My secretary said you needed some information about one of our properties."

"Thank you for speaking to me, Mr. Colthurst. I'm not sure whether you handled the villa at some point, but I thought I'd start with your firm since your clientele is British. The name of the property is Villa del Nido Cuervo. Does that ring a bell at all?"

He chuckled aloud. "Yes, I remember the Villa of the Raven's Nest."

"Wh-what? Villa of," she stammered, as she moistened her lips with the tip of her tongue.

"That's the English translation of the name. It sticks in my mind because the buyer and I joked that it sounded like something out of one of those old Errol Flynn films."

Raven's Nest. It couldn't be a coincidence.

"I see," she murmured. "Can you tell me how to contact the owner? As I told your secretary, I'm working on a feature and need to interview him." She crossed her fingers. It was a tiny white lie. Colthurst would never know.

"Let me see," he mumbled. His voice was muffled as if he had pressed the receiver between his ear and shoulder. She heard him tapping on a keyboard and held her breath.

"Ah, here it is. The villa was purchased by an Adam Royce in May 2000."

She didn't hear the rest of what Colthurst said. The room began swimming before her eyes. He offered to e-mail her all the details of the sale. Somehow, she managed to make her mouth form words and to thank him for his trouble.

The bitter taste of bile rose to her throat and a wave of nausea roiled her stomach.

Colthurst was mistaken. That's all there was to it.

But how do you explain the fact that Adam's name appears on the deed of sale? a horrid little voice whispered

"You can go to the Devil. No one asked for your opinion," she argued aloud to her empty office.

She had to talk to Adam. He was the only one who could clear up this…this disturbing revelation.

Her hand shot out and grabbed her phone. First, she tried his mobile. Unfortunately, he had turned it off because it went straight to voicemail. Although she left a message, she immediately punched in his number at the office.

She was relieved when it was answered on the second ring. "Good. I've caught you. Adam, I—"

"I'm sorry, Emmeline," his secretary Delia apologized. "I'm afraid Adam isn't here."

She squeezed her eyes shut and pinched the bridge of her nose with her thumb and forefinger. "Oh, I see. I need to speak to him about an urgent matter. When will he be back?"

Delia hesitated a moment. "It's difficult to say," she replied guardedly. "He left town unexpectedly this morning." Emmeline sucked in her breath. "He came in with a face like thunder and told me to cancel all the meetings he had scheduled for the next few days. Then, he locked himself in his office for about half an hour to make some phone calls. I've never seen him in such a foul mood."

Emmeline's spine stiffened and her eyes flew open. "That's odd. When I saw him a few days ago, he didn't mention any upcoming trips. Where did he go?" She tried to keep the worry from creeping into her voice.

Crossing her fingers, she silently prayed, *Please let it be anywhere but Spain.*

"He didn't say. But as he was storming out, I overheard him on his mobile booking a reservation on the first flight to Madrid. He must be in the air by now."

No, no, no. This is not *happening.*

Emmeline jumped to her feet. One jumbled thought after another chased itself across her mind.

"Are you still there?" Delia's voice dragged her back to the present.

"Ye-es, I'm here. Never mind. I'll just try calling Adam again later." She strove to make her tone light, so that the other woman wouldn't hear how upset she was by this unexpected news.

"Right. If there's anything, I can do…" Delia's sentence trailed off.

"No, it's fine. Thanks."

She mumbled a hasty goodbye and rang off before Delia decided to ask awkward questions she couldn't answer.

Emmeline plopped down heavily into her chair again. She felt as if the walls were closing in on her. This was a cruel joke. First, Adam's name appeared on the deed of sale for the villa in Torremolinos, the Raven's Nest. She groaned and shook her head. And now, Adam had gone off to Spain.

Why had Spain become such a popular spot lately?

She had to tell Gregory about these developments, even though he didn't deserve it. However, if he was off to Madrid tomorrow, then she would have him track down Adam to find out what the devil was going on.

She sucked in her breath as a thought struck her. Did Gregory find out for certain that Adam was the Raven and he wanted to confront him alone? Was that the reason for this impromptu trip?

There was a nervous flutter in the pit of her stomach. It was too horrifying to even contemplate.

The insistent peal of her mobile interrupted these dark musings. Her hand shot out and she scooped it up. Perhaps, it was Adam. He had better have a good, a *very good*, explanation for his strange behavior. She felt a stab of disappointment and sighed when she saw the number.

"Hello, Superintendent Burnell." She pasted a smile on her lips, even though he couldn't see her. She flipped open her notebook and held her pen aloft. "Do you have any new information about McCallister's murder that I can print?"

"No comment," he replied tersely. "Emmeline, this is off the record."

She grumbled inwardly and set her notebook aside. "I see."

A short silence ensued before Burnell reluctantly admitted, "The body of a woman has been discovered on a houseboat in Little Venice." She sat bolt upright in her chair. "The victim fits your description of Stephanie. I'd like you to come down here to confirm whether it is or not." He told her precisely where the boat was moored.

With her mobile pressed between her ear and shoulder, Emmeline was already on her feet and slipping an arm into the sleeve of her coat. "I'll be there as quick as I can."

✑✑✑

"Have you nothing better to do than to trail after me all over London?" Villiers demanded acidly, as Gregory stepped into his path, preventing him from reaching his car.

"Don't flatter yourself," Gregory shot back in a clipped tone. "We need to talk."

Villiers frowned. He saw his driver hurrying toward them. He lifted a hand to wave him off. "It's all right, Ralph. An unexpected matter has come up. I won't be needing the car at the moment. Wait for me back at the office."

"But, sir—" Ralph protested.

"Just go. This is liable to take some time." Out of the corner of his mouth, he muttered at Gregory, "Especially if it has to do with your tiresome wife. Which I suspect it does."

The driver gave a curt nod and returned to the car. Within a minute, he had merged into the traffic on Whitehall and was gone.

Villiers rounded on Gregory. "I don't appreciate being accosted on the pavement."

Gregory gestured toward the wrought-iron gate behind them, where a police officer stood guard. "It was either that or pounding on the door of Number 10, until you came out," he snarled.

Villiers smirked, a hard glint in his eyes. "More your

wife's style I would have thought to barge in when I was in a meeting with the PM. She has no sense of propriety or restraint."

Gregory clenched his fists at his sides and drew in air through his nostrils. He would not allow himself to be baited.

"I very much doubt that whatever you came to discuss is for public consumption." Villiers cast a pointed glance at the hustle and bustle around them. "Therefore, I suggest we go somewhere private."

Gregory flashed a nasty smile. "Your club again? I found it rather cozy. In an anachronistic sort of way."

"No," the other man snapped.

"And here I was hoping you could put me up for membership, *Papa*." His voice dipped on this last word.

Villiers's cinnamon gaze, which mirrored Gregory's own, smoldered with irritation and disapproval. He made a rumbling sound at the back of his throat.

Gregory arched an eyebrow. "No? Ah, well. No need to get your knickers in a twist. I rang Acheson. I thought it wise to apprise him of the situation. He graciously offered his office for our *tête-à-tête*. He's expecting us. Shall we?" His arm made a sweeping arc that encompassed the Foreign Office, which was a short distance down the block.

Villiers drew himself up to his full height and braced for unpleasantness.

Chapter 33

Pamela, Philip's secretary, looked up from her monitor and murmured a polite greeting when Villiers entered the antechamber. However, her face lit up considerably as her eye fell on Gregory.

"Hello, Mr. Longdon. It's been a while since you've popped by the office. May I say how delightful it is to see you?" she gushed.

Villiers sniffed and pressed his lips into a thin line. Gregory ignored the censorious expression on his face as he stepped around him.

"Ah, Pamela"—he pressed a hand to his heart—"you grow lovelier every time I see you."

A pink flush spread across her cheeks and her smile grew wider.

Villiers groaned and shook his head. "What utter drivel. Women can be so gullible."

This observation had an immediate dampening effect. Pamela cleared her throat and reached for her phone. "Mr. Acheson," she said in her most efficient tone, "Mr. Villiers and Mr. Longdon have arrived." She listened for a few seconds. "Right. I'll tell them. I assumed it was important, so I've rescheduled your meetings."

She replaced the receiver in the cradle. "Go straight in, gentlemen."

Villiers strode into Philip's office without another word. But Gregory gave Pamela a cheeky wink over his shoulder. Before he pressed the door closed behind him, he thought he heard her murmur, "Mrs. Longdon is a lucky woman."

His smile vanished, though, as he settled at one end of the claret leather Chesterfield sofa to the right of the door. Villiers, his features clouded with strain and the fine lines around his eyes more pronounced, was ensconced at the other end. Philip was lowering himself into one of two matching armchairs flanking a highly polished oval coffee table made of cherry. This nook was nestled next to a large window that overlooked King Charles Street. On the opposite side of the room near the elegant mahogany desk were two bookcases with glass doors.

Philip leaned forward in his chair, hands clasped together, his gaze alert. "I gather this has something to do with the Raven." Gregory gave a curt nod. "Burnell rang this morning when I was in conference with the Foreign Secretary. I was about to return his call."

Villiers propped one elbow on the armrest and brushed a fleck of lint from his immaculate trousers. "I, for one, can't wait to hear how a meddlesome reporter has mucked things up. Again."

Gregory's head whipped around and glared at him. Through gritted teeth, he shot back, "As usual, *your* fingerprints are all over this mess."

Villiers grunted dispassionately. "I do what I do to preserve the country's security. I will not apologize to you or anyone else. On the other hand, your wife fails to grasp the concept of discretion, which makes her dangerous."

"Sir," Philip interrupted before tensions boiled over, "you're not being fair to Emmeline."

Villiers refused to relent, though. He wagged an admonishing finger at Philip. "You, of all people, should be more wary. I've warned you time and time again not to allow that woman to pull the wool over your eyes." He flapped his hand impatiently in Gregory's direction. "Toby is a lost cause."

Gregory swallowed hard and was silent for several seconds. What he sorely wanted to do was to walk out the door. But for Emmy's sake, he couldn't allow things to go to hell in a handbasket.

He took a deep breath. "I'm leaving town tomorrow and I need to know Emmy's safe." His tone was quiet and calm. "For that reason, I came to tell you about some developments."

He proceeded to give them an account of Stephanie's unsettling entanglement with the Raven; the contents of Verena's will; the letter that Verena had left for Emmeline detailing her dealings with Villiers to set a trap for the Raven; the empty safety deposit box; and Stephanie's link to McCallister.

"We're quite certain," he concluded, "that Stephanie stole the letter to get past the bank manager and into the safety deposit box. Obviously, she and McCallister attempted to blackmail the Raven. Now, McCallister is dead and Stephanie has disappeared."

Villiers stared at some spot on the far wall, his jaw clenched and his long fingers drumming an angry tattoo on the sofa's armrest.

The silence was claustrophobic and suffocating. The muted ticking of the antique carriage clock on Philip's desk seemed to beat in time with Gregory's heart. Each stroke sent a flutter rippling across his chest and stripped away another layer of his patience.

He gripped his knees hard and whirled his head around. "Right, I've had quite enough of your impression of a sulking statue, dear Papa. It's time to tell us what you have up your sleeve because, as always, you know far more than you've divulged. I'm not interested in state secrets. My only concern is for my wife, who seems to have stumbled into one of your twisted Machiavellian plots."

Villiers sniffed and slowly turned to stare him directly in the eye. "That's because her unhealthy curiosity is compounded by her predilection for meddling." He held up a hand to forestall the volley that was about to fly from Gregory's tongue. "However, I'm left with no choice but to put you in the loop, in the hope that you'll appreciate the gravity of the situation and muzzle your wife once and for all."

Gregory leaned back and smoothed down the corners of his mustache. A ghost of a smile played about his lips. "Emmy is a free spirit and I wouldn't change her for the world."

"More's the pity," Villiers grumbled. He took a breath and plunged ahead, "As I told you the other day, we suspect the Raven of assassinating several Russians defectors who were in protective custody here in the UK." Gregory nodded. "We believe that he was also helping in other ways to further the Kremlin's efforts to sow dissent in this country and Europe."

Gregory frowned. "Verena's letter not only accused you of knowing that the Raven had killed her father, Sid Cranbrook—"

Villiers gave an indifferent shrug. "One less criminal walking the earth. I haven't lost any sleep over it, I assure you. Verena is the only one who mourned his death."

Gregory made a dismissive gesture with his hand and went on as if he hadn't been interrupted. "—but it mentioned something about a diamond scheme Sid had conceived and the Raven had stolen. Any idea what she was referring to?"

Villiers and Philip traded a guarded look.

"Sir, I think we had better tell him," Philip advised. "He's pieced this much together."

Villiers gave a reluctant nod and Philip picked up the thread. "In one of its rare sharing moods, MI6 deigned to inform us that the Russians were seeking to infiltrate the London Diamond Bourse with the goal of setting up a new pipeline to launder its filthy money. We've been keeping a close eye on the Bourse for the past two years. Thus far, we haven't seen anything remotely suspicious. We didn't want to alarm anyone unnecessarily. However, we felt it prudent to warn someone at the Bourse about the potential threat. David Nussbaum, one of the board members, is our man on the ground."

Gregory arched an eyebrow. "David? He didn't whisper a word."

"We vetted him carefully," Villiers chimed in, "before we approached him. Of course, we discovered your connection to him. Still, I couldn't allow that to influence the situation. We needed someone with the utmost discretion and integrity.

"That certainly describes David. He's a good man." Gregory crossed one leg over the other, as he turned over this new information in his mind. "From the outset, my instincts told me that Verena's murder had something to do with her husband's connection to the Bourse." He flicked a glance at Philip, before his gaze settled on Villiers again. "It appears I was right. I think the Russians, through the Raven, were attempting to pressure Craig Sheldrake into having his company act as a front. Naturally, they didn't give him a choice in the matter. Either through stupidity or bravado, he didn't take the threat seriously and they killed Verena as a lesson.

"The evidence that Oliver and Finch have uncovered seems to suggest that McCallister killed Verena, but she had been drugged to ensure that she wouldn't put up a struggle. The pathologist found hydrocodone in her system. It's a common prescription, but it also causes sedation and euphoria while slowing the central nervous system. The postmortem indicates that she likely ingested it half an hour to forty-five minutes before she died. So, that would put it at sometime during the intermission when we were all in the bar. The police believe that the Raven slipped it into her drink."

Philip settled back in his chair and steepled his fingers over his stomach. Two vertical lines had formed between his brows. "If this McCallister conspired with the Raven, that means he's working for the Russians as well."

"It appears that way," Gregory concurred.

"Scott McCallister," Philip mumbled. "The name rings a bell. I saw it recently."

He pushed himself to his feet and crossed to his desk. He sifted through a neat stack of files. "Ah, here it is," he said, drawing one out that was toward the bottom.

He began leafing through the pages, as he rejoined the other two men. His lips moved silently as he read. The lines on his brow deepened.

"Bloody hell," he swore and handed the file to Villiers, who had a similar negative reaction.

"Why are we only finding out about him now?" the deputy director of MI5 demanded.

Philip shrugged. "I'm afraid I can't answer that question. I received the file yesterday. I haven't had a chance to review the details in-depth."

Gregory's gaze shifted between the two men. "What does it say about McCallister?"

Philip lifted an eyebrow. Villiers exhaled a frustrated sigh. "Oh, go ahead."

"It seems Scott McCallister never existed," Philip explained. "This new intelligence"—he tapped the report with his forefinger—"indicates that he was really Feliks Kuznetsov. He was the grandson of KGB spymaster Kolya Ostrovsky."

Gregory shook his head in disbelief. "That's why Finch was unable to find out anything about McCallister's background before he arrived on the scene in London in 2005."

"With his connection to the higher echelons of the Kremlin," Philip ventured, "I suspect that Kuznetsov was the Raven's handler. Perhaps, he was sent here to keep the Raven in line."

"That's plausible," Villiers agreed. "But the Raven turned the tables and now Kuznetsov is dead.

"Ostrovsky and his boys in Moscow are not going to like that," he observed with a touch of spite. "They had better not be making reservations on the next Aeroflot flight to London. We already have enough Russians running about the city."

"McCallister called Emmy last night."

Villiers threw his hands up in resignation. "Speaking of stirring up trouble. How does your wife manage to be everywhere?"

Gregory ignored him and directed his comments to Philip. "The police believe McCallister was poisoned by some sort of nerve agent. But with his dying breath, he tried to tell Emmy about the Raven."

Villiers sat forward, immediately alert. "He *told* her the man's identity? And you wasted all this time sitting on your bum and didn't think to mention it? What the devil are you waiting for? Spit out the fiend's name."

Gregory held up a hand. "I'd like to remind you that McCallister was likely in pain and far from lucid."

"I don't bloody care," Villiers snarled. "What did he *say*?"

Gregory took a deep breath. "Royce…Raven…watch… Devarest…Spain."

"Royce? That family again. Your wife's bloody family." Villiers's voice was steeped in scorn. "It's no wonder you didn't come straight out with it."

"It beggars belief that Adam Royce could be the Raven or involved in this in any way," Philip countered. "His life is an open book."

"Open book, my foot. The man was sleeping with Verena. She made no secret of it. And she had this McCallister warming her sheets at the same time. It's amazing how she juggled the two men."

Philip blinked twice. "I see. Still. We've never had a reason to investigate Adam. Unlike his brother Jason who was as thick as thieves with Swanbeck and the Russians."

"Jason Royce," Villers muttered bitterly. "He's more trouble than he's worth."

"What's that, sir?"

"Never mind. The fact that McCallister/Kuznetsov brought up Spain worries me. There's been far too much chatter lately about Spain."

"Indeed. I was speaking to a contact at MI6 just last week and he told me that they're concerned about the separatists in Catalonia. Apparently, tempers are flaring and the rhetoric is becoming more incendiary. He feels the region is about to implode. Of course, you're both well aware that ETA, the militant group, wants a Basque homeland in northern Spain and southwest France. They've killed over 800 people in their forty-year reign of terror to get it." Philip paused as a thought occurred to him. "I see Putin's hand in all this. The situation in Spain must be part of the Russians' calculated effort to destabilize the West."

"Putin," Villiers spat the name. "Why doesn't someone do the world a favor and kill the smarmy bastard?"

The three men retreated into brooding silence, each contemplating the ominous ramifications of the Kremlin's involvement.

"I don't understand what Devarest has to do with any of

this," Villiers said at last more to himself than to the others. "He dropped off the radar over forty years ago."

Gregory shot a questioning look at Philip, who shrugged.

"Who's Devarest, sir?"

Villiers's head snapped up. "What do you mean?" he asked incredulously. "Rodney Devarest, of course." His tone softened when he met their blank stares. "No, I forget that the two of you weren't born at the time"—his gaze slithered to Gregory—"Well, you were, Toby, but you were still crawling around in nappies." He lifted a hand in apology and corrected himself. "Sorry. Gregory. You know I will always think of you as Toby."

"That's your problem. Now, get on with it and tell us about Devarest."

Villiers leaned back and sighed. "I'd only met him on a handful of occasions. He was a rising star in the Foreign Office and had cultivated a coterie of admirers in diplomatic circles. He was intelligent, handsome, and could charm both men and women. However, he was thoroughly merciless and used anyone to get ahead. His family bore the brunt of his ambitions, but he was careful to keep the ugliness from prying eyes. Whitehall is a small world and everyone knew, of course. They chose to hold their noses and avert their eyes because Devarest was an asset when it came to navigating the international political landscape, ensuring that Britain remained on top. But in 1967, his behavior had become an embarrassment for the government. The police had been called to his Belgravia home one too many times because he decided to exercise his fists on his wife Jacinta. I'm baffled why she never filed any charges against the brute. My guess is he threatened her and she was terrified for their two sons. Gavin, the older boy, was sixteen and a bit wild, while Robert was only eight. She was barely nineteen and Devarest was twenty-six when they married. Gavin was born just shy of their first anniversary."

Villiers pursed his lips and shook his head in distaste. "Devarest was beginning to offend the sensibilities of even some of the more jaded politicians roaming the cutthroat corridors of Whitehall. So, the mandarins in all their wisdom came up with a plan that would keep his wicked ways from tarnishing them and the government. He was shipped off to Spain as a cultural attaché at the embassy. In one tidy stroke, the matter was swept under the rug.

"No doubt Jacinta was pleased by this turn of events. She was Spanish, the only daughter from the well-respected and wealthy Moncada banking family in Madrid. Things were quiet for about eight months. Then just after the new year in 1968, the trouble started. Jacinta had met an old flame, Dario Texidor, at an embassy party. From what I gather, it didn't take long for the sparks to fly, and soon they were having a torrid affair. I can't blame the poor woman. She was lonely and yearned for a bit of kindness. To be fair, she was discreet."

"She could have divorced Devarest and made a new life for herself in Spain among her family and friends," Philip pointed out.

"She was a devout Catholic and didn't want to bring that shame on her family."

Gregory shook his head. "So, she chose to be a martyr. How sad."

"Not quite. Yes, she felt trapped and desperate. But Texidor persuaded her to come live with him in Barcelona. Although they could never marry, she readily leaped at the chance to snatch some happiness. She took young Robert with her. She couldn't bear to be parted from him. He had been a sickly toddler and grew to be a sensitive boy. In many ways, he was like her. Devarest, on the other hand, lavished all his attention on his brother. Gavin was a useless, arrogant layabout from all counts.

"In any case, Jacinta and her lover managed only a week together before Devarest came after her. He beat the lover senseless and left him for dead, and dragged Jacinta back to Madrid with him. By the time they arrived at the embassy, one of her eyes was swollen shut, and she and the boy were covered in bruises."

Gregory ground his teeth and his fists curled into tight balls. "The filthy swine. Someone should have taken him down a dark alley and given him a lesson in the proper way to treat a lady." Philip nodded in agreement.

"Unfortunately, no one could touch Devarest because he had diplomatic immunity."

"That's outrageous," Philip exploded.

Villiers threw his hands up in resignation. "I can tell you that there was a good deal of acrimonious dialogue between London and Madrid. Ultimately, Devarest was recalled and the two countries set off on the long road to repair the damage that had been done to their relations.

"The authorities here couldn't prosecute him, but Devarest's career was finished for all intents and purposes. He was transferred to some minor position in an obscure department. The Foreign Office couldn't formally make an example of him because it would have meant putting the whole sordid incident on public display and that was the last thing anyone wanted. So, it was hushed up and Devarest faded into oblivion. Half of society shunned him because one can never really keep things completely quiet in Whitehall. But the old boy network always comes to the rescue of one of its own. Within two months, he was hired at a prestigious law firm and invited to become a member of several boards of directors. However, his ego was still smarting from the scandal in Spain. To prevent Jacinta from ever turning to another man again, Devarest packed her and his sons off to the family's Georgian mansion in

Hampshire. It will come as no surprise that the house was bought with the money Jacinta's father showered on her as a wedding gift. Devarest was now free to do as he wished in London without fear of his wife embarrassing him again. He came down on weekends simply to keep up appearances. Needless to say, Jacinta was a bundle of nerves during those visits. From what I understand, Devarest set the staff to watch her and provide reports on her movements and who she saw in his absence. She was essentially a prisoner in that country home."

"I have never felt such contempt for another person, with the exception of Swanbeck, in my life," Gregory interrupted, bile rising to his throat. "How is it possible that a bully and a beast like Devarest was allowed to behave in such a manner without being held accountable for his actions?"

"He even managed to turn his recall to London into a lucrative coup," Philip pointed out in disgust.

A spasm of dark emotion flitted across Villiers's features. "It gets worse."

"Worse? That's hard to fathom," Philip replied.

"Texidor turned up in Hampshire. He was still recovering from the beating Devarest gave him, but he came to take Jacinta away. She resisted at first because she was afraid of what her husband would do if word reached him before they could make their escape. In the end, she agreed. They arranged for Texidor to return that evening. Jacinta was going to take Robert with her. She had no qualms about leaving Gavin behind. He was his father's creature and could fend for himself."

A pained sigh escaped Villiers's lips. "She was right to be frightened. One of the staff must have called Devarest to tell him what she was planning. He came down from London and confronted her. They had a violent row, which ended in her tumbling down the staircase. Her neck was broken and she died instantly. Texidor vanished that night. No one ever heard from him again."

"Bloody hell," Gregory exclaimed.

"This couldn't be covered up and Devarest went on trial for murder. Despite the evidence, the jury found him not guilty." Villiers huffed a bitter laugh. "A perfect example of *blind* justice, don't you think, gentlemen?"

Gregory and Philip shared an outraged look.

At last, Gregory spoke. "Blind my foot. The jury was paid off. There's no other explanation."

"No one wanted to look into the matter too closely. Everyone wanted the ugly circus to end," Villiers told them.

"What happened to Devarest?" Philip asked.

"The last thing I heard was that he left these shores for the warmer climes of the French Riviera."

"And the two sons?"

"Gavin went off to Cambridge. His father pushed him to read law, but he had aspirations of becoming England's greatest actor and was more interested in the amateur dramatic club. Meanwhile, he fell in with the wrong crowd. His other pursuits were drugs and alcohol. Although his father was livid, he offered a generous donation to the university and Gavin's puerile indiscretions were overlooked. Ultimately, he was sent down for a cheating scandal. I'm certain that the university was happy to finally see the back of him. I don't know what became of him afterward.

"I believe Jacinta's relatives took Robert under their care. And thus, the loathsome Devarest saga disappeared from public consciousness. Until last night, when our friend McCallister/Kuznetsov died with the man's name on his lips. Why?" Villiers scowled. "I'm at a loss to see how Devarest could possibly be connected to the Raven."

"Spain holds the key," Philip noted. His blond brows

knit together. "We're still missing so many pieces, though."

"Mind you," Gregory chimed in, "the mere suggestion that Adam Royce could be the Raven is ludicrous. Nor could he commit treason or concoct a plot to target the London Diamond Bourse and use it as an illicit bank account."

"Hmph," Villiers grunted. "Don't be naïve. Royce may *look* like a decent chap on the outside, but the most ruthless criminals wield their charm as a weapon. The best policy is to trust no one."

"What a jolly outlook on life," Gregory replied facetiously as he rose to his feet and slipped into his coat. "Well, I must be off. I have a few matters to take care of before I leave." He inclined his head at Villiers and to Philip he said, "Watch over Emmy for me."

"No need to ask," Philip murmured.

Satisfied, Gregory nodded and crossed to the door.

His hand stilled on the doorknob, when Villiers called, "You never said where you're going."

Gregory tossed a smile over his shoulder. "Didn't I? Need-to-know basis, I'm afraid. You're not the only one who can keep things close to the vest, *Papa*."

Chapter 34

Even if Emmeline hadn't known the precise mooring of the *Wanderer*, the crowd of uniformed constables in yellow reflective vests and the scenes of crime officers, or SOCOs, covered head-to-toe in white protective suits and booties would have given her a clue that something evil had trespassed upon the peace of this otherwise glorious winter day.

She shaded her eyes against the honeyed strands of sunlight tumbling from the cerulean sky onto the towpath. Her footsteps slowed as she approached the blue-and-white tape that screamed POLICE LINE DO NOT CROSS. She hadn't trusted and resented being manipulated by Stephanie. But no one deserved to be murdered.

Perhaps, this woman isn't Stephanie after all? the optimistic part of her brain suggested. However, the knot in the pit of her stomach predicted a different outcome, crushing all hope.

She hitched her handbag higher on her shoulder and took a deep breath.

"Excuse me, miss, this is a crime scene," declared a rather beefy constable with a round, haggard face and pale blue eyes clouded by fatigue. "I'm afraid you can't pass this way."

"My name is Emmeline Kirby. Superintendent Burnell

asked me to come down. He thinks I might be able to identify the victim."

The constable gave a curt nod. "Please wait a moment, Miss Kirby. I'll let the superintendent know you're here."

Five minutes later, Burnell was lumbering from the deck of the long, forest green canal boat and onto the towpath. Sergeant Finch was close on his heels.

The two detectives hurried toward her. She could see that their jaws were set in hard lines and their features held the same grim expression.

"Thank you for coming, Emmeline," Burnell said gruffly.

He lifted the tape so that she could enter the cordoned-off area. He wordlessly handed her a pair of plastic blue booties and a pair of gloves to prevent her from contaminating the crime scene, which was still being processed. She quickly slipped them on.

"Good. I must warn you that this won't be pleasant, but it shouldn't take long." His eyes searched her face. "Ready?"

She swallowed hard. "Death is not something anyone is ever prepared to confront. I just want to get it over with."

Burnell nodded. Finch took her by the elbow and guided her toward the stern of the narrow boat, where a door was propped open.

As they neared the boat, male and female voices from the interior floated to her ears. Finch climbed aboard first and held out a hand to steady her as she stepped onto the slippery deck.

"Make way," Finch called through the door. "Miss Kirby is here to identify the body."

All conversation ceased abruptly. Then to Emmeline, he asked, "All right?" She nodded.

He gestured for her to enter the cabin. It was a narrow, rectangular space comprised of a tiny kitchen area with a refrigerator, sink and stove on the left, and a compact table nestled between two half banquettes at the far end. Everything was neat and tidy.

Aside from the forensics officers huddled in a corner, the only thing that marred the cozy scene was the dead woman half-sprawled on the caramel-colored sofa just inside the door. Strands of her chestnut hair dangled inches from the highly polished hardwood floor. Emmeline couldn't tear her gaze from the woman's waxen face. The glassy, smoky-blue eyes stared back at her and seemed to hold an accusation in their vacant depths.

For an instant, the image of Verena's lifeless body in her seat at the theatre danced before Emmeline. She stumbled backward, her shoulder blades colliding with the solid bulk of the superintendent's broad chest.

He gripped her arms to steady her. "Emmeline," he whispered in her ear, "is this Stephanie?"

She pressed a hand to her mouth and gave a vigorous nod. She couldn't trust herself to speak.

"Right. Finch, take Emmeline outside in the fresh air. I'll be along in a minute. I just want a word with the head of the forensics team."

Finch touched Emmeline's elbow and gently prodded her toward the door. Once back on the towpath and several hundred feet from the *Wanderer*, he gave her a kind smile. "Take a deep breath. Come on. It helps, at least a little." His brown eyes scanned her face in concern. "There that's better, isn't it?"

"Yes, a bit." Her voice held a tremor. "How do you and Superintendent Burnell deal with violence and all manner of crimes on a daily basis and still remain sane?"

"By making sure we catch the guilty and put them behind bars so that they never harm the innocent again." His words were infused with his unwavering belief in the rule of law and his dedication to duty. "It's not very different from the way you view your job as a reporter and your loyalty to the truth."

Despite the glimpse she had just been given of man's depravity and her growing worry about Adam, Emmeline smiled for the first time that day. "Thank you for that. I wish more of your colleagues were as broad-minded. Many police officers view the press as the enemy."

The sergeant chuckled. "That's because most are. They merely want titillating headlines to sell more papers or to boost television ratings. You're the exception. Mind you, there are times when you tend to be a tad…overzealous, which makes the guv's ulcer turn somersaults."

"I'm only trying—" She broke off when she caught sight of Burnell.

"Did you tell her?" he demanded of Finch, when he drew level with them.

"No, sir. I thought it best to wait for you."

A frisson of unease slithered down her spine. "Tell me what?"

The intensity of Burnell's stern gaze made her wince.

"Meadows confirmed that McCallister was indeed poisoned. The money was coated with a sophisticated nerve agent that he hasn't been able to identify yet. However, Finch traced the serial numbers on the notes." He paused, seeming to choose his next words carefully. Emmeline held her breath. "They came from a Royce Global Holdings account. An account controlled directly by Adam."

An icy tendril of fear curled around her heart. Her legs felt like water. Surely, her knees were going to buckle beneath her any second.

She moistened her lips with the tip of her tongue and forced her brain to concentrate on what the superintendent was saying.

"Finch called the bank. The manager confirmed the

transaction."

The sergeant flipped open his notebook and picked up the thread. "I quote, 'Mr. Royce himself collected the hundred thousand pounds in cash. The family has been doing business with us for years. I would know him anywhere.'"

She gave a violent shake of her head. "No. It's not possible. The bank manager was paid to lie."

"Perhaps, that's true. But whether it is or not," Burnell answered matter-of-factly, "Adam has a good deal of explaining to do. He was Verena's lover. And twice in the last twenty-four hours his name has come up in connection with the Raven and two murders."

Her mouth went dry and her voice was a hoarse croak. "Two murders?"

"Yes, McCallister and now Stephanie. Adam's name and number were in her mobile. That's not all. Sheldrake has gone into hiding."

"Wh-what? Why?"

"He vanished in the middle of the night. Mrs. Fairchild, his housekeeper, found a scrawled note saying that two thugs had paid him a visit yesterday and threatened to do him bodily harm or worse if he didn't agree to sell CS Gems to Stonecrest." She opened her mouth to offer an argument, although a wave of nausea assailed her. "Ah, ah. Let me finish. Since Stonecrest keeps popping up, I had Finch do some digging. Do you know what he found out?" She gave a mute shake of her head. "Stonecrest is a subsidiary of a shell company that is owned by Adam. That's not all. The housekeeper told us that she overheard a call Sheldrake received yesterday afternoon from Adam. She described Sheldrake as extremely shaken afterward."

She put a hand to her lips and felt the blood drain from her cheeks. "We need to speak to Adam. Where is he? His secretary said that he left town in a hurry this morning."

"If he's not at the office, I...I have no idea." Which was the truth in the broadest sense. A suspicion did not count as knowledge.

Burnell's wispy brows knit together and a hostile scowl transformed his features into a terrifying mask. "Emmeline, this is an official investigation," he growled. "Please don't insult my intelligence by lying to me."

"I...I would never lie to you. I don't know where Adam is."

"We're checking the airports, trains, and ports. We'll find him eventually. It would go easier for him if he came to the station of his own volition. Tell him that when you speak to him," he replied tersely.

"I will, but I doubt he'll call me. You can't focus your inquiries solely on Adam. Need I remind you that McCallister also mentioned a man named Devarest? Who is he? What's his link to this lethal business? Why aren't you hunting him down?" she challenged.

"We will. We are," the superintendent snapped. "But at every turn in the case, we find Adam as large as life. His sudden disappearance only makes him look guilty. You do realize that, don't you?"

Her chin jutted in the air. "It's all circumstantial," she stubbornly asserted. "The Raven has carefully orchestrated all of this to deflect attention from himself. And you've fallen into his trap. He's probably scarpered already." She felt the salty sting of tears against her eyelids, but she was too angry to cry. "Well, I'm going to prove you wrong."

Chapter 35

Her journey on the Tube back to the office was a blur. Fury had ceded to reason, allowing her brain to objectively assess the crimes of the past few days. It would be a waste of time to follow up on the bank account. She had no doubt that the Raven had performed some electronic conjuring to make it appear that the money had come from Royce Global Holdings. For the moment, she would set aside the bank manager's unsettling contention that Adam had collected the money. Instead, she was going to channel her energies on the newest clue: Devarest. He must play an important role in this web of intrigue. Otherwise, why would McCallister bring up his name out of the blue? Did Devarest pose another threat or was he one of the Raven's victims?

Blood thrummed through her veins, as she began scouring the *Clarion*'s archives to discover any morsel she could about this man.

Soon, she was drowning in the cascade of sordid details about the meteoric rise and fall from grace of the reprehensible Rodney Devarest. Each new fact peeled back the layers until a portrait of a selfish, arrogant bully emerged. Her stomach churned with anger, as she made notes about the murder trial and the jury's ultimate decision to declare him not guilty.

Not guilty? she seethed silently. *When the evidence against him was overwhelming?*

The jurors must have been a collection of inept fools. She frowned. Or, did the seven men and five women trade their souls for filthy lucre? Her eyes narrowed. Yes, it was all frightfully clear.

She glared at the black-and-white photo of a beaming Devarest outside the courthouse just after the verdict had been announced. He had a hand clamped on the shoulder of each son. The older boy, Gavin, stood next to his father, a blank expression on his face. But young Robbie's eyes stared back at her in bewilderment. Her breath caught in her throat at the profound sadness. It was painful to see how his mother's death had affected him. The look was so intimate and familiar.

Poor little boy. And poor Jacinta lying cold in the grave.

Emmeline ground her teeth and slumped back in her chair. At least now she knew *who* Devarest was, but she was still at a loss to see how he was linked to the Raven. She cursed McCallister. If only he could have lived a few minutes longer.

Question upon question rattled around her head. Each raised new possibilities.

Was Devarest the Raven? She dismissed this thought almost immediately. She guessed that he must be in his seventies now. She very much doubted he'd be rushing about the globe as an assassin. Devarest was too fond of a life of leisure to exert himself. No, it must be something to do with Spain. Perhaps he crossed paths with the Raven when he was stationed in Madrid?

She roused herself and began trawling the Internet again for any information about what became of Devarest. A man with a shred of decency and self-respect would have gone quietly. Not Devarest. He appeared to revel in his newfound notoriety.

She came across several interviews he gave in the aftermath of the trial.

One was a BBC video clip that captured the moment that he and his sons emerged from the courthouse into a throng of reporters. Devarest made a brief statement portraying himself as the victim of a cruel world. Then, he happily took questions. Even Gavin relaxed a bit and responded to the reporters. Little Robbie, on the other hand, was clearly overwhelmed and tried to slink off. Devarest grabbed the boy roughly by the nape of the neck and drew him to his side again. He made a joke about the boy's shyness. He ruffled his son's hair affectionately, then his heavy hand clamped down on Robbie's shoulder. She could see that the boy was trying bravely not to cry, although Devarest's signet ring was digging into his skin.

She pressed her tongue against her cheek and shook her head. The man didn't deserve to have children. However, the clip did yield one clue. When asked about his future plans, Devarest discussed his intention to leave the UK for Europe because he had been profoundly traumatized by the trial.

Emmeline rolled her eyes heavenward and moved on. A few clicks later, she found a *Le Monde* exclusive with a spread about France's newest citizen in his villa on the Côte d'Azur.

Would Devarest have dared to take jaunts to Spain, despite the scandal a few years earlier? she wondered. *Emboldened by his acquittal in his wife's murder, he could have convinced himself that no one could touch him.*

Even if that were the case, how could Devarest's squalid domestic travails be relevant to the murders here in London in 2010?

She simply didn't know. She was grasping for anything.

Her eyes felt gritty and heavy. She had been staring at her computer screen for too long. She squeezed her eyes shut and pressed the heels of her palms against her temples because her head was beginning to throb.

A frustrated sigh escaped her lips. None of this was helping her to clear the cloud hanging over Adam. There had to be something, she stubbornly told herself. She wasn't going to give up until she found it.

She blinked a few times and renewed her search. Her fingers stilled on the keyboard when a series of articles related to the Devarest trial started popping up.

She greedily scanned each story. Her hand flew as she filled several pages with careful notes of dates and personal background details on a group of men and women.

They had two things in common. Each was now deceased *and* had served on the jury at Devarest's trial.

Her journalist's instinct cheered in triumph. She *knew* that she was on the right trail at last. Like Burnell, she was not fond of coincidences. The *entire* jury couldn't have died one after another over the course of several years. She conceded it was possible but highly improbable. Someone had methodically killed off each person. That took audacity, planning, patience, and a certain degree of cold-bloodedness.

That description fit one person like a glove: the Raven.

But why kill the jurors? Could it be as retribution for giving in to greed and allowing a guilty man to go free? That was the only plausible explanation.

And yet…Why would the Raven care? There was an undercurrent of highly charged passion running through these murders. Meanwhile, the Raven had a stone for a heart. To him, a human life was a commodity.

She sat bolt upright. Unless someone with a personal stake hired the Raven. She nodded. Yes. Someone who wanted justice for Jacinta. Her boyfriend Dario Texidor was the most obvious choice. He had disappeared the night she was murdered, though. Did Devarest kill him too? He nearly did in Spain. Or had Texidor been in hiding all these years wielding the Raven as his weapon of revenge?

She gave a dissatisfied shake of her head. Why not go after Devarest directly? Was it part of the punishment Texidor was meting out? To rattle Devarest's nerves every time another juror was picked off? To make him look over his shoulder, never knowing when it would, at last, be his day to die?

On the other hand, she mused, the bond between mother and child is one of the strongest. The boys were young at the time of the murder and trial. Gavin was sixteen and Robbie eight. They were helpless and still dependent on their father. However, hatred could have been festering in their hearts, growing and mutating until it became a desire to punish. Perhaps, that's why it was several years before the jurors started dying. For the tragic story to end, the *coup de grâce* would have to be Devarest himself. Was he still alive?

A few keystrokes yielded the answer. She put a hand to her mouth. He died nine years ago at his villa in Mougins, just north of Cannes. The news account revealed that a maid found him in his bedroom. He had been shot in the head. The police had briefly considered Gavin a suspect because he and his father had been known to have heated rows about the son's choice of career and money, which went through his fingers like a sieve. Devarest had finally put his foot down and turned off the spout. Ultimately, the police ruled it a suicide.

Emmeline was not so sure.

William Faraday, who they now knew was the Raven, surfaced mere months after Devarest's suicide.

What was it that Villiers had told Gregory the other day? The Raven always assumed a new identity before killing his victims. Isn't that what actors do? Play different roles to broaden their artistic range.

Gavin Devarest had become an actor. What if his most rewarding role was the Raven?

And now, the Raven is tangled up with the Russians. What if it wasn't by choice? What if the Russians discovered who he is and threatened to expose his crimes to the world? Unless he put his lethal talents to work on the Kremlin's behalf.

Royce...Raven...watch...Devarest...Spain

McCallister could have been trying to warn her that the Raven was Gavin Devarest and he was watching Adam. Why? She couldn't fathom a reason and pushed the thought aside for the moment to focus on a more worrisome matter.

What did the Russians want the Raven to *do* in Spain?

She knew that Putin had been systematically fomenting political unrest in Europe in recent years. Perhaps, the Raven was the Kremlin's secret tool in this campaign. But how would Putin do it from behind the scenes?

She leaned back in her chair and tilted her head to stare up at the ceiling. Her thoughts raced in a thousand different directions.

Of course. She sat up suddenly and kicked herself for not making the connection sooner. The Basque separatists. The Russians were using the separatists' cause as a way to discredit Spain on the international stage. Putin hoped that while the government in Madrid was distracted, he could swoop in and...and...She threw her hands up in the air in exasperation. Only God knew.

Her nerves tingled with excitement. She always enjoyed the hunt for the truth.

"Madrid," she murmured, as she hastily scanned the editorial calendar. Yes. She gave a satisfied nod and snatched up her phone to ring the editor-in-chief.

"Hello, Emmeline," he answered tersely. "Please don't tell me there are problems with that piece we're going to run on Friday. Nigel went over the story with a fine-tooth comb."

"No, Jeremy," she assured him. "The article is solid. I want to discuss something else with you."

"Good. Make it quick. I have a meeting in five minutes."

"Right. I want to reassign Dennis to the bill the prime minister has proposed and I'd like to take his place covering the international security conference in Madrid."

Jeremy hesitated a fraction of a second. "What about the Verena Penrose murder? And the suspicious deaths of that chap McCallister and the woman in Little Venice? Only this morning you were telling me that they were all connected to the mysterious Raven."

"They are. I'm more certain of it now."

"Then why go to Madrid? Stay in London and follow up on the leads. Simply because you're the editorial director of investigative features doesn't mean that you have to investigate *every* important story. You're not the only reporter at the paper. I've told you more than once that you have to delegate more."

"Yes, yes," she said quickly. She didn't have time for a lecture. "It's a theory, but a strong one based on what I've been able to piece together. I think the conference or someone attending it may be the Raven's next target."

She went on to detail what she had learned about Rodney Devarest's turbulent life and ignominious death; her deductions about the son Gavin and the Raven; and her suspicions about the Russians' machinations in Spain.

Jeremy listened without interrupting. When she was done, she heard him expel a long sigh. "I resent the fact that you are always so bloody efficient and never give me a reason to reprimand you." His words may have been blunt, but his tone was light. "Pack your bags for Madrid. I think your reasoning is sound. But be careful. The Spanish authorities have to be warned about the potential threat since top security officials from a dozen countries will be attending the conference. It must be done through official channels. No one would believe a reporter. The Spanish might think you were angling for a major scoop and there's no substance behind it. I suggest you ring your contacts at MI6 and MI5. Let them handle the delicate interagency logistics. We wouldn't want to step on anyone's toes."

No, certainly not, she conceded. That was a prudent course of action. Security was of the utmost importance always. Lives were at stake.

While it would be unconscionable to keep mum, she was not looking forward to broaching the subject with Philip. Her hand hovered over the phone. She took a deep breath and steeled herself for his inevitable reaction to her plan of action to trap the Raven.

No matter. It was her civic duty and a courtesy to inform him. She would listen politely to whatever Philip had to say. But in the end, she was going to Madrid.

There was *nothing* he, or anyone else, could do to stop her.

Chapter 36

Gregory took a cautious step into the hall and bolted the door behind him. He cocked an ear and heard Emmeline moving about upstairs. He hadn't liked the way they had left things that morning. However, he couldn't very well tell her that Jasper had called him the previous afternoon to say that a meeting had been arranged to sell the Blue Angel and Pink Courtesan to the Raven.

A reservation had been made for him at the Hotel Princesa Plaza in Madrid. Instructions would be left in his room about where and when the exchange would take place.

He grimaced as Jasper's words echoed inside his head. He knew he was playing with fire. But it was a risk he was willing to take. The Raven's reign had to come to an end. And the farther away from England and Emmy, the better.

Emmy's tuneless humming tore him from these disturbing musings. A smile tugged at the corners of his mouth as he hastily shed his coat and hung it on the peg.

To get himself back in his wife's good graces, he had bought an enormous bouquet of coral roses, which were her favorites. He scooped up the flowers. He was confident that their heady scent would help to melt away any vestiges of anger Emmy was still harboring. He hoped. The alternative would be to smother her with passionate kisses until their argument became a distant memory and marital bliss was restored.

His smile grew wider, as he took the stairs two at a time. Mind you, he could still ravish her with kisses to seal their reconciliation.

"Emmy," he said softly from the doorway of their room.

She spun around, a broad smile spreading over her face. "Darling, you're home."

She flew toward him. Her hands twined themselves about his neck. He slipped one arm around her waist and bent down to kiss her upturned lips. They lingered in the embrace for several delicious minutes.

When they broke apart, Gregory quipped, "I'm relieved to see all sins are forgiven."

She pressed a kiss to the tip of his nose. "I wouldn't go that far. You are merely on probation." Her dark eyes glimmered with amusement.

He cleared his throat. "I see. Perhaps these might help." With a flourish, he drew out the bouquet from behind his back.

"Oh, they're lovely," she gushed, as she buried her nose among their velvety petals.

She gave him a peck on the cheek and then scooted past him to get a vase and put the roses in water. After she left the room, he noticed an upright suitcase open on the floor and sundry clothes piled on the bed.

She returned within minutes and was humming once again.

"You've been a busy bee this afternoon. Thank you for packing for me, but I could have done it myself."

He couldn't miss the gleam of mischief in her eyes and felt a flutter of apprehension in his chest, when she replied, "Yes and you will. Now if I can just get on with *my* packing—"

He held her gaze. "Emmy, what are you up to?"

Her eyes widened in innocence. "Up to? I have no idea what you could possibly mean, husband dear. I'm going on assignment."

He raised a skeptical eyebrow and folded his arms over his chest. "Oh, yes? This *assignment* is rather sudden, isn't it?"

One shoulder rose in a shrug. "It's the nature of the news business. Stories break all the time. A reporter has to be prepared at a moment's notice."

"Hmph. The more you natter on, the more certain I am that you're hiding something."

"Ha," she snorted. "This coming from a man whose past is mired in layer upon layer of dark secrets."

He waved off this comment. "We're not talking about me, darling." He crossed to her and took her by the arms to prevent her from escaping. "Where are you going?"

An ember of anger kindled in her gaze. "You have no authority to interrogate me."

"Shall I ring Oliver?" he shot back. "Scotland Yard's finest is an expert in winkling out the truth from recalcitrant suspects."

At the mention of Superintendent Burnell, her fire extinguished itself. She sighed. "I'm going to Madrid." She held up a hand to forestall the avalanche of protest that was about to burst forth from his lips. "No. Come sit down. A lot has happened today."

She laced her fingers through his and led him to the bed, where they perched on the edge. She quietly told him about Stephanie's gruesome murder and what she had uncovered about the detestable Rodney Devarest, which led her to speculate that his son Gavin was the Raven and he was working to help further Putin's grand scheme to destabilize Spain.

Finally, with great reluctance, she disclosed the unsettling news that the poisoned banknotes had come from an account controlled by Adam and the bank manager's unequivocal affirmation that Adam collected the money.

"No one will convince me," she concluded on a ragged breath, "that Adam is involved in this mess." She fixed her stare on Gregory's face. "I'll admit that his sudden trip raises questions. But there is a perfectly logical explanation."

He dropped his arm around her shoulders and drew her to his side. "Of course, there is. It's obvious to anyone with eyes and an ounce of brains that Adam has been set up." He paused, resting his chin on her head. "If I didn't know better, I'd say that it was some sort of revenge plot. But that makes no sense."

Emmeline lifted her head and held his gaze. She swallowed down the lump that had lodged in her throat. "Gregory, I'm frightened for Adam." She clutched his hand between both of hers. "And I'm worried about what the Raven is planning. However, you'll be happy to hear that I rang Philip. He knows everything now. He made some calls to his counterparts in Spain. Can you believe that they were skeptical and questioned the source of his information?" She shook her head incredulously. "They said that there had been no credible threats against the conference. They assured him that the security service was prepared for any contingency. In the end, they brushed him off with a polite thank you."

Gregory chuckled at the thunderous expression etched into her features. "Darling, I'm sure you're more upset by the official Spanish reaction than Philip was. It's a matter of pride. They can't be seen to admit that they allowed something to slip through the cracks."

"Do you really think that's the case?"

"Undoubtedly. They've probably had their analysts scrambling to sift through any new chatter no matter how innocuous. ETA, the militant group, has been very active in recent years. The authorities can't afford to ignore the possibility that the Russians and the Raven have entered the playing field."

He went on to give her a brief account of his meeting with Villiers and Philip, which confirmed some of the details that she had uncovered separately.

She nodded and pushed herself to her feet. "Right, I have to finish packing."

"Emmy, in light of everything, it would be better if you remained in London."

She gave him a wry smile. "Think again. I'm *going* to Madrid to cover this story. I have to see it through to find the truth."

He rose as well and stared down his nose at her. "I married a deranged, obstinate woman. Why do you insist on placing yourself in harm's way?"

Her dark eyes narrowed. She squared her shoulders and drew herself to her full height, which would have been comical if the situation weren't so serious.

She poked him in the chest. "You're one to talk. There's so much of your past that remains a mystery to me. I find it deeply infuriating that you don't trust me." Another poke. "You go off on secret forays, like this sudden trip of yours. I *know* it has nothing to do with Symington's. I haven't figured out what precisely you're up to, but it must be connected to the Raven. So, you can stop all the pretense. Just tell me if you're on the six-twenty British Airways flight tomorrow morning from Heathrow to Madrid."

He smoothed down the corners of his mustache. *Oh, Emmy*, he groaned inwardly.

The wheels of his brain began spinning. It was going to take a delicate balancing act to keep her safe, while he made himself bait for the Raven.

On the other hand, life would be too dull without a few challenges to spice things up.

He gave a resigned sigh as he looked down at her expectant face. "Yes, I'm on the six-twenty."

Her mouth curled into a smile. "I thought as much. Perhaps someone would be willing to switch seats on the plane, so that we can sit together."

He slid his arms around her waist and drew her to him. "It shouldn't be a problem. My devasting charm will brighten the day of the flight attendants and they'll scramble to accommodate my humble request."

She leaned into his embrace and couldn't help smiling. "Just remember you're a married man."

He kissed the top of her head. "As if I could forget. The image of your face is burned forever in my heart."

She gave him a gentle shove. "All right. That's enough of that." She pointed at his empty upright. "Get on with your packing."

He executed a sweeping bow. "Your servant, my lady."

Chapter 37

As luck would have it, the British Airways flight was not fully booked and Emmeline was able to switch her seat at the gate before they departed from Heathrow the next morning. The flight left on schedule and there was no turbulence. Gregory dozed for about half an hour, but Emmeline remained awake the entire time. She could never sleep on a plane. Besides, she was too anxious about what awaited them in Spain.

She tried to distract herself by reading the thriller she had brought along, but the words kept blurring before her eyes. In the end, she gave up and leafed through the file of clippings about Devarest for the hundredth time. She could cite all the details by heart. And yet, a memory at the edge of her consciousness kept dragging her back. It was staring her in the face. She had missed an important clue. What was it? She read each article again from beginning to end, her gaze combing over every inch of the photos.

Devarest, exuding supreme arrogance, was always trim and impeccable in Savile Row suits, crisp custom-made Egyptian cotton shirts, and silk ties. No wedding band on his manicured hand, only a signet ring adorned his left pinky. By contrast, Gavin and Robbie appeared solemn, unsure, and awkward at his side. They were in awe of their father.

By the time they touched down at Madrid–Barajas Airport at 9:55, her mind was still chasing ghosts. At the same time, she wondered how they were going to track down Adam if, indeed, he was in the city. Which she hoped he was not.

୧୬୧

They were among the first passengers off the plane. Fortunately, the line through customs was short. Since they hadn't checked any bags, they breezed through the airport. However, Emmeline's skin prickled with goosebumps and her nerves tingled with apprehension. She couldn't shake the feeling that someone had been watching them from the instant they set foot in the terminal. Her gaze darted to her right and left, but no one stared back. In fact, the travelers around them were either rushing to catch flights or ambling slowly until it was time to go to their gates. She cast a surreptitious glance over her shoulder. Nothing. She shrugged. It was probably a lack of sleep that was finally catching up with her. She had been so consumed by intrigues and murder the past few days that her imagination was running wild. And she couldn't have that. She had to keep her wits about her.

A taxi rolled up to the curb at virtually the same moment that they came out onto the pavement. Gregory told the driver that they wanted to go to the Hotel Princesa Plaza. The traffic was light and the driver nattered on cheerfully, asking them all sorts of questions about England, which he hoped to visit one day. Before they realized it, half an hour had slipped by and they had arrived at the hotel. Gregory quickly settled the fare and gave the driver a handsome tip. With his face wreathed in a broad grin, he wished them a pleasant stay in Madrid and within seconds was merging into traffic on Calle de la Princesa.

The hotel lobby was bright, spacious, and ultra-modern. From the columns coated in a gray-veined marble to the blond hardwood floors, everything gleamed. Emmeline wandered down the corridor to take a peek at the restaurant, as Gregory headed to reception to check in.

When he joined her again a few minutes later, he handed the press packet for the security conference that had been left for her at the desk.

She glanced at the schedule of events as they rode up in the lift. "The conference is being held at Galería de Cristal del Palacio de Cibeles. It's in El Retiro Park, which according to this is not far from the hotel. Once I drop my bag in the room and freshen up, I'll have to go over to the gallery. Apparently, a number of panel discussions will be held this afternoon." She grimaced. "Just my luck. I was hoping I'd have a chance to do a bit of investigating on the Raven before I had to go cover the blasted conference."

Gregory arched an eyebrow. "Emmy." His tone held a note of warning.

"What?" she asked innocently as the doors slid open.

"You are not to do any *investigating* on your own. Do I make myself clear?"

Her eyes narrowed, as they came to a halt in front of their room. "That sounds suspiciously like an order. I never promised to obey when we exchanged vows. This is 2010. You are not my lord and master," she retorted tartly.

A pained sigh escaped his lips as he inserted the plastic card into the slot and unlocked the door. "Infuriating woman," he muttered, "haven't there been enough murders already?" He stepped aside to allow her to enter their room.

"That's precisely the reason why I have to find the Raven. *Before* he carries out whatever nefarious plot ETA and Russians have devised."

"How do you intend to do that on your own in an unfamiliar city, where you have no contacts, and government officials refuse to admit there is a threat of any kind? Hmm."

She plopped down on the bed and gave him a sly smile. "Where there's a will, there's a way."

Gregory made a moue of displeasure. "How very profound. Just do the job you came here to do and cover the conference."

"Huh," she grunted, folding her arms over her chest. "The *real* story is Verena's murder and how it is tied to the Raven. The conference was merely a way to get me to Madrid so that I can finish what I started." She bit her lip, as a wave of worry washed over her. "Well, primarily that and to clear Adam's name."

The tension in Gregory's shoulders eased and he came to sit next to her. "Darling, I won't lie. Things do look black for Adam at the moment." His tone softened and he laced his fingers through hers. "But the truth will come out. It always does."

"Yes, you're right." She wasn't sure whether she was trying to convince herself or him. "Adam is as steady as they come. He must have had a compelling reason for leaving London as he did. Granted, he's been distracted lately. He admitted the other day that there have been problems with the company. Then of course, I know he's concerned about the possibility that Jason will be released from jail. But it doesn't explain why he rushed off to Madrid. *If* he's actually here."

They fell into a brooding silence, their thoughts swirling round and round as they tried to make the disparate pieces of the puzzle fit together.

Her head dropped onto his shoulder. "Why is the Raven trying to implicate Adam? The Raven—or to call him by his real name, Gavin Devarest—is an actor. Adam has no links to the theatrical world, so how could he possibly know the Raven? And yet, it all seems very personal. It's almost as if—"

She sat bolt upright and stared back at him.

"As if what?" Gregory prompted.

"As if he's seeking revenge."

"Emmy, I trust your instincts. But even if they had crossed paths by some extraordinary chance, Adam is not the type of fellow to antagonize someone else, let alone provoke a desire for revenge."

"Revenge, revenge," she mumbled. "Oh, my God." Her hand flew to her mouth and her pulse quickened. "I just had a horrible thought. The only person who ever made Adam's blood boil was Jason. Jason has always resented Adam. Jason would seize the first opportunity to mete out revenge. Like all those who are weak, he felt he had been wronged his entire life by his brother."

She searched Gregory's face. The expression in the depth of his eyes confirmed that her theory was not far-fetched.

"Jason would do anything to discredit Adam. Once that occurred, he could step in and take the helm of Royce Global Holdings and no one would be able to stop him."

"The only way that would be even remotely conceivable is if he were able to get the charges against him dropped."

"From what Adam told me, that is appearing more likely by the day. He's managed to hire a *very* expensive, high-flyer lawyer."

"That still does not explain how Jason would have joined forces with the Raven."

She leaped to her feet and started prowling around the room. "He was arrested because he latched onto Swanbeck's coattails. We know Swanbeck was hand-in-glove with the Russians. Jason could have met the Raven through Swanbeck's Russian cronies."

Gregory inclined his head in affirmation. "That's terrifying, but I have to admit highly probable."

She halted in her restless perambulations. "The more I think about it, Jason could have lured Adam to Madrid. That would mean…" Her voice dropped to a hoarse whisper. "That would mean Jason is here. Out of jail and wandering around the city free as a bird." She flapped an arm in the direction of the window.

Gregory rose and went to her. He placed his hands on her shoulders and gave them a reassuring squeeze. "This is all conjecture. We don't *know* anything definite."

"Darling, it's staring us in the face. You know I'm right. Now, everything is beginning to fall into place. The only thing I don't understand is why the Crown Prosecution Service would make a deal with Jason."

A snippet of conversation stirred in Gregory's memory. It was a slip of the tongue by Villers.

Jason Royce…He's more trouble than he's worth.

His jaw clenched. "Bloody bastard." The words were like two bullets flying across the air.

Emmeline pressed a hand to his chest. "What is it?"

His nostrils flared with fury. "Villiers," he spat the name. "It wasn't the Crown Prosecution. It was Villiers. Turning Jason loose is part of one of dear Papa's grand schemes."

Emmeline's complexion turned ashen. "Wh-what? Why?" She drew a ragged breath. "He…he didn't tell us anything."

Gregory smirked. "And that surprises you?"

She swallowed hard. "No, it just makes the situation worse. Jason feels vindicated and emboldened. He's been given *carte blanche* to do whatever he likes, without fear of reprisals."

Her body shuddered with revulsion and sheer terror.

"The Raven is floating in ill-gotten gains. He could have paid for Jason's lawyer and pulled some strings behind the scenes."

"Jason would have no qualms about making a pact with the devil," Gregory observed, "if it meant being set free."

"And in exchange, he agreed to help the Raven." Her hands curled into balls at her side. "Jason will never learn. He's merely traded one prison for another. The Raven owns him now. He'll never be free."

"Unfortunately, he doesn't view the situation in that light. It's more than likely he will help carry out whatever the Raven is planning to do here in Madrid and not even realize that it means certain death. His obsession with Adam has blinded him to everything else."

An overwhelming sense of helplessness was pressing down on her chest, suffocating her. "I feel as if precious time is slipping through our fingers. If the plot involves ETA and the Russians, as we suspect, then it must be a major target. They'd want to make a bold statement that would send ripples across the world stage."

Her gaze fell on the press kit lying open on the bed.

"Dear God, it's the security conference. The Raven is planning an attack on the conference."

Chapter 38

No one will believe us," Emmeline said as she snatched up the folder and leafed through it until she found the list of speakers.

With every name she read, her muscles coiled into ever tighter knots and nausea roiled in the pit of her stomach. Wordlessly, she handed the list to Gregory and pointed to one name in particular.

His countenance was strained and grim. Rage was radiating off his body in waves.

"Villiers," he hissed. He lifted his gaze to meet hers. "He's a last-minute replacement. It must have taken a great deal of arm-twisting through back channels. He must have started making calls the minute I left Acheson's office. He's been chasing the Raven for so long he tastes blood."

"In this respect, we can't really blame him," Emmeline remarked.

He blew out a hard breath. "No, but damn him all the same. The Raven has survived by cunning and sheer audacity all these years. He must know that Villiers has been hounding his trail. Verena's murder served a double purpose: to prevent her from exposing him and to draw out Villiers."

"I'd ring him," she said tentatively, "but we'd both end up losing our tempers, which won't help matters."

He touched her arm. "Leave it to me. You go to the Galería de Cristal del Palacio de Cibeles." He held up a hand to muzzle her protest before it burst forth. "If you don't make an appearance at the conference, it will arouse suspicions. Most likely, the Raven is already there. Remember he's an actor. He's probably assumed the identity of one of the attendees. That would give him easy access to the venue."

This chilling thought set her heart thumping wildly against her rib cage. "If Stephanie hadn't tricked me, we would at least have had a recent photo of Gavin Devarest. I discovered that he's part of a traveling theatrical troupe, but I couldn't find a single photo, which was odd."

"It might not have been of much use if he's in disguise," Gregory pointed out. She gave a glum nod.

"There must be something here"—she glanced down at the press kit in his hands—"that will give us a clue to the Raven's plan. Does he plan to assassinate one attendee or several at one blow? To date, bombing hasn't been part of his CV. But if he's working with ETA, they'd want a high body count."

"I think he's set in his ways, despite the dubious company he's been keeping." He paused, his forehead furrowing in concentration. "What if Villiers is the target? He'd made the Kremlin his enemy long ago. His death at the conference would be blamed on ETA. And the Raven wouldn't have to look over his shoulder anymore."

It was a clinically logical deduction. Villiers was connected to every aspect of this case. The problem was Villiers would scoff at the mere suggestion of going into protective custody until the Raven was apprehended.

That meant it was up to her and Gregory to prevent a tragedy. They would have to make the authorities listen. First, though, they had to determine when the Raven planned to strike. They scanned the day-to-day conference schedule. They reasoned that the Raven would want an event that attracted the largest number of people. Something with a bit of cachet to serve as a stark contrast to the ugliness of the hit and therefore make it even more memorable. That would appeal to the Raven's sense of irony.

She tapped her finger against the paper. "That's it. I'm certain of it."

The welcome reception the following evening would be a black-tie affair at the Palacio Real de Madrid, the official residence of the Spanish royal family. Nowadays, the palace was only used for state ceremonies. A grand dinner would be held and there would be a special performance of Flamenco dancing.

ꝏꝏ

When Emmeline asked for directions for the fastest way to get to Galería de Cristal del Palacio de Cibeles, the Crystal Gallery, the enthusiastic young woman at reception had told her in no uncertain terms that Madrid was a city where one strolled leisurely to savor its wealth of charms and history. Emmeline tried to protest when the woman pulled out a map from underneath the desk and started marking sights that were "a must" for all visitors.

"You have to go to the Prado to see the masterpieces of Velázquez, El Greco, Rubens, and Goya." The woman wagged a finger at Emmeline. "Promise me you won't leave Madrid without visiting the museum. Another place I'm sure you will like is the Plaza de Cibeles, which is in the center of the city at the intersection of the Paseo del Prado and Calle Alcalá. It is one of the most beautiful squares in my opinion. You will find a fountain there of the Greek goddess Cybele on a lion-drawn carriage. Did you know that it was designed by the architect Ventura

Rodríguez in 1782?" She breezed on without giving Emmeline a chance to offer a response. "The Old Town area around the Plaza de España, where the monument to our great writer Cervantes is located, is very interesting too. The plaza is at the western end of the Gran Via, our most famous street. It has many shops and restaurants. If you like architecture, you will enjoy all the magnificent buildings." Her eyes gleamed with pride. She took a breath, but she wasn't finished extolling the virtues of her beloved city. "The Palacio Real. You can visit the palace, if you want. I suggest that you do. It is only a short walk to the south of Plaza de España. Nearby is Plaza Mayor, another square full of history. The square is huge, one hundred twenty-nine meters by ninety-four meters. For centuries popular entertainments, bullfights, beatifications, coronations and…and the sometimes an *auto de fe*."—she crossed herself and sent up a little prayer to the Almighty— "were held there. The *auto de fe* were public ceremonies, organized in the Inquisition, involving prisoners condemned for crimes against religion." She gave a shudder but quickly continued in a more cheerful tone, "You will also see the statue of Felipe III on a horse. It was a present from the Duke of Florence to the King of Spain and—"

The last threads of Emmeline's patience snapped. She rolled up the map. "Thank you so much for all of the information." She tried to keep her voice even. "But right now, I just want to get to the Galería de Cristal del Palacio de Cibeles. I have work to do." She flashed her press pass. "I'm covering the security conference."

The woman clucked her tongue. "*Madre di Dio*. Why did you not say that from the beginning?"

Emmeline clenched her jaw but managed what she hoped was a polite smile. Finally, the woman gave her directions and she was out of the hotel. Gregory had departed separately. He'd received a mysterious call half an hour ago. She hadn't liked the expression on his face when he left the room. He was extremely evasive when she'd asked where he was going. In response, he had given a distracted kiss on the top of the head and said that he would ring Villiers. They agreed to meet back at the hotel later in the afternoon.

Once out on the Calle de la Princesa, Emmeline glanced at her watch. It was too early to go to the Crystal Gallery, so she decided to take the advice of the woman from the hotel and walk. She ambled along Calle de la Princesa and followed it until she reached Gran Via. The woman at reception had been right. The street thrummed with life and the elegant Belle Epoque buildings with tile facades were a feast for the senses. She spotted one or two restaurants along the way where she and Gregory could have a romantic meal.

She took a brief turn around Plaza de España, which she had to admit was lovely. She admired the monument to Cervantes, who is widely considered to be the greatest writer in the Spanish language. The monument featured several statues carved into the pedestal representing characters from his writings. The section she found most enchanting was the statue of a gypsy girl. It was so full of life. Emmeline had the impression that the gypsy and her companions would leap off at any moment and continue their jig before her. As a tribute to his most celebrated work *Don Quixote*, a bronze statue of Don Quixote and his squire Sancho Panza stood sentinel in front of the monument. This was flanked by stone statues of Dulcinea, whom Don Quixote idealized, and the peasant girl Aldonza Lorenzo.

She was so absorbed in soaking up all the details of the various carvings that at first she didn't notice the tall, balding man in his late sixties who stopped next to her. He inclined his head, when she flicked a glance in his direction. He had an angular face, whose many deep lines emphasized his dour expression. His complexion was sallow and bloodless. His lips twisted into what she supposed passed for a smile. However, his gray eyes were hard as steel. His spectacles only made them appear even larger. She gave him a watery smile in return. But something about the way he carried himself and his intense, watchful gaze put her on her guard.

The hairs on the back of her neck prickled. She hitched her handbag higher on her shoulder and started to walk away.

"A moment if you will, Miss Kirby," the man called.

The sound of her name on his lips made her back stiffen. She pivoted slowly on her heel to face him again.

"Who are you? What do you want?"

He took a half-step toward her, but stopped short when she ordered, "Stay right there."

He held up his hands in surrender. "As you wish. I come as a friend."

He spoke English fluently, but he had a heavy Russian accent. Her past experiences dealing with Russians had been far from cordial. In fact, they had been downright menacing. So, for this man to deliberately seek her out in a foreign city was more than a bit disconcerting.

"Friend? We've never met," she shot back. Her gaze snaked to her right and left. "I'll scream for the police, if—"

"Please don't." He was about to advance toward her but then thought better of it. "I'm not going to hurt you. Quite the contrary, in fact. I merely want to give you a word of advice. For your own good, you and your husband should go back to London. You're in over your heads. If you stay, you will most certainly die."

She sucked in her breath at the bald audacity of the statement.

"You will understand that we don't value your

journalistic zeal. I suppose it's a matter of different political philosophies. But please believe me when I say that it would be a great pity if you sacrificed your life. Leave now, while you still have a chance."

Once he had said his peace, he gave her a curt nod and strode away without a backward glance.

We? she chortled to herself. *I must be getting too close for comfort if the Russians sent a thug to frighten me off.*

This thought both exhilarated and terrified her.

She half-ran, half-walked the rest of the way along Gran Via. The Teatro Lope de Vega and the other graceful buildings all became a blur. She only stopped to draw a shaky breath, when she reached Calle de Montalbán, where the Crystal Gallery stood on the left. The Russian's unexpected warning rattled her more than she realized.

She tilted her head back, allowing her gaze to travel over the large, irregularly-shaped vaulted dome of the imposing Crystal Gallery. However, only one part of her brain took in the clean lines of the architecture. The other part was completely focused on Gavin Devarest, the infamous Raven.

"Gregory and I will stop you," she said aloud. "This ends here."

One way or another.

෬෨෬

Gregory had arrived early in Plaza Mayor to get the lay of the land and ascertain whether he had acquired an unwanted shadow. The rectangular square was surrounded by three-story, red-brick residential buildings with balconies facing the plaza. An arcade went all the way around its perimeter. Gregory noted the nine gates and ten entrances, which would provide an easy escape if needed. The plaza was brimming with activity at the restaurants and tapas bars alongside the arcade. It was the Christmas season and everyone seemed to be in a festive mood.

He had taken two turns around the arcade. No one stood out. But instinct told him that the Raven was watching him. Perhaps the bastard was at one of the tapas bars.

Gregory glanced at his watch again. Five minutes before the exchange was to take place. He broke from the shadows of the arcade and crossed the square to the bronze statue of Felipe III in the center. The Blue Angel and Pink Courtesan were burning a hole in his pocket. His gaze never stopped roaming over every inch of the square. Would his gamble pay off? Would the diamonds prove too tempting a prize that the Raven risked showing himself?

Greed was a powerful motivator. And yet…

A frisson of unease slithered down his spine. Deep in the marrow of his bones, he could sense that something was wrong.

"Toby," a male voice called.

He spun around.

Bloody hell. Villiers was striding toward him.

"What the devil are you doing here?" Gregory demanded when the older man had drawn level.

"Making sure that you don't make a great big cock-up," Villiers snarled. "As usual."

Gregory dropped his chin to his chest and groaned. "You've probably scared off the Raven, you do realize that?"

"You're welcome, by the way."

"For what?"

"Keeping you alive. For the present at least." Villiers exhaled a frustrated sigh. "I don't know why I bother, though. Your inquisitive wife is going to lead you to an early grave at this rate."

Gregory took a step toward his father. "Stuff it," he said through gritted teeth. "What are you doing here?"

"Have you forgotten that you left a rather urgent voicemail for me?"

"So—what? Instead of returning my call, you went into full-on MI5 mode and decided to follow me. How did you even know we were in Madrid? I didn't mention it in my message."

Villiers made a dismissive gesture with his hand. "Never mind." His gaze darted around the square. He took Gregory's arm and gave him a nudge with his elbow. "Let's walk. We're too conspicuous here."

"And whose fault is that?" Gregory hissed.

However, he tamped down his anger and exasperation. The Raven had flown. There was nothing to be done on that score at the moment. On the other hand, the stakes were high. Any miscalculation would be lethal for all of them.

Chapter 39

Emmeline was cool, calm, and collected, the epitome of journalistic professionalism when she flashed her credentials inside the Crystal Gallery's cavernous hall. One of the conference coordinators showed her to a room set aside for the press.

The low murmur of voices reverberated off the walls. Cameramen checked their equipment. Some journalists had their mobiles plastered to their ears, while others lounged in chairs chatting or making notes. She nodded a greeting at a few of the colleagues she has met in the past. However, she loitered by a table at the back of the room where coffee and tea had been set out to avoid being drawn into conversation. She had too much to do.

She pretended to study the schedule that the coordinator had handed to her. The second round of panel discussions would be held in half an hour. Villiers was not participating in any of today's panels. She gave an inward sigh of relief, although she was still certain that the Raven intended to strike at the welcome reception the following evening. Still, Villiers's absence from today's events reduced the stress level a notch or two. She could channel her energies into convincing the authorities that the conference was under lethal threat. In the interim, she hoped that Gregory had managed to track down Villiers and persuaded the deputy director of MI5 to withdraw from any public appearances in the near future. The voice of reason told her this was a lost cause.

Keeping her eyes on the room, she surreptitiously took several backward steps until her shoulders brushed against the wall. The next second, she slipped out the door and into the hall.

Her footsteps echoed on the marble floor, which was dappled by strands of golden light streaming through the glass dome.

She popped her head into a room that looked like a private cinema, where some sort of documentary was playing. She exited almost immediately and continued her perambulations. One of the panels was being held in the next room. A man nearest the door lifted his head and shushed her even before she took a step inside. She gave him an apologetic smile and left.

"May I help you?" a male voice floated to her ears.

She turned around to find herself looking up into the scowling face of a tall Spanish stranger, whose brown eyes pinned her to the spot. His gaze held something she couldn't quite define. It was unsettling and vaguely intimate at the same time.

"I…I," she stammered. She cleared her throat and tried a friendly grin, before starting again. "I'm Emmeline Kirby of *The Clarion* in London. I'm here to cover the conference."

She proffered a hand. The man hesitated for an instant before he took it. His handshake was cool and firm. In fact, she had to flex her fingers for a few seconds to get the blood circulating again once he released them. She could still feel the imprint of his signet ring in her palm.

He gave a curt nod. "I am Hector Melgoza. I am the head of security for the conference. May I see your press pass?" He didn't even wait for her to take it off her neck. "Yes, it seems to be in order. I've been watching you. Is there a reason you are sneaking around?"

She drew herself to her full height. "I wasn't 'sneaking.' I was merely trying to familiarize myself with the layout of the gallery."

"I see. Was the map missing from your press kit? If so, I will get one for you."

"No, no. I have it," she replied hastily. "I like to get the feel of a place first-hand. To form my own impression." The smile on her lips died, when it clashed with the stony expression etched on his features.

"Not here. The security for the conference is extremely tight. We do not want the press sticking their noses everywhere. If you do not follow the rules, I will have to revoke your pass and you will be escorted out of the building."

Well, that's put me in my place, she thought. She couldn't afford to antagonize him further.

"Please return to the press room."

Before she could acquiesce to his command, someone called, "Emmeline, there you are. You've kept me waiting for ten minutes. I did tell you I had a busy schedule today. Please don't make me regret agreeing to the interview."

Emmeline's eyes widened in surprise and she was left momentarily tongue-tied by Philip's unexpected appearance.

She recovered quickly. "I do apologize, Mr. Acheson. I was"—she cast a sideways glance at Melgoza—"I was unavoidably detained. If that's all, Mr. Melgoza, I have an interview to conduct with Mr. Acheson."

She had the satisfaction of seeing the security man looking suitably chastened. He turned to Philip. "It was my fault entirely. A minor misunderstanding."

Philip smiled. "Of course." Then he shot his cuff and looked at his watch. "Are you ready, Emmeline?"

She dug out her notebook and pen from her handbag and waved them in the air. "Yes. Lead the way, Mr. Acheson."

"There's an empty room down the corridor at your disposal. You can speak without being disturbed," Melgoza informed them

They thanked him and started to walk away. She could feel Melgoza's mistrustful gaze trailing their footsteps.

They exchanged pleasantries until Philip closed the door and they were alone.

"I see that you and Longdon can't resist jumping into the fire." Philip's voice held a fierce edge.

He dropped heavily into a chair and impaled her with a hard blue stare.

She took the seat next to him. "That's unfair and you know it. We're not here on some lark. We're trying to prevent another murder. *Villiers's murder.*"

She folded her arms across her chest and glared at him. "Yes, that's right. We're quite sure the Raven is going to kill Villiers and make it look like it was ETA. That way the Kremlin's hands are clean, while it sows dissent in Spain and disposes of a nemesis in a single blow."

Philip exhaled a weary sigh, relenting at last. "The minute you came to me with your theory about Gavin Devarest, ETA, and the Russians, I went straight to Villiers. We had heard chatter about Spain recently and came to the conclusion that the conference would be a prime target. Villiers huddled with his counterparts at MI6 and it was decided that he would go to the conference as a replacement speaker. They reasoned that no one would bat an eye at the change because there are so many high-profile participants. Besides, Villiers has been chasing the Raven for years. He knows him inside out." He shook his head. "That's what the Kremlin was counting on. We played right into their bloody hands. Meanwhile, it was ludicrous to think that anything would hold you back once you were on the scent. I should have known that you would manage a way to come to the conference."

She flashed him a smug smile. "Indeed, you should have."

"The only thing I can't work out is what Longdon came to Madrid to do. Is it connected with the Raven? Or is he playing some other game?"

Emmeline bit her lip and remained silent because she didn't have an answer and it was driving her to distraction.

"Perhaps Villiers found out when he met with Longdon."

"What? Gregory's mysterious meeting was with Villiers? Why didn't he tell me?"

"Likely because he went out to confront the Raven on his own. But Villiers has had the two of you under surveillance, since you landed in Madrid so he knew that Longdon would be in Plaza Mayor. The Raven aborted the meeting once he saw Villiers."

Emmeline's eyes narrowed. "I see," she murmured. Gregory had a good deal to answer for once they returned to the hotel tonight.

She pushed aside her annoyance with her husband's covert personal missions and told Philip about their theory that the Raven would try to kill Villiers at the welcome reception the following evening at the Palacio Real.

"Yes," he concurred once she had finished. "I think you and Longdon have hit the nail on the head. Villiers reckoned that the hit would occur at a high-profile event, rather than at the conference itself." He paused for a moment to mull this thought further. "Well, it's good we brought reinforcements with us."

She brightened. "I'm relieved to see that our government is taking the matter seriously. What kind of reinforcements?"

Bang on cue, the door opened and Superintendent

Burnell and Sergeant Finch walked into the room.

Chapter 40

Hello, Emmeline. What a surprise to find you and Longdon in Madrid," Burnell drawled, as he crossed toward them.

She was trapped in the liquid netting of his glacial stare, which never left her face. Her cheeks suffused with heat, as the two detectives settled into nearby chairs.

"I…I'm sorry," she offered contritely. "We never intended to deceive you. It's just that…" Her voice trailed off.

"It's just that you didn't trust me enough about Adam and decided to swoop in to his rescue."

The hurt expression reflected in his eyes made her wince.

"I'm sorry," she mumbled again. "You were so…intransigent. You wouldn't listen."

The superintendent's mouth curled into a crooked smile. "I'm bound to follow the letter of law, no matter my personal opinions."

She nodded. "Yes, I know that." Her gaze flickered to Finch and then back to Burnell. "You're both conscientious and dedicated. A credit to the force. I was desperate to clear Adam's name. He's not the Raven. It's a man called Gavin Devarest. I told Philip what I had uncovered before we left London."

She caught the guarded look that Burnell and Finch exchanged. She was sure once they heard what she had pieced together, based on McCallister's cryptic final words, they would be convinced of Adam's innocence.

They listened without interruption to the information she had gathered about the Devarests. She concluded with what she and Gregory had speculated about Jason's involvement with the Raven.

"Don't you see? It all makes sense now." Her voice rose in excitement. "Adam is being framed. As we all know, Jason has always been consumed by jealousy and is willing to do anything to destroy Adam to get his hands on Royce Global Holdings."

She drew a breath and waited. The two detectives were slow to react, which set off an alarm in the back of her head.

The superintendent pursed his lips and cleared his throat. He spoke slowly. "Philip told us about Gavin Devarest, so we did some checking." He paused and regarded her steadily. "Devarest is dead."

All the wind was knocked out of her lungs. "He can't be dead." Her gaze raked over the faces of the three men. "He can't be. I followed up. His theatrical troupe was in each of the cities, where one of the Raven's victims was killed."

"I assure you he's dead. He was an alcoholic, who tried to shake his addiction. But after being pickled for most of his adult life, it was too little, too late. He died in a private rehabilitation clinic in Merseyside. Gavin Devarest is not the Raven."

"But…everything pointed to him." She held Burnell's eyes. "The facts all fit together." She choked on this last word.

This unexpected blow set her mind reeling. She had been so sure.

"Emmeline, you can't punish yourself. The Raven is as cunning as a fox. He left a trail of false breadcrumbs to deflect attention and give himself time to assume another identity. He knew the authorities would have to start their search from scratch. In the meantime, they had wasted months and years."

She swallowed hard. "Well, one fact remains." She straightened her spine and tossed her chin in the air. "Adam is *not* the Raven." Her tone held a challenge edged in steel. "The evidence that has come to light is all circumstantial."

"None of us believes Adam is guilty," Philip offered gently. "Granted, the Raven has spun an extremely sophisticated web to misdirect us. But after years of outsmarting the law, criminals like him become careless and leave a loose thread. Our job is to find it and pull until the entire ball of yarn unravels."

"Philip's right," Finch chimed in. "Officially, the guv and I are in Madrid to follow up on a lead on Adam, who is a person of interest in an active case. That will lull the Raven into a false sense of security. He'll believe he's free and clear to move forward with his plans for the welcome reception. He doesn't know that we're really here to help Philip set a trap."

"Now, thanks to you," Burnell interjected, "we know that Villiers is the Raven's target. It will make it easier to hone our plans. We can also keep an eye out for Jason."

"How can Gregory and I help?" she asked eagerly.

"You've done your part. The best thing the two of you can do is to go home." Although the superintendent's words were uttered softly, they held a firm command.

She raised an eyebrow. "Respectfully, Superintendent. You must be joking. I've worked far too hard on this story. I'm going to see it through to the end. I need to know the truth."

"Perhaps Longdon will see reason," Finch suggested.

Her mouth curved into a wry smile. "Gregory and I are of one mind."

God help us all, Burnell griped silently. *Why do I feel like two grenades are about to explode in our faces?*

Chapter 41

The pearly white confection of the Palacio Real, otherwise known as Palacio Oriente, rose above the flagstone forecourt and gleamed against the velvety cobalt sky. Emmeline's breath caught in her throat when she laid eyes on the graceful sixteenth-century Baroque architecture.

And yet, she thought as they ambled up the gravel path of the Oriente gardens toward the palace, *a criminal with a mercenary black heart is planning to commit murder in this beautiful setting.*

Gregory stopped a few paces before the entrance to the courtyard. One eyebrow quirked upward. "There's still time to change your mind, Emmy. It's no shame to let Oliver and the others handle things."

Philip had wrangled invitations for them to the reception since Villiers proved intractable in his refusal to keep his distance. There had been a good deal of grumbling and debate among Philip, Burnell, and Finch, before they reluctantly resigned themselves to the inevitable. Needless to say, Villiers was displeased with all of them.

She straightened Gregory's bow tie and then caressed his cheek. "No." The word was unequivocal. "We're going to this party. As Caesar said when he led his army across the Rubicon, '*Alea iacta est.*' The die is cast."

A smile curled around his lips. "That's my girl. I was merely checking."

He looped her hand through his elbow. "Shall we, Mrs. Longdon? It would be impolite to keep a murderer waiting."

"I can't think of anything I'd rather be doing on a lovely December evening in Madrid."

He patted her hand and they proceeded to the door. The beating of her heart sounded extraordinarily loud. She slid a glance out of the corner of her eye at Gregory. She hoped he couldn't hear it thudding against her ribcage. She took a deep breath and placed one foot in front of the other.

Alea iacta est.

She hoped those words wouldn't be the epitaph on their tombs.

ভোষো

Emmeline and Gregory were in awe from the moment they crossed the threshold of the grand hall, which was dominated by a magnificent double marble staircase where lions guarded the bottom steps. The carving was so life-like that she could almost hear them roar. Meanwhile, radiant frescos framed in gilded moldings spied down upon them from the vaulted ceiling.

The guests were given a brief tour of the palace. Emmeline's neck ached from swiveling it in every direction, as she tried to burn into her memory the gleaming elegance of the Hall of Mirrors, the Royal Armory, and several other rooms. Her senses savored the vibrant colors of the rich tapestries hanging on the walls and marveled at the works of such masters as Goya, Velazquez, Caravaggio, and Battista.

Far too soon, they were ushered toward the dining room. With a sigh of regret, Emmeline cast one last look at the

Hall of Mirrors. Then, she squared her shoulders and mentally prepared herself for the hunt that lay ahead.

The crystal facets of the chandeliers captured the embers of light and sent them skittering across the highly-buffed parquet floor, gray-veined marble columns, and the gilded ceiling of the dining room. Huge porcelain urns were framed like a painting in curtained nooks at intervals along one side of the room.

To her dismay, she found that Gregory was seated opposite her at the long table. Philip was placed to her right, while Villiers was on her left.

Philip gave her a crooked smile and gallantly drew out the chair for her. She murmured her thanks and lowered herself onto the creamy gold velvet-button cushion. Villiers, on the other hand, grunted something unintelligible. She assumed it was "Good evening," but she couldn't be absolutely sure.

Her gaze snaked to Gregory, who gave her a cheeky wink. This brought a smile to her lips, while a warm glow spread over her body and eased the knot in the pit of her stomach. She couldn't see Burnell or Finch anywhere, but she knew they were at the palace coordinating with the Spanish authorities. She did find herself the object of the surly Melgoza's scrutiny at one point, but she quickly averted her gaze.

During the first course, Villiers hissed out of the corner of his mouth, "This ridiculous plan of yours is doomed to fail. There are too many holes in it. I've waited far too long to catch the Raven and in one night you're going to ruin years of painstaking work."

"Yes, sir," Philip replied without moving his lips. "You've made your feelings quite clear on the matter. But we all agreed—"

"I especially object to this woman's involvement. Not only is she a civilian. She's a bloody reporter." Villiers gestured with his chin across the table. "Toby shouldn't be here either. They're both amateurs."

"*This woman*," Emmeline snapped in a hoarse whisper, "is not deaf. You don't have to like me, nor am I seeking your approval. But for Gregory's sake, I think we should try to be civil to one another. We owe him that much." She pretended to take a spoonful of soup. "As for tonight, I'm here to do a job. I'm going to see this story through to the end. And despite your constant barrage of disparaging remarks, I don't want to see you murdered in cold blood. So, we're stuck with each other, like it or not."

This little speech kept Villiers silent for the rest of the meal.

When the plates were being cleared for dessert and coffee, a waiter bent down close to Gregory's ear. "I hope you're enjoying the evening, Señor Longdon," he said politely.

Gregory inclined his head. "Yes, thank you."

The waiter's voice dipped even lower. "A certain gentleman would like to know whether you have the blue and pink items with you."

Gregory's neck whipped around to stare into the fellow's onyx eyes. "Yes."

"Very good. The gentleman has the money. The exchange will take place tonight. The gentleman will be waiting in the yellow salon. I will come to get you during the Flamenco performance."

He glided away without another word.

A dozen thoughts jostled with one another in Gregory's consciousness. Was the waiter one of the Raven's lackeys or merely an innocent messenger? Why the devil had the Raven decided to take possession of the diamonds here in the palace?

He frowned. The diamonds made him wonder yet again about the Raven's identity since their theory about Gavin

Devarest had been shot to pieces. He had an idea, but it required confirmation from his friend David Nussbaum at the London Diamond Bourse. When he missed David at the office, he tried his home number. To his frustration, David's wife Marjorie answered. He asked her to have David call him the instant he set foot through the door. He stressed that the matter was urgent.

Gregory had set his mobile on vibrate and cursed every minute that ticked by during the dinner. He drew it out discreetly under the table.

Come on, David, he silently implored.

The heavens must have taken pity on him because the next instant it began vibrating in his hands. David's number flashed across the screen.

He pretended to drop his napkin on the floor and answered the call, "David, hold for just a moment."

When he sat up again, a waiter was setting down a plate of *Tocino De Cielo*, a traditional Spanish dessert that was similar to flan.

He snatched the fellow's sleeve. "I must take this call." He waved his mobile. "It's urgent. Is there somewhere private I can go?"

"*Si, señor*. I will show you. Please follow me."

Emmeline's head popped up, when he rose. A shadow of worry rippled across her face.

"It's all right. I'll tell you later" he mouthed.

She nodded, but her expression telegraphed that she was unconvinced. At least she had Acheson and Villiers to keep her occupied until he returned.

The waiter led him to a small, exquisitely furnished reception room. He gave a curt nod and withdrew immediately, leaving Gregory alone.

"David," he said. "Sorry about that. I didn't want anyone to overhear."

"It's all right. How can I help you? Marjorie said it was

important."

"It is. I can't explain now. You'll have to trust me. I have one question."

"After all these years, you must know that you can ask me anything."

"You mentioned that the board was considering offering a seat to Craig Sheldrake and another candidate? Who's the other chap?"

"This stays between us."

"You have my word," Gregory promised.

When David told him, everything clicked into place.

❧❧❧

By the time he had finished his call, dessert had been devoured and the guests were rising from the table to gather at one end of the room. The air reverberated with the low hum of excited anticipation as the lights were dimmed over the table. Only one chandelier was left burning to create a spotlight over the Flamenco troupe. The women were arrayed in long red dresses that clung to every curve and curled into a thick ruffled flounce around their ankles, while the men wore crisp white shirts with flowing sleeves, black vests, and fitted black trousers.

The head of the troupe gave a brief explanation of the dances they were going to perform. And then, it began. Precise heel tapping movements and rhythmic hand clapping that were accompanied by guttural cries from the men. The guitar music thrummed with fiery passion and melancholy. All conspired to mesmerize the audience.

Gregory saw none of the dancing. He was intent on finding Emmeline. The semi-gloom was not making it easy. Finally, he spied her across the room. She was dwarfed by Acheson and Villiers.

He threaded his way through the crowd on the balls of

his feet and grasped her lightly by the elbow.

Startled at first by his touch, she let out a soft gasp and then relaxed. "Where have you been?" she demanded.

"Emmy, come with me." He lowered his voice to a conspiratorial whisper so that the guests nearby would not eavesdrop. "I have something important to tell you about the Raven—"

He broke off when the waiter who had given him the Raven's message at dinner sidled up to him. "It's time, Señor Longdon."

He swore inwardly.

Emmeline peered at the waiter and then her gaze settled on Gregory. "What's going on?"

"It may be another ploy or it may not." Her eyes narrowed. "I'll soon see."

"I'm coming with you," she insisted and took a step toward him.

"No," he hissed, "it's better if you stay here." Philip became aware of their hushed conversation and shot him a questioning look. "Acheson, I have to take care of something. Watch over, Emmy."

Philip nodded and mouthed "Go"

She shook off Philip's hand. "I don't need anyone to watch over me."

This earned a snort from Villiers, who had been following every word. However, he held his counsel and pretended that he was enchanted by the dancing.

൙൙

Gregory and the waiter wended their way down a labyrinth of seemingly endless corridors. Gregory's breathing quickened with every footfall that took them farther away from the dining room. At last, they came to halt before a thick, mahogany door.

The waiter bent in a half-bow and gestured at the door. "Please go inside and place the items on the table. The gentleman will join you shortly. Have a good evening, señor."

Gregory listened for several seconds as the fellow's silhouette faded into the shadows, before reaching for the doorknob and giving it a flick of his wrist.

As Emmy said, "Alea iacta est." This is the point of no return.

The salon was small by comparison to the rooms he had seen that evening. Its yellow damask walls were covered in paintings by Goya and Caravaggio. A plush carpet with a pattern of flowers, medallions and curlicues in hues of crimson, azure and cream muffled his footsteps.

He removed the Blue Angel and Pink Courtesan from his inside pocket and placed the two blue velvet boxes on the marble-topped console table set against one wall. Then, he crossed to the gilt-edged mirror hanging above a small fireplace.

The Raven found him calmly straightening his tie.

Gregory glanced up at the murderer's reflection in the mirror. "I knew it would be you," he drawled.

Chapter 42

P ardon me, Señor Acheson," one of the young waiters said, as the performers were taking a short break before their second dance.

Philip glanced around. "Yes?"

"I have a message from Superintendent Burnell. He must see you about an urgent matter. He said you would understand."

Philip shot a worried glance at Villiers, who was scowling, and then replied, "I'll come straightaway."

Emmeline stiffened and clutched at his sleeve. "Perhaps I should come too."

"No. Don't move from this spot," Villiers commanded. "I'll go with Acheson. Obviously, this is a security matter, which is none of your concern."

The protest died on her tongue, when Philip remarked in a more diplomatic tone, "It would be better if you remained behind. If it is the Raven, you'll be safer among the rest of the guests."

He patted her arm and flashed a smile, which did nothing to soothe her frayed nerves.

Heads bent in conversation, they strode off without a backward glance.

Hmph, men, she griped to herself and damned the entire species to hell.

Speaking of men, where was Gregory? She craned her neck around, but he was nowhere to be seen.

She glanced at her watch. He'd been gone far longer than she realized. Her chest began to swell with fear. He had started to say something about the Raven. Now, her husband was trapped within the walls of this gilded cage. Even if she had an inkling of where to begin searching for him, she had been abandoned here. Alone. If she went roaming the corridors on her own, she would surely be arrested for trespassing or worse.

She needed the assistance of someone in an official capacity. But she was a foreigner. Who would listen to her?

As she was debating this question, she caught a glimpse of the gruff Melgoza on the other side of the room. She could approach him. He was the head of security for the conference, after all. She would implore him to help her. He appeared distracted. She supposed that he was preoccupied with all the preparations for the reception. He must have sensed her gaze upon him because he looked round suddenly. In that moment, he let his guard down and she saw something approaching regret reflected in his eyes. Then, the lights were dimmed and the dancers stepped out again.

Damn and blast.

The other guests surged forward like a tidal wave and she lost sight of Melgoza.

The dancing became a blur and the music, which she had found so captivating a short while ago, now made her temples throb with worry.

She had to find Gregory. What could he have found out about the Raven?

Unconsciously, she began twisting her pink sapphire engagement ring around her finger as she reviewed all the details she had pieced together. She had been convinced that Gavin Devarest was their man. All the clues had pointed to him.

Had she become obsessed and arranged the facts so that they fit her theory? God help her. If she lost her objectivity, it would be the death knell for her career.

She wallowed in bitter recriminations.

Ouch. Her ring had scratched her finger. While it didn't draw any blood, the pain was the shock that she needed to lift the fog in her brain.

She hadn't been wrong. Not entirely.

"Of course, there were two," she murmured. "The Raven was hiding in plain sight. He was taunting me."

Her fists curled at her sides, her ring digging into her palm keeping her alert. It was all so obvious.

Until now the Raven had been the puppet master, but she was finished dancing to his tune. She had to find Gregory and tell the others.

She whirled around and collided with the gentleman behind her.

Oof. She was momentarily stunned.

"I'm terribly sorr—" Her mouth went dry and the rest of the sentence would never be uttered.

Her body stilled. Only ice sluiced through her veins, as she stared up into Jason's green eyes.

"Hello, Emmeline." His odious voice dripped with contempt. "It's been a long time. We have a great deal of unfinished business."

A scream clawed at her throat, but his next words prevented it from escaping.

"If you'd like to see your thief of a husband one last time, I suggest you come with me. Quietly. Do I make myself clear?"

She nodded dumbly. "I'm glad to see that you're being sensible for once in your life."

His fingers bit into the fleshy part of her upper arm with unnecessary pressure. "Smile. This is a party after all. We wouldn't our hosts to think that you weren't enjoying yourself."

☙☙☙

"Ah, there you are, Emmeline," the Raven greeted her. "You're the guest of honor. Now, the festivities can begin."

She shook off Jason's grasp and flew to Gregory's side the instant she entered the yellow salon. "Are you hurt?" she asked him.

Her husband offered a sardonic smile and slipped one arm protectively around her waist.

"I must admit I've never spent a more stimulating evening." He turned to the Raven. "However, I regret to say your hospitality leaves a good deal to be desired. You haven't even offered us a post-prandial *aperitif*. A Crema Catalana would be nice." He clucked his tongue in admonishment.

Although the Raven remained outwardly nonchalant, with one elbow propped casually on the mantelpiece, she was pleased to see one of his eyelids fluttered in annoyance.

"I must congratulate you, Sheldrake," she said facetiously. "I was a fool not to see it."

Sheldrake inclined his head, as he pulled off the makeup and wig that had transformed him into Melgoza. "Please don't reproach yourself. I've never had such a worthy adversary. You added a delicious piquancy to the chase. I enjoyed myself enormously if it makes you feel any better."

"It doesn't, Sheldrake," she growled. "Or do you prefer William Faraday? Or the name you were given at birth, Robbie Devarest?"

He raised a hand in a silent salute.

"You were there at every turn. In the bar at the theatre,

you contrived the argument with Verena and slipped the poison into her drink." He gave a slight nod. "I'm not sure. Did you kill her or was it McCallister?"

"Verena's death is on McCallister's conscience." He pressed a hand to his heart and said solemnly, "God rest his soul."

"Hmph," she sneered. "Neither of you has a soul."

He wagged a finger. "Ah, ah. Let's not sink into personal attacks. You're better than that."

She glared at him, but went on, "Judging by McCallister's reaction at the reading of the will, you must have promised him half of Verena's fortune, once you discovered they were sleeping together." She chortled. "You were never going to honor the agreement."

Sheldrake shrugged. "You really shouldn't cry over either of them. The world is better off without them. Believe me. When I first met, Verena she was like a breath of fresh air. She gave life the zest that it was missing. However, it was time to move on. Verena's charms were beginning to pall. I needn't have to remind you that the bitch wanted to kill *me* at one point and then she decided to ruin me instead. I couldn't have that. I merely made a preemptive strike, so to speak.

"As for McCallister—his real name is Feliks Kuznetsov—the Russians sent him to be my handler. His greed was his undoing."

She picked up the thread of the tale. "I'm guessing they discovered that you murdered your father and the jury that set him free." She received a nod of confirmation. "So, they gave you an ultimatum: either kill for them or they would make sure that proof of your previous crimes fell into the hands of the authorities."

"I must admit it chafed at first being under the Russians' thumb. But I've always been good at anything I turned my mind to. Dad never understood that. Because I had been in poor health the first years of my life, he thought I would always be weak. Gavin was his pride and joy. Gavin could do no wrong in his eyes. He didn't want to recognize that my brother was as thick as two planks. All he wanted was the easy life. His dream was to become an actor. But he barely applied himself to that.

"Only Mum loved me. However, Dad took her away from me. It was Gavin's fault. He called Dad in London the night Dario was going to take Mum and me away. Dad swooped down to the country all in a lather. I heard him and Mum having a row in the hall. I was a coward because I didn't go out to help her." There was a catch in his voice and his eyes pleaded with Emmeline for understanding. "But she told me to stay in my room until he'd gone. I had the door open a tiny crack and saw the whole ugly scene. Dad pushed Mum downstairs and then Gavin helped him cover it up. For the rest of his life, my dear brother held that over his head."

He swallowed hard and paused to regain his composure.

"Dad took Mum away. Therefore, I made him suffer and took his life. And the jurors. They shared his guilt. It seemed only fair. Flesh of my flesh, as the saying goes. Dad's blood runs through my veins. He made me what I am. That's why I had to rip him out like a cancer. You do see that, don't you?"

Emmeline's body shuddered at the detached manner in which this man sought to justify his crimes. She was glad of Gregory's warm arm about her. It reminded her that there was goodness and love in this world.

It gave her courage. She gestured with her chin. "You kept your father's signet ring as a trophy, didn't you?" She breezed on before he could answer. "I recognized it from the photos taken outside the courthouse after he was acquitted and I remembered you playing with it when we spoke at your flat. Then yesterday, I saw a flash of it when

'Melgoza' waylaid me at the conference. It just didn't register until a short while ago. You really shouldn't have kept it. It was a mistake."

Sheldrake glanced at his hand. "Perhaps. But it reminded me that Dad was cold in his grave where he belonged."

"And Adam?" Gregory prompted. "You had to sully his reputation because you were worried that he would be invited to join the board of the London Diamond Bourse instead of you. That would have ruined all of your plans." He jerked his thumb at Jason. "And you played on that fool's jealousies to do it.

"Tell me, Jason. You're the one who gave Sheldrake access to the Royce Global account number and you were the one who collected the money from the bank?"

Jason's mouth curled into a lupine leer. "The plan was perfect."

Gregory chuckled. "Not quite. You were merely a pawn." He turned to face Sheldrake. "Correct me if I'm off the mark. You sent Adam off on some wild goose chase on some pretext or other—"

Sheldrake cut across him. "I believe his twin sister is in some sort of distress."

"—Yes, Sabrina always is so that would seem reasonable. Of course, you've planned all along to make it look like Adam and Jason masterminded this whole plot with ETA and the Russians. And then you're going to do what you do best, reinvent yourself in another city under a new identity."

"That's a lie," Jason protested. "Tell him."

Sheldrake clapped his hands. "Bravo. You're both a marvel. It's a pity you'll have to die now." He shrugged. "Ah well, sacrifices have to be made in this world," he concluded cheerfully. "Emmeline, I must say that I'm going to regret it. I really did like you."

A wave of nausea roiled her stomach and her head was swimming.

They all froze when a light tapping echoed off the door.

Without waiting to be bidden, the unexpected arrival came into the room.

Emmeline gasped and pressed her body closer to Gregory.

It was the Russian who had accosted her in Plaza de España. In his wake was a lumbering hulk of a thug, who was carrying a silver tray with a sparkling bottle of some sort of spirit and two crystal balloons.

The Russian inclined his head. "Miss Kirby, we meet again. I did warn you of the consequences if you remained in Madrid. You really should have listened to me." He nodded at Gregory. "I assume you are the infamous Gregory Longdon."

"Remember the old adage, 'You should never assume. It makes an ass of you and me,'" Gregory quipped.

The Russian chuckled good-naturedly. "I have always admired your dry British wit. Even when facing death, you retain your stiff upper lip."

"I can see how it would stand in sharp contrast to the FSB's boorish threats," Gregory observed with one of his most charming smiles.

Emmeline elbowed him in the ribs. They were in enough hot water as it was, without antagonizing their captors.

The Russian waved to his lackey. "Andrei, put the tray down on the table before you drop it." Then, he turned to Sheldrake. "Forgive this intrusion. I came bearing a gift." He gestured at the bottle. "Henri IV Dudognon Heritage Cognac. Two million dollars." He smiled when Emmeline's jaw dropped. "The bottle is dipped in twenty-four karat gold and sterling platinum, and it is decorated with 6,500 brilliant cut diamonds."

Sheldrake crossed to the table in two strides. "I'm honored. To what do I owe the Kremlin's generosity?"

Andrei carefully splashed a measure of the tawny liquid into each balloon. He handed one to Sheldrake and the other to the Russian.

"Not the Kremlin," the Russian replied. "This is a personal gift from me. A payment for the job the Raven did in London. It went beyond my expectations."

Emmeline could see Sheldrake's ego swelling with pride. "One does one's best," he murmured.

The Russian lifted his glass and swirled it in the air to warm it, before bringing it to his lips. Sheldrake followed suit and took a deep swig.

The Russian watched him in silence for several seconds. When Sheldrake began to choke, he said, "I neglected to tell you my name. It's Kolya Ostrovsky. Feliks was my grandson."

Sheldrake stared at him in disbelief. The balloon slipped through his fingers and the precious spirit spread over the carpet. He clutched at his throat and crumpled to his knees.

"You will die in another minute," Ostovsky intoned phlegmatically.

His prognostication came true with cold-blooded accuracy. Andrei gave Sheldrake a half-hearted kick in the kidneys just to be certain, but it was quite obvious the Raven was dead.

Ostrovsky gave a nod of satisfaction. "A waste of an excellent bottle of cognac, but it was in a good cause."

Then he turned to a stunned Emmeline and Gregory. "You can't be found here. Take the corridor to your right. Follow it to the staircase. At the bottom of the stairs, make a left and it should lead you back to the dining room."

Emmeline blinked at him and remained rooted to the spot.

Ostrovsky jerked his chin at the door. "Longdon, take

your wife and *go*. We have special expertise in cleaning up messes."

"What about him?" Gregory asked, pointing at a dumbfounded Jason.

"Take him with you. The Kremlin doesn't want him. Let the Crown Prosecution Service deal with him."

They shared a conspiratorial smile. Then, Gregory propelled his wife and her half-brother toward the door.

"One thing," Ostrovsky called before they quitted the room. Gregory tossed a glance over his shoulder. "Please thank Villiers for me. Tell him I will not forget his courtesy."

Gregory raised an eyebrow but refrained from comment.

Epilogue

The "incident" at the Palacio Real sent Madrid into an uproar in the following days. Across the world, the press was reporting that the Spanish security services had received a tip that the notorious Raven was planning to assassinate a prominent British official at the reception and had set a trap for him. He chose to take his own life, rather than be captured. The authorities were surprised to discover the famous Blue Angel and Pink Courtesan diamonds when they searched the Raven's body. They concluded that he had stolen the diamonds and was planning to sell them, possibly to one of the guests at the reception. However, he took that secret to his grave.

Burnell and Finch took Jason into their custody and made a reservation for him in a nice, cozy cell until the Crown Prosecution Service could decide what new charges to bring against him.

Philip and Villiers had returned to the corridors of Whitehall and the opaque milieu of spying.

Emmeline and Gregory had decided to take a week's holiday. They went to the Prado, strolled in El Retiro Park, and made a point of visiting the Plaza de Cibeles, where the fountain of the Greek goddess Cybele on a lion-drawn carriage resided. They also ventured to Plaza Mayor and Plaza de España. They found that the squares were much more pleasant since they were no longer being hounded by assassins and spies. She also was able to relax because she had at last spoken to Adam and was satisfied that all was well. But she was still going to pop by his office the minute they returned to see him with her own eyes.

Every evening after dinner, they took long walks along Grand Via.

Now, Emmeline was feeling wistful because tomorrow would be their last day.

"I wish we could stay longer. Madrid is beautiful."

Gregory threw his arm around her shoulders and kissed the top of her head. "We could return in the spring if you like."

She tilted her head back to smile up at him. "Ooh, yes. I'll start making some plans when we get home."

Gregory chuckled and drew her closer to him.

"Excuse me, señor," a man called behind them.

They stopped and turned around. "Yes?" Gregory asked.

"You're English, are you not?"

Gregory's eyes narrowed in suspicion. "Why do you want to know?"

Beads of perspiration were sprinkled across the man's forehead and his breath was coming in rasps. He fumbled in his pocket and drew out a black velvet pouch.

His hands trembled as he shoved it against Gregory's chest. "Please take these to London. Give them to Alexander Colefax."

His gaze seemed to dart in every direction at once. "Only to Colefax. It's very important."

"Look here—" Gregory began, but the fellow cut him off.

"They will kill me if they find them. Please help me," he begged.

He shot a glance over his shoulder. "*Madre di Dio*, it is

too late."

He scurried off, leaving Gregory staring down at the pouch in his hands. He slowly loosened the drawstrings. His heart stopped between beats, when six luscious red diamonds tumbled into his palm. The tip of his tongue flicked over his lips. Red, the rarest variety of natural fancy colored diamonds.

Emmeline's hand flew to her mouth and Gregory hastily stuffed the gems back inside.

He took her elbow. "Come on," he commanded. "Let's go back to the hotel."

A horrifying screech followed by a sickening *thud* shattered the peace. Chaos broke out as people scattered in different directions a couple of blocks ahead of them. Women started shrieking and men were shouting.

"What happened?" Gregory asked an older man, who was hustling away.

"A terrible accident, señor." The stranger crossed himself. "A young man was hit by a car."

Emmeline and Gregory traded a wary look, as the stranger bolted off.

Good sense dictated that they should go directly to the hotel. But curiosity drew them like a magnet to the scene of the accident.

An ambulance arrived and the paramedics were clearing a path to the victim.

It was too late.

The young man who had entrusted the diamonds into Gregory's care was dead.

About the Author

Daniella Bernett is a member of the Mystery Writers of America New York Chapter and the International Thriller Writers. She graduated summa cum laude with a B.S. in Journalism from St. John's University. *Lead Me Into Danger, Deadly Legacy, From Beyond The Grave, A Checkered Past, When Blood Runs Cold, Old Sins Never Die* and *Viper's Nest of Lies* are the books in the Emmeline Kirby-Gregory Longdon mystery series. She also is the author of two poetry collections, *Timeless Allure* and *Silken Reflections*. In her professional life, she is the research manager for a nationally prominent engineering, architectural, and construction management firm. Daniella is currently working on Emmeline and Gregory's next adventure. Visit www.daniellabernett.com or follow her on Facebook or on Goodreads.

CPSIA information can be obtained
at www.ICGtesting.com
Printed in the USA
LVHW031143151222
735213LV00010B/1338